I0689227

BJ Watson

The Glare

Rapier
PUBLISHING COMPANY

The Glare

Copyright © 2016 by BJ Watson
stintleg36@outlook.com

ISBN 978-0-9977029-4-1
Library of Congress Control Number 2016953676

Published by
Rapier Publishing Company
260 W. Main Street, Suite #1
Dothan, Alabama 36301

www.rapierpublishing.com
Facebook: www.rapierpublishing@gmail.com
Twitter: rapierpublishing@rapierpub

Book Cover Design: Damany Leggett
Book Interior Layout: Rapture Graphics.

Rapier
PUBLISHING COMPANY

This book is dedicated to my brother Ronald Watson and family.

Prologue

The storm continued throughout the evening, as gusts of wind and torrents of rain smashed against the windows of the small brick townhouse. The house was empty now, whereas, only hours before it had been filled with buzzing conversations, handshaking, hugs, and laughter in the midst of tears. Gazing out of the window, her eyes welled up with tears, Sage could hardly see. She stood staring blindly through the large picture window in her living room. Holding onto the letter, with tears falling from her eyes, streaming down her slender face, her mind continuously replayed the scene of every moment of this miserable, and sorrowful day.

Earlier that day, drops of rain had begun to fall intermittently during the graveside service at the cemetery. At the end of the benediction prayer, several friends and relatives walked over to Sage and her brother, who were still sitting under the tent, to give their last condolences, words of encouragement, and embraces of consolation. Soon after, she got up and stood next to the casket crying softly, still clutching the stem of the flower that had been given to her by one of the funeral home attendants. As she stood silently glaring at the casket, her brother walked over to her side and put his arm around her shoulder, both of them still in disbelief. She sighed deeply and with a remorseful heart looked up towards the cloudy, graying sky. A raindrop fell right into one of her already tear-filled eyes. With her tissue, she wiped the mingled water from her cheek and looked again at the casket for the very last time. By this time, the casket was hardly visible. It had almost been completely covered with flowers that had been placed there by relatives and friends, one by one, as they walked by. There were an array of flowers of all colors and types. Roses, lilies, carnations, baby's breath and more, that had been taken from the myriad of flower arrangements that had been brought from the church. So many people had attended the internment that the casket appeared to have been covered with a thick, colorful, flowery quilt. Her sight had become a little blurred as she again wiped her eye. "Something must have gotten into my eye from that raindrop," she thought as the eye continued to tear. Her brother broke away from her to place his flower on the casket. Slowly, he began to walk towards the awaiting black limousine. She laboriously walked closer to the casket; her feet seemed barely able to move. Finally, she placed the flower that she had been holding onto the mound of others. She had been grasping it so tightly that the stem had become limp. There she remained standing as the groundsmen, who far from their sight, were impatiently waiting. They wanted to get the casket prepared to be lowered into the ground, especially now, since it was beginning to rain harder. They were prohibited from proceeding with descending any caskets into the ground until everyone had left the area, as this could be very upsetting to family members. From a distance, one of the men glanced over at Sage with a subtle, miffed look. Her brother, Casey, noticed him from where he was standing and walked back over to get her. Placing his arm around her shoulders, he gently tugged her away towards the limousine. "Come on, Sage. We have to go now," he said softly. As the limousine drove away, it had begun to rain even harder. Riding by, looking in awe at the incredible number of graves, the ultimate sight of the future, Casey pointed out to her a taller headstone close to the road, which stood out amongst the others around it, not only in stature, but because of the words on it. They looked at each other with a tacit stare.

Finding her way to the white wooded wicker chair, which was situated, adjacent to the large picture window in the living room, she sat there, lifeless. She had been staring thoughtlessly through the rain-drenched window in a trance until a not too distant sound of a thunderclap brought her back to her sorrowful melancholy. It had been at least two hours since everyone had gone as she sat recalling the evening. The out-of-town relatives and friends had gone to meet their scheduled times of departure. Toni and her husband had flown all the way from California and had reluctantly left with promises to keep in better touch and to continue to take care of their grandmother. They had come as soon as they could which was only two days before the funeral. Toni wanted to drop everything and get there as soon as she had received the news. However, in her current state of mind, her husband felt it necessary to come with her, whereas, initially he was going to stay at home with the children. It was at their wedding, where he had first met Ally, so their acquaintance hadn't been close. They mostly saw each other on occasion when she and her children came to visit her parents during her marriage to Greg and some correspondence through phone conversations. His attendance had been primarily for Toni, who had become so deeply distraught over her dearest and closest friend's death that he was afraid for her to travel alone. Ever since she got the devastating news, she had been extremely heartbroken and gravely depressed with grief. Drowning in feelings of guilt for not being with her long time friend during her illness caused her to sink into a pit of self-reproach and remorse.

The small townhouse was packed with the many people who had come to the funeral to pay their last respects. A number of church members, friends, and neighbors old and new, who had come to her home had brought food and beverages which added to the vast amount that had already been sent. Several of them had also pitched in to help with serving the other guests and many even stayed to help with the clean up. These gestures of kindness overwhelmed Sage and filled her with heartfelt appreciation and surprise, especially because some she had only seen in passing and others she hadn't met until today. Co-workers from both her past and current jobs were there, as well as friends and co-workers of Casey's. Even some of her classmates from college attended when they got the news, as did her college counselor, now friend, Mrs. McFarland. She had met her years before when she first attended Glasslane University. Of all her friends there, she especially wanted her family to meet Mrs. McFarland. She had had such great influence on her at school and in helping her get her first job. After introducing her to her father and uncle, they both stared strangely at her while smiling as they both shook her hand. As she continued walking through the crowd talking and hugging those who she apparently knew, Greg and Jack watched her from a distance. Standing on the side, away from the rest, Greg said to his brother, "I know her."

"Yeah, she looks familiar to me too. And she's kinda hot for her age."

"Jack, you will never change. But I have to agree, she is a looker."

"What are you saying? This is your wife's repast for God's sake!" he whispered, edging up closer to make his point known.

"Ex-wife, mind you. We were divorced almost twenty years ago."

"Well, anyway, for her I could make a change."

Still discussing their new interest, trying to jar their memory of how and where they both could have possibly met her, they plotted and competed as to who would make the first move on her. Their eyes followed her every move throughout the crowd searching and staring at her as if they were hunting for prey. Jack wanted to know if she was married, even though he noticed that she was not wearing a wedding ring, he thought he had better find out before he advanced. He couldn't believe how he could have forgotten someone that attractive. Sage thought maybe it was just her imagination, but noticed her father and uncle watching her friend. She didn't think it was her imagination because it seemed as though she was trying to avoid them as well. She couldn't really blame her even if she had been keeping her distance; their stares were a bit unnerving. By the time they had gained enough confidence to ask her after searching throughout the crowd of mourners; they realized that she had already left. "Sage thought besides the rain, their stares probably also prompted her to leave.

"I still can't figure out where I know her from. Somehow, I even remember talking to her," Jack said, walking away. Noticing how the two men had been staring at her, Mrs. McFarland left to avoid any encounter with either of them.

Sage's very close friends stayed long after everyone else. They were very concerned, seeing how distraught she had been during the funeral didn't want to leave her alone. After a few more hours had passed, they too left, but only upon Sage's insistence.

"Are you sure that you're going to be okay?" one of her friends, Rachael, asked. She assured them all that she would be all right.

"Go-o-o. Get out of the rain. I'll be fine. Thanks, you guys for everything." Though reluctantly, they left.

"Okay, we'll be in touch," one of them told her, as they threw up their umbrellas and rushed to their cars out into the torrential downpour. She also insisted that Casey leave as well, even long before her friends had. Neither had gotten very much sleep.

"Casey, why don't you go home, go to bed, and try to get some sleep."

For both of them, sleep was elusive. It was difficult to stop the mind racing thoughts of all the sorrowful events from beginning to the end. The loss of their mother had been totally unexpected. They both were very deeply grieved and were still in utter disbelief.

From all the business of preparing for the funeral, Sage was totally exhausted. It had only been she and her brother Casey, who notified and contacted all of their relatives, friends, and their mother's acquaintances of her untimely and unexpected passing. She thought of how by phone and email they had gotten in touch with everyone in addition to arranging accommodations for those who were coming from out of town. Coming out of her thoughts, she stood up. To get some relief she rolled her head around to try to loosen the tightened muscles in her neck and shoulders. Wringing her hands together, she began talking to herself as she paced slowly around the glass top, white wicker coffee table that was centered in the living room. "I just can't believe it." She began speaking out loud to herself. "I can't believe that she's gone. Oh, God… so many times I wished for this day, but now I feel so…so sorry that I'll never see her again," she said in a soft, muffled tone. She paused, staring through the glass top table, yet not really seeing anything.

Terrible memories began to replay and thoughts that were coming back into her mind from the past that crushed her heart. She was trying not to remember the many times she even had thoughts of killing her mother. Through those horrible years, she had begun to hate her for all she felt her mother had put her and her brother through. Finding out about her mother's prior ambulance trips to the hospital had been an annoyance before; she had no compassion only hatred. She felt that her mother even deserved whatever happened to her. She and Casey had been through unimaginable tough times after their father decided that he no longer wanted to be married or be a father for that matter. She always felt it was her mother who had driven him to that point in the first place. With feelings of remorse and shame, Sage walked into the bedroom and fell across the bed weeping uncontrollably.

BJ Watson

Chapter 1

It was eleven years ago that Greg and Ally had been married. She hadn't yet graduated from high school by the time Greg had already acquired two degrees in the Master's program at the University of Pennsylvania. It was at Huntington Beach in California when he first met her. On the beach was where he had first seen her. He was spending the weekend there for a business trip. She and two of her friends from work, Toni and Jessica had gone there on a girl's weekend getaway. While taking a stroll along the shore to get his feet wet, he spotted her dragging something along the sand through the multicolored plethora of umbrellas and people. He couldn't take his eyes off her once he got a good glimpse. He wasn't a female predator combing the beach for women, although there were a myriad of alluring body types in bikinis and swimwear of all colors and designs at every angle of sand. He wasn't interested in any of them. Currently, he wasn't interested in any woman. There was a time he had once been engaged, but his fiancée abruptly called off the wedding two weeks prior. He couldn't understand the reason for the sudden breakup. There had been no signs of reservation or cold feet, but only eagerness to finally be together as husband and wife. Greg was so devastated and hurt that he vowed he would never let another woman get that close to him again. Marriage was no longer an option, no, not for him. That had been almost five years ago. That's why he couldn't understand the inexplicable feeling he got when he saw Ally. She stirred something within him. It was neither physical nor sexual. He obviously knew nothing about this woman, only seeing her for the first time.

Through the years, he had dated many women, but they were meaningless to him. He had never seen this woman before and yet felt compelled to say something to her. "I've got to meet her," he thought.

It was a beautiful Friday morning in the summer of 1987, sunny, hot, and breezy. The traffic was intensely congested on the highway that day. It seemed as though everyone was headed to the beach. A gentle, warm breeze quietly flowed into the car with harmonic cadence along with the intermittent slow movement of traffic. Ally, Jessica, and Toni had crammed their suitcases, beach umbrellas, and coolers into Ally's 1981 white Ford Fairlane. Somehow, they all managed to get Friday off from work with ease and left their coworkers green with envy. From the three choices of transportation, they concluded that Ally's car had more space to put everything in the trunk. Jessica's two-seater MG Midget was completely out of the question and Toni's car everyone decided was just too old. It barely got her to work every day. They talked about how wonderful it was to be able to get away from work, if just for a weekend. Feeling lighthearted, they laughed, joked, flirted and waved to truckers while nibbling on snacks all the way to the beach. They were having so much fun acting like silly high school teenagers.

Although traffic was heavy, they made pretty good time getting to the beach. They got there early, only to find that the parking lot was almost full. After combing the lot, they finally found a parking space; checked in and quickly rushed to their condo to unpack only what was necessary for a day at the beach. The girls decided on the way that they didn't want to waste a minute and would head straight for the beach as soon as they arrived. Quickly changing into their bathing suits and briskly grabbing their already packed beach gear, they hurriedly tossed everything into the car and were on their way. Since on Sunday afternoon, they would be leaving, and Friday had already begun, they wanted to get a head start to get as much out of the weekend as they could. Fortunately, the room was ready for check-in when they arrived, so their fun weekend had already begun.

The beach was very close to their condo, only about three minutes away if driving. Although walking would have saved their "so-hard-to-find" parking space, they had to drive because there was just too much to carry. Luckily, they found a place near the beach, which seemed to have again, taken forever. Seeing the many beach umbrellas got them excited; they grabbed everything and raced onto the sand, dropping and picking up their things along the way. Not stopping to set up, they dropped everything at the first sight of water, kicked off their sandals and started running wildly onto the hot white sand like little children towards the sparkling, turquoise-colored ocean. They splashed, kicked, and threw water in each others' faces, diving in the waves and flirting with the guys who were coming in on their surfboards. After playing in the water for awhile, leaving Jessica and Toni still in the water, Ally decided to head up to try and find the things they had dropped along the way and to look for a permanent place to set up their umbrellas and chairs. She wanted to hurry before the few spaces that were left on the beach were taken.

"Hey, guys, I'm going to head up to find us a spot."

"Okay," yelled Toni.

"We're going to stay out here a while longer, okay?" Ally turned slightly around balancing on the sand she waved to them and preceded up the sandy incline. Her feet buried in the sand with each step, making her trek more laborious.

Looking around for where she thought they had dropped their belongings, all the while she continued to search for a clear space to settle. She finally found them sprawled about, nowhere near where she thought they were. By this time, she had walked quite a ways away from the water. Turning around to see where her friends were to where she was standing, she was suddenly caught off guard by the awesomely beautiful sight before her. It was almost too magnificent a sight to behold. It was a living photograph of a glimpse of what heaven could look like, she thought. The colors of the sky, the water, and sand matched harmoniously perfect and brought over her a sense of tranquility. This combination of colors was that which only God, Himself could have put together. The clear azure sky, met by the rippling line of turquoise blue water, gently kissed the white sandy shore was a breathtaking scene. Far out on the calm surface of the ocean, the water sparkled as the sun placed its finishing touches to this masterpiece. The ocean seemed to glisten as if sprinkled across the top with diamonds, which intermittently appeared and disappeared across the calm waves. On the shore, the rushing waves crashed and rolled onto the sand, erasing any tracks in the sand where footprints had once been. This was a scene of the awesome power of God, she thought. Regaining her thoughts, Ally continued to look around for a clear place to set up.

At last, she found a place and dropped everything that she was able to carry. She felt lucky that it was no more than ten yards away from where their beach gear had been thrown. It took a couple of trips, but she managed. Exhausted from the drive and having to haul their belongings across the sand, she decided just to lie back on a blanket and rest for the remainder of the afternoon once she was finished with getting everything done. They had brought their beach chairs, towels, umbrellas, radios, books and magazines along. Gazing at everything that they had brought, she couldn't believe that she had lugged it all in only a few trips. As soon as she found the area, she was again thankful that it was not too far from the same angle as where the girls were who were still out enjoying themselves in the water. She started jumping around and waving to try to get their attention so that they could see where she was. Finally, after getting their attention, she turned back around and began the task of getting settled. First, turning on the radio, she then began spreading out the blanket while singing along with the song that was playing when a long shadow appeared over her as she was leaning over.

He first spotted her from a distance as he strolled along the beach. Stopping in his tracks, he watched how the breeze from the ocean blew through her light brown hair, brushing it ever so gently against her face and how she slowly moved it from her eyes with a slight movement of her hand. Advancing his position closer for a better look, he was being careful not to be conspicuous. Simply out for a little morning exercise, decided to walk along the cool water close to the shoreline of the beach when he noticed someone looking around down at the sand. Apparently, she was searching for something that was lost in the sand. Walking towards it, she smiled with joy having found whatever she was looking for and reached down to retrieve it. He stayed where he was and watched her every move while dragging items and carryalls to an area between clusters of beach umbrellas and even contemplated going to help but decided to wait. By this time seeing now that she could be alone, he closed in as she picked up one of the blankets and was shaking off the sand. Trying not to startle her, he inconspicuously stepped up from behind. Standing there quietly, clad in a plaid yellow and blue Ralph Lauren short-sleeved shirt and a pair of khaki shorts, he nervously contemplated whether he should approach her or just keep walking. Unable to resist, he closed in. He started to tap her on the shoulder, but cautiously decided not to.

"Can I give you a hand?" Ally was so startled that she froze dead in place. She hadn't seen or heard him because he had walked up from behind. She jerked her head around so quickly that she had to take a step backwards to balance herself. After catching her balance, she saw a tall male figure against the brilliance of the sun. "This was the shadow," she thought. It appeared as if light shown around his entire well-built body. Raising her hand to her eyes to block the sunlight, she fixed her gaze on his face. She thought that she had somehow stepped onto Mt. Olympus. He must have been over six feet tall. She stood speechless staring into the eyes of a Greek god with blue-gray eyes and dark brown hair. "This guy is gorgeous," she thought. Glaring without a word for so long Greg repeated his question, but this time more loudly.

"I'm sorry. I didn't mean to startle you. Do you need some help?"

Ally answered, stuttering, "Uh, uh, I didn't know that you were behind me. And, uh, ye-ye yes, if you don't mind." She answered hesitantly, but really needed the help. Even though he was a stranger, she decided it would be safe for him to help her. What could he do in broad daylight, especially with thousands of people around? Plus, he seemed like a nice guy, and he did offer to help.

"Okay, what can I do?" he asked eagerly. "And by the way, my name is Greg, Greg Tyler," he said with an out-stretched hand.

"Pleased to meet you, Greg, my name is Ally." She hesitantly extended her hand, still stunned by the abrupt encounter. Greg reached out further. She brushed the sand from her hands and shook his hand. Shaking her hand, he was thinking of how soft it was. Ally felt somewhat awkward and uncomfortable shaking his hand, especially since it was still coated with grains of sand. She wondered if this handshake gesture was even proper. "What am I thinking? What does it matter?" she thought. Finally recovering from her momentary stupor, she replied,

"Oh, and yes, yes. That will be great. And thank you for asking."

"Okay, so what can I do?"

"Oh, ah… could you please help me with the umbrellas?"

"Sure."

She had finished spreading out the beach blankets and began setting up the chairs. Greg took off his shirt and laid it across one of the chairs exposing his well-built muscular, tanned body. Glancing inconspicuously over at Greg while he stuck the last and third umbrella pole into the sand, she could see the muscles flex in his arms as he pushed the pole down firmly and adjusted it trying to blot out the direct sunlight. Standing up and looking at Ally, Greg asked, "Anything else?"

"Oh, no. That was such a big help, thank you very much."

"So Ally, where are you from, if you don't mind my asking?"

15

"No, I don't mind at all. I live in a little area just outside of Orange County, called Irvine."

"Oh, okay. Then you're not too far from here, huh?"

"Yes, you're right. It's not far from here." She didn't want to give too much information to a stranger, even if he was kind and handsome.

"I'm sorry, Ally, I didn't even ask you if you were with anyone. I didn't see anyone and uh… I guess you are since you have all these umbrellas, but that doesn't mean you're not…uh… I don't want to get anyone upset by standing here talking to you. So, are you with …?", hesitantly asking.

"Well, yes…kinda," Ally replied, "…but I'm only with a couple of girlfriends from work." "Phew," Greg said.

"Why… what's wrong?" she asked, being a bit coy.

"Because I was hoping this wouldn't be the end of our conversation," he answered.

"Do you mind if I hang around a while? I mean…I don't want to impose or anything." "Oh, no, I don't mind," she answered, "As long as you aren't with anyone. Are you?" "No, I'm not. As a matter of fact, I'm here on a business trip. I'm meeting with a few of my business partners and a client here."

"Why don't you sit down under the umbrella and get out of the sun."

"Oh, okay. Thanks. What was I saying? Oh yeah… I was saying that I reserved a conference room for our meeting over at the Hyatt Regency, which is where I'm staying."

"Wow, nice place for a conference," she joked.

"Where are you staying? Again, if you don't mind my asking."

Cautiously, Ally responded, "Oh, I'm staying at one of the condos down the beach." Understanding her response, from his shirt pocket he handed her a Hyatt business card on which he had already written on the back, his room and phone numbers. They talked for another twenty minutes when Greg saw who he surmised must have been her friends, waving and walking up towards them from the beach. Not wanting to become an imposition, he stood up as they got closer and stayed only a short while longer, but only to be introduced, as Ally had politely insisted him to do when she saw them heading their way.

As Toni and Jessica headed away from the water towards their umbrellas, they could see as they got closer that Ally was talking to someone. As they began to close in, Jessica asked with a tone of excitement, "Toni! Do you see that?"

"Yeah... that hunk looks like he's right off the movie screen."

"Yeah,...and that body too," Jessica added.

Thinking that Ally maybe had run into a friend, they wanted to find out if he had any other friends with him. Jessica, the more bold and vociferous of the two, began to scurry across the scorching sand and had gotten farther ahead of Toni, trying to get to this unfamiliar visitor first to meet him and get a better look. Ally introduced her friends to Greg and noticed how polite and courteous he was to them as well. He displayed such gentlemanly qualities, she thought. She was truly impressed and wondered if she would ever see him again. He had given her a card with his name on it, but she had been in these same types of situations before. When Greg shook Jessica's hand, she asked shamelessly,

"Anymore from where you came from?" Ally was embarrassed.

"Oh Jessica..." But Greg only laughed and apologized for his imposition. He then invited them to come over to the Hyatt for dinner that evening as his guests. They gleefully accepted the invitation. Ally was shocked and felt that her prayer had been answered.

"Okay great, then I'll see you ladies later on tonight," he said enthusiastically. As Greg walked away towards the parking lot, he wondered if he had done the right thing. In five years, he hadn't met anyone that he even wanted to have a serious conversation with, let alone someone that he wanted to see again. Yet, there was something different about her. He knew when he first saw her. Did he really want to let himself go? Did he really want to find out the 'what and why'? Maybe at dinner he would find out. He hadn't felt anything like this for any woman since he had first met Janice, his ex-fiancée.

After Greg had gone, the girls stayed at the beach a few more hours. They laid out in the sun listening to the radio, singing along with the artists, giggling and joking about Ally's great find. Toni and Jessica talked about what the evening was going to be like and if they could be as lucky as Ally and meet someone. Ally was embarrassed but was secretly feeling lucky herself and grateful that she chose not to go swimming. "Was this meant to be?" she thought. Jessica, feeling that she was getting a little sunburned, suggested that they pack up and get back to the condo.

"Let's go. I feel like my skin is beginning to get burned." They all agreed.

"I can't make a good impression if I look like a tomato tonight. Anyway, red clashes with the color of my dress." They burst out laughing. Packing up their things, they kept laughing uncontrollably all the way to the car.

"Jessica, you're so crazy," Toni joked.

The girls had gotten a real bargain on their recently remodeled condo, and conveniently and pleasantly close to the beach. The price was also reasonable, especially since it was being split three ways. One of Toni's coworkers had recommended it one day at work when a discussion had come up about vacation spots and places to stay. It had a huge bedroom with one queen-size bed, a dining area, and a large sofa in the living room, which pulled out into a full-size bed. As the girls busied themselves showering and getting ready for their most anticipated event, they couldn't stop talking about Greg. In and out, back and forth they went from the bathroom to the bedroom, from the mirror to the closet babbling and chattering along the way. Jessica had gotten her dress from the closet, looking closely over it to make sure that it was okay. She said excitedly, "So girls, we've been invited to dinner at the Hyatt-Regency. You know, it's a good thing we decided to bring something dressy for our "one-time-going-out-to-a-nice-restaurant" night." "Oh, my gosh… that's right," said Ally, thinking of what could have been while sliding her dress over her head. She walked over to the full-length mirror that hung outside the bathroom door to get an overall view. "Yeah…or else we would have had to go out and buy outfits or decline the invitation."

"Are you kidding me? No way decline," said Jessica, as she walked into the room fully dressed.

"There was no way that we could have missed out on this once in a lifetime opportunity." "You're right about that, Jessica. This isn't even a once in a lifetime chance. It's more like a miracle. It was a miracle," Toni responded.

"But can you imagine having to buy something to wear from here on our salary?" added Ally.

"Yeah, especially since we hadn't planned on even going out to a place like that," Toni, remarked.

"Even if…I would have spent the money before I would have missed an opportunity like this. Wow, speaking of…that guy must really be rich," Jessica said.

"Well, he did tell me that his family owned a business," Ally gloatingly responded, standing in front of the mirror but looking at the reflections of her friends' faces of wonderment. At that point, Toni and Jessica rushed over to Ally wanting to hear more about everything that he told her about himself and all that they had talked about. Of course, Jessica wanted to know if he had any brothers, cousins, uncles, or any other of the male species relative or friend.

"Wait a minute, guys, I forgot something." Stopping in the middle of putting on her makeup, she went to the phone in the bedroom to call Greg. She remembered that he hadn't told them the exact time or where to meet him. She had already put on her dress. It was a black polyester blend V-neckline pullover. With scrutiny, looking over her outfit in the mirror and glancing at the phone, acting as if he would be able to see her, she wanted to make sure that every part was in place. It wore perfectly on her with capped sleeves and a high waist gathered in the middle held together with a wide band to give the dress a twisted pleated appearance just under the bust line. There she had pinned a green quartz and quartzite floral brooch that she had purchased during a huge jewelry sale that was held at work several months ago. It was payroll deductible. This was the only way she ever could have afforded such a piece. It took about four paychecks to finally pay it off. Smiling in the mirror, she thought this gave her outfit a look of nobility. "The brooch actually cost more than her dress," she thought, as she laughed to herself, still gazing in the full-length mirror. Stepping out on the deck for more privacy, she dialed Greg's number. He answered the phone immediately. Thanking her again for accepting his invitation, he gave her the time and directions. Delighted that she had called, he offered to send a limo to pick them up but Ally politely declined. He was disappointed but understood. When she went back into the living room, she told the girls about Greg's instructions and his generous offer of a limousine pickup that she declined. They immediately stopped what they were doing and with their mouths wide open turned simultaneously towards her and stared directly at her face in total disbelief. Jessica, who had been sitting on the sofa fastening the buckle of her multi-strapped four-inch sandaled heels around her ankles and Toni who had gone into the bathroom to put the finishing touches on her hair style, came to the living room where Ally was standing. They couldn't believe what they had just been told. The revelation that she had declined an offer of a limousine ride to the Hyatt was incredulous to them. Both stared at her. Their facial expressions reflected amazement and disbelief. Unintentionally, but in unison, they yelled out loud. "What?"

"Are you crazy?" asked Jessica. "How could you have turned down such a generous offer?" Toni chided her. But Jessica asked again in disbelief.

"You turned down a limousine ride to the Hyatt Regency?" She turned around walking away, saying, "I don't believe it." Ally, being more circumspect, told them they needed to stop and think about her decision. She tried to explain that they had to be more cautious, because firstly, they had just met Greg only a few hours ago.

"Oh, yes, we can't forget your old fashioned Christian values," Jessica said sarcastically.

"No, Jessica, I'm serious, we..." Ally was saying defensively, as Jessica interrupted.

"Oh, Ally, you're such a prude. Let it go for a change," her voice elevated.

"Listen, Jessica, we don't really know this guy. Yeah, he seems sweet, and yes, he's polite…"

"…and good-looking," Toni playfully interjected.

"You never know, he could be a serial killer or something. We really don't know," Ally continued in a very serious tone.

"Then, Ally, why the hell did you accept the invitation?" Jessica nastily asked.

"Okay, Jessica, take it down a notch," Toni warned.

"Well, for one thing, the three of us are going and we're going in our own transportation!" Ally exclaimed. "And I don't want to talk about it anymore," she added, which ended the discussion.

"She does have a point, Jessica," Toni said.

"Oh, whatever," said Jessica crassly, and whisked away into the bathroom and slammed the door.

"Hey, wait a minute. I was in there," Toni shouted standing at the door.

After they had gotten fully dressed, they paraded around the room. The limousine argument had died off, and they resumed looking in the mirror, critiquing one another's hair and dress. Checking their purses for necessities, they went down to the front desk and asked for directions on how to get to Pacific Coast Highway. Standing behind the desk was a short, heavy middle-aged woman wearing deep red lipstick, with thick eyebrows and a very pretentious smile, but a pleasant personality. She directed them to a tall, slender male who was straightening the brochures and maps across the room near the door.

"He's the concierge on duty for the evening." The young man explained that he was not the real concierge, but he would try to help as best he could. They thanked him for his help and left to get into the car. Even though they lived there, neither of them had ever ventured out anywhere except around this part of the beach area, especially at night. Getting their bearings together while driving, they had in just a short time come to the area of the Pacific Coast Highway. The parking lots and streets were lined and filled with limousines and cars of the affluent. There were also regular cars, even those like the one they were riding in, which was Ally's old, used Ford Fairlane, but those were very few and far between in this area.

Greg had told Ally to come to the Red Chair Lounge at the Hyatt where he would be sitting at the bar with some of his clients and couple of friends. He told her when she called him earlier that he wanted to invite his client and partners to join them for dinner after they arrive, of course, with her and her friends' permission, for which she had given. Continuing their drive on the way to the hotel, Ally asked Jessica and Toni what they thought of Greg's guest request.

"I don't care, as long as it's not with some fat, old, bald, married man," Jessica answered.

"That's right, Ally. We don't want our time being wasted on some old farts, excuse my French," chimed in Toni. Ally joined Toni as she and Jessica burst out laughing.

"Look guys, I've never met those men. I don't know what they look like," she said defensively.

"We just want to have what you have."

"What are you guys even talking about? I don't have anybody. Greg isn't even a date. And besides, these guys aren't our dates. We were just invited to dinner by a very nice guy."

"And rich," Jessica interjected.

"Hey, I thought we came to have a weekend of fun at the beach," Ally responded again in her own defense. "Remember, we just met this guy."

"That's right, Jessica," and added facetiously, "And he could even be a serial killer."

They burst out laughing hysterically, even Ally.

The view was majestic, as more palm trees, lamps with fountains of colorful waterfalls added to aesthetically enhance the entryways to the edifices of architectural artistry. The architecture had a flare of Spanish influence. They were all so brightly painted with oranges, whites, and tans, even at night the colors shone brightly. The girls were in awe as they continued their drive through the streets on the way to the Hyatt-Regency. The Mercedes, BMWs, Jags, and limousines, signified the type of clientele these visions of opulence attracted. They watched limo drivers who were standing around together, some smoking, engaging in male palaver as they waited with laxity for their occupants.

"Man, I have never seen so many people from so many different countries in one place all at the same time in all my life," Ally said, pausing between each phrase with excitement. "It's like we're at the U.N."

"There are a lot, but if you think about it, this is becoming the face of America now," Toni said. "In Irvine, where we live, it's so small that all we see are regular Americans."

"You are sort of a home body, Ally. Aren't you? You really haven't seen much of what's really going on in the world, have you?" Jessica added condescendingly. Ally was becoming a bit irritated with Jessica taking jabs at her, but she decided to just blow her off. She couldn't understand why she had agreed to go away for a whole weekend with her anyway. It wasn't that she didn't like her, but Jessica sometimes… no, most of the time didn't know how to be discreet. No, discretion was not one of her qualities. In fact, qualities were what she lacked all together. She was such an egotist. If it hadn't been for Toni's big mouth, blabbing one day during a conversation at work about she and Ally's plan of a weekend trip to the beach, Jessica would never have found out. Jessica had overheard Toni's conversation and approached her later that very day to find out the details of their trip, during which she somehow invited herself along. Toni tried to redeem herself by persuading Ally that by letting Jessica come along, it would work out to their advantage, financially, anyway. If Jessica came along, they could then split the cost three ways instead of two, Toni had explained. Ally was sure that these were Jessica's words to Toni verbatim. Toni had always been the neutral one in the bunch. She was always the mediator in any dispute, always there to help settle many of the coworkers' constant disagreements and complaints. Contrarily, there was Jessica, who was such an egregious and vile individual, really didn't have many friends, not at work anyway. Reluctantly, Ally yielded to the plan.

It was almost two years ago that Ally had come to work at the firm as one of the secretaries for one of the lawyers. She hadn't known or met anyone when she first came to work at the Carter, Dunhart and Wintham Law Firm. Ally and Toni seemed to hit it off as soon as they met and had become friends as quickly. On her first day while everyone only stared and whispered, Toni walked over, introduced herself, and took her around to meet the other employees. Through many weeks of working together, the two women talked and shared stories about their families, resolved job-related glitches, and discovered other similar interests, as they got to know each other. Toni would ask Ally to go to lunch and take breaks with her every day. In the beginning, only she and Ally would be together, but after Ally had become more familiar with everyone else, Toni would invite some of the other coworkers to join them. This was how Ally met Jessica and found out just how rude and vociferous she could be.

Having the gift of discernment wouldn't be a necessity to figure out Jessica's character. She was often loud and obnoxious, notorious for her vulgarity. Her bold, shameless attitude was often an unwanted display that had caused her to be omitted from many functions held in other departments. Everybody joked and debated about why she had never gotten fired. Noticeably quite friendly with the office manager, Mr. Clancy, it was rumored that his friendliness towards her was not just limited to hours spent at work. Fortunately, for Ally, Jessica didn't have to work in the same office area that she and Toni worked. One day during lunchtime at a nearby café, while waiting for their carryout order, Ally saw firsthand the infamous Jessica in action. She was causing a blusterous scene at the lunch table with the manager of the restaurant all because she thought the rolls should have been warm when they were served. Jessica had somehow manipulatively invited herself out with some of her coworkers.

"What an idiot! She's certainly not someone that I would like to have as a friend or even know," Ally thought to herself as she was leaving the restaurant. But because of her association with Toni, Ally had gotten to know Jessica a bit better and became more tolerant of her.

They were really enjoying the sights at the beach. Had it not been for Greg's invitation, they never would have even driven in this area. They had only seen it from their balcony and knew from the names, that this affluent area of Huntington Beach was certainly out of their league. Looking through the car windows like little children out for a Sunday drive, they also saw along the streets, couples walking hand in hand, arm in arm, smiling, laughing, and appearing to be enjoying one another. The girls were trying to guess which couples appeared to be married, engaged or just lovers. Jessica blurted out that some of those couples probably didn't even know each other past the bedroom. "Look at that old geezer over there with that young chick," Jessica snickered. "He looks like easy money." There was a young woman walking along side an obviously older man. She was scantily clad in a flimsy purple skirt that was mid thigh with a very low cut tee strap multicolored top. With her arm through his, she trotted in her five-inch heeled sandals appearing to be laughing at something he said to her.

"She won't have to do one thing for that gig. He looks like the only thing that he could do for her is to sit back and watch …or die," She burst out laughing. Looking at Jessica in the rear view mirror, Ally blurted, "Oh Jessica, you always have to add a hint of vulgarity to everything." Jessica looking back at Ally in the rear view mirror from the backseat replied, "You know Ally, you need to stop trying to be such a Miss Goody Two Shoes. She's obviously a hooker. And sweetie, at the rate you're going, you'll just blow any chance of ever talking to that guy Greg again after tonight, or anyone else for that matter!" Jessica said snidely. Ally looked at Jessica angrily from the rear view mirror.

"Who said that I even wanted to see him again, Jessica?" Ally exclaimed defensively. She hadn't expressed to them her thoughts of hoping that she and Greg would be a couple. She knew that her thoughts were only fantasy. She never thought that she could be impressive enough that he would want to see her again after tonight, anyway. Rationalizing her thinking, she thought it was pretty stupid that she would even have allowed herself to think that way about a stranger. Toni was silently looking at Ally beside her and then at Jessica in the rear as they verbally sparred back and forth. Having finally had enough Toni yelled, "Jessica! Ally! Stop with this petty bickering, will you? I just want to get there and have a good time. Don't let some guy that none of us even know, destroy our fun. In fact, I'm enjoying myself already, knowing that we'll be having dinner at the Hyatt Regency and it's going to be free. Free!"

They all laughed together in agreement that this would probably be the highlight of the weekend. But Ally and Jessica could still feel the tension between each other.

As they approached the driveway to the entrance of the Hyatt Regency, there were palm trees encased in diaphanous columns of light leading to the entrance. Greg had told Ally to come to the Red Chair Lounge at the Hyatt where he would be sitting at the bar with some of his clients and friends. The girls had never seen anything of this magnitude of splendor before.

"I can't believe that we're going into this place," Toni said with amazement.

"Yeah, this place is incredible," Ally said.

"I'm almost afraid to see the inside," Jessica said. "This is really more than an upscale resort hotel, you know."

"Yeah, more like off the scale," Toni laughed. People with matching outfits were getting in and out of expensive cars. Many of the women wore semi-formal attire and men were decked out in tuxedos and designer suits.

"Talk about elegance, did you see those dresses? We don't belong in this place Ally," Toni said with feelings of regret.

"Oh, come on, Toni," Ally said, assuring her. "We're just as good as they are. Plus, we don't have to worry about money.

And that's what you need in a place like this," Jessica said with confidence in her voice.

"That may be true, but neither do they," Said Toni.

"Yeah, Toni. Jessica may be right about that, but we were invited, so we belong," Ally added with reassurance, trying to overcome her own disbelief. When could she ever remember agreeing with anything that Jessica said?

When they drove up to the entrance of the hotel, a valet stepped up wearing a black jacket and white shirt to open the door and helped them get out of the car. They were not expecting this. "This added cost was not in their budget," Ally thought to herself. Just as Ally and the girls were beginning to reach into their purses to check for money for the valet, Greg intercepted from out of nowhere and placed a bill into the valet's hand. He looked at it and bowed as he backed away with a gracious grin towards the driver's side of their car. Greg was casually clad in a white cotton Calvin Klein shirt, black slacks and Giorgio Armani sports jacket. After greeting them, he placed his arms through Ally and Jessica's arms, as Jessica shamelessly forced him to, and guided them into the Red Chair Lounge where he had been waiting for their arrival. Toni followed closely behind them looking around in awe of the luxurious display. When they approached the entrance of the lounge, there were huge fireplaces structured within the red painted walls. Situated around the huge room were love seats and red leather high backed chairs positioned around low-level cherry wood coffee tables. There were also tables throughout for light casual dining. Slow, soft jazz was playing quietly in the background, which seemed to untangle the muffled chatter of the day's events. As they were walking in, Greg reached back for Toni who had been trailing behind and pulled her gently up to where the other two girls were.

"Hey, get up here, Toni. It is Toni, isn't it?"

"Yes, that's right," she responded. Ally thought to herself, how courteous that was of him to have done that. Before they walked in, Greg turned to all three women to welcome and thank them for not standing him up. The girls all chimed in with their grateful comments for his kindness for inviting them. As they all ambled over toward the bar counter to where he had been sitting, Greg stepped over to Ally and said, "You never told me your last name, Ally."

"Oh, I'm sorry," she apologized. "I was just being cautious."

"I understand."

"It's Morris," she answered.

"Well, I'm pleased to make your acquaintance again, Miss Ally Morris. It is Miss?" Greg teased as they walked over to the men.

"It's still Miss," Ally answered melodically. He took them into the area of the lounge where he and his friends had gathered at the bar earlier for drinks and introduced them. Evidently, he had been talking about them. "These are the three beautiful women that I told you about that I met on the beach earlier today," and proceeded to introduce them one by one to his guests. Two of the men got up to offer their seats. Greg took Ally to where he had been sitting. The place was busy with people strolling throughout with drinks in their hands going in and out of the lounge. Many sat on the sofas relaxing by the fireplaces, engaged in conversation, some obviously waiting to be seated for dinner. Greg had made dinner reservations himself, so they all just sat a little while longer at the bar, becoming more acquainted with each other until it was time to go to their table in the main dining room.

The Californian was where Greg had reserved their table. It was the most exquisite restaurant within the Hyatt. He had requested a table that would accommodate additional guests after Ally agreed to include his clients for dinner. The restaurant was ornamented with an awesome setting of palm trees, stately gardens, and a dynamic ocean view. The host came over to the bar to guide them to their table as Greg had requested. He and his male guests politely pulled out each of the girl's chairs to seat them properly. Having been seated, Greg started the conversation by asking them if everything had gone okay with the drive over. Ally answered, telling him that everything went fine and thanked him again for offering a ride. Jessica thought as she gave Ally a sneer, "She should have let Toni and me have a say in that decision." Greg began to give a little background about his friend and the two clients. Jessica migrated to a gentleman who she had been attracted to when they met in the lounge. The fact was, he was the only one left. Ken reintroduced himself and started a casual conversation with Jessica. He seemed to be in his late forties or early fifties. His wedding band was obvious, but this was only one night anyway, and it was only for dinner. He was not looking for anything more.
"Toni and Sean seem to be hitting it off well," thought Jessica. "Probably because they're both African-American, but who cares, he's cute. Too bad she got to him first. Greg is the youngest of all it seems, but Ally has him. I guess I'm stuck with good ol' Ken," Jessica thought, as she weighed her options. Greg had assured Ally that there were no strings attached when she spoke to him on the phone earlier. He explained that those guys were pretty harmless characters and only wanted to hang out to enjoy the evening.

Greg told them after they had been seated at the dining table for a while that his brother, Jack, had flown down unexpectedly, and politely informed them that he had invited him to join them for dinner as well. Looking directly at Ally, Greg said, "I hope you don't mind."

"Oh no...not at all," She quickly responded. He explained that Jack had gone to Colorado on another business venture for the company, but didn't know if he would be able to make the conference at Huntington Beach. His plane had gotten in only a couple of hours ago and would be running a little late. When Greg got up to speak to the waiter about his brother as a possible addition at the table, Jessica said in a low tone, "So now he tells us."

"What are you talking about Jessica? What did he tell us?" Toni asked.

"...his brother?" Jessica said, grinning like a Cheshire cat. "That's what I wanted to hear. He has a brother. He said that his brother is going to join us. And if he looks anything like him, I'm going in for the kill." said Jessica whispering in a firm tone.

Ally whispered to Jessica sternly, "Why don't you calm down and stop acting like an animal on the prowl. Don't be rude to Ken."

"Oh, Ally, you're such a bore," Jessica said with a tone of growing intolerance. Ally whispered to Toni,

"Yeah, and she's such a whore." Toni covered her mouth and snickered unnoticeably with Ally. When the maitre d' saw that Greg's guests appeared to be settled, he sent the waiter to their table to take them their menus. Greg ordered a bottle of champagne to begin with and whatever the girls wanted. The girls were profoundly impressed. It was top of the line. They looked at each other with wide eyes at all the wonder that was before them. They knew that this would probably only be for one night. As they looked around, they wondered how it must feel to be rich, especially after looking at the prices on the menu and the clientele. Jessica whispered to her friends,

"The price of the steak dinner is what I could pay for a dress, a pair of shoes, and dinner." The three began to snicker again. All the guys looked at them with puzzled faces and shrugged their shoulders. Greg encouraged them to order whatever they wanted. Ally asked Greg if they should wait for his brother. Not knowing exactly when he would arrive, Greg decided not to wait. By the time the group was ready to order, Jack, Greg's brother, walked up to the entrance of the restaurant. When Greg saw him speaking to the Maître d and being directed to the table, he excused himself and got up to meet him. They both walked back to the table together as Greg leaned over as if talking directly into his ear until they got to the table.

"This is John Tyler, my brother I was telling you about. Everyone who knows him calls him Jack," said Greg.

"Hi, everybody. Sorry, I'm late," Jack, said apologetically. Greg proceeded to introduce his brother to the girls and the one client, Sean Barnes, who Jack had never met, but the other gentlemen he had seen at the New York office. Greg had invited him to Huntington Beach to talk business in a more casual and more personal setting. Jack shook hands with everybody then sat down in the vacant chair in front of Toni and Jessica. The waiter came over to Jack when he was seated to place a menu before him and waited for his affirmation. Jack nodded. Greg was the eldest son by two years. The difference in ages couldn't have been seen by appearance. Greg was a couple of inches shorter at six-one with dark brown hair and blue-green eyes. Jack was also good-looking with a firmly built body to match at six three with light brown hair and deep blue eyes. As kids, Jack was more of the athlete than his brother. They both played basketball because of their height and were always pursued by coaches of other schools to play on their team. Greg played lacrosse as well, but Jack loved playing basketball. He also had more of an intensive competitive spirit and always, always had to win. Being handsome and athletic, he had always had a following of admiring girls in high school and college, which helped to perfect his already conceited and vain personality. Even now, a woman to him was only an unnecessary commodity.

Jessica combed Jack over with her eyes from head to toe. Both Toni and Ally noticed and looked at each other with looks of disgust about Jessica's actions. Ally, loathing Jessica's wanton behavior thought, "She is such a slut. Discretion is not one of her attributes." Jack reached out to shake everyone's hand, but when he shook Jessica's hand, she held him with a lengthy hold and a lustful gaze. Toni nudged Ally with her knee under the table. Ally looked at Toni, acknowledging that she was aware. She was trying to get Jessica's attention to give her a look to back off, but Jessica pretended not to see her. She continued her optical advances toward Jack. She then began to interrogate him.

"So, Jack, do you lift weights? You look kind of muscular underneath that jacket."

"Well, I do work out at the gym every chance I get, but bodybuilding is not something that I'm really into."

"Does your wife get to travel with you?" she continued.

"No, she doesn't." Shocked, Jessica's face suddenly changed to regret. "…

especially since I'm not married," he answered with a flirtatious glance. With a look of relief, she started with another question.

"Well, do you ha…" Greg, who also noticed what was going on abruptly and intentionally cut her off.

"Did everyone make their selections yet? Maybe Jack will have to look a little longer since he just got here," giving his brother a spurious smile.

"Yes, Greg, I've already selected what I would like to have," Jack said, looking up from the menu and realizing Jessica was staring straight into his eyes.

"And so have I," she said. Ally was so embarrassed and ashamed. She looked around to see if anyone else had picked up on Jessica's overt and indecent proposal. At this time everyone began to converse with each other to break up Jessica's advances toward Jack. He also tried by avoiding any eye contact with her, but she was always looking in his direction. Ally tried by bringing up the name of an old boyfriend of hers and asked, "Jessica, aren't you still seeing Rob? Just the other week I saw him when he came to take you out for lunch, right? Yeah, the two of you walked right by me on your way out."

"Rob…Rob? Who's Rob? Ohhhh, that Rob," she said sarcastically. "I was never really dating him. We went out a couple of times, and maybe had lunch but that was it. No. He wasn't my type," she said, looking at Ally with a sneer and a tone of annoyance. She turned her head from Ally.

"Besides, he was too short," she said while looking back at Jack. At this time, the waiter had come over to take everyone's order. The waiter finally took their request and left. While they were waiting for their food, Greg began to make small talk with the girls as they passed around the bottle of champagne. He began by asking if they were enjoying themselves so far and how long was their stay at the beach. He was trying to keep the conversation going to make everyone feel comfortable. He had noticed the look of embarrassment on Ally and Toni's faces when Jessica went after Jack with her obvious lascivious behavior. His client, Ken, though stoic in manner, seemed to be quite amused. Greg knew that his brother could hold his own, but didn't want the evening to go in the wrong direction. Not only was he physically fit, but also he was experience and competent in handling sexually aggressive women. "He would give them just what they were asking for," as his brother would say, hardheartedly. He took no prisoners.

Earlier that day, Jack had phoned Greg to tell him that he would be joining him in Huntington Beach. Greg told him about Ally, a girl he had met on the beach earlier that afternoon and found her to be most attractive and sweet. He also told him that he had invited her and her two friends to dinner. In the presence of women, Jack used his looks and charm to titillate their mind and then use their bodies, so Greg wanted to caution his libidinous brother to be respectable in their presence, as he also had reminded him as they walked to the table together when Jack first arrived.

Speaking on the phone, "Look Jack, I really want to make a good impression on Ally, so be on your best behavior."

"Come on, Greg, what do you think I'm going to do?" asked Jack innocently.

"Remember, Jack, I'm your brother. I know you," he only laughed.

"I'll see you soon," Jack said. They both hung up the phone.

After everyone had ordered and the host walked away, Jack excused himself and went to the men's room. Almost immediately, Greg also got up, excused himself and followed briskly behind Jack. Ally watched them with concern as they walked away. She whispered to Toni, "This is her fault."

Greg was trying to catch up with Jack. He had gone to remind him and reiterate what they had spoken about earlier on the phone. Things were getting out of hand, and this was an opportunity to get the situation cooled down. As Greg walked through the door, Jack was coming out of the stall towards the sink to wash his hands. Greg turned Jack around by his shoulder and stood nearly three inches from his face. Just then, a short, stocky man walked out of a stall, still zipping up his pants. The man turned and walked hurriedly out the door. Not knowing what was going to happen, he headed straight for the exit without bothering to wash his hands.

"Listen Jack, I know that little wench is coming on to you, but I don't want you to cause me to blow my chances with this girl."

"What? I haven't done anything. You should be talking to her. And am I hearing you right? What happened to your vow? I thought you never wanted to seriously get involved with women again…ever. So what's up with this?"

Backing off and turning to look in the mirror holding onto the sink with both hands, he began speaking in a low tone, "I don't know. For some reason I felt something when I first laid eyes on her. And it's not what you think," Greg said in a serious tone.

"Hey, I didn't say anything," Jack said innocently, backing up, holding both palms up in front of him. "You know what, Greg, from the reaction of your girlfriend Ally towards this Jessica, I really don't think they're such good friends anyway. Heck, they're probably not friends at all. Not like she seems to be with the other girl, Toni. Besides, Jessica's no baby; she's an adult. If she keeps coming on to me, she's going to get what she's asking for. Besides, she's kinda cute. Nothing I'd want to take home to Mom though," drying his hands with the towel that the attendant who had just walked in handed him as he continued. "I'll try to deter her and avoid her, but if she steps over the line, sorry, brother, she's mine," he said as he slapped a twenty dollar bill in the heavy sized attendant's hand and dropped the towel into the bin. "Thannnk you sir," the attendant sang, his voice deep, with a large smile.

"Why don't you stop trying to play the field and settle down with someone?"

"What? You mean like… a wife?" Jack asked with a frown on his face. "Nah. Not me. I haven't been particularly interested in anyone that seriously… ever. Maybe someday to someone very special," Jack said smiling. "Maybe I will someday, but I'll guarantee you one thing, it won't be that trash."

"Aww, come on, Jack," Greg pleaded. Jack was so tempted to bring up Greg's engagement and breakup, but he didn't want to hurt his brother's feelings.

"Look, don't hurt this girl. She's still with Ally, even if they're not friends," he said firmly. Noticing how long they had been gone, with urgency in his voice, "Look, we have to hurry and get back so as not to cause any concern. I don't want Ally to think that you got upset about her friend chasing after you. Man, if she only knew."

"Well, she just might find out," chuckling. He was so egotistical. His heartless behavior in the treatment of women had always been appalling to Greg.

When they had gotten back to the table, Greg apologized and lied with some explanation that they were catching up on the outcome of the business trip that Jack had flown in from.

"We didn't want to bore anyone with shop talk at the table," Jack concurred. While they were gone, Ally decided not to castigate or reprimand Jessica at the table about her behavior for fear of how she might react. She didn't want to arouse any concern from the other guests at their table, although she was sure that it was obvious to anyone around them. Her thoughts were of how Jessica's behavior had really gotten noticeably out of control. Ally had given her a disdainful look that Jessica only ignored. While they were gone, she had been laughing and giggling with Ken, one of the clients who was sitting on the other side of her. He was really enjoying her. Jessica acted as though she didn't even know her two coworkers. Sean had seen that both Toni and Ally were getting quite perturbed with their friend. He tried to distract their attention from Jessica in conversation, but could see Ally constantly glancing in the direction where Greg and his brother had disappeared. By her short responses, he knew that her mind was not there. To her, it seemed as though they had been gone for hours. She began to feel anxious for the night to end. Jessica had ruined everything. When the brothers had gotten back to the table, Ally tried to read their faces. They repeatedly apologized for taking so long. Soon everything had gotten back on track. Greg looked at Ally and smiled. He showed no signs of irritation or regret. The men began talking amongst themselves about sports, business, and the unpredictable stock market. They were in their world where women preferred not to go. Even so, Ally had to find a chance to apologize to Greg for Jessica's embarrassing behavior. She hoped that her actions hadn't influenced what he thought about her.

About twenty minutes after the waiter had taken their order, the food arrived. It was so beautifully garnished and attractively arranged on large elegant plates. The appearance suited only for the regal as the combined aroma bellowed into the air, titillating their senses. The myriad of meal choices almost covered the entire area of the table. Jessica hastily ate like a ferocious animal as if she had somewhere to go. By this time, she had had several glasses of Champagne as well. Fortunately, she was eating which is probably why she was not totally inebriated. Still annoyed by Jessica's behavior, Ally told Toni that this would be the first and last time that she would ever go anywhere in public with Jessica.

"I'm really sorry that I persuaded you to let her come with us, Ally," Toni whispered in a sorrowful tone. "This is the worst I've ever seen her behave. I don't really know what's gotten into her. Maybe it's the excitement of being around all of this affluence."

"That's okay, Toni. Now we know what she's really capable of."

They were speaking softly to each other when Sean, who was another client, began to focus his attention on Toni, whom he found to be a very enjoyable person to talk to. Their conversation was enjoyably benign. It was casual and friendly.

The time simply seemed to have quickly flown by. Everyone raved about their choices of food, offering one another a sample for confirmation. They all were in awe and raved about the ingeniously designed rooms, innumerable amenities that the Hyatt offered of which the guests attested to, and the perfect weather for such a night as this. Noticing that everyone had finished their meals seeing the nearly empty plates, Greg urged his guests to order anything else they wanted. Toni and Sean decided to order dessert and continued with their conversation about their careers and goals in life and whatever other subject came up to fill the space with idle chatter. Greg ordered a pot of coffee for the whole table to offset the alcohol, if necessary. The drink orders and champagne had doubled since they first sat down for dinner. With an artificially coy look, Jack turned to Jessica and asked if she would like some dessert.

"I'll have my dessert later," she said, gazing right into Jack's eyes and touching him with her foot under the table, reaching for the private areas of his body. He stared right back, hardly intimidated. When the waiter came back with the coffee, Ken reached to prepare a cup. Greg took Ally by the hand and asked if she would like to see the patio. He had boasted that it was a most spectacular view and a must see. Ally turned to Toni and before she could ask, Toni told her to go.

"Go ahead…of course, I don't mind. You don't have to ask me. I'd like to see the patio myself before we leave," Toni answered. "But for now, I'll just sit here with Jessica."

"For what? I'm a big girl, Toni. I don't need a sitter," Her words were a bit slurred. Ally looked at Jessica with piercing eyes, turned her head with a start and walked away. Greg took her hand as she walked alongside him towards the patio.

It was an awesome sight as he had said. The architecture with its Spanish flare was obvious at this resort. Each entrance was built with an archway. Everything had been painted with light pastel colors and white. There were palm trees everywhere, aligned strategically to bring out the majestic view. The water spewing from the mouths of fish statuettes were fountains that lined the lighted elongated pool of blue water. Greg and Ally talked and laughed for quite a while. Greg hadn't felt this happy in the company of a woman in a long time. It seemed that whenever he met someone, the memory of Janice would somehow crop up and he would end the relationship. This time, he noticed that he didn't feel that way. He couldn't even make himself think about her. He didn't want this night to end. Not wanting to believe it, but knew that she had to be the one. He didn't even care if his mother agreed or not. Boldly, he asked Ally if she would allow him to see her again. "Was this a dream?" she thought. "I know I'm going to wake up at the condo. This has to be a dream." Even though she prayed that he would want to see her again, it was still too incredible to believe. They exchanged phone numbers and addresses. He talked about growing up and how the family business had begun by his father with the help of his mother. As his father was getting older, he had passed more of the responsibilities to him and his brother, most of which was in the field. Ally listened attentively as he explained how he nor and his brother really minded traveling because they got to see so many different places. Sometimes their travels even took them out of the country. His father was still active in the running of the business, but tried not to invest as much time as he had in the past, especially in travel. He chuckled when he mentioned how his mother sort of just sits back now and reap the benefits of its success after all of her years of sacrifice during the beginning stages of the business. Ally had spoken well of her parents too, expressing the love and respect for them for all they had done for her. She was their only child; her mother had conceived late in their marriage, not intentionally, but that was how God had allowed things to work out, she explained. As a family, they went to church almost every Sunday. When she was a little girl, they would attend services, while she was sent to Sunday school class. She smiled as she told him how much she enjoyed every minute. Greg smiled too, as he could see on her face the happiness those memories brought to her. She explained how they tried their best to follow the will of God, and continue to do so to this day, she expressed with pride. At this point, Greg knew that she was someone to be respected and that he wanted her to be in his life. He listened to her with curiosity. He couldn't remember religion ever being discussed by anyone else he had ever been out with. He could hear in her voice the love for her parents and the compassion she felt for others. He admired her values, the love and empathy that she explicitly personified. She was surely the person he wanted to be his wife and to be the mother of his children. Not having felt like this in such a long time, he fumbled at thinking about commitment almost immediately. Overcome by strange emotions for even thinking in this manner, he was still taken aback by her integrity and honesty. Knowing it was necessary but pressing in the back of her mind, she wanted to apologize for Jessica's behavior while they were still in the garden out of her presence but didn't want to ruin the moment. After a while, she finally told him that it was time to get back to the table to see about the other guests even though her thoughts were the contrary. Slowly they headed back to the table. Approaching the table she saw Toni and Sean still relaxingly, sitting at the table talking over an after dinner cup of coffee. Ally gasped when she saw that Jessica was not there. "Where's Jessica?"

"I don't know. All I know is that she's with Jack." She had totally forgotten all about Jack while they were in the garden. Greg's stomach sunk. Wiping his brow, he began to sweat from anxiety and asked, "Where's Ken?"

"He said that he was tired and was going back to his room to go to bed," Toni again replied. He knew that if they were both missing, he had taken her to his room. He thought to himself, "I guess she crossed the line. Surely Ally couldn't blame me for Jessica's, nor Jack's actions." He decided that unless she said something to him about it, he wouldn't say anything.

Ally turned to Greg, "I'm sure Jessica is with your brother, probably in his room, knowing her," Ally said, sounding angry and disgusted.
"Greg, I think we better leave now," frustrated about this news. "I really don't want to, but I don't want to be selfish and leave my friend Toni sitting out here. Could you please call your brother so that he can tell Jessica that we're leaving now?" Greg was so relieved to hear what Ally said about Jessica.
"So Jack was right," he thought. "They're not really friends after all." He actually felt blameless.
"All right Ally, I'll go call right now," Greg said. He went out to use one of the hotel phones hoping that Jack might answer seeing "Front Desk" as the caller on the phone in the room. The phone seemingly rang for more than five minutes before he answered.
"Hello." Jack finally answered, practically out of breath.
"Jack, what's going on?" Greg firmly whispered into the phone.
"I was wondering why the front desk would be calling my room. If you're looking for Jessica, she's with me. Look, Greg, she crossed the line!" he said panting. He spoke softly not wanting Jessica to hear. Greg could hear Jessica moaning in the background.
"You know.., you're disgusting and apparently have no dignity or shame," Greg said with anger in his voice. Infuriated by his brother's behavior, he slammed the phone down. The sudden noise startled the clerk at the front desk, who looked at Greg with raised eyebrows.
"Sir, is everything okay?" Realizing his noticeably angry actions, he apologized and assured the concerned man that everything was all right.

When Greg got back to the table, everyone had just about finished everything that they had ordered. The busboy continued to remove their dinnerware from the table as those who left were sitting and waiting for news about Jessica.
"Uhh, sorry to keep you waiting, but Jessica said to go on without her," Greg told them sheepishly. "She said that she'd have Jack bring her to the condo later," Greg was lying. He wouldn't dare let on as to what was really going on in that room, although he thought Ally probably already knew.

"Okay, sounds like her to me. Let's go, Ally," Toni said in a manner, which showed that she was utterly fed up with Jessica at this point.

"Greg, I am so sorry about Jessica. Her behavior has been atrocious all evening," she said apologetically. With a look of anger, she turned her head to reach down for her purse that she had left on the chair and in a low tone uttered under her breath, "She's such a…"

"So is Jack," Greg interjected. Embarrassed and surprised, she had no idea that she could be heard. With a look of disappointment and grief, she turned and looked up into his eyes.

"Greg, I hope that Jessica's actions haven't made a bad impression on you concerning Toni and me. She's just a co-worker."

"Don't worry. She hasn't impressed me at all," he said jokingly. "But I also know my brother." Everybody looked at each other, smiled and began walking towards the entrance of the restaurant.

While waiting for the valet to bring the car, the three talked about the events of the evening. Sean had already expressed his gratitude inside the dining room, said his goodbyes, and proceeded to go to his room. In spite of Jessica and Jack, they all agreed that they had a wonderful time. Toni told Greg with genuine appreciation, "Had it not been for you Greg, we would have never known what it's like to be on the other side."

"What do you mean, Toni? The other side of what?"

"The side of the rich and famous!" she exclaimed.

"Toni, let me tell you something. Not everybody that you've seen around this area is rich and certainly not famous. You'll be surprised at how far a little plastic card can go and how far people will try to take it."

"But it is true what you said about everyone around here not being rich. We're here, aren't we?" Toni said laughing.

"You know Toni, money isn't everything."

"True, but it sure helps," again responding with a chuckle. They all joined in the laughter.

"But really… on a more serious note, remember, having money does help, but loving it can contribute to your own demise." Ally stood between Greg and Toni as they debated. She had zoned out into thoughts of her own. She was thinking of how truly wonderful this guy was.

"He is so down to earth and with such wisdom. He's a successful businessman and he wants to see me again?" She couldn't get over it. She felt like she did in high school when the high school's quarterback, the most popular guy at school asked her out. This whole night was so incredible to her that she knew at any moment she would wake up. "This is crazy," still fantasizing over Greg wanting to see her again.

"Earth to Ally," Toni said laughing. "Where were you?" Just then, the valet came driving up with their car.

"Here's your car, ladies," Greg said as he opened the door for Ally and handed her the keys. The valet had opened the door for Toni on the passenger's side. Again, he thanked them for coming, apologized for Jack, and expressed that he hoped to see them again before they left as he waved good-bye.

"You have my number," he yelled, as they were driving away. "I'll call you as soon as I see Jessica."

Until he said that, she had almost forgotten about Jessica's disappearance.

As they were driving along the driveway back to the street, Toni and Ally talked about how disgusting Jessica was and how her salacious behavior even attracted the attention of the patrons sitting nearby in the dining room. "I was so embarrassed when she went after Greg's brother like some kind of animal in heat looking for a mate."

"I was too," said Toni. "Did you see that older couple faces' sitting on the right of us? I could see the woman constantly staring at our table out of the corner of my eye."

"Well, it seems that Jessica has met her match. I guess she got what she was asking for."

"That's true, but she did come with us, Toni, and we have to make sure that she's okay. I think when I get to the room I'm going to give Greg a call and ask him to have Jessica call us so that we can pick her up, rather than for Jack to bring her. I kinda feel responsible, but not for her actions. Those belong to her."

"She is a grown woman. But I know what you mean."

They got back seemingly quicker, even though they were unfamiliar with the area. This time, however, the scenery was not a distraction. The rest of the ride back as they drove on Pacific Coast Highway had been silent with thoughts of their disastrous night's end. As soon as they got inside, Ally grabbed the card with Greg's number, went into the bedroom and called his room.

"Hi, Greg, this is Ally Morris."

"Oh, hi, Ally, I'm glad you called," Greg said.

"Really? Why? What's wrong?" Ally asked in a voice anticipating some impending doom. "Have you heard from Jessica?"

"No, I'm sorry to say."

"Listen, Greg, I'm sorry to bother you, but I really feel responsible for Jessica since we drove here together. I'd like to pick her up myself when she's ready to come back to the condo. So could you please give her this message when you see or hear from her? I'm sorry…so why were you glad that I called?"

"Calm down, Ally. Nothing's wrong. I was just glad that you called so that I could hear your voice again." There was momentary silence. "Hello?" Greg said, wondering if they had suddenly gotten disconnected, or worse, that maybe she had hung up.

Ally was speechless. Finally, she said, "Greg, stop joking. You don't even know me."

"But, that's what I intend to do. I want to get to know you. Do you think we can get together tomorrow night?"

"I don't know. Remember, I did come here with friends. I don't want to abandon them. That wouldn't be too kind or fair. In fact, it would be quite selfish."

"You're right. But still, I'd like to see you before you leave. How about on Sunday…maybe for breakfast or brunch? You could bring your friends if you like."

"That sounds like a possibility. I'll call you Saturday afternoon to confirm. And Greg, please don't forget to give Jessica that message for me."

"I won't."

"Okay, then. We're going to stay up and watch TV a while, so I don't care what time it is that she wants us to come. We'll be there. Good night Greg, and thanks again."

Greg told her good night, and they both hung up.

Toni had taken a shower while Ally was on the phone. After her brief conversation with Greg, she walked to the bathroom and yelled through the fully mirrored door, "Toni, you won't believe this,"

Toni yelled back, "What has she done now?"

"No. Not her. I'm not talking about Jessica. It's about me. Greg said that he was glad that I called because he wanted to hear my voice again. Can you believe it?" Ally said, almost losing her composure.

"Ally, can you wait until I get out of the shower?" Toni yelled through the running water. "I can barely hear you."

Ally was looking at herself in the mirror, staring and wondering just what Greg saw in her. With all those other girls on the beach why her? She was no blond beauty. She was not even wearing a bikini. She was flattered, even feeling quite honored. Ally never thought of herself as any great beauty or anything, but indeed, she was beautiful. Her parents had raised her in such a way as not to look totally on the outside for beauty, but to look mainly on the inside of a person. If there is beauty on the inside, it will manifest and show itself on the outside. They also impressed and emphasized it is the outside beauty that does not last. "That kind of beauty only lasts for a short time. It's the beauty on the inside that will always be there and that's what will carry you through long-lasting years in any relationship." She could hear the voice of her mother as she thought of those words. While looking at herself in the mirror, she reflected on how her caring parents had so lovingly disciplined her so that she would be equipped and prepared to deal with the many encounters of life to sustain her when she decided to leave home and live on her own. She caught herself imagining being married to Greg, when suddenly, the door swung open and startled her out of deep thoughts.

"Now, what were you babbling about out here?" Toni asked, walking towards her suitcase with a towel wrapped around her body and one wrapped around her head. She was looking for her comb.

"I just got off the phone with Greg. He told me that he was glad that I'd called and do you know why?"

"No, why?" Toni answered quickly, feigning curiosity.

"…so that he could hear my voice again! Can you believe that?" Ally said excitedly. "Wow, you must have really made quite an impression on him," Toni responded with delight for her friend. "Ally, I'm sorry, but I have to get to bed," as she walked into the bedroom to put on her nightgown. "I can't stay up to wait for Jessica to call. We probably won't hear from her until tomorrow anyway," pulling the covers back to get in bed. Ally, who had been following right behind her, was still talking about her phone conversation with Greg. "And yeah, one other thing, he also said that he wants to see me again before we leave. In fact, he invited all of us out for breakfast or brunch on Sunday after checkout," she said turning to walk back to the living room. Toni was back to the living room now with a big grin closely following Ally trying to get all the details of what she said about a Sunday brunch.

"He wanted to go out tomorrow, but I told him that I couldn't because I had to spend time with you guys," sounding somewhat regretful. "Our reason for coming here was to have a weekend of fun together."

"That's true, but if you want to spend time with him, it's okay with me. I guess after this evening, we can rule out that he's a serial killer, huh?" said Toni jokingly. She pushed Toni, and they both fell on the sofa laughing.

"Seriously, there's no way that I would abandon you guys. But if it was only Jessica here, now that's another story. No, I'm just kidding. Besides, I just met him. I don't want to appear too anxious." While they both sat on the sofa, seated on opposite sides from one another, both with one leg hanging over the armrest, they began to recall the events of the evening again. They talked about how truly beautiful the Hyatt-Regency was. How awestruck they were to see firsthand such opulence. The furniture, the décor, the guests, it seemed to them that they were living inside a Hollywood magazine. Quickly, Jessica became the main topic.

"Can you believe that Jessica?" Ally asked. "I was sooo embarrassed," she expressed angrily while frowning at the thought. "How could she have acted so rude and uncouth in a place like that…bringing that kind of attention from all those people sitting around us?"

"Yeah, she was making a real fool of herself," Toni said.

"Knowing her, she'll deny that she did anything wrong and will probably act as though something's wrong with us if we say anything to her about it," Ally responded.

"That's right, knowing her," Toni added, thinking of past encounters with Jessica.

"Yeah, she probably would."

"Toni, I meant what I said earlier. I will never, ever go anywhere with her in public again. Did you know that she could be so reckless and go this far? You know her better than I do."

"You know, Ally, there aren't a lot people that really care for Jessica at work or anywhere else that I know of. I don't think she has many friends. She's never mentioned any other names to me except the names of people that we work with. And I'm sure you've noticed that. People at work only tolerate her just like we do. Truthfully, I think she's a very lonely person. I really hate to see anybody lonely, even if they are obnoxious at times, so I tried to be friendly to her. You know, like going to lunch sometimes or do happy hour or something every now and then. That's just how I am." Toni tried to explain that she truly felt pity for Jessica.

"Yeah, I know that's how you are. I know firsthand. That's why I liked you when we first met. And now consider you as a real friend…my best friend." They gave each other a hug.

"Well…," continued Toni, "I've never seen Jessica take off with someone that she'd just met before although, mind you, I don't go out with her all of the time, so I really don't know for sure if she has ever done this before, or what she's capable of doing."

"Even so…" Ally interjected, "…her behavior tonight was despicable." Her facial expression displayed the acrimony that she felt. "I really don't want to talk about her anymore." Ally was becoming extremely angry at how their evening had ended. The evening had gone from one of gaiety, excitement, and awe to an embarrassing finale of apologies and regret. With thoughts seesawing, the two women again diverted their conversation back to the breathtaking sites, the spectacular resort where they had been, joking about Greg's guests, and the delectable foods that they had eaten and confessed that they probably would never experience anything of that caliber again. Realizing how late it had gotten, Ally left Toni, who had dozed off on the sofa to take a shower and prepare for bed. Awakening when Ally got up, she saw her heading to the bathroom. "What if she calls tonight?"

"Well, I guess we'll just have to get up and go get her," Ally answered with intonations that she was dreading the possibility as she stepped into the bathroom and closed the door. She had a feeling that they were not going to hear from her that night, just as Toni had said. Toni got up and slowly walked back towards the bedroom.

Chapter 2

It was almost eight o'clock Saturday morning when Toni got up. Ally had gotten up earlier because she hadn't slept well. All night long, she tossed and turned replaying the previous evening, wondering and imagining where and what was going on with Jessica. It wasn't that she thought Jack would harm her, but she felt responsible that she was out with a stranger. It was she, who had introduced them to Greg in the first place, although it had been Jessica's decision to go with his brother. Because of Ally's upbringing, she couldn't fathom a woman being so promiscuous, even though it did seem to be the norm these days. She wanted to call Greg again, but she didn't want to disturb him again so early in the morning. Maybe around 10 o'clock would be more appropriate. Toni walked into the living room still in her nightgown to where Ally was sitting. "I guess she hasn't called yet, huh?"

"No. Not yet. I'm going to call Greg again around ten. Do you think 9:00 is too early?"

"No. Even if he's not awake by then, 9:00 is not too early to call someone," said Toni. "What do you mean? Eight o'clock isn't too early especially in these circumstances. Besides, it's almost 9:00 now. Look at the clock."

Ally picked up the card that she had left next to the phone. She dialed Greg's number.

"Hello?"

"Good morning, Greg. How are you? I hope I didn't wake you. Listen, I'm sorry to be such a pest, but I haven't gotten a call from Jessica. Have you seen or spoken to your brother yet?"

"No, I'm sorry to say. I haven't seen Jack or Jessica since last night when we were at dinner, but I know that he's in his room. I saw a "Do not Disturb" sign hanging on the doorknob last night as I walked by. I got off on his floor first before going to my room. Since it was so late, I didn't knock because I didn't want to disturb the other patrons. Feeling at fault, he said, "Ally, I am truly sorry for all this. I hope that your weekend hasn't been ruined because of me."

"Oh no, it hasn't been ruined. I just thought that we were going to get to hang out today like we had originally planned since we have the whole day. Now we have to wait. I didn't want to go off without Jessica…leaving her here alone with no transportation. And tomorrow we have to check out by noon," she explained, while simultaneously thinking of a plan. "I'll tell you what, Toni and I are going to go out for breakfast. This should give Miss Jessica more time to get in touch with us. Then we'll check back here, or with you before we go out for the day. Call my room if you see her or hear from her or your brother. If we're not here when you call, could you leave a message at the front desk? Thank you. You still have my number, don't you? I gave it to you last night, remember?"

"Oh yeah, of course, I have it."

"Also, if you should see or hear from her, tell her to please call our room and if we're not back to please leave a message at the front desk?"

"Sure."

"Thanks, Greg."

"No problem. Go on with your plans and don't worry." Greg, too, was getting annoyed with Jack and Jessica. Their antics were disrupting everybody's plans. He was beginning to feel sorry for Ally, though. He could hear disappointment and frustration in her voice.

Toni had gone to the bathroom to quickly get washed up and dressed to go out for breakfast while Ally was on the phone with Greg. She put on a bright flowered pullover top with a matching green cotton skort. From her suitcase she got her almost wallet size brown suede fringed shoulder bag and slipped on her sandals. They decided to go somewhere close for breakfast. They wanted to find a place within walking distance to eat and get back quickly in case they got a call from Jessica. On the way, as they drove down the street to get to the highway the evening before, they noticed a number of restaurants. "I'm really not that hungry," said Ally, as they walked along, stopping to read the menus on the fronts of windows and on the sidewalk stands in front of the restaurants. It was early and the streets were not very crowded. In between checking menus as they walked, Toni said in a daring tone, "I hope you're not losing your appetite over Jessica."

"I don't know. I don't think so. But there's a lot going on now, you know. And I keep thinking about Greg, too."

Toni pulled Ally by the hand to the edge of the sidewalk near the curb, out of the way of any pedestrians. "Look, Ally, Greg is a nice guy. He's successful, handsome, chivalrous, polite... I could go on and on with the superlatives, but you've got to keep everything in perspective. You just met him. You don't really know him, as you said yourself or anything about him except what he's told you. For all you know, he could be just like his brother. I'm not trying to dissuade you, but I just think that you should slow it down, step back and play it by ear."

"Yes, I think you're right," Ally agreed with a sigh. They started walking again. Toni occasionally glanced at Ally to try to read her mood.

Soon they found a little diner down the street about a half block from their condo that served reasonably priced food. Immediately, they were met with the aroma of breakfast and a courteous hostess. She led them through a maze of wooden tables occupied by an array of patrons. There were whining children, crying babies, and sleepy teens picking at their food as their incognizant parents sat beside them. In seconds, a little bubblegum waitress whose hair was a myriad of tiny blond braids pulled back into a ponytail was there to take their order. Ally ordered a bagel with cream cheese and orange juice. Toni got the hot cakes big breakfast. After collecting their menus, she disappeared in the maze of tables. In about fifteen or twenty minutes, they could see a huge brown tray headed toward them. Underneath was the tiny waitress with their order. After placing their food in front of them she asked, "Is there anything else?"

"Not right now, thank you."

Ally sat mulling over her food thinking of Jessica's lustful behavior.

"I still can't get over her," she blurted out, breaking the silence. "Jessica's conduct was just plain lewd. She doesn't even know that guy. How could she spend the night with him?"

"I guess that's what sluts do," Toni responded with nonchalance. "Like I said before, Jessica has always been an unscrupulous person."

"Yes, but that's no excuse for her not calling us. She could have let us know something by now. This weekend has become a real nightmare. Because of her, our plans have really gone out of whack."

"That's right. Now we have to keep bothering Greg to find out if he's seen her and try to hang around the room to wait for her call. This isn't fair to us to waste our time waiting for her," Ally said angrily. "She's acting as though she doesn't even care."

"Well, maybe that's the answer to this whole thing," said Toni. "She doesn't even care."

"Well, now it's almost 10, and we still haven't heard a word from her unless she's called since we left," Ally said, looking at her watch. "We'll go back to the condo and if we haven't heard from her by 11:00, we'll just go on with our plans. It's already later than what we'd planned. We can't let her ruin our weekend."

"That's right. "Even if she has to sit around in the room for the rest of the day, then that's just too bad. It's her own fault. I really don't want to talk about her anymore, Ally."

"Neither do I."

"And I'm going to finish my breakfast. And I'm not going to rush either," Toni emphasized.

"That's right. We can't let her ruin our weekend," Ally concurred. They talked about their plans for the day as they finished their meal. Already behind in their plans, the girls unconsciously scurried back to the hotel.

Not being able to get Jessica out of her mind, Ally began mulling over her again. Her being an uninvited guest had actually commandeered the planning of their trip. At her persistence, a week before they were to leave, Toni, Ally, and Jessica had gotten together after work at Jessica's apartment. She convinced them to meet there to plan their activities for their weekend getaway and offered to cook dinner for them as bait. The apartment décor reflected Jessica's personality. A yellow, faux leather loveseat with a matching chair was positioned in almost the center of the room. There a black round, faux leather ottoman, all of which surrounded a rectangular white shag rug that was spread out in the middle of the living room. Huge pictures of male celebrities clad in skimpy beachwear hung on the walls. After their Italian dinner, which included garlic bread and red wine and tea for Ally, they sat in the living room to discuss their itinerary. Jessica insisted they try parasailing the Saturday morning of the trip. Not one of them had ever been, but they agreed that it probably would be fun. Other things had been included, but this would be the highlight of the weekend. They would get up early around eight o'clock, have a light breakfast and get started before the crowd got there. They wanted to do something exciting, although not to this extreme, but decided to try it anyway. So now, that they were here, they had to rush and play catch-up because of the time lost trying to locate Jessica. As they continued their walk back to the hotel, Ally asked Toni, "Why did you get such a big breakfast knowing that we were going parasailing?"

"Toni answered. "Hey wait a minute. It was after I ordered that we decided not to wait for her...remember."

"Well, hopefully, you'll be okay, and soon, because we're not waiting a minute over 11 to hear anything from her. Do you think that I should call Greg one more time before we leave? I did use the word 'call' and not 'wait', didn't I?" Ally asked rhetorically.

"No, absolutely not. We've given her enough chances. Once we find the parasailing place, we can leave the number with Greg, and at the front desk. And if he doesn't call, then he hasn't heard, and if she hasn't called, then she doesn't care," answered Toni, still a bit miffed about the whole situation.

"Again, Toni, you're right. She's wasted enough of our time. You know, she may try to blow us off, but she's going to hear it from me anyway," Ally said angrily, as visions of the previous night replayed through her mind.

"You're not the only one. I hope she doesn't think that she's just going to waltz in here and act as if nothing ever happened," Toni added.

Chapter 3

As Jack rolled over to look at the alarm clock on the night table, he quickly sat up on the side of the bed. It was eleven o'clock. He looked over at Jessica sprawled out on her back. She awoke and saw how he was staring at her. Trying to read his eyes she asked, "What's wrong?"

"Nothing's wrong. I just thought you might want to call your friends," he said.

"I will," she answered, pulling on his arm, trying to reach for his hand. Without being obvious, he tried to move away saying, "Don't you think they're worried about you?"

"You didn't seem to care about that last night when you lured me into your room," she said, caressing his long, muscular arm.

"I lured you? You practically molested me at the dinner table. What are you talking about?" He was insulted but constrained himself from blaring out some hurtful insult. Jack was not going to let some sleazy woman think that he desired her. He never had to chase anyone in his life. The choice was always his. He always had his pick of the litter.

"Well, I did think that you were kinda cute," she confessed.

"What is it with you and those girls? Aren't they your friends?"

"I wouldn't say 'friends.' I work with them. They're my coworkers and we go out together sometimes, but that's about it. And what do you care anyway?"

Thinking about what Greg had asked of him, he said in a more tender tone, "It's my brother, Greg." He's worried that I'm blowing his chances with Ally. So I think that you should call them at least to let them know that you're all

47

right."

"Oh, so now you're concerned. I don't get you. Last night you were all over me and didn't care whether I left with them or not. And now you sound as if you're trying to throw me out. Are you?"

Holding back the truth, he answered, "Look, Jessica, I didn't say that. I just think that you should call your friends, just out of courtesy. I'm sure they're worried about you. Unless they're used to you abandoning them when you go out together," Jack said, trying to make her feel like a bimbo.

"What do you think I am, some sort of a slut? ... easy, or something?" she asked, feeling that she had just been insulted.

He looked at her with a smirk. In his mind, he was insolent with an answer to her question, but he held back and didn't say anything.

"I've never gone off with anyone I didn't know before," she continued

"Well, you could have fooled me."

"What do you mean by that?" she asked defensively.

"You have to agree, Jessica. No one would have known that by your behavior last night," he said, intending to insult her again. She got up and wrapped the sheet around herself, staring angrily into his face from the other side of the bed. Noticing her anger and needing to appease her for the sake of his brother, he walked around the bed and dishonestly apologized for what he had said. He assured her that she took it the wrong way. With his arms wrapped around her, he persuaded her to call her friends.

It was almost 11:30 when she tried to call the room. She'd gotten the business card from her purse where she had written their phone number. Since there was no answer, she called the front desk to find out if there were any messages. Toni and Ally were driving down the highway on their way to go parasailing.

They located a place in the yellow pages and left the number with Greg and at the front desk. There were a few to choose from along this stretch of the pier in between fishing charters, sailboats, and small cruisers. They walked into a small shed. Standing at a tall desk was a couple that was talking to a male voice from behind the desk. After they were handed papers, they sat down to fill out the forms. When the girls stepped up to the desk sitting low on a small swivel chair was a young tan fair-haired muscular young man who greeted them. They looked askance at him when they saw him then looked at each other. They were hoping to see someone who at least looked experienced. The young looking lad asked if they had ever been parasailing and then proceeded to tell them all about such an experience and explained what precautionary measures they had to adhere to. They looked at each other and shrugged their shoulders. He sounded knowledgeable even if he wasn't. While they were still reading and filling out the disclaimer forms, the phone started ringing behind the desk.

"Wonder if that could be her," Ally whispered with anxiety into Toni's ear.

"Good Morning, this is Slide Glides Parasailing. Can I help you? Did you just ask if there was anyone here named Ally or Toni? I don't know. Hold on and I'll check." He stood up and looked at them. "Excuse me, but are your names Toni and Ally?"

"Yes," answered Toni.

Looking at her strangely, he said, "Okay, you have a call."

"Thank you. I'm sorry about this," Toni said as she took the phone receiver from his hand. "We have a friend who was supposed to meet us here." Ally tried to explain. He only peered at her with a disinterested look on his face, turned and disappeared behind the desk.

"Hello, Jessica? Where are you?" Toni said sternly, but softly. "Where have you been? We have been worried about you all night. What's going on?" Lost in the moment, Toni heard the young man clearing his throat as an indication that her time was up.

"Okay, listen, don't go anywhere. I have to get off this phone. Give me your number. I'm going to call you right back." Ally glanced at the young man, "Sir, we're still going. We have to speak with our friend first."

"Okay, sure. I'll be right here when you get back. I'm not going anywhere," he responded sarcastically. Gathering up their papers, they hurried out the door. They scanned over the area hastily looking for a payphone. Catching their eyes was an area where there were about six payphones in a row that were several yards away from the parasailing company. Practically running, they reached the payphones. There were only two available. Talking on the phone next to one of the unoccupied ones was a hairy-legged man in flowered shorts wearing a straw Fedora who had given them such a queer look that they decided to move to the next one. Ally scrambled in her change purse for coins and quickly put them in Toni's hand. Dropping the coins in the slot, Toni rapidly dialed the number that Ally called out to her. "Hurry up, answer it." Toni said to herself with impatience. The phone rang and rang, finally a tired voice said, "Hello."

"Hello, Jessica," Toni blasted.

"Yes, it's me again," Jessica said softly, but with sarcasm as if being annoyed by the call. Toni answered while looking over at Ally.

"Jessica!" Toni called again sternly.

"You called my name twice, now what do you want?" Toni looked at Ally who was livid. She could tell by Toni's conversation that Jessica was being a smart aleck. She began shaking her fists, reaching out, gesturing for Toni to hand her the phone. Toni shook her head, "no" to Ally as she continued trying to speak to Jessica. Toni had never seen Ally display this much emotion of any kind. She couldn't let her talk to Jessica in that state of emotion. If she did, Jessica would probably have angrily hung up before they could find out what her intentions were. Ally was so filled with anger that she walked through the small parking lot and into the street. Toni could see her pacing back and forth and walking around parked cars. Car horns began to blow with drivers yelling for her to get out of the street.

"Where are you?"

"What number did you dial?"

"Look, don't be so smart. It's obviously not our room number. We have been worried sick about you all night! So where are you? Are you with Greg's brother? And what are you going to do, Jessica?" Toni asked again persistently.

"Where are you guys? I called the room and you weren't there."

"We're here on our way to go parasailing like we had planned. Remember? You haven't answered my question, Jessica," Toni said in harsh tone.

"Toni, stop talking to me as if you're my mother. I am an adult, you know, and I don't have to answer to you," she said while looking around the room to see where Jack was. She certainly didn't want him to hear her or see her blow up. Containing her anger, she was trying desperately to end the conversation so that she could hang up.

"Now go ahead. What were you saying?"

"Listen, Jessica, I'm not trying to pry. And I know you're an adult, but you could have been considerate enough to have called us last night to at least let us know that you had other plans."

"I do apologize for not calling. That was thoughtless and selfish of me, wasn't it?" Jessica said, as she smiled at Jack, puckering her lips as if to kiss the air toward him. She thought she was showing Jack how considerate and selfless a person she truly thought herself to be. "You guys go on with your plans and I'll see you back at the condo later on," she said with a kind voice and pretentious smile.

"You know Ally and…"

"Oh, okay." But Toni had sensed the mockery in her voice. "Bye now." interrupting Toni's reply, she hung up the phone as she attempted to explain. Trying to impress Jack, she feigned sweetness in her voice to appear to be pleasant. Removing the receiver from her ear, she stared at it. Toni couldn't believe that she had just hung up on her while she was still talking. Angrily, she then slammed it down on the hook. Finally, having quelled her anger, Ally walked back over to Toni seeing that she was now furious. She stood right in front of her and waited for her response. Toni was dumbfounded and stood still, biting her bottom lip staring at Ally. "So what did she say?"

Breaking her silence with a look of defeat, she answered, "Nothing. She said absolutely nothing."

"What do you mean nothing?" She could see on Toni's face that she no longer cared. "So, what's going on, Toni? She had to have said something. What did she actually say?"

"I can't believe that hussy," Toni said in amazement. Toni started flailing her arms around as she ranted. "That is the most inconsiderate tramp I have ever known. And to be honest, I don't know any other tramps. I couldn't believe her. She had the nerve to tell me that she was an adult and didn't have to tell us anything. We have thought of nothing all night long, except whether or not she was okay, and this ingrate has the gall to act as though we are out of line for even being concerned about her. Then she hung up on me." Toni's nostrils were flaring. She was breathing like a raging bull. "She hung the phone up on me while I was still talking to her. Can you believe that?"

"Okay, Toni, calm down. You know we'd already talked about this. How did you not expect it? We'd already known that she would try to turn the tables around and blame us. Just let it go. She's not worth getting upset over," Ally said, after having gotten herself under control after her own tirade. She was upset with herself for even allowing someone to make her lose her self-control, especially someone that she hardly knew or cared for.

Jack had listened and heard the conversation she was having with one of her friends. He couldn't understand why she told them to go on with their plans without her. How could she have gotten the idea that he wanted anything more than what he had gotten from her the night before and continued those lustful acts of porn throughout the morning? They had only just met. Had it not been for his brother he would have thrown her out. Now that his sexual appetite had been satisfied, he desperately was hoping that she would leave soon on her own accord. Didn't she get the hint when he asked her to call her friends? He really didn't want to embarrass her, so he asked, pretending that he had no idea about her conversation on the phone.

"So, Jessica, are your friends coming to get you?"

"No, they're on their way to go parasailing," she answered nonchalantly.

"So didn't you want to go?" Looking straight into his eyes as she slowly walked towards him, she said, "No, not now."

"Then how were you going to get back to your condo?"

She stopped in her tracks with a look of surprise and amazement. "I didn't think that I was going back yet. I did what you asked me to do. I let them know that I was okay. Now I'm free for the day. So, are we going out for breakfast, or are we going to get room service?" smiling as she opened the sheet that she had been covering herself with. Wrapping them both in, she then pushed him onto the bed. Jack thought to himself, I was finished with her, but if she's giving, then I'm taking. And if she thinks that it's any more than this, I'll have to let her know about it…but later. He ravenously attacked her like a sex-craved lunatic, and she loved every moment of it.

Jack and Jessica hung out in the resort all morning and afternoon. They had ordered room service for their meals. It didn't take long to find out that her sex drive was insatiable, but by the latter part of the afternoon, he had had enough of what Jessica had to offer. He had been lying there in between their lascivious acts trying to contrive an excuse to get rid of her. Suddenly, he jumped up, sat on the side of the bed and said to her with urgency in his voice, "Jessica, I have to leave for a few minutes. I have to speak to my brother." He made up some excuse to leave the room.

"Why, what's wrong?" she asked with concern.

"It's a personal matter that I can't discuss with you, but I have to catch him before he leaves his room." He stood up grabbed his pants from the floor where he had dropped them the night before and then proceeded to look for his shoes. After searching the room for his shirt, he finally found it in the sheets. He put in on and buttoned it while hurriedly walking out the door. With a puzzled look on her face, Jessica had sat up on the bed, watching him scurry around the room as he got dressed piece by piece. She even handed him the shirt from under the sheets.

"Can't you just call him? How long do you think…" She heard the door close.

"…you'll be?" she continued in a very soft and saddened voice after hearing the door shut. Jack desperately needed to talk to his brother. He had to get rid of this sex maniac. She was getting out of hand and he had had enough of her.

He didn't want to hurt her because she was a friend of Ally's. He needed some advice from Greg as to how to handle the situation without being callous, so he went down to his room. Already he anticipated that Greg would reprimand him for having gotten into this situation in the first place, especially since he had already been warned.

Jack took the elevator up to Greg's floor. He knocked on the door. This time looking up and down the long hallway as if he was being followed, he knocked again. Greg opened the door. Jack quickly stepped across the threshold, went over to the sofa and plopped down. Greg walked directly behind him and stood in front of him.

"What's going on Jack? Where's that girl? Do you know that her friends have been calling and calling me about her for half the night and again this morning? Why didn't you have her call them? She may not be Ally's best friend, but they're here together. Ally feels responsible for her. So what's going on? Why hasn't she called them?" Greg turned around and slowly walked away with his arms folded. Turning back around he said, "You know, I warned you not to get involved with any of those girls."

"Okay. Now wait a minute, Greg. I did try to persuade her to call them."

When? …after you were finished with her?" Greg asked sarcastically, and with contempt. Jack leaped off the sofa, walked to where Greg was standing and looked straight into his face.

"Look, that little nymphomaniac didn't even want to call them at all. She finally called after I persuaded her to. I overheard her telling them that she was an adult and didn't have to answer to them. Then she told them to go on with their plans without her. Now she thinks that I'm interested in her and that she's going to spend the rest of the day with me. Greg, I'm not in any way interested in her. I don't know how she got that impression."

"You don't?" asked Greg again with sarcasm. And again, he walked away from Jack and sat down in the huge dining area. He glanced at the bar cabinet tempted to get a drink. Jack walked over and sat across from him.

"She's old enough and has been around long enough to know that having sex doesn't mean commitment, especially if you don't even know the person. She can't be that stupid. I mean naive." He corrected himself, trying not to sound so insensitive.

"You know Jack, you're sick!"

"And you can talk?" Jack retorted. "You've certainly had your share of women."

"Don't you dare try to compare me to you, Jack."

"Listen, I didn't come here to argue. Truthfully, I need your help. I've got to get out of this mess without any hassles. I don't want to hurt her, even though that little floozy deserves it. I don't want your friend Ally to think harshly of me which could make her think badly of you," Jack explained.

"Okay, maybe we can get you out on a quick flight back home. Let me think about this," said Greg. An idea had already popped into his mind. "Yeah, I think that will do it."

"Okay, now let me in on it." They both sat at the dining table quietly for a moment to quell their anger. Greg had again started castigating him for getting into this latest quagmire. Jack's only defense was that at least this one wasn't married. Jack got up to make coffee hoping this would help to clear the air. While Greg sat at the table, he began giving Jack the scenario as he was envisioning how they could get his infamous brother out of his dilemma. Jack was nodding his head and smiling conceding to the idea that Greg was playing out to him. They continued sitting and drinking their coffee concocting their plan. After almost an hour had passed, Jack went back to the room to play out their deceitful scheme.

Greg and Jack had fabricated a plan for Jack to have to take an urgent flight back home to the main business office, in New York. The plan would begin with an urgent call from their father who needed Jack to return home right away to straighten out a very crucial business deal, in which one of their top clients wanted to close by Monday morning; consequently, Jack had to get back in order to prepare for the meeting. After the plan was fabricated, Jack went back to his room to await the call from Greg, which would commence their guileful plan. This little scheme brought back to Jack the nostalgia of the good old days, something that Greg didn't want to remember.

When Jack got back to his room, Jessica was dressed and sitting at the dining room table having an early dinner, which she had taken upon herself to order from room service. "So where have you been?" Her question was curt. Clearly, by the tone of her voice he could tell that she was upset. Sounding annoyed, yet confident that he probably would never have to see her again, "I told you I had to go out for a while."

Sharply, she replied, "Well, I didn't know you'd be gone that long."

"Wait a minute, Jessica. What's going on here? Remember we just met last night and you're talking to me as if we have something going. You wanted to come to my room last night. You had your eyes and your hands all over me the whole evening. I mean, you seem to be a nice person, but I'm not looking for anyone special right now, so if that's what you think then..."

"I'm sorry, Jack, if I sounded like that. It's just that you didn't say where you were going and just left me here in this room all alone for such a long time, and..."

He cut her off. "Wait a minute. I did tell you that I needed to see my brother. Anyway, you had every chance not to be stuck in this room. I told you to call your friends. But when you called, you told them to go on without you. You chose to be here. I didn't ask you to stay," still annoyed. "Like I said, Jessica, you're a nice person but..." The phone rang. It was Greg calling to initiate their plan. "Hello," Jack said. "Oh, hey, Greg. Nothing really. Wait a minute, didn't I just speak to you?" he said pretending to be joking. "Oh, he did?" he said feigning surprise. "How did Dad even know I was here? I didn't call him. Okay, you're right." He looked over at Jessica with a pretentious sensual smile. Greg was working through their plan with this bogus conversation so that Jack could make the appropriate responses. "He did? When do I have to be back?" Jessica was listening, trying to figure out what was going on. "He wants me back by today?" Jack sounded as if surprised. "Well, if he says it's urgent then I guess I have no choice. Okay, I'll start packing right now. Yes, of course I'll stop by to see you before I leave. I know I need to get more details. Okay, see you later." He slowly put the receiver on the hook and looked at Jessica who was waiting to hear what caused Jack to look so somber. She had an idea of what he was going to say but waited to hear him say it.

Jessica had been listening to the whole conversation. Jack hadn't bothered to leave the room because it was his intention for her to hear everything that was said. He thought to himself that Greg's call was in perfect timing. He was wondering how long he would be able to hold back from telling her the real truth about how he felt about her. She was really beginning to push the wrong buttons at this point. All he wanted from her was sex. She gave it to him and he was finished with her... for now, anyway. And since she was that easy, he might as well get her phone number for future use. But after the way she performed, he began to have second thoughts.

"Jack, what's going on?" she asked very politely. She had stopped pushing her food around on the plate and continued sitting at the table waiting for his response. She didn't want to get him upset again.

"I'm sorry, Jessica."

"What... what happened?" she asked reluctantly, waiting to hear the answer.

"That was Greg." He continued talking to her as he walked over to the table. "He just got a call from my dad. He told him that I have to fly back home today to prepare for a major deal on Monday," he lied.

"If you don't mind my asking, why didn't he call you?" she asked.

"Who?"

"Your father."

He didn't mind answering her at all this time since the plan was to get rid of her. "Dad didn't know that I had come to Huntington Beach, remember?" looking at her and smiling, "I only came here because I'd finished my other assignment early. He gave her a phony sensuous gaze again brushed his knuckles softly across her jaw. Mendacity was his gift. His glib lies flowed so fluently from his lips with no consequence. She smiled back. "I'm sorry, honey, but you're going to have to call your friends again."

"I can't. Not after the way I talked to Toni."

"Sorry, Jessica, but I know you must have heard my conversation with my brother. I have to get out of here today," he said, feigning urgency in his voice. "I can have someone drive you back to your hotel."

"Okay. I guess I'll just have to eat crow," she said, feeling like an idiot and dreading having to look at their frowned up faces.

"I guess you'd better start getting yourself together." Disappointed, she began looking around for her pocketbook to get her comb.

"I'm going to send you back there in style." He picked up the phone. "I'll call for the limo service." Putting the phone down, he walked over to her from behind and put his arms around her. "But before you get yourself totally together, let's have one last go round," as he turned her around and began unbuttoning her blouse. She didn't resist… at all.

Chapter 4

Jack had been the most popular kid in high school, even more than his older brother. His popularity was mainly with the girls, although because of his athletic prowess, he was both admired and envied by some of the guys, especially due to his many talents and abilities in sports. He was a true jock. Their motherly influence and the boys' sublime good looks didn't always work in their favor, though. Jack and Greg sometimes, through no fault of their own, wound up in some pretty compromising situations as they were growing up during their high school years, primarily due to Jack's arrogance.

Their mother, Nancy, was from an average, middle-income family who lived in a modest single-family home just over the city line in Philadelphia. Her father was a pharmacist, who worked at a pharmaceutical research company, and her mother started a daycare service, which was constructed in the basement of their home. She had been a teacher and was the director of the facility. They didn't have the finer things in life, but they had what the majority of middle-class Americans had in those days. Still, Nancy was always envious and jealous of others' possessions, even their looks. She was also very unpopular which only nurtured her low self-esteem. Always focused on others she never found, nor developed, her own abilities and talents. She was such a self-deprecating individual. Reading was her only escape; she loved to read. Through reading, her imagination always took her to places of high standing and opulence. She indulged herself in stories of the rich, complete with kings, queens, princesses, and palaces. She would often imagine herself as the damsel in distress to be rescued by the handsome prince. He would marry her and take her to his castle where she would be showered with jewels, go to balls, have parties, and mingle with nobility. In the midst of her daydreams, she would be brought back to reality by the children at her mother's daycare, which annoyed her immensely. There was no way she could see children anywhere in her future. But as fate would have it, the prince who rescued her wanted children. She had two boys out of that union that she grew to love more than anything, and zealously protected them.

When the boys were growing up, she always taught her sons that they were special. She not only made them feel special, but she made them feel superior. She made sure they would always know this about themselves and live this way. Nancy lived vicariously through her sons' lives. She didn't allow them to feel the desire for anything they wanted, and then be denied as she felt had happened to her in her life. In her eyes, her boys could do no wrong, nor was anything ever their fault. Nancy never denied them anything, nor did she ever use the word "no" to them. They had no boundaries, which resulted in having no fears. They were never able to develop any sense of either guilt or responsibility. Jack and Greg lived under this protective umbrella for most of their young lives. But in Greg's development to maturity, his character was innately different from that of his brother. Unlike Jack, there was warmth within him. He had a sense of compassion, which sometimes confused him, because his feelings conflicted with the teachings of his mother.

As teenagers, the boys found out just how beneficial their looks and money were to them, especially when it came to dating. There was no one around to either bridle their thinking, or correct their actions. In fact, this behavior was even encouraged by their mother. Their mother was the first to introduce them to condoms. When their friends complained about not getting dates, the Tyler boys would boast about never having such a problem. In fact, they had to have separate phones and phone numbers so they wouldn't tie up each other's phone calls or tie up their parents' phone line. They were always being pursued. Never were they given the opportunity to pursue. She cautioned them that because of who they were and what they had, they could never trust anyone, especially women. Her teaching was inculcated with the caution that they should never get emotionally tied down to any one female. Jack learned this instruction very well. He showed little respect for girls and sometimes this didn't go well with the parents, especially girls' parents.

Nancy Tyler was not very well accepted in their community during the blossoming stages of the business. Where they lived was a friendly middle-class neighborhood and its people dwelled together nicely. As a child, she and her brother had lived in a middle-income dwelling too. In Hopatcong, New Jersey, theirs was the traditional household, with mother, father, two children, and the proverbial pet in the yard home, as were most. There were manicured lawns and flowered gardens. The parents were active in the PTA, mainly the mothers, and most of the families attended the community church. Most of the neighbors got along well with each other. It was a quaint little community, but because of Nancy's haughtiness, condescending attitude, arrogance, and her non-disciplinary parenting style, some of the neighbors, especially the women, didn't take very kindly to her. However, everyone in the community admired her husband John. He was very kind and respected by all, whereas, she was only tolerated.

In the early years, around the late '60s and early '70s, John Tyler worked extremely hard to get his business off the ground. Nancy helped early on with the bookkeeping. She scheduled his meetings, contacted clients, arranged for transportation, and did most of the accounting. They entertained many prospective clients, mainly in their home during those times. She felt ashamed and embarrassed of their little three-bedroom cottage. It was a very lovely home with a garage and was situated near a small lake. When the boys got old enough, they spent a lot of time playing near that lake along with the other children in the neighborhood. In spite of all of her other obligations of running a household and helping with the business, Nancy found time to work in the yard. She had planted rose bushes just outside the entrance of the house. Sometimes she would even plant a few vegetables in the back of the house during springtime. Every spring she would plant colorful annuals to mix with the green. She so admired her creation of shrubs and flowers. This she felt was the pinnacle of her self-worth. All her life, she never gave herself any credit for anything, yet when she saw her flowers, she felt a sense of worth.

When the boys began to grow a little taller, around the ages of seven and nine, John set up a basketball net by the garage. It was here where they acquired their outstanding basketball skills. He would play with them whenever he was in town; they loved it. They really missed their dad when he was away.

Unfortunately, for them, he had to travel sixty percent of the time during their growing up years. They were mainly in touch by phone. When he was home, he was constantly reminded of his parenting inadequacies by Nancy. She constantly complained about them not being able to afford many of the things that some of the other neighbors had. She felt that she couldn't dress her sons like the other boys, and was embarrassed to go anywhere because she couldn't dress like the other women in the community. "Why can't you get a regular 9 to 5 job like other husbands, and not try to have your own business?" she would nag. "And you're never at home. I'm left here to do everything alone. I'm practically a single parent raising two children." She would cry in frustration. "Nancy, Nancy, please try to be a little more patient. I believe that this business is going to take off one day and soon," he would plead, as he held her in his arms. "You believed in me when we first got married. Believe in me now," he would say with importunity. When they first got married, she was always encouraging him, which was what made him persevere. To him, she was his strength. But what were truly initially behind her encouragement were her selfish dreams of someday becoming rich. Then she could show all those women who she envied that she too could have what they had, and be invited to social gatherings of the affluent because then she would be one of them. The truth was that Nancy's feelings of rejection were from her own paranoia. These were not affluent people as she thought and imagined. They were middle-class families, just like hers and her parents. Most of the wives were housewives and preferred being at home to be with their children. When asked to come to fundraising events, community affairs meetings, women's socials, or join a woman's organization, she would turn down their invitations because she felt they were insincere and derisive. Her bizarre imagination caused her to be unsociable, unfriendly, and disliked. Her ostracism was largely self-inflicted.

John Tyler was a man of great integrity, honesty, and trustworthiness, which were innate qualities of his character. Because of these wholesome assets and his indefatigable spirit, John's computer software business' growth was phenomenally rapid. During the beginning years, this increase in growth was due to the quickly changing technology. With him keeping up, this caused him to be away even more than before. He frequently had to travel out of state to learn this new technology, which he managed to incorporate into his own company's development. Some of those times, he would be gone for weeks if within the country. As the business grew, he sometimes had to leave the country, which meant in those times he would have to be away for at least three to four weeks, traveling from one country to another. As a result, his wife was left with the responsibility of having to do most of the rearing and upbringing of the children. She took them to their practices and games, attended school conferences, especially if summoned because of a disciplinary concern, and she would attend some PTA meetings. Those were the times that she had become very angry and resentful, for having to do all of the social activities alone. Her feelings of inferiority were almost too overwhelming. There were times though that she could get John to schedule his meetings around these events which helped her to contend with her anxiety. Strangely, if she felt that her sons were at risk, her whole demeanor would change. Her over protectiveness disallowed many situations to be revealed to their father about their sons' behavior, especially if she thought any corrective action needed to be taken, even if it may have been deserved and necessary. Their father never learned about any quarrels or contentions, in or out, of the home. John knew that his sons were not perfect. They were boys. He was rarely around to have the face-to-face father and son talks on mutual respect, relationships with girls, dating, good sportsmanship, and friendships from a male perspective, and for that reason, he often felt extremely guilty. They didn't have the male influence necessary to develop them into becoming wholesome, well-rounded men. He convinced himself that what he had done, and all he was doing, was to give them a chance for a better life. That was his saving grace. By the mid-70s, John was able to spend more time with his sons and they were both in high school. He did what he could for them between trips, but their mother kept a protective shield around them, even from him. When he was home, they seemed so perfect and would always be on their best behavior. She never revealed any of their mischievous behavior, and tried to bury their past. All those negative, momentous events in their sons' lives that had happened when he was away were erased from memory. There was never a reason for lectures or be reprimanded by their father from what he could see. They were perfect during those times, though it did make him a little suspicious of such perfection.

By 1976, Jack was a sophomore in high school; Greg had graduated and was beginning his freshman year in college. As with most kids, Greg wanted to go away to college and chose Georgetown University in Washington D.C. While in college, he began to learn the family business, especially during the summer months when both boys were out of school and would sometimes go to work with their dad. John had started them learning the business when they reached high school and continued through their college years. He wanted to some day pass the business on to them. During this time, John had bought a three-story building in downtown New York, which became the home office of Tyler Enterprises. He had also established smaller sites in several states and in other countries. His staff of employees grew along with the business. It seemed to their parents that time had gone by exponentially when Jack began packing for college. He too decided to go to Georgetown. In the summer just before his sophomore year, Jack told his parents that he wanted to start living in an apartment off campus.

One windy, chilly autumn day of his freshman year in his first semester, Jack met a girl named Amy Sandler from Bedford, Ohio. It was early in the morning, and he just couldn't seem to concentrate on the morning lecture. In his boredom, he began scanning the huge stadium classroom to see to if anyone else felt the same way as he. Around the room were a few yawns and faces resting on elbows, and then his eyes landed on Amy. She was diligently taking notes and following the professor's every move as he walked back and forth in front of the blackboard. In his mind, he remembered seeing her before, when she was walking into the classroom. She was a tall girl with a thin figure like a model. Her face was quite pretty, even without makeup. She had large green eyes and thick strawberry blond shoulder length hair. He couldn't understand why she never really had any effect on him before that day. After class, he approached her. During their short conversation, joking about her attentiveness during the lecture, while he, on the other hand, almost fell asleep, they exchanged phone numbers and dorm locations. After that day, they began calling each other often and became very good friends. The school canteen became their meeting place where they enjoyed the greasy, grilled burgers and fries. They even started studying together and took a few of their required classes together the following year. He really liked her, and she liked him as well. They were not a couple, but made a great team and enjoyed each other's company. Jack and Amy went out together quite often, but always parted ways at the end of their outing.

As it was in high school, Jack showed himself to be an accomplished basketball player during tryouts. He was becoming very popular. Many colleges and universities had scouted him in high school and even more nearing graduation. He was offered full scholarships to play for a number of them and become a member of their school's basketball and lacrosse teams.

However, his father turned them all down since he could afford to pay for his son's education as far as scholarships went. He could pay for any school of their choice, so he urged the school board to give the scholarships to lesser-privileged students, whose only means to attend college was through sheer talent of playing sports. Along with his athletic prowess, came his notoriety with the women and sometimes Amy felt herself becoming a little jealous. When these feelings came over her, she had to remind herself they were merely just good friends. By the end of the year, Amy unintentionally began to feel affection towards Jack in a way that had gone beyond friendship.

When school ended for summer break after the last exam, Jack started packing up to head home. He walked over to Amy's dorm on the other side of the campus to say goodbye; as she too was packing. He helped her finish, putting away the last few items in her car. As he placed an apparently old desk lamp into the box, he wondered why she bothered to pack it, along with a toaster and an outdated video player. Taping the box up and grabbing it under his arm, he picked up the larger luggage bag and took it to the awaiting cab. As they parted their ways, Jack gave Amy a hug and a little peck on the lips and wished her a great summer. Amy felt a tingle throughout her body and wondered if Jack felt the same. And why shouldn't he have? She thought something had happened between them ever since the one night when they had been out partying and having had a little too much to drink had found themselves in his dorm bed naked the next morning. She had felt enormously embarrassed awakening and realizing the unintentional, but longed-for situation, yet Jack acted as though it was nothing out the ordinary. He was totally indifferent. He joked about it and casually got up and went to take a shower. She was puzzled about his reaction but blew it off as his way of shielding his embarrassment.

During the summer, they stayed in contact through mail and phone calls. They also sent pictures to one another of their vacations with family and friends. Once, Jack sent a picture to her that Greg had taken of him with a girl in whom she and Jack were engaged in a very awkward position by a pool. Amy was puzzled as to why Jack would send such a picture to her, but tried not to jump to any conclusions, being as though they were just friends, but she still had to stifle her feelings of jealousy. She decided to give him a call to let him know that she had received the photo. She casually stated that the girl was cute and then left matters alone to see if he might elaborate about the stilled event. His response was that they had just met and were just hanging out for just that one day.

Jack and Amy, after having gone out on several dates and often hung out exclusively together in their freshman year, appeared to be very comfortable with each other. They had many similar interests. Towards the end of the last semester, he had even brought up the possibility of the two of them getting an apartment together the following school year, but she didn't take his suggestion very seriously. But early during the summer vacation, Amy got a letter in the mail from Jack, along with some pictures that he had sent, asking her if she was still interested in moving in together. She again acknowledged receiving the pictures and gave him a synopsis of her vacation thus far, and a one-sentence response to his question. "I'll think about it over the summer," even though she couldn't remember giving him any reason to believe she was interested in living together. One day a few weeks after the last correspondence, she and her mom had just sat down to have lunch at the mall in between shopping. Wanting to get away from the noises of the mall, they decided to dine in a restaurant. Standing there waiting to be served, she remembered that she had received another card from Jack which was still unopened in her purse. Now seated and waiting for their order, Amy put her shoulder bag on her lap and took the card out to read the note that was inside. Before she read the message, she looked at the pictures that were enclosed. "Come on, Amy, that's rude. Is it that personal?" her mom said, jokingly.
"Okay, Mom. I'm only going to read this one message." It was from Jack, but she didn't tell her mother who it was from.
"Hi Amy, how's your vacation going?" She stopped reading aloud and read the rest to herself. "Are we still moving in together when we get back to school?" She hadn't thought about the subject again since the time before. She quickly put the envelope back into her shoulder bag, closed it, and hung it on the back of her chair without responding to her mother's question. To her mother, she looked like a deer in the headlights. "Are you okay?" her mother asked. "Who was that from?"
"Oh no, I'm okay. It's just from a friend reminding me of something that I'd promised to do that I had completely forgotten about." Trying not to be noticed, she put the envelope back into her purse.
"So, Mom what do you think is going on with our order? What did you order anyway? I forgot. It's really taking them quite a long time. Don't you think?" she said trying to divert the conversation. Her mother repeated to Amy what

she had ordered. Figuring that it was something that she didn't want to talk about, her mother dropped her pursuit about the contents of the card. Amy had totally forgotten all about Jack's question about moving in together. Even when he first brought up the subject, she tried to blow it off. She had never thought of living with anyone, not with a guy anyway until she was married. But how could she say no? Later that day when she was alone, she bought a postcard with a beach umbrella of a "happy face" and gleefully answered with a big "OK, and I'm having a great time," as the message. She mailed it that same day.

When classes resumed at the end of the summer, they discussed over the phone their plan to meet up in a specific place off campus to go together to look for an apartment. After Jack received the ok from Amy to be his roommate, he decided to go back to school a week early stay in a hotel so he could search for a place for them to move into; he found what he thought would be the ideal place. So excited when he found it, he called her immediately, recounting every step of how he found it to a full detailed description of the interior. "Hey, Amy, I couldn't wait to tell you. I found the greatest place to move into. It's close to the school. So close that you could practically walk across the street to the campus."
"Really?" she responded.
"Yeah, you're going to really love it. It's perfect for us."
"That's great, Jack. I can't wait to see it." Surprised and delighted to hear from him, but also disappointed that he had gone ahead and gotten a place without waiting for her. Her thoughts wandered back to the first time he seemed serious about living together, but it wasn't until the day she received the card to get her final answer to share an apartment that she knew. She remembered being somewhat surprised that he was that serious about it and urgently persistent when she read the card.

Amy liked Jack a lot and thought about him often over the entire summer. Since they seemed to have gotten along so well and had spent a great deal of time together, she considered this as the confirmatory reason she finally accepted his offer believing maybe there was more to their relationship than what she had previously thought. Thinking over her decision, she now felt very comfortable about living together. "Now, I'll get to be with him even more," she thought being filled with bliss. But unbeknownst to her, she was only one of the many women that Jack was seeing. Yet, for some reason, which he was not really sure of himself, preferred being with her and seeing her more than any of the others. However, the true reason for his live-in plan was out of his own selfishness. He felt that since he didn't mind having her around and they got along so well it was better than living with and hanging around a bunch of guys. Besides, she would make a better roommate and a convenient one, as well. They had already been intimate in their freshman year after several dates ever since that first weird encounter when they inadvertently spent the night together, so why not beat the hassle and live together, he thought. To him, she seemed to really enjoy being with him, anyway this way he could keep the other hounds away from her and have her all to himself.

After living together for just a few weeks, Amy thought she and Jack were actually complimentary to one another. But it was all one-sided. If Jack wanted anything, Amy was willing to get it. If he needed anything, she was there to fulfill his every desire. She even offered to do his laundry. He thought she was such a great buddy. She could even have been a good companion if it wasn't for the fact that she didn't meet the mandatory qualifications his mother had embedded into his brain all of his life. Amy was an extraordinarily beautiful girl and he knew she liked him more than he liked her, but her family didn't meet the financial requirement. His mother taught him and his brother that being loved was not enough to have a good relationship, not as important as having money. She stressed to him that this was paramount in a relationship to be certain they were not being pursued just for what they had or could give. Drilled into his mind was that he should always be the one in control in a relationship, and must always remain in control. Money was the major factor that gave them that control and power. If a woman showed any sign of aggressiveness, she surely wouldn't be considered as a choice. They both were taught this, but throughout his childhood, Greg would struggle with this concept and suffer deep internal conflicts of emotion because of it. Sometimes he would become physically sick with the very thought that he had hurt someone. It was sometimes difficult distinguishing who he could even become friends with, especially when it came to females. He was very trusting, but yet with apprehension. It seemed that the ones he liked didn't fit the criteria of his mother. For that reason, he didn't have a lot of girlfriends or a lot of friends of either gender. His mother noticed this "softness" about him, as she described it, and tried to teach him otherwise, but Greg had more of his father's personality, unlike Jack who was more like her. This created a conflicting and constant battle within him, which would spill over even into his relationship with his brother. This laborious internal turmoil would later cause problems for Greg in future encounters.

That fall, in the beginning of his sophomore year Jack and Amy moved into their apartment. Amy hadn't been totally honest with her parents about her living arrangements. Because of her deceitfulness, her feelings of comfort became very uncomfortable moving in with him. She had a very close relationship with her parents and had always been honest and sincere about everything with them. The first time they had heard of her even wanting to live off campus was when she had already returned to school and told them she had already found an apartment and someone to share it with. She told them she met a fellow classmate who in conversation was looking for someone to rent an apartment with. After seeing the place and wanting to experience having her independence, moving off campus was the best idea, so she agreed to sign the lease, share the expenses and the upkeep, which was not really a total lie. This was her reasoning, which was how she could alleviate some of her guilt. Even though they were completely caught off-guard, they agreed to pay her share of the expenses. On the contrary, Jack could freely tell his mom and dad. At this age, his dad felt that his sons had reached manhood and should be capable of making their own decisions. Their father often felt guilty though about not having been more a part of their upbringing, and of which Nancy had so often reminded him of that regretful fact. She cautioned Jack to only use this girl for his personal needs and not get emotionally involved. This was something that his father would never have approved of had he known. But with his advice, he didn't discourage him by warning him of the risks of living together with a female and the relationship issues that could ensue with possible legal consequences of living together without benefit of marriage. Stressing again not to get involved, his mother said to him, "If she's willing to live with you, then that is what she expects." With affirmation, she told him, "It's her choice." When they became teenagers, she had also warned both Jack and Greg to be careful not to make any mistakes of creating unwanted pregnancies, which she reiterated often. These girls would only try to use this predicament as a method to try to trap them, she would caution. Because their real interest was money, a baby would insure a life of security and dependence. She inculcated these warnings when they became teenagers and put condoms right into their hands. "Don't ruin your life before it even begins," she warned emphatically.

As the days went by, Amy became more relaxed living with Jack. Initially, they agreed to split the rent and share other expenses as was agreed on the lease. With these arrangements, they were getting along extremely well. It was their sophomore year and mostly part of their junior year when they began their live-in arrangement and continued as a couple, even though Jack managed to get his alone time in as well. Never giving up going out with other women, he did whenever he felt the desire. Amy never found out about those outings because he always managed to return to the apartment in time for the night. During the Christmas holidays, they both went home to spend time with their own families. It was in their junior year, right before the Christmas holiday, after the last exam, Amy packed a few things and flew home to Ohio. She had planned to invite Jack to visit her home but changed her mind when Jack began first by telling her about his plans for going home to New Jersey. She had hoped to introduce Jack to her parents since she had already met his one weekend he had invited her to his home. All this time she still hadn't found the courage to tell her parents about who her roommate really was. "If only they could meet him," she thought,
"They would get to love him as much as I do."

On the flight home, she decided that for spring break she would ask Jack to come home with her. This time she planned to ask early before he had a chance to make any plans of his own. But she didn't know that Jack had already made other plans. He and some of the guys had planned to go to Miami for spring break. One of the guys from Florida knew about a few racy clubs they were sure to be able to get into. They all had gotten their flight tickets had been ecstatic about it for weeks. Jack had just gotten in from a late class when she approached him about the possibility of going home with her. It was then that he proceeded to tell her of his own plans of going to Miami with his buddies. Amy was deeply disappointed by this unexpected news. He hadn't said one word to her about this before, yet decides to tell her now, just after she asked him about coming home with her. This was when she found out what Jack was really like. He proceeded to keenly let her know that he didn't have to tell her anything. Looking into the refrigerator for the carton of milk, he said, "Amy, we're only roommates. We're simply sharing this apartment together, that's all." He got a glass out of the cabinet and poured a glass of milk. Amy followed him as he walked away into the living room to turn on the television. With tears rolling down her cheeks, she declared, "But I love you! I thought that you felt the same way about me."

Not surprised by her confession, he responded. "Amy… I never told you that I loved you. What made you think that? I care about you a lot…" he said, "…but I can't say that I love you. What? Did you think that just because we share a bed together that I love you? Grow up!" he shouted. Amy started crying audibly now. He got up and walked over to her. He never expected that reaction. Trying to show compassion, he spoke softly. "Amy, look, I'm really sorry that you got the wrong impression." She continued to cry at his every word, which by now was beginning to irritate him. Frustrated, he went back and sat down to finish his milk. At this point, he said very callously, "Look, it's not that I'm your first lay, for crying out loud. You weren't even a virgin. You're not some innocent young girl. You've been down this road before, so why would you go falling in love this time? Or maybe you have been in love before, or thought you were," he stated rhetorically and cold. He put the glass on the wooden coffee table, stood up and went back into the kitchen. She followed him and answered anyway, "I don't know why, or even how. It just happened. And no, I haven't been in love before," she said sobbing. "Maybe I fell in love with you because you treated me as if I were special to you," Amy answered through her sobs.

"Where are those cookies? I know they're in here." Apathetic to her obvious hurt, he continued diligently searching in the pantry for cookies. Suddenly, he halted his search, turned and looked at her as if he had just been insulted. "When? And how?" he asked sternly, as if interrogating her. "Why, because I'm polite to you … or was it because I opened the door for you? I use proper etiquette. I do have manners, you know. I wasn't raised by wolves, Amy."

Muttering through her sobs, she said to him, "But you took me to meet your parents and…."

"So what!" he interjected loudly, walking back into the living room with the cookies, one hanging out of his mouth. "I just wanted them to meet the person that I was living with, that's all! My roommate." His voice had gotten louder as he was yelling insults. "Jack, it's as if I don't know you. You've never talked to me this way before," Amy said, crying profusely.

"I never had any reason to until now," he responded apathetically. "You sounded like you were getting all possessive or something, and I just wanted to set the record straight, that's all." Wanting to end this matter, he said in a more gentle voice, "Amy look, we're not married, and I don't plan to get married… not any time soon anyway," he said. Then he smiled, turned the television off and walked over to her, wiping her tears with the napkin he had the cookies in. "And now that we've gotten that all straightened out, can't we get back to where we were before all this started?"

She could smell the cookie flavor in the napkin. He leaned over and tried to kiss her. Amy pushed him away and stepped backwards as if she would be poisoned by his touch. She couldn't believe what she had just heard. Her face contorted with feelings of absolute revulsion. Staring into his deep blue eyes she stood, tears streaming down her face, her neck red with fury. He looked back at her, stunned as if looking at someone he had never seen or known before. With deep hatred in her heart, and rage in her voice, her fists clasps tightly by her sides, so tightly that her knuckles were white, she slowly screamed, "You used me!" She turned with a jerk, ran into the other bedroom and slammed the door sobbing incessantly.

While Jack was in Florida, Amy moved out of the apartment. There was no way she would ever be able to look at him again. She managed to avoid him before he left for Florida and moved out before he got back. On the advice of her parents, she went back a few days before Jack was to return to pack and remove all of her belongings. The following day after their heated argument, she had finally confessed to her parents about her living arrangements and the heated altercation she had with him. Taking her parents' advice, she flew back to school a few days early to rent a van and remove her things and have them put into storage until she could decide what to keep or sell. On the flight back, gazing out the window, she thought of how one decision had altered her life. She couldn't believe what had happened to her and how adversely all her plans had changed. All that time she had spent with Jack played over and over in her mind. "How did I miss it?" she thought. "Am I that naive?"

A few days before she left for the airport, while still cleaning out the apartment, she started crying while remembering the good times she thought she had had with Jack. "It was all fake!" she shouted in anger. Still humiliated, she thought of how she had allowed herself to be used as she packed up her things, grabbing and angrily tossing everything she touched that belonged to him. She felt like such an idiot... a fool. Amy decided the ill-treatment she had gotten from him, she deserved, because she allowed it, and whatever she wanted of his, she would help herself to it, whether she wanted it or not, because she deserved that too. He only wanted her there for his own convenience anyway. While he was away, she also found out about all the other women he had been sleeping around with. No one told her about the others until they found out that she and Jack had broken up. After calling a few of her girlfriends to tell

them about the breakup, they told her what they had seen and heard. At first, she was upset with them for concealing what they knew, but they explained they didn't want to be the cause of a breakup. "I didn't want you to be angry with me, Amy," her friend Andrea told her, who had gone away herself for spring break. "Suppose I had told you and then the two of you made up. Then, both of you would have been angry with me and I would have been blamed."
"I understand, Andrea. I'm just glad I found out before I introduced him to my parents. They would be even more furious if they knew him. It's okay, Andrea, I have to finish packing. I'll call you later,"
"Sorry I'm not there to help you pack."
"Oh, that's okay. I'm fine. Enjoy the rest of the break." She hung up the phone and continued packing. Whenever she found pictures they had taken together, she ripped them in half, leaving only the part with his image behind. Most of them she just ripped into tiny pieces and scattered them all over the bedroom, mostly on the bed. Amy was so gorged with hostility that she tried to destroy everything of his in her path. When she left the apartment, it was her intention not to lock the door, hoping someone would come in and finish the job. She never wanted to ever see Jack's face again. When she arrived home, she told her parents everything, from the time she first met Jack as a freshman, to their tumultuous argument. They were disappointed, but not unforgiving for not being told about who this mysterious roommate was until her junior year of college. She was so ashamed and remorseful for having deceived them for so long. Wisely, they not only advised her to pack up early and come home, but they also urged her not to return to school for the next semester and recommended that she even transfer to a different school, in a different state when she felt ready to continue with her education. It was obvious to them that their daughter was hurt and distraught.

Jack had tried to call Amy several times from Florida, but never got an answer. He left messages and never got a return call. A couple of days before the end of spring break, Jack came back home to the apartment. He had missed Amy by one day. When he tried to unlock the door to the apartment, he realized the door was not locked. He couldn't believe his eyes when he walked in. Remembering that he had never gotten an answer from Amy, and now the door being unlocked, he became very alarmed that maybe something had happened to her. He searched the apartment calling out her name, going from room to room. At first, it looked as if there had been a break-in, except the lock was not broken. When he went into their bedroom, there were broken lamps, the mattress and sheets had been ripped to shreds, pillows were cut up and tossed; but finally when he saw the pictures that were torn in half, and the half with his image only, he knew. It was apparent from the looks of the apartment that Amy was angry and had moved out. He was furious. He became so irate and enraged that he began slamming doors, throwing objects, tossing furniture, and screaming obscenities throughout the apartment. He couldn't believe what she had done to him. Even some of the things that belonged to him were gone or destroyed. When he managed to calm down, he found the ripped beanbag he had previously tossed, placed it near the phone where he sat down and immediately called his mother.

"Mom, do you remember the argument that I told you about between me and Amy? Well, it looks as if she was still upset. She moved out. This place looks as if it was hit by a tornado. She practically demolished the whole apartment. Yeah, and she left me here alone to pay the rent and all of the other expenses that we agreed to pay together, and now for damages. We both signed the lease. She took just about everything and even took some of my things... I guess the things she hadn't destroyed. I should take her to court for breaking the lease and for her part of the other expenses, and the damages. Mom, she had no right to take my things too," Jack said angrily. "Jack... Jack don't worry about it. Let it go. Your father and I will make sure the rent gets paid and pay for any damages," his mother assured.

"Mom, can you believe her?" asked Jack, as if he had been duped.

"This is why I tell you not to get involved with those kinds of girls," she said, trying to console him. Nancy knew in her heart of hearts that any girl would have been hurt. "Jack, I think that you should try to find a guy friend or a male roommate to share a place with. Don't you think?" Nancy asked, using her subtle, persuasive influence.

Chapter 5

In the early years of their marriage and the business, between cooking for the boys, refereeing their squabbles, washing clothes, cleaning the house, doing the bookkeeping, making appointments and calls for the business, Nancy somehow found the time to dream. She found out everything she could about the life that she was going to live. She got high fashion and glamour magazines, posh designer furniture magazines and catalogs and learned their name brands. She began searching for expensive real estate and sought out exclusive locations where she wanted to live. Nancy enjoyed reading celebrity magazines and reading about how the rich and famous lived and all of their scandalous escapades. She read where the stars lived, how much money they had, how much their houses cost, and where they vacationed. Forbes was another one of her favorites. She would keep up with who were the top millionaires and billionaires. Nancy's life-long dream was to be one of them, and after nearly twenty years of struggling, finally her dream came true. She was one of them.

The Tyler Software Company had made it big in the business world when Jack and Greg were nearing their last years of high school. John was not one to flaunt, but because of the years of promises to Nancy, he got her what she felt she deserved. They moved into an affluent area in Montville, New Jersey. Nancy didn't want to take anything from the old house with her. Nothing to her had any sentiment. She wanted everything new. John remembered from where he had come and wanted always to remember. He knew material things didn't last forever, and without integrity, all that he had was useless. He tried to teach these things to his sons in the little time that he had been able to have with them between traveling as the business was growing. However, what their mother had taught them had already been embedded into their lives, so his teachings were practically useless. Through the years, he had spoken to his wife about developing good character in them, but to the boys, his discipline seemed harsh and uncaring. They felt that he didn't care about what they wanted, but rather he chose to think about the needs of others. Greg often listened, but Jack only ignored his father's advice. "What sense does that make?" Jack said, complaining to Greg after one of their rare father-son talks. Yet, their father sincerely tried instilling positive values and morals into his sons by telling them that everyone was important and they have to put others first sometimes. He shared with them to always do the right thing, which meant that sometimes they would have to make sacrifices.

"Why should I? What about me?" Jack would say, "What about what was important to me and what I want." Jack loved his father, but couldn't understand why he couldn't leave things alone and continue with the way their mother had taught them. Greg could understand what his dad was trying to convey. He was fascinated by his words. He loved, trusted, and admired him immensely. He could understand why he always seemed to feel compassion when he saw someone hurt. He was a magnanimous person in helping others and always gave large amounts of money to charities. To attempt to make Greg feel better when he would feel pity for someone's misfortune, his mother would tell him that it was Karma and that they were getting what they deserved. She said that they probably had done something bad and deserved their misfortune as pay back. This only confused Greg more. John knew his wife well. He knew why she felt the way she did and why she seemed so unkind and uncompassionate. He felt sorry for her. Early in their relationship, he tried to persuade her to leave the past behind and let him make a better future for her. He did, but her self-inflicted hurt was deeply planted and she was determined not to let her boys experience what she had felt in her youth.

They moved into a large eight-bedroom mansion that was situated on twenty-five acres of land and a magnificent garden that was managed by a grounds keeper. There was also a maid and a cook that she only used for special affairs. Nancy liked her home, but she would have preferred something bigger if John had permitted. The kitchen was almost as large as her old kitchen, dining room, and living room combined. It was so much more than what they needed but well within their means to afford. They moved into the house a year before Greg graduated from high school. The business had kicked into high gear at that time and John felt secure enough to invest in something he was sure to be able to keep. Nancy thought he shouldn't have waited so long to buy the home of her dreams. She felt the boys wouldn't get to enjoy the fullness of their wealth while they were still boys. John more than made up for that. Both sons, when they had come of age had their own cars while they were still in high school. They bought whatever fashions they wanted. He also took the family on luxurious vacations at least once a year. John had been doing this before they purchased their new home. By their junior year in high school, he decided the boys had matured enough to have their own cars, Greg first, then Jack. And when it came to a higher education, he wanted to make sure they would get the very best, even before buying a house, if needed. To him, in order for them to have a chance in life, their education would have to be first and be the best.

Long before Greg was in junior high school, John had put money aside solely for their education. It was enough for both to have the best that college had to offer. John was a realist. Even though the business was beginning to thrive, he always prepared for the worst. Even in junior high school, Greg knew where he wanted to attend college even though they could afford for him to go anywhere else. He chose to go to Georgetown University in Washington D.C. Since toddlers, the boys had always played some kind of ball sport. Basketball became their favorite sport and Georgetown had one of the best teams. When their father put up the basketball net in the driveway at the old house, they played every day, mostly competing against each other. They were both gifted in playing sports, and they loved it. In high school, Greg watched all the games, especially the college games whenever they were being televised. He grew to love the Georgetown Hoyas and longed to play on their team. Jack chose to follow his big brother when he graduated from high school and also attended Georgetown. They had completely different personalities but in spite of this, they were very close. Besides playing basketball, every summer when he could, John would take them from their sports and take them with him to the office to learn how the business worked. They loved being around their dad. They had done this since high school. It was John's hope that they would someday take the reins and run the business when he no longer could.

Throughout high school, Greg and Jack got through fairly smoothly, with the exception of a couple of incidences at the recreation center. They were well respected by the other kids, except for a couple of guys who were jealous of their popularity and abilities on the court. They had a tendency to be condescending at times, especially Jack, who was, at times, unrelenting. Greg would wind up shaking hands, whereas Jack would ruthlessly walk away with pride, not wanting to give any impression of equality. The two of them were even more intimidating when they were together. Greg being the elder was always protective of his younger brother, although Jack could pretty much hold his own. Confident in their abilities, they usually took command, especially when they played together on the court. This was prior to moving to the new house. When they moved to New Jersey, the kids at the new school were their peers, so their status didn't mean anything. They too were the kids of CEO's of large businesses; owners of entire businesses, some were even kids of celebrities. John became a member of an exclusive athletic club where the boys would meet some of their friends for a game of tennis, racquetball, or just to hang out at the pool.

The first summer at the new house, Greg and Jack found out that some of the kids they had met at school also went to the club during the summer months. One day, they saw two of the guys who they had met on the first day of school. There were also kids from the club whose parents worked at the club. The employees were mainly from the urban area of New York. In the summer at the end of the school year, they would come to help their parents and some kids were hired for summer jobs. Most of the kids preferred going to a fast food restaurant after working out, but on this particular day Greg, Jack, and two other guys from school, Pete, and D.J., decided to have lunch at the club. Immediately, Jack spotted a little unattractive, plain-looking girl who was waitressing that day. The boys had been acting disorderly the entire day, all but Greg. When they sat down and looked at the menu, their antics continued. They started making fun of everything on it. Greg threatened to leave if they didn't stop with their ridiculous antics. The same waitress timidly walked over to their table to take their order. Jack and the other two boys snickered, "So what's your name, cutie?" said Jack, with a pretentious smile. The other two boys snickered again, covering their faces with the menus. The girl was hurt, but she pretended not to notice. She had been through this type of treatment before. After she took their order and walked away, they got louder. Greg was embarrassed, said to Jack, "Why do you try to humiliate people? I'm sure that girl knows you're laughing at her. It's because of people like you that some people become introverted, hurt, and lonely."

"What are you talking about? I'm not doing anything. People probably laugh at her all the time. Besides, you have to admit she's no beauty and she knows it," said Jack callously.

"That doesn't mean because she knows it, she doesn't get hurt when people like you make fun of her, you dope!" Greg said, reprimanding him. The other two boys really started laughing then. "What are you two laughing at? Find a mirror and you'll wipe those silly smiles off your own stupid faces." Greg scolded. When the girl came back with their order, Greg thanked her and smiled at her sincerely. The girl could tell his smile was genuine.

After their meal, the guys decided to go to the sauna before they left. Greg told them that he would meet them there. He saw the waitress standing by the register. He walked over and introduced himself and began to have a short conversation intending to gently make up for the other boys' behavior. Greg told her this was their first summer there, but often he and his brother had gone to the club after school.

"Well, I guess that's why you haven't seen me here before," she said. "I come to help my parents out only during the summer months. Now that I'm old enough, they let me work to earn my own money. Both of them teach and are off for the summer. They come here to work as well, while they're off from school to make a little extra money. Actually, we live in upstate New York, but my parents rent a little place not far from here. It's like a summer home."

"I'd like to talk to you sometime when you're off," Greg said. She was stunned. She hoped that her expression didn't reveal her disbelief. Did she hear him right? "Excuse me?" she said. "I didn't hear what you said." He repeated it. She figured he was trying to be derisive and was trying to humiliate her again. Then she looked carefully at his face. There was a look of honesty there. "He looks and sounds sincere," she thought. He asked for her phone number and with some suspicion she gave it to him. "If he doesn't call, it won't matter. No one does anyway."

Greg felt sorry for the girl. He was glad she had written her name by the number so that he would know whose number it was. Sticking it in his wallet with the rest of his credit cards, he went to the sauna. Later in his bedroom, he was going to put it in his pocket-size phonebook.

"What took you so long?" Jack asked as he saw Greg coming towards them in the sauna.

"I walked over to the treadmills. I thought I saw Shannon there, but it wasn't her." Greg lied. He wasn't going to tell Jack he was talking to that waitress so he could tell their mom he was fraternizing with the help. He already knew Jack would tell her everything. He always did. Verbatim, he would blab to her how defensive he was of the waitress.

"I thought I saw you walking away from the register," Jack said accusingly.

"What do you think? I'm socializing with the help?" Greg asked, trying to sound indifferent. Jack couldn't understand why Greg always looked guilty in situations like this. What was wrong with him? Greg couldn't understand how Jack could make fun of people the way he did, and why he felt as if he had done something wrong for sticking up for them. Why couldn't he be more like Jack? There was nothing wrong with that girl, but there was surely something wrong with them. How did he really feel? Greg was confused. He couldn't seem to get it right in his mind. But he knew in his heart he was right.

Chapter 6

The guys hadn't gone back to the club for a couple of weeks. Since then, John had taken the family to Cancun, Mexico for a weeklong vacation. Greg was in the bedroom of their resort looking in his wallet for a code for a video game he was playing and ran across the waitress' phone number. He had forgotten all about her and forgotten to put her phone number in his phonebook. Reading the note, he thought, "Her name was Beth, that's right." Greg felt awful because he hadn't thought anymore about the incident that afternoon at the club, until now.

"I'm no better than those other guys," he shamefully thought. "I'm sure Beth thinks I was making fun of her too," thinking of how hurt she must have felt. "As soon as I'm alone, I'm going to call her. "I can't let Jack or Mom know about this," he thought.

Jack told their mother about the waitress, just as Greg knew he would. He told her how he and a couple of guys had been teasing the girl and how Greg reprimanded them for it. Feigning innocence, he explained how they were only just having a little fun. His mom pretended to chide him.

"Jack," she said, "you shouldn't bother the help. Let them do their job."

Then turning to Greg, "And you too, Greg. Don't lead these girls on. Nothing will ever become of you trying to befriend them. Your worlds are just too far apart."

"Why couldn't they just be nice to everyone?" he thought to himself. Why be nice only to certain people? They were only pretending anyway, so why not just at least pretend to be nice to everyone." As a kid, Greg would go to his dad and ask why he couldn't visit his friends from the old neighborhood, or even have them stay over sometimes. He would ask why he and Jack could never stay over their Uncle Todd's house, his mother's brother. Uncle Todd and his wife had three children. The two boys were around the same age as he and Jack. The girl was just a baby. That had been years ago when they first moved into the old house. Uncle Todd had even helped them move in. John tried to reason with Nancy about this matter.

"Todd is your brother, Nancy."

"I don't care if he is my brother. Our boys are just not used to that type of environment," she would say. Todd's family was middle class, no less than what they both had been raised in. Only on special occasions would she invite her brother and his family to their home. But after a while, there didn't seem to have been any visits. Sometimes, only if the boys begged, would Nancy permit her nephews to stay overnight. Most of the time, there were always excuses. John tried to explain to Greg that because he had more, he should try to have friends that had the same as he. The kids who didn't have as much would feel bad that they didn't have the same as he, and it may cause jealousy and envy. Nancy always insisted that John explain to the boys about issues of disparity.

One afternoon, the family had planned to go out to dinner at one of the restaurants not far from their resort. "This would be just the right time to be alone, to call Beth," Greg thought. To get out of going with them, he pretended to be sick and pleaded to stay behind. He was in bed, but got up and went into the living room as soon as they left. Greg decided to sit near the door so he could hear them when they came back. When he was sure they wouldn't return, he dialed her number. Relieved that it was a local New Jersey number and not a number from the clubhouse, he dialed.

"Hello?" she said.

"Hello, Beth. Remember me? I met you at the club about two weeks ago."

"Yeah, I remember," she said in a perfunctory manner. She knew it was Greg because there was no other guy who would have been calling her. "So what's wrong, are you bored?" she asked, being a little sarcastic.

"Listen, Beth, I'm so sorry I didn't call you. Truthfully, I'm in Cancun right now. If I were there, I'd even ask to come over to see you. That is, if you wanted me to."

"Was this guy in his right mind? What was he up to?" she thought, "I'll just go along with him to see what he really wants. No one else is going to call."

Their conversation was pleasant and went on for quite a while. Beth couldn't believe this handsome guy had called her. Who could she tell? She had no one to confide in. There was no one to share in her exhilaration. She wanted someone to know that a boy had called her. She couldn't believe this conversation was even happening.

"Beth, when I get back, would you go out with me?"

"Who me?" she asked in disbelief.

"Yes, you. No one else is on the phone, is there?" Greg replied with a chuckle. "Where did you want to go?"

"What about a movie?" he asked.

Of course, it would be a movie. Somewhere out of the public eye, she thought. "That sounds great," Beth didn't want to tell her parents about Greg but knew she would have to get their permission to go out with him. She didn't want to sneak out.

"You know Greg, you're going to have to meet my parents before I can go out with you. "That's okay. I don't mind." Suddenly, Greg thought that he heard voices outside the door.

"Uhhh, Beth, I'll call you again another time, okay? Probably, when I get back home, okay?" he said hastily.

"Okay, Greg." After the first call, he didn't wait until after he had gotten back, but called her continuously during his entire Cancun vacation. Whenever he thought someone was near, he'd end the conversation quickly. Beth wondered whether or not this was her imagination that Greg seemed to always end their conversations so abruptly. Was he ashamed of her? Was he with someone else? He had nothing to hide. Not from her anyway. Extremely tired of not being able to trust people, she had also become paranoid, due to people's relentless mistreatment of her. Afraid to ask for fear of hearing the truth, she decided to say nothing about it.

Greg told Beth he would be home on Friday, and would call her then. She was so excited. She even bought something new to wear for the occasion, although there were no plans for a meeting. As the end of the week neared, Beth felt she needed to tell her parents about Greg. She told her mom all about the polite young man she had met while working at the athletic club one day when she was waitressing. She could see how jubilant her daughter was as she talked about her phone conversations with Greg and that he wanted to take her out. She was truly happy and excited for her daughter. She was entering the twelfth grade in the fall and had never even been asked out on a date. Not knowing how her husband would react, she decided to tell him privately that evening as they prepared for bed. When she told her husband who the guy was, he was livid.

"My daughter will not see, nor go anywhere near either one of those rich brats!" he said angrily. "I've heard enough about those two, especially the younger one."

"Calm down, Don. He only wants to take her to a movie," his wife said, startled by his reaction. "Beth says he's a very nice young man. Listen, we're only here for three months anyway, so let her have a little fun. She doesn't get to go out that often. After all, she's almost seventeen."

"I'm telling you now, I don't like it," her father said sternly.

"Don, she said he only wants to take her to a movie. What is wrong with that?" her mom asked firmly.

"It's like I said, I don't like it. I don't trust those two scoundrels," her father said, his face displaying the immense anger in his voice. "End of discussion."

Greg had begun to enjoy his conversations with Beth. He found her to be interesting and entertaining. As she and Greg talked, she began to feel more comfortable and trusting of him. Oddly enough, they had a lot in common. She never told him how her father felt about him and his brother, and he never told her how his mother would feel if she ever found out about her.

"What was wrong with having someone like Beth for a friend?" he thought. The other girls who were the so-called upper class and "on the same level", were very superficial and phony. On the outside, they looked so sweet, charming, and innocent, but on the inside, they were promiscuous, arrogant snobs. They had only one thing on their minds. He had gone out with quite a few and found out that most were more sexually aggressive than he. Most of the guys at school had already had sex with them. None of them seemed to function with a brain, nor did they feel they had the need to even have one. Their only interests were guys and the latest fashions. Beth may not have been as attractive as some of them, nor did her family have money, but she had qualities that were of more value. She had kindness and integrity. He was beginning to like her. What was he going to do? He couldn't have any relationship with her nor did she fit any of the qualifications. Like his mother said, "Nothing could ever come of it."

On Thursday afternoon before their departure from Cancun, he managed to secretly call Beth. He wanted to let her know that they were leaving Cancun soon and would call her as soon as he got home around four. They didn't talk long, because his dad wanted to take the family out for one last evening together for dinner in Cancun, especially since he had missed so many other family dinners.

Greg had been home for three days from their Cancun trip and had spoken to Beth every day. "When will I be able to see you, Beth?"

"I don't think that my father is ready for me to date yet, Greg,"

"What? Beth, it's not like we're dating. Don't they allow you to go out?" he asked with bewilderment.

"Greg, it's obvious I don't go out much, so the issue has never come up for my parents."

"What are you saying? Don't say things like that about yourself. You're a nice, sweet person, and I really enjoy talking to you. I'd like to see you and I don't mean at the sports club," Greg insisted. "I don't want to keep talking on the phone either. So would you speak to them again? If you like, I could come over to meet them first."

"Please don't. Not until I get the okay from them. My dad wouldn't take it very well if you just showed up."

"Look Beth, I don't want to ask you to meet me somewhere." She was silent. How could he dare ask that of her, he thought. But the only way he could see her without creating a family crisis would be in secrecy. What would he say to Jack if he found out? These thoughts crossed his mind as he spoke to her. He felt like a real hypocrite. He was beginning to feel as if he was pushing her. Was he acting like the rich kid who had to have his way? "Beth, are you still there?

"Yes, I'm here," she said softly.

"Beth, I'm sorry. I'll call you tomorrow." He hung up before she could respond.

Beth wondered why Greg never gave her his phone number. Again, those thoughts of doubt began to crop up again. What was he hiding? Was it the fact that he was calling her that he was hiding? Was he deceiving her? Maybe he was embarrassed about her. She remembered how obnoxious his brother had been at the club that day. Was he hiding from him? Should I ask him, she thought. I don't want to run him away. She enjoyed talking to Greg and was beginning to like him a lot. She didn't want to do anything that might end it all, so she decided again to let it go and say nothing.

The next day Greg called as he had promised. Beth still hadn't gotten an answer for him. She really felt stupid. How could someone like her put off such a handsome guy like him? He probably can't believe it himself, she thought. How could such a plain Jane like her jerk this handsome jock around? Why did her dad have to be so unreasonable? Coming back from her wandering mind, she told him she would be going into the city later to buy a book from a new bookstore that had just opened. She knew this was just an excuse to possibly see him, but she didn't tell him that. He asked her if he could meet her there. There was a book he could possibly get that he actually needed to have for a summer reading assignment for school. Truthfully, he had procrastinated getting it until now. He took the bait as she had hoped.

"Sure, why not? It is a public place. If you just happened to be there, well, that would only be purely coincidental."

"What time are you going?"

"I'll be there around one; I'll probably stop in one of those nearby sandwich shops afterwards for lunch."

What was he thinking? The city is a public place. I don't know who I might run into, he thought. My mother and brother aren't the only people who are bigots around here. "Beth, why don't you save your money and try to find the book at the library? I could meet you there and help you find it. As a matter of fact, I could also save some money myself and try to find the book that I need there." He didn't want her to know he couldn't be seen with her, so he justified his actions through self-deceit by convincing himself that he didn't want her to go through any more harassment, nor be humiliated again, nor suffer any embarrassment by any other snobs.

"That sounds like a great idea. I could at least try there first," she agreed. They discussed the time to meet and where at the library.

"Okay, Beth. See you there soon." She hung up the phone and immediately felt as though she was beginning to have a panic attack. She was so excited. Soon she would be seeing Greg again and under completely different circumstances. This happened so quickly and unexpectedly she was virtually unprepared. Never had she experienced anything like this before. Frantically, she combed through her tiny closet to find something nice to wear. There was a pair of blue jeans and in her drawer a yellow pullover cotton shirt. Also in the very back of the top drawer (her very private things) where she kept her underwear, she found the makeup kit her mother had given her as a gift last Christmas, along with a bottle of perfume, neither of which she had ever used. She couldn't understand why she brought them with her but was glad that she had. After gathering everything, she jumped in the shower.

Her face was made up as best she knew how. Being this was her first time putting on makeup, she used the pictures of the models from her Seventeen magazines as an example. After looking in the mirror, with a satisfied smile, she concluded that she did quite well. She made a neat ponytail, pulled it together with a rubber band and then tied a ribbon that matched the color of her shirt. She always bought ribbon and fancy barrettes for her ponytails. This was the only way she ever fixed her hair. Looking at the clock and becoming more panicky, she quickly picked up her shoulder bag from the dresser and taking one last glance in the mirror, headed for the door. As she grabbed the doorknob, her mother came scampering from behind. She had seen her briskly walking toward the living room from where she was in the kitchen.

Hurrying out to the living room, still holding the dishtowel in her hand, her mom called out, "Hey, wait a minute. What's going on? Where are you going, young lady?"

"What do you mean? I'm on my way to the bookstore, remember? Remember the book I told you I needed to buy?"

"I remember, but you didn't say you were going today. Besides, that's not what I'm asking about. What's with the makeup?"

"Nothing, I think it's time I try to make myself look a little better. Don't you?" Her mom walked over to her and hugged her.

"Beth, you are beautiful with, or without, makeup. You have no need to improve on who you are, or what you look like. Always love yourself for you and nobody else. Remember that."

"Thanks, Mom."

"Now, how are you getting there?" her mom asked.

"Remember you said I could drive the car when I needed to?" dangling the keys in the air while walking away towards the door.

"That's true, but you still have to get permission first."

"I'm sorry. Can I? I shouldn't be too long."

"Drive carefully," her mom yelled, as Beth was pulling away. She wondered if her new look had anything to do with this guy that she had met.

Nervously driving to the city, she remembered the area for studying was on the lower level of the library where they had talked about previously. Down there, the desk arrangements were for study partners and small rooms for group study. Greg told her he would be sitting at one of the desks designated for partners. During this time of the year, there would only be a few people on that level and probably those were attending summer school. Greg sat at the desk anxiously waiting for Beth's arrival. He couldn't understand why he felt this way. He had been out with plenty of girls before; girls who were rich and beautiful. Was it their clandestine plan that was causing this excitement? Could it be the secrecy of their friendship? Or was he embarrassed to be seen with her?

Beth didn't want to deceive her parents. As she drove to the library, she started having second thoughts. Her parents were still bickering about her wanting to go out with Greg. She even began to feel guilt and regret for telling him that she was going to the city. If her parents found out, they would feel betrayed and not trust her anymore. She was beginning to feel deeply remorseful as if she was deceiving everyone. But it's not like we planned to be there to really meet there. She thought, trying to convince herself. It just so happened they were both fulfilling a school assignment. What was wrong with that? What could they possibly be afraid of? Why would someone like him ever want to be with someone like me anyway? Her thoughts were beginning to ricochet back and forth until she began wondering if she should just turn around and go back home. The library was only another five-minute drive from the bookstore, and she was trying to save a little money, just as Greg had said. I'm not doing anything wrong, she thought. Then why am I feeling so guilty?

Finding a parking space quickly, then reaching the top of the steps was an arduous effort. She nervously opened the library door. It's true, she thought, still trying to convince herself of her innocence, she was going to get a book and if the library didn't have it, then she would go to the bookstore to buy it. The library was also a public place and she had no control over who would be there. Still trying to persuade herself, she was not doing anything wrong, she walked towards the stairs to descend to the lower level of the library. Feelings of guilt made her imagine she was being watched. As she passed the different areas of the library, she saw children sitting in tiny chairs at the knees of their mothers, old people, young people, some were sitting and reading, and others were searching the shelves. But why did they stop to glance at her as she walked by? Or was it her imagination? A library aide came seemingly out of nowhere and walked over to ask if she needed any help. Beth couldn't understand why she came to her or even where she had come from. She faked a smile and said,

"No thank you." Did her feelings show on her face? She continued towards the steps with her head down trying to avoid the stares. The less than fifteen-second walk to the steps seemed to take an eternity. With thoughts of consolation, she took the first step to the lower level. Beth's heart pounded so hard she thought she felt the beats vibrating against her chest resonating echoing sounds down into the quietness of the hollow decline as she went step by step to the bottom. Taking the last step to the floor, she looked straight ahead and there she saw Greg sitting at a table near the back of the room. She hadn't seen him since the day he had spoken to her at the athletic club when she first met him. His hair was still brown with the same friendly smile as when she last saw him. She thought she was going to faint. Thoughts of seeing him for the very first time streamed through her mind. She never thought a day like this would ever be and meeting him was certainly nowhere in her wildest dreams, let alone a reality. This cannot be true. Why was he doing this? She had to be dreaming. She even pinched herself. Whenever she looked at herself in the mirror, she thought she was unattractive and really nothing much to look at and couldn't imagine how she must look to him. As she continued to walk towards him, she tried but couldn't tell if she was smiling. She was hoping her expression was not one of fear, although that was how she felt. He was absolutely the most handsome guy she had ever seen. His thick chestnut hair was cut so perfectly around his ears. He looked at her, his blue-gray eyes seemed to smile at her and immediately took away the fear she felt.

Greg thought as he saw Beth approaching, "What have I gotten myself into? I don't want to hurt this girl, but I do like her. She's such a nice person." He stood up, as she got closer to him. "Hi, Beth. Did you find your book?" he asked.

"No," she answered, shyly looking away. "To tell you the truth, I haven't looked yet. I just got here," she said nervously.

"Here, why don't you sit down?" he said kindly. "What kind of book are you looking for?" "You know, I'm actually trying to find a book to help me study for the SAT's," bashfully turning her head.

"Oh, so you're going to go to college? Which one? Have you taken the test before?" he asked in rapid session.

"Yes, I am, but I haven't really decided yet which one. What was your last question?" she asked, looking down at the table again to avoid any eye contact. Not bothering to ask again, he proceeded to update her on his future plans. "I'm going to college too." The people at the table adjacent to them looked over and frowned. "I guess we're talking too loud," he whispered, and smiled. "Hey, my car's parked right on the back lot. Let's just go somewhere where we can talk." Beth was shocked. She was not prepared for this offer.

"Okay," she said nervously. She must have looked reluctant because Greg assured her it was okay. She smiled shyly, looking away. They got up and headed towards the steps.

"Have you eaten yet?" he asked, as they walked up the stairs.

"No, not yet." She was so anxious to meet with Greg she had forgotten about eating.

"Do you want to take a ride to get something to eat?"

"All right, but I still have to get my book," she said politely. She had to get that book for proof to her parents that she really was going into the city to get the book she needed. To make matters worse, her father had already been acting suspicious of her ever since she asked about going out with Greg. Greg took Beth by the hand and led her to his car in the parking lot. She could have melted when his hand touched hers. He was actually holding her hand. 'It was so warm and soft,' she thought. Leading her over to the passenger side, he opened the door and she slid in. Beth had never gone out with any guy anywhere. She couldn't believe the treatment she was getting from someone like him. He had his choice of any girl, but he was with her. It was surreal.

Greg was looking forward to being with Beth, but couldn't understand why. She was not what his family wanted for him, nor was she what he thought he wanted for himself. Although he had just met her and had only gotten to know her on the phone, he really liked her. She was so down to earth, not snooty or sex driven like the other girls he knew.

"There's a Pizza Hut right over the hill. Is that okay?" Greg asked.

"That's fine," Beth answered softly. They pulled into the parking lot. Still looking over his shoulder, Greg gave a quick scan to see if there were any familiar cars there. There were hardly any cars in the parking lot. He pulled into a parking space and stopped. Still inside the car, he looked over at Beth and smiled. "Are you ready to go in?" he asked. Beth smiled and said she was ready. He came over to open the door for her. Greg's courtesy and charm made her feel a little distrustful, yet she was exhilarated. This was one day in her life that she would never, ever forget.

When the greeter walked over to them, a smiling, short elderly woman, Greg asked if they could be seated in a booth. Surmising they wanted to be alone, she seated them near the rear of the restaurant. After waiting for

Beth to sit, he sat directly in front of her. A young woman soon came to their table and introduced herself as their server. She handed them the menus, took their order for beverages and walked away towards the kitchen.

"Do you realize this is our first date?"

"I don't know. I thought dates were planned," she shyly responded. "I guess you could call it an unofficial date," she added, not wanting to appear negative.

"Okay, we'll call it unofficial. You know, Beth, I really enjoyed the conversations we had when I was away in Cancun. I kinda got to know you just by talking on the phone." "Yeah, I have to say I enjoyed our talks too. And…uhh…and I also must admit I was quite surprised. I never expected to hear from you at all," she said, looking down.

"Why did you think that?"

"Uhh… probably because I don't get many calls from guys…well, really not any calls." This was an awkward moment for Greg. The waitress had come back with their drinks just in time and he managed to dodge having to respond. After placing their glasses on the table, she asked if they were ready to order. Greg answered, no and asked for a few more minutes. The waitress sighed, turned and walked away.

"Believe me, I know how she feels," Beth said, as the waitress walked away. They both chuckled.

Smiling he said, "I guess we'd better be ready when she comes back, then."

Looking down at the menu, "I still somehow can't believe this is really happening to me."

Greg took his hand and gently lifted her face. "What do you mean, Beth? He askcd softly.

"Well, no one has ever… well, anyway, no guy has ever talked to me kindly before. Let alone ask me out. And then someone like you… I mean, you could have any girl you want…not that you've chosen me or anything… and I'm sure you do have a girlfriend… Well, anyway, I just think it was nice of you to have even called me," she said humbly. "You certainly had no obligation to me. You didn't even have to call."

"Beth, I did have an obligation to you. I took your phone number and I said I would call you. I felt horrible that I had forgotten. I didn't want you to think I was that type of guy. Do you know what I mean?"

"You see. What you're saying to me is just so strange for someone like you to be saying those things to…to someone like me," she said, feeling unworthy.

Greg could see how unattractive she felt she was. He was beginning to feel pity for her. At that point, he wanted to hug her and hold her to comfort her, but he knew not to.

"Beth, please stop saying things like that. From what I've gotten to know about you is that you're a great person to talk to, you're funny, and nice to be around too." The waitress walked back to their table to hopefully get their order. This time they were ready. They gave her their selections and she walked away this time with a grateful smile.

Looking right at Beth with a smile, Greg said, "Let's get off this subject, okay." After taking a deep breath, he said cheerfully, "So, how's your summer going?" She laughed. All through the rest of their meal, they talked about their schools, their future ambitions, hobbies and favorite music artists just as they had done while he was on vacation. They were both astonished to find out how much they both had in common.

As they finished their meal, playfully and blinded by enjoyment, Greg asked, "So, when are we going out on a real date?" Again, Beth was taken aback. She didn't expect to ever see Greg again after this, other than at the athletic club where she worked. He had already upheld his promise. Why would he want to see her again?

Out of nowhere, she asked, "Greg, why can't I call you?" She was shocked at her own words. They seemed to have just blurted out.

Greg knew she was bound to notice he'd never offered to give her his phone number. "I don't know why? I guess I never thought about it before," Greg said, feigning innocence.

"Oh, I'm sorry. I have no right to ask you. Forget I even said that." Beth was really and truly sincere in her apology.

"I thought that we had exchanged numbers…maybe not," he lied. He took out his phone book from his pocket, tore out a page, and wrote down his phone number, thinking as he wrote. He had his own phone line anyway and his own phone. No one else should answer his phone. When he tried to hand it to her, she told him it was okay and that she understood. But he insisted and apologized for not giving it to her before. Taking the paper and putting it into her pocketbook, she thought to herself she would never call him. The waitress came back to see if they wanted dessert or anything else. They both declined and he asked for the check. She offered to pay for her meal, but he insisted on paying since it was his suggestion to go to lunch anyway. Looking at her watch, she was alarmed at how much time had elapsed. She didn't want their time together to end, but she had to get that book and get back home. She didn't want to arouse any more suspicion from her parents, so she told Greg that she needed to get back to the library to look for the book. With no curfew or restrictions hovering over him, he offered to help her find it. When they got back to the library, Beth had become a different person than when she first entered. She felt more confident and self-assured, not caring if anyone was staring. With Greg by her side, she went directly up to the librarian and asked for the book she needed. In a few minutes, the librarian found the book and they both went over to the checkout desk.

Beth's car was on the other side of the parking lot so he offered to drive her there. She told him the type of car and pointed to where she had been parked. He drove up right beside it. Putting the car in park, he stepped on the emergency brake and sat looking at her sitting beside him. Beth thought he was getting ready to get out to open the door as he had been doing, but he only sat there. She could see him from her periphery staring at her. Breaking the silence, she said, "Okay, here's my car. Thanks." She looked directly at him this time. "Thank you for lunch and for helping me find my book."
"You're welcome. It was my pleasure. You know, I had a great time today."
She responded in the same manner and proceeded to open the door. Greg asked her to wait. He got out of the car and went around to open the door for her. When she stood up, he being much taller than her bent over and kissed her on the cheek. Again, he thanked her for the date and opened the door of her car. Still in shock, she secured herself in, put on her seatbelt, started the car and drove off in pure ecstasy. They both waved goodbye. Then Greg got into his car and drove home. He completely forgot about his book and the assignment.
"It was just an excuse anyway," he thought.

Beth was almost in tears as she drove home pondering over what had just happened. The music from the car radio was softly playing. No one had ever treated her so kindly. She could not stop thinking about the kiss. It was so gentle. He was the nicest person she had ever met. Somehow, she felt he genuinely liked her. She had to speak to her parents again about Greg. She didn't want to lose his friendship. Greg was equally astonished about how much he liked Beth. How was he going to explain her to his parents? Did he even need to? His father wouldn't be the problem; his mother would be the one who he had to contend with. But then again, his father would probably give in as always and take sides with his mother using the "disparity" lecture. Conceding was always his way of keeping the peace. When would his father ever get the courage to stand firm for his own beliefs? Greg was beginning to have feelings for Beth, but what kind of feelings? It couldn't be love. He had just met her but a couple of weeks ago. Was it sympathy... empathy? His mother would certainly think so, that or pity. Whatever it was, he wanted to continue to see her at least until the summer was over. "After all, she'll be going back to her home all the way in Plattsburgh, New York at the end of the summer, which is a long ways from where I live," he thought.

When Beth arrived home, she decided to confess to her parents after dinner that she had been with Greg earlier that day.

"You what?!" her father exclaimed, as he slammed the newspaper on the sofa and stood up. "I told you how I felt about those boys, Beth. You deliberately disobeyed me."

"But Dad, I saw him at the library and he asked if he could buy me lunch. Dad, Greg is not the person you think he is. You don't know him. He's a nice, kind, and polite person. He's nothing like his brother," she pleaded

"Listen, Beth, you don't know anything about them. People talk, I've heard about the type of characters they are, and I don't want you around them!"

"Tell him, Mom!" looking to her mother for support.

"Okay, Beth, your father and I will talk about this later."

Beth stared at her parents with anger, saying nothing. She swiftly spun around, went to her room and slammed the door.

"Look, Don, Beth is sixteen and will soon be seventeen. She's growing up. She's not a little girl anymore."

"Yeah, that's the point. She's not a little girl. I've heard things about those boys and they aren't pleasant things, either."

"Look, I also work at the club and I've heard things as well, but Greg, I've heard, is not like the other brother. In fact, I've even heard compliments about him. He's very polite and respectful to all the employees. Furthermore, they seem to like him. Look, there aren't any other boys banging on our door if you haven't noticed. So I don't think you have a lot to worry about. Let her enjoy herself and have a little fun. We're only here until the end of the summer."

"A lot can happen in a little time," Don said.

"What are you worried about? We taught our daughter the difference between right and wrong, and she's heard it in church all of her life. I'm not at all worried about her making the right decisions. She always does."

"I'm telling you, Jan, I don't feel comfortable about this boy."

"How about having him come over for dinner one evening then? That way, we can determine for ourselves if we can trust him with her or not. I don't want her to start sneaking around to see him. This encounter was close enough."

"Okay, but if I see one thing I don't like about him, I will not allow her to go anywhere with him. And that will be final. You can tell her that."

     The next day at the athletic club, Beth and her mom were in the kitchen preparing the lettuce for the salads. They hadn't spoken any more about Greg since the evening before. Jan told Beth her dad had given her permission to invite Greg over for dinner on Friday. Beth got so excited she dropped the head of lettuce in the large metal strainer and was beginning to take her gloves off.

"What do you think you're doing, young lady? Her mom asked.

"I was just getting ready to call Greg."

"Not now. You have a job to do. Maybe you can call during your break." It was already Tuesday. Beth was elated. Then she began to worry. What if he can't come? What if he doesn't want to come, she thought. It was getting close to eleven o'clock. Jan looked at her daughter's face and saw expressions of anxiety. This poor girl, her mother thought. She told Beth to go ahead and break away for an early lunch. A smile returned to her face.

"Thanks, Mom. I love you. I'll see you in a while."

She hastily walked towards the door of the kitchen. Pushing the door open, she almost bumped into a little, burly man carrying a platter of rolls. Pardoning herself she kept going hastily to the ladies' locker room. As soon as she got in, she went to the payphone to call Greg. With emotions heightening, she realized she had to first get the number from her purse. Nervously opening her locker, she found the paper still pushed in her purse. Recalling her reluctance to take it was now thankful she had decided otherwise. Looking at the paper she thought, this was the number she had first refused to accept and vowed not to call. Thankfully, no one was in the locker room, she thought. It was eleven o'clock in the morning. Hoping not to awaken him, she dialed the number.

"Hello?" Greg said sleepily, as if asking who it was.

"Hi, Greg, this is Beth. I hope I didn't wake you."

"Not really," he answered, concealing a yawn. "What's up?" He quickly got up to lock the door. He didn't want anyone bursting in while he was talking to her. He hadn't yet told anyone about her.

"I told my parents I was with you yesterday," she said.

"Well, what did they say?"

"My mom was okay, but my dad was not happy. He said he'd heard bad things about you and your brother. What was he talking about?"

"Yeah, what was he talking about?" responding in disbelief.

"Well, Greg, I do know a little about your brother myself, from my own experience." "Yeah and I'm sorry about that," he said in defense. Not responding to his apology, she resumed her thoughts.

"And from other things I've seen, he can be a bit obnoxious, so I can see why he'd say such things about him. But you, Greg, I don't know how anyone could say anything bad about you."

Greg was becoming a little uneasy. He was not what her father thought of him, especially with girls…in fact, he was nothing like his brother. His mind began to wonder about his generation. His peers' actions were not really their fault. But some of those girls deserved what they got, he thought, and they even expected it. Most of them were not even looking for a meaningful relationship. But there was something different about Beth. She was so sweet, so innocent, and truly sincere.

"So Greg, will you be able to come Friday? You didn't answer."

"What? Friday? What did you ask me about Friday?"

"My parents asked if you could come over for dinner Friday?" He had been so caught up in his thoughts of being sized up and compared to his brother that he had completely tuned out their conversation. What would he tell his parents about Friday? Would he tell them the truth? His mother would absolutely forbid it. He would have to make up an excuse just in case they should want to know his whereabouts.

"Greg? Are you still there?" He hadn't realized how long he had drifted off into his own thoughts.

"Oh… ah… yeah. I'm here. What time's dinner?" he asked, pretending to be enthused. "Can you come around six? Everyone is off that Friday. What luck, huh… including my dad. I'm sure you've already met him. You may have even worked out with him in the gym. He's a trainer in the body building area. His name is Donald Tinsley. Everyone calls him Don."

When she told him her father's name, he just realized he didn't even know her last name.

"My mom's name is Janet. Of course, she's called Jan, for short. I help her out back in the kitchen sometimes. She's a real gourmet cook, you know," Beth ranted on.

"Yeah, I've seen your dad there, but I've never worked out with him. Okay, so it looks like we're set to go then," he said being facetious.

"Okay, I'll see you then," She responded with a laugh. She was ecstatic. She felt as though her life was turning into a real fairytale. Thinking about her mother's advice, she knew she needed to be cautious and not to expect much. After all, he was only a boy she had just met and would meet many more by the time the right one comes along. Her mom reminded her also they would be leaving at the end of the summer. But despite what her mother told her, for the first time in her life a boy found something worthwhile in her and it made her feel special.

This friendship was beginning to snowball into something deeper than he had intended. Greg was becoming apprehensive about the possibility of having to confront his family about Beth. He was beginning to feel a little regretful that he ever spoke up and apologized to Beth for the way she had been treated by his brother and his friends. Then thought he probably would have felt worse had he not, because that was certainly not in his character. He knew he had done the right thing, but should have let it go after the apology. He didn't have to get her phone number and start this telephone relationship, but he did. What were his intentions? Initially, he only felt sorry for her. His brother had been so cruel to her that day at the club; he thought he should at least call her to apologize for his behavior since no one else did. That was supposed to have been the end of it. How did he get this involved? But as it turned out, she was a nice girl and someone with enough intellect to have a real conversation with, especially while he was away. Anyway, there was no one else he was interested in at the time. Something was unexplainably different about her that seemed to stir something within him. Their worlds were totally different as far as affluence and social status were concerned; yet, there was something more significant than that. The difference was not only material acquisitions between the "haves" and the "have-nots." This was something that seemed to reach down into the very depths of one's soul. Greg couldn't grasp his own thoughts or his feelings about this. There was something significant and intangible between these two types of people. This was of greater value than those things which can only be purchased by the rich. Wealth can acquire much, and possessions are only empty gains that only create boredom, deceit, and distrust of the financially inferior. There is something far more meaningful in life for those who have accomplished goals by effort, rather than those whose gains were handed either by birth, inheritance or sheer luck. These accomplishments can only be seen or touched. Fulfillment of life cannot be purchased. At this time, he could only have the sense of how he felt, but couldn't comprehend what it was. He was drawn to it and yet confused by it.

Greg told Beth that he and his brother would be going to the office with their dad on Thursday and Friday and probably wouldn't be home to answer the phone if she needed to call him. He also mentioned if he didn't get to speak to her before Friday, he would see her on Friday evening and would give her a call before he came. What he needed was time. With Friday closing in fast, he needed to think about that evening and be ready for what her parents were going to present him with. He also needed to figure out what he wanted out of their friendship.

The guys went to the office with their dad as he had said they would. They were both standing by the copy machine when Jack told his brother he and some of the guys were going to get together over a friend's house to shoot pool and hang out a while on Friday and asked him to come along. Man, why did she have to ask me over to dinner this Friday? This would have been a great opportunity to straighten some things out in his head. Greg made up a lie and said he met a friend who lived in the city while he was at the library the other day. Jack suggested he bring the friend along with him. Greg told him the friend was a girl.
"Well, bring her and share the wealth," he said laughing.
"You're sick. Is that all you ever think about when girls are involved?"
"Ah, come on, I'm just kidding. Well, is there anything else?" he said laughing again. He knew how to get Greg's goat.

As soon as they got home on Friday, almost simultaneously, they both jumped in their showers. Greg searched his closet for something appropriate to wear. He wanted to make a good impression. He found a nice blue Ralph Lauren golf shirt and jeans. Jack was in his room getting dressed as well. As they were getting ready for their night out, Nancy had long been in the kitchen preparing their favorite Friday night meal as soon as she saw they were home. She had come to the foot of the spiral staircase by the time Jack, who was just putting on his jacket, came walking down towards her.
"Aren't you guys going to eat something? I made your favorite." Jack was almost midway to the bottom by the time she finished announcing her last persuasive plea. When he reached the bottom, he kissed his mom on the cheek and apologized. He told her he was going to meet a few buddies to play a game of pool and would be eating there. He also told her Greg was going out as well. By the time Greg had come downstairs, Jack and his mom had gone into the kitchen. He walked in.

"So you guys are going to leave me here to eat alone, huh?" she asked somewhat jokingly.

"Aww, come on Mom, Dad, will be home soon. He told us to go on home and he would be leaving soon after we left," Jack said.

"So where are you going, Greg? Jack told me about his plans."

"Who me?" Greg said nervously.

"Yes. I did say, Greg."

"Oh, I'm going over to see an old friend from school I saw at the library today. I hadn't seen her in a long time," he answered.

"When, since school ended?" she asked, but she was smiling.

As he was walking out the door, his mom said, "Remember what I told you."

"Yeah, Mom, I'm prepared. But that's not my intention," he said with a sigh.

"It doesn't have to be, just be prepared."

"I know, Mom."

Parting ways to get in their cars, Jack yelled. "Always be prepared," and burst out laughing while closing the car door.

"Man, is that all these people ever think about around here when you're going out with a girl," he thought.

Beth had given Greg the directions to their summer cottage when he called her from his dad's workplace earlier that day. Greg parked his black Mustang in front of the house. It was situated on a slight incline where three other small cottages were structured contiguously, one to the other. He thought about sitting in the car until exactly six o'clock but thought it was more impressive to be a little early. After waiting five more minutes, he slowly got out of the car and strolled up the walkway, bending so as not to bump his head on the tree limb which hung over the walkway. He climbed the six wooden steps that led to the porch. Reaching the door, he looked around for the doorbell. Not finding it, he knocked gently on the door. Through the pale blue diaphanous curtains, he could see the figure of a male coming towards the door. Her father opened the door. He cordially greeted Greg, but the look on his face revealed otherwise. Greg reached out to shake his hand. Smiling, he said, "Good evening sir. I'm Greg Tyler."

"Yes, I know. I've seen you at the club. Well, dinner's just about ready. Please have a seat."

There were two armchairs in the small living room. One faced the sofa where her father had been sitting. He saw the newspaper opened where he had left it when he came to open the door. Greg not wanting to sit face to face with her dad, headed for the one facing the wood burning fireplace. He wondered if it was ever used. Just as he was about to sit, Beth walked into the living room smiling. She had heard the knock at the door and ran to take one last look at herself in the full-length mirror on the bathroom door. Looking at Greg for any signs her father may have been rude, she greeted him. "Hi, Greg, how are you?"

Looking surprisingly comfortable to her he answered, "I'm fine, thank you."

"I see you've met my dad."

"Yes, I did."

"Well, why don't you have a seat? Dinner is just about ready." Again, just when he was about to sit her mother also stepped in. She was a gorgeous woman, he thought. She was tall, thin, with shiny blond hair and hazel green eyes. Beth had no resemblance to her mother at all except height, Greg thought. What happened to her daughter; I wonder if she's adopted. Immediately, he felt guilty with feelings of shame for having such thoughts.

She walked over to Greg. Wiping her right hand with the dishtowel, she reached out to shake his hand.

"How are you, Greg? Pleased to meet you."

Immediately he responded and reached out to shake hers. Her hands are so soft, he thought. He couldn't believe she worked in a kitchen. He couldn't recall ever seeing her at the club. A face like that he wouldn't have forgotten. Probably because she was always in the back, in the cooking area was probably why he had never seen her.

"I'm fine, thank you, Mrs. Tinsley. And I'm pleased to meet you also, ma'am," he responded with a smile.

"Beth, bring Greg to the table. I'm about ready to put the food out." Greg was so relieved he didn't have time to sit alone with Beth's father.

"Okay, Mom. Do you need any help?"

"No sweetie, I'm fine."

She led Greg to the dining area. Beth saw how Greg looked at her mom. She knew what he was thinking. Just like everyone else whenever they were seen together. Some would even express their rude comments out loud. "Your mother is beautiful," they would say. "You don't look anything like her." She remembered how hurt and embarrassed she would be, but her mother would always defend her daughter with a clever response. Beth's father, watching Greg's eyes could also tell what he was thinking about his wife. Don could remember the first time he saw Beth after she was born.

"Are you sure that's our baby?"

"You know she's ours. You watched the birth yourself. Isn't she beautiful?" Jan adored her daughter.

Everyone gathered in the dining room with Beth's father leading the way. When all were seated, Don said the prayer to bless the food. Greg had never witnessed this ritual before. He knew people went to church and said prayers, but he had never encountered the act directly. His family recognized themselves as Christians, but they didn't go to church. They began passing around plates of meat and vegetables to each other. The conversation was general.

"Mrs. Tinsley, this food is the best. Beth told me how great a cook you are. She wasn't exaggerating."

"Thank you, Greg. That's very kind of you to say."

"No, it's true, ma'am. Everything is really good."

They continued with the basic questions about grades, plans after graduation, pursuits and ambitions, and career goals. Greg asked them what they did back home in New York.

Then Beth's dad asked the dreaded question.

"So Greg, I'm told that you want to take my daughter out on a date."

"Ye-ye yes sir," stuttered Greg nervously.

"What did you have in mind?" he continued with the interrogation.

"Well, sir, I was thinking about going to a movie."

"Well, what kind of movie did you have in mind, Greg?" Her father couldn't get those thoughts of the rumors he had heard about those Tyler boys out of his mind.

"Well, sir, uhh…that would be up to Beth, sir."

The response was very clever, her dad thought.

"Dad, Greg isn't on trial," jumping to Greg's defense and feeling embarrassed about her father's behavior.

"So Greg, what show did you have in mind?" her mother interjected to demonstrate her approval.

"Well, ma'am, I think a matinee would be good. Then I would have time to take Beth to get a bite to eat before bringing her home. That is, if that's what she'd like, and, of course, with your approval."

"And what time would that be?" her father asked, looking at Greg with a stern face.

"Sir,…that would be your call. I mean, that would be up to you and your wife." Again, a very clever response he thought.

"Okay, my wife and I will talk it over with Beth about what we feel is an appropriate time to get her back home and she'll get back to you."

To change the subject, her mother asked, "Anyone for dessert? I made an Apple Clafouti."

"I'll have some, thank you. It sounds good. I'm sure it tastes just as good as it smells." Beth and her mom laughed. Her dad only eyed Greg with suspicion. Everyone had dessert and talked about how wonderful it was. He had been at their home for over two hours and was beginning to feel a bit uncomfortable after the showdown with her father. He could feel his eyes on him at every move.

Looking at Beth with a smile, Greg said, "I guess I'd better be leaving. I left my mother at home by herself. My dad hadn't gotten home from work by the time I left." There was no way he would mention his brother. Beth knew this was only an excuse to leave, but she understood how he felt.

"Would you like to call her, Greg?" her mom asked.

Getting up from the table, he turned to Beth's mother who was removing the dishes from the table.

"No, thank you, ma'am. It won't take that long to get home. But thank you anyway. And thank you both again for inviting me to your home for dinner. It was nice meeting you both."

"Oh, you're quite welcome, Greg, and thank you for coming."

"Yes, Greg, it was nice meeting you," her dad added with a stern look. As he reached out to shake Greg's hand, "Like I said, Beth will let you know about the movie and the time," He was trying to sound more pleasant.

Beth walked Greg to the door and went out on the porch with him. To Beth, it seemed as though it took almost an eternity for the door to close. She could see her mom had walked away, but her dad stood there longer. "Thanks again, Greg, for coming. I'm sorry about my dad."

"That's okay. I guess he's just being a dad. He is tough, though," Greg said, as he walked down the steps down to the walkway. As he ducked to avoid the branch in the walkway's path, he heard Beth say, "I'll call you."

Getting in his car, he began to reexamine his situation. What is going on? Why was he still letting himself get deeper and deeper into this dilemma? It was not his intention for this to have gone this far. If Jack ever found out, he would probably squeal like a pig and tell all of his friends and then he would be the laughing stock at school. He could never let that happen.

Beth was very disappointed with her dad. When she went back in the

house, she proceeded to let him know it. "Dad, why did you have to treat Greg as if he was some kind of a criminal or something? He has been so polite and kind to me ever since I met him. I've never been so embarrassed in all my life."
"Yes Don, you were quite harsh."
"Listen, I just want that kid to know I want him to respect my daughter, that's all."
"Dad, he's been nothing but respectful to me. He's really a nice person."
"And I want him to stay that way."
"Oh, Don, give the kid a break," his wife said.
"Dad, I really want to go to the movies with Greg. What's the big deal?"
"The big deal is I don't want you to get involved with him."
"Come on Don! She only wants to go to a movie, not get married."
"Well, I'll consider it as long as you go see something decent. And I want you home no later than eight o'clock."
"What? Eight o'clock? Are you kidding me? Dad, I'm not a baby. I'll be seventeen in a couple of months. I'll be graduating from high school next year, for crying out loud."
"Come on Donald, at least until ten."
"Mom!"
"Beth, you are going to a matinee. Let's not push it. You'll even have time to get a bite to eat afterwards." She looked at Beth and winked. "This is your first date," her mom said.
Beth looked at her mom and smiled, holding her index finger to her mouth, indicating not to talk about it as she pointed to her dad with her eyes. She didn't want to get him stirred up again.

It was not until the following Thursday afternoon that Beth got a chance to call Greg to let him know she had gotten the okay from her dad to go to the movies with him. Ever since that Friday evening's dinner, Beth was obsessed with preparing for her date with Greg. She knew her dad would accede. She had even gone shopping to buy something special for the occasion and also had been searching for a hair stylist. She wanted to make a good impression on Greg. There was such excitement in her voice when she called Greg. At that very moment, he was getting ready to drive over to a friend's house, named Shelley Allen. Shelley was not a girlfriend, not to him anyway, but maybe she thought so. He had been intimate with her a few times since the day he met her at a friend's party. It was just about the time they had initially moved into the area. They had exchanged phone numbers and called each other several times, but he never considered their relationship serious. The first time she called was when she invited him over for a swim in their pool. Her parents were away for the weekend. What innocently began as a parting "thank you-for-coming" kiss quickly became an all out orgy. She called him several times after that, each time her parents were away. The evening before his plan to go to Beth's, she had called to ask if he would like to come over for a game of tennis the following afternoon. Wednesday was usually one of the days he and his brother didn't have to go to the office with their dad.

"Hello, Greg, it's Beth."

"Hi, Beth, what's up?"

"My dad told me I could go out with you," she exclaimed.

"Oh, that's good," he said nonchalantly.

"Greg, did you hear what I said? I can go out with you," she said with exhilarating joy. "Did I interrupt you or something?" Beth sheepishly asked.

"No. I mean…yeah, Beth, that's great news." Noticing how disinterested he must have sounded, he tried to enliven his voice. "So, when do you think we can go?" he asked.

"Well, soon I hope. But I'll call you as soon as I find out and let you know exactly when." "I'm actually on my way out right now, Beth, but I'll call you later. Okay?"

"Oh, okay. Greg, is anything wrong?"

"No. Nothing's wrong. I'm just kinda in a hurry right now, that's all. But I will call you. Okay?"

Trying to only sound curious, but feeling a little jealous, she asked, "Oh, where are you going?"

"As a matter of fact, I'm on my way over to a friend's house to play a game of tennis, and I'm running a little late. So, I'll give you a call later. Okay?" he reiterated, trying to conceal his annoyance with her questions.

Catching the hint she was going too far with her questioning, she ended the conversation. "Okay, I'll talk to you later. Bye."

"Bye, Beth."

Greg was just about at Shelley's house. He was pulling into her driveway when he saw Shelley lying out on the patio. She was stretched out on a lounge chair sunbathing, wearing a very skimpy bikini. There was a pitcher of iced tea on the picnic table shaded by a large umbrella. He got out of his car and walked over to the patio.

"What's going on Shelley?"

"Oh, nothing. I'm just out here enjoying the summer sun."

"Yeah, me too, but I thought we were going to play tennis. I'm dressed to play tennis. I didn't even bring my trunks for a swim."

"That's not a problem. I could get you a pair of my brother's. You know, Mike." Greg sat on a patio chair underneath the umbrella and poured a glass of iced tea. "Sure, I know your brother. He's on the basketball team."

"Or you could use a pair of my dad's."

"No thanks," he said with an expression of disgust. "Where is your brother, by the way?"

"He went to visit a friend in Florida. He'll be gone for about two weeks. He'll be back just in time for school."

"So, where are your parents? Where'd they go this time? They really travel a lot, don't they?"

"It's my dad who has to travel so much. My mom just gets tired of being left behind. So she tries to take advantage of the summer months when my brother and I are out of school and uses that opportunity to be with my dad."

"So what about you guys? Don't you miss your parents?"

"Maybe you should have asked if our parents miss us," Shelley said sarcastically.

"I'm surprised they leave you home alone for so long."

"Well, that's not totally true. I'm supposed to be staying with my aunt who lives about a forty-five minute drive away. I told her I wanted to come home to get some more clothes and hang out at the pool a while, although they have a pool. She didn't want to argue, so she said okay. And that's when I called you," as if telling the end of a story.

"I guess you never had tennis in mind then."

"Obviously not," she cooed, as she leaned over from behind and kissed Greg on his neck. He pulled her over his shoulder until she sat in his lap, as if he were holding a baby. The kisses became more intense. She stood up and guided Greg into the house, both dropping their clothes along the way.

While Shelley and Greg were ending their climactic interlude, Shelley's cordless phone started ringing. She wanted to ignore it, but Greg hesitantly urged her to answer it.

"Hello. Oh hi, Aunt Kate. Yeah, I'm still here. I decided to hang out at the pool a little while longer. I won't be much longer. No. No one's here, except me. Yes, in fact, I'm getting dressed right now. I know I promised to bring the car right back, but you said you didn't have any plans. Okay, I'm on my way. See you in a bit." She hung up the phone and tried to climb back onto Greg, who had been lying on the bed listening to the conversation. He pushed her off and got up, proceeding to put his clothes back on.

"What are you doing?

"What does it look like I'm doing? And you should be doing the same from the sound of that conversation." She walked over to him naked, trying to unbutton his pants.

"Stop it, Shelley. This wasn't why I came over here."

"Well, what else did you come for? Don't try to come off like you're so innocent. You're just like the rest. You got what you wanted, so now you leave," she said angrily. She picked up his shirt and threw it at him, standing by the bed crying profusely.

Greg put his shirt on and then got a towel and put it around her. He put his arms around her to comfort her. "Shelly stop crying and get your clothes on. You don't want your aunt not to allow you to drive her car anymore, do you? Come on now. Put your clothes on." She wiped her face with the towel and started gathering her clothes to put on. "Truthfully, Shelley, this was not why I came over. I'm sorry. Call me later to let me know you're okay." In his heart, he really felt sorry for Shelley. She was a lonely girl and vulnerable. He felt angry with himself because he allowed his lustful feelings to overtake his reasoning. He was no better than the rest, just like she said, "…taking advantage of a perfect situation." He got into his car and drove home thinking about his date with Beth. He wouldn't allow this to happen with her. And why should it, he thought. He has never had any sexual thoughts about her when they were together or when they spoke on the phone. He could never imagine himself being intimate with her. To him, she was just a nice person, someone to talk to and have as a friend. Maybe this was what drew him to her. With her, he could enjoy being with a female without having sex… and it was relaxing and fun. Sex was not the ultimate enjoyment in life.

Shelley had called Greg later that evening trying again to set up a date. He cautiously made excuse after excuse, trying not to further injure her already hurt ego. He couldn't go through that again knowing how really lonely and vulnerable she really was. He failed before, but needed to and wanted to uphold his ethical principles. While he was talking to Shelley, he could hear another call trying to come through. "Good," he thought. He wanted to end this conversation anyway, but didn't know how. In the middle of her sentence, he said, "Shelley, I have to go. I have another call."

"All right, if you have to, but call me back later. I hope it's not a girl," she quickly responded before he switched over.

Clicking over to the new call, found it was Beth. "Hi, Beth, what's up?"

"I have a date and time you can pick me up for the movie."

"Okay, so when?"

"How about next Saturday? Do you have any plans?" she asked.

"I don't recall anything. No, I don't think I have any plans," he responded.

"Okay, but I won't tell my parents until I hear from you. Did you want to come over so we can tell him together?"

"Are you kidding me? I'm sorry, Beth, but I don't want to see your father again until I come to pick you up. You know how he feels about me."

"I do, Greg, and I'm sorry about that. I guess he's just being a father, just like you said."

"Okay, I'll check and let you know soon. …talk to you later."

"Bye, Greg."

What's going on? Will this summer ever end? In just a few weeks, life seems to be strangling me, Greg thought, as he tossed and turned during the night. With the fear of his secret relationship with Beth, he would wake up from dreams of being taunted by Jack, and his mother pointing her finger in his face with warnings to "leave her alone!" Why did he feel so guilty? Why was he feeling so confused? Why couldn't he be more like Jack? Jack was enjoying the summer. He was hanging out with the guys, going to the pool, playing tennis, going to the mall to pick up girls and just hanging out without a care in the world. He was having a ball. A couple of times he asked Greg to go with them, but he seemed to not want to be bothered, so Jack stopped asking. But he did ask him what was wrong. Teasing and jesting that he was probably in love. Jack couldn't have been further from the truth. The fact of the matter, he was not in love with anyone. It was too bad he couldn't confide in his brother. There was no one he could confide in to tell what was really going on. He couldn't wait until summer was over.

Chapter 7

Sitting at his desk in his locked bedroom, Greg had taken the entertainment section of the newspaper to look at the movie listings. Always needing to select the right venue for obscurity, he remembered there were movie theaters over in Suffern, New York, which was about a thirty-minute drive. He had to be sure there would be no possibility he would run into any member of his family or any acquaintances, especially from school. He started thinking about Beth. She was such a sweet girl and so nice. Why did he have to treat her differently? Was he embarrassed to be with her? In his complex situation and befuddled emotions, he honestly didn't know. This was becoming a real ordeal and a battle. His very integrity was being challenged and he couldn't find the guts to be a man. He felt like a real worm, a criminal, sneaking around as if he was committing a crime. Trying to convince himself otherwise, he began making excuses. Not realizing it, he began seeing images in his mind, eyes of friends, family, even visualizing himself in these confrontations. "It's not that I'm afraid of standing up for my beliefs," he thought, "I just don't feel like having to explain myself to anyone. It's none of their business anyway. I can go out without having to tell anyone where, or with whom, I'm going out with. Anyway, I'd like to spend a little more time with Beth and going over to Suffern would be a nice little drive. She's really going to enjoy it. She doesn't get that many dates anyway. She told me so herself. Hey, I'm doing what those others guys wouldn't do. I don't know why not, she's really a fun person to talk to and be around. So, why should I feel guilty?" This mental soliloquy did nothing for his conscience. He felt nauseous with guilt.

Finally, he got his mind and eyes focused back on the newspaper. Oh, here's a movie I think her parents will be pleased with and the show time is perfect. "Now, let me find a nice restaurant in the area," he said softly to himself. "I don't want her parents to wonder why I'm taking her so far. I want them to think I want to show her a really nice time, which I do."

The doorknob of his bedroom began to twist and jiggle. "Hey, Greg, what's going on in there?" his brother asked through the door. "I was just walking by your room and I heard you in there talking. I know you're in there. Who's in there with you? "

"Hold on a minute. I was just getting ready to take a shower and I didn't want mom or anybody bustin' in. You know how she is." He jumped up and unlocked the door.

Jack barged right in, in his usual barge-in manner.

"What's going on with you? Who's in here?"

"Nobody, I was just thinking out loud."

"Anyway, big Bro', it seems like we don't get a chance to talk or hang out anymore. It's like you're avoiding me or trying to like… hide something. You haven't gotten anybody knocked up have you? You know Mom would freak out."

"No way. I'm not as stupid as you look."

"Ha, ha." Jack laughed sarcastically.

Greg exclaimed jokingly, gently pushing Jack's head, "Jack, you know sometimes you guys goof around too much. Like playing silly little games, like teasing people, whistling and yelling at girls from the car windows. You know, all that's crazy, don't you? It's stupid, immature, childish stuff."

"Awww, come on, Greg. Don't be such a schmuck. We just like to have a little fun, that's all."

"Look, I'll be graduating next year, and I guess I'm becoming a little too mature for you guys," he said as he took a playful jab at Jack's stomach. "Anyway, I'm spending a lot of time researching about the different colleges and ways to get scholarships and stuff."

"Get outta here, Greg. We don't need any handouts. Dad can send us to whatever college we choose. You know that," Jack said in a haughty way. Jack saw the newspaper spread out on Greg's bed. He noticed it was open to the movie pages. "Yeah, colleges my ass. These don't look like any colleges I know," picking up the paper from the bed and laughing.

"Can't a guy go to a movie? Give me that paper. And what do you want anyway?" he asked snatching back the paper.

"There's no more soap and I was going to take a shower," He knew Greg was a hoarder.

"Turn your head and I'll get you some. Don't think I'm going to let you know where I keep my stash," Greg gave him a bar of soap. "Now, would you please leave? …and I'm locking my door," he said, while gently pushing his brother out of his room.

Turning around outside Greg's closed door, he jokingly said, "Well, I never…" and went laughing down the long hallway to his bedroom.

Again, more lies and secrecy, Greg thought. If Jack was not such a jackass, he could talk to him. He went back to the newspaper to get the information about the movie so he could be prepared for when he would see Beth's father again. Highlighting the choices and times, he thought this would be a good time to call Beth, especially since Jack was in his room taking a shower. Finding his phone that had fallen under the desk chair, he called Beth. "Hi Beth, it's Greg. I found a great movie you might want to see. There were several theater choices showing it and many other movie choices as well, if you don't like this one." They talked about the latest movies that were playing and what they had heard and read about them. She picked the same one that he thought would be most appropriate before he even mentioned it to her. "Hey, that's the one I was thinking about." She had checked on some possibilities herself. But when he mentioned where the theater was, he was met with apprehension. She had no idea they would be going so far, especially since there were several local theaters nearby showing the same movie. While they talked, her thoughts were on what her father would say. "Look, Beth, I thought since we're going so early, we could make a whole day of it. It's a nice scenic route. Plus, you'd have an excuse for not coming back so early, or did you want to go right back?"

"No…not really. I didn't want to, but it's my father that's the problem."

"Look, Beth, one day you're going to have to stand up and not be a little girl. You are going away to college next year like you said, aren't you?"

"Yes… I am," she sheepishly responded.

"Your dad can't hold on to you forever. He has to learn to trust you."

"He does trust me. He has no reason not to."

"So, what's the problem?"

"You're right, Greg. I'll be graduating next year. They both are going to have to let go and stop treating me like a little kid. I'm going to tell them about our decision. Don't worry. This is something I need to do. I'll call you later." She said all this with audacious authority.

"Listen, Beth, I'm not trying to stir up any trouble, so…"

She cut off his sentence, "No, you're not stirring up any trouble. This conversation was bound to happen sooner or later. We may as well start sooner rather than later."

"Okay, then. Call me so I'll know what to do."

"I will."

They said good-bye and ended their call.

Beth didn't call back until the next day. A meeting was called by Beth to discuss her date with Greg. Her father was not happy about where they would be driving. It became a pretty heated discussion. He wanted to know why they couldn't just go in town, have an early dinner and get back home. Beth's mother jumped to her defense. She explained that it was her first date and being a high school senior, it was long overdue. She rationalized there was nothing wrong with driving a half hour away, because when she goes away to college it could be a half hour in flight. With apprehension, her father finally acceded. When their discussion ended, which had commenced directly after dinner, Beth felt it was too late to call Greg. They would have more time to talk the next day.

At work the following day, Beth took an early break to let Greg know about the outcome of their meeting. Hoping no one would be in the locker room again; she slipped in quickly to make her call. He was lying out at the pool when she called. His mom was out pulling weeds from a little garden not far from the pool area, which she maintained herself. She wanted her work of art to be seen whenever anyone came to the pool to lounge around or take a swim. Even though the gardener attended to the grounds of their estate, Nancy still enjoyed planting flowers and cutting fresh ones to bring into the house. She would place them in beautiful vases. Some of them were handmade by residents of some rescue organization. Those, among other items she had purchased from fundraisers and charity auctions that she periodically attended. Most of her finds that she purchased, she would simply just give away, mainly to the help, which only helped to feed her egregious condescending attitude. This gesture of giving things away, along with other financial contributions, filled her with pride and was soothingly self-gratifying.

These humanitarian gestures, as she called them thinking herself to be modest, made her feel as though she had lifted some poor family out of great poverty and ultimate destitution. It really gave her a tremendous sense of pride and accomplishment, especially when she would decide to put one of her charity purchases on display inside the house, but never got any farther than some place in the kitchen. His mom glanced over at him and smiled as he talked on the phone.

"Hi, Greg. I hope I didn't wake you."

"No, you didn't. I'm just hanging out by the pool."

"Well, I just wanted to tell you that my dad gave the okay. Not without a little nudging, of course."

"Okay, that sounds great. Sooo, I'll pick you up on Saturday... let's say around one o'clock? The movie starts at two-thirty. That should be enough time to get there, park and buy something to drink and eat before the movie starts. How's that sound?" "Sounds great. Thanks again Greg for asking me out. You don't know what this means to me." Beth said sounding to be in tears.

"Come on, Beth. It's only a movie. But, you're welcome anyway. You're making me feel a bit embarrassed."

"I'm sorry. I didn't mean to."

"I'll call you before Saturday, of course. Have a good day," Greg said to end the conversation.

"Okay," still sitting on the bench in the locker room. Finally, she came out of her transfixed state when she heard the door to the locker room open and hung up the phone. Quickly wiping the tear that had run down her cheek, she jumped up. Almost late getting back from her break, she briskly pranced back to her station.

To discredit Jack's suspicions, Greg decided to go out with him and some of their friends on Friday night. Bradley, a high school friend and neighbor, was having a late evening cookout. Brad, as the kids called him, was going to Paris with his parents for the rest of the summer and wanted to spend some time with his friends before school started. He and Jack decided to drive over together. As they drove up the long driveway to Brad's house, they could hear the loud music. As soon as Jack stepped into the enclosed Quartzite slated patio, everybody cheered, greeting him by name. They started high fiving and shaking hands with each other. They also acknowledged Greg, but Jack was the more popular brother. He received more attention than the host. When Greg saw the look on Brad's face, he felt a little embarrassed for him. The patio was well lit with extra lighting around the pool. About fifty people attended, and everybody seemed to be having a great time. Soon Jack was lost in the crowd. Greg walked around watching everyone and having short conversations with those who he knew. There were several pockets of activity going on. Some people were just standing around talking, some were eating and talking, others were dancing and some just clowning around pretending to be dancing. There were all types of foods on the grill, including meats of all species, seafood and vegetables and tables covered with an array of salads and desserts.

Sitting alone near the pool at one of the many tables under an umbrella eating a piece of steak, he was finally beginning to feel relaxed. Thinking to himself, "So this is what I've been missing." Scanning the crowd, he found Jack cornering one of the girls against the stone patio wall. She appeared to be enjoying his company. When he could finally get a clear view of her face, he saw that it was Shelley. She saw him and smiled. Returning a quick grin, he went back to eating his steak. He had been avoiding her calls and didn't want to give any impression that he was at all interested. Walking back over to the salad and dessert table, he got another fill on his plate. Feeling a finger tap on the shoulder, he looked around to see who it was. There Shelley stood in her Liz Claiborne cuffed white shorts and royal blue halter-top. "Hi Greg," she sang. "I haven't heard from you since that day you came over for a game of tennis," giving him a seductive wink.
"I know. How's your aunt?" he asked, trying to divert the conversation.
"She's good."
"Are your parents back yet?"
"No, not yet, but they should be getting back next week though. Why?"
Trying to look enticing and moving closer to him, Shelley looked into Greg's eyes and asked, "Did you want a rematch of tennis?" She was being sensually sarcastic. Just then, Jack walked over.
"Are you trying to trade me in for my brother, Shelley?" Jack asked teasingly.
"You know Shelley, Jack plays a better game of tennis than I do," he said and smiling as he went back to his seat under the umbrella. He was thoroughly enjoying himself just being alone. There were no lies being told, no clandestine places to meet anyone, and no secrets to conceal from those unsuspicious guests. After eating, Greg found a chaise lounge to lie on and dozed right off. He slept right through the loud playing music, the loud laughter and wild dancing. It was the best sleep he had had in weeks.

Chapter 8

The days seemed as if they had gone by so quickly. It was already Friday, the day before the movie date with Beth. During that whole week, Greg's mind had been inundated with thoughts of regret and then contradicted with feelings of compassion, which gave rise to pity. By Friday, he thought the day couldn't go by fast enough. Going to Brad's party was a much needed distraction. He really wanted to get it over with and go back to the way things were... uncomplicated.

On Saturday, Beth had already called twice. First, to make sure the date was still on and the other to let him know if he wanted to back out, she would understand.

"Beth, why would I want to back out? Remember, I asked you out."

"I know," she said in a shy low tone, "but..."

"Beth, I'm all set to go, so let's go out and have a good time."

When she said those words, Greg's heart broke. Whenever she talked like that, he would feel so guilty, as if he was responsible for her unhappiness. He felt that he should try to build up her confidence and self-esteem.

"Thanks, Greg. I'll be ready when you get here. See you later. Bye."

When he hung up, he looked at the phone and shook his head slowly side to side in sadness. A feeling of pride began to come over him. He felt as though he was treating her just as he would a regular friend and that it was okay if two friends who had common interests spend some time together. She was like one of his buddies. But deep in his subconscious mind, something else was there.

Beth only had three hours to get ready. After taking her shower, she and her mother were in her room hastily making sure that her hair was in place, her outfit was in order, and her makeup was perfect. Her father had already asked her if Greg was still coming, which is why she called Greg to confirm their plans. He still harbored distrust and resentment for those Tyler boys. He didn't believe Greg's interest in his daughter would last this long, nor was it genuine. Her mom was different. She was very intuitive. When she first looked into Greg's eyes, she could see something kind and gentle in them and told her husband so. He merely blew her off as just being a softhearted female. He had come to Beth's bedroom door to find out what was taking so long and to give advice through the door. From behind the closed door of Beth's bedroom, "Don, just because they're brothers doesn't mean they have to be alike. I've seen them both, and I can see that they're very different," his wife said, affirming her trust in Greg. He went grumbling down the hallway back to the living room where he usually sat to read.

"Don't mind him, sweetie, he's just being a dad. He loves you very much and wants to protect you. This is a new experience for him, you know."

"I know, Mom, but it's getting to be annoying."

"He'll get use to it. Just give him a little time," said her mom. Walking out to the living room and snatching up yesterday's folded newspaper from the coffee table where he had left it, he sat down, jerked it open and began trying to find where he had left off.

Looking in the mirror that hung behind the bedroom door for a final analysis, Beth and her mother stood side by side. Her mother was as excited as she was. Turning to Beth and looking straight into her eyes, she told her how beautiful she looked. She looked at her mom, and said, "Mom, you're beautiful. I hoped and prayed so many times that I would grow to look like you." Still standing face to face, her mom put her hands on her shoulders, "Stop it, Beth. When I say you are beautiful, I really mean it. And I am so proud to have you as my daughter and wouldn't want you any other way. Plus, you have much more valuable qualities than just physical beauty. Those qualities are forever, but physical beauty is only temporary. I'm sure Greg has recognized all of these." Beth grabbed her mother and hugged her tightly. She hugged her back, but pulled back gently, and said, "Be careful, you don't want to wrinkle your outfit." They both laughed. "Now turn around and let's see how you look." Her mother stood back and looked at her daughter with a huge smile said, "Perfect." By this time, it was twelve forty-five.

Beth and her mom walked into the living room. Beth went over and stood directly in front of her dad. Looking up from the paper, he asked, "What?"

"How do I look?" she asked.

"You look fine, but why do you have to put that stuff…that war paint on your face?"

"Don, why can't you just tell her how nice she looks and leave out the questions?"

"You look very nice Beth. Just remember everything that you've been taught. And if you need me to come…"

"Don!" her mother interrupted, she'll be just fine."

"Oh, I forgot my bag," Beth said, and frantically ran back to the bedroom. Just as she turned to run back down the hallway, there was a knock at the front door. It was Greg. He had gotten to Beth's house a little early and had been sitting in his car about three houses away. Fearful of stumbling over his words, he had been rehearsing what he was going to say to her parents, especially to her father in case he was questioned about his choice of venue. As he walked up the now familiar walkway with the hanging branch, he was softly practicing his script. "Sir, I know it's a bit farther than where we could go, but I wanted to show Beth a nice time by going for a little drive. The scenery along the drive there is very beautiful."

By the time he finished his last word, he had reached the front door. As before, he could see her father sitting in the living room on that sofa in the same place with the newspaper. He knocked gently on the door and stepped back. When her father opened the door, he immediately reached out to shake his hand. "How are you sir?" Don reciprocated and shook his hand. In a stoic demeanor, he said, "Come in and have a seat. She should be ready."

"Beth," he called, "the young man's here."

"Okay," came a melodic voice from down the hallway. Greg was hoping that he wouldn't have to talk to him anymore. He just wanted to wait silently.

Clearing his throat, "So… ah, Greg… " He was reluctant to say his name, "Beth told us the name of the movie that you two selected. We thought it was a good choice."

"Thank you, sir. I had hoped that it did meet with your approval."

"Yes, and the location was a good choice as well. Yeah…the historical Lafayette in Suffern, New York. What's that… about a thirty-minute drive? Well, it seems that you put a lot of thought into this. Yes, and Beth told us that you'll be going out to eat afterwards not far from there?"

"Yes sir."

"Well, I think that'll be just fine, just be mindful of the time, son."

"Oh, yes sir. By all means, I'll have her back here at a very reasonable time." Beth's mom had walked in before Beth. She wanted to make sure that Don was not intimidating Greg or making any threats. She walked over to Greg. He immediately stood up to greet her. They shook hands and cordially greeted one another. "Hello Greg. It's so nice to see you again."

"Thank you, ma'am. Nice seeing you again also." Just then, Beth walked into the room. She didn't look like the same person. She really looked quite attractive.

"Wow," he thought. "She's been transformed." She still was nothing like her mother, but it was indeed an improvement. He started to walk over towards her but was careful not to touch her, especially in her father's presence. "Hi, Beth, are you ready to go?"

"I'm fine, thanks. And yes, I'm ready." Not wanting to walk in front of her, they walked together until they got to the door. He quickly stepped out onto the porch ahead of her and extended his hand. He was taught that this was proper etiquette and in order. She took his hand and stepped out. Again, Beth was greatly impressed by his well-mannered behavior and so were her parents.

"Have a good time you two," Jan called out.

Don yelled, "…and drive carefully."

"Yes sir, I will," Greg answered. The door closed, but both parents stood there peering through the thin curtain as the couple walked down the steps to the walkway. Remembering the branch, Greg held it out of the way until both had gotten by. Jan looked at her husband and rolled her eyes. They watched him walk her to the passenger side of the car, open the door, and close it for her. Motionless, they stood until he got in and drove away. Jan elbowed her husband in his side again nodded her head with an "I told you so" jerk and walked away to the kitchen.

"Hey, what'd you do that for?" But he knew why. He was also cautiously impressed by Greg's polite behavior and treatment of his daughter.

As they drove away, Beth said, "I know they were watching the entire time. They are so embarrassing."

"They're okay," interjected Greg. "Don't be so hard on them. They only want you to be safe."

"You know, Greg, you're a nice guy. I've never met anyone as nice as you. I'm glad that you let me be your friend."

"There you go again, Beth. Now I am embarrassed. You should stop belittling yourself and selling yourself short. You're a nice person to know and a good friend to have." "Thanks Greg, I guess that's something I'll have to work on." They rode for about ten minutes in complete silence but for the radio, which was playing The Doors softly in the background. Greg could see from his periphery Beth staring out the window, but he couldn't see the elation in her heart. Suddenly he spoke, and the silence broke like a rock thrown through a glass window. Beth was startled back to reality. She had been gazing out the window but not seeing anything. She was deep into the dream that she thought she was in. "This can't be true. I'm really still asleep in my bed. Me... out on a date... with a guy more handsome than Paul Newman?"

"You look really nice, Beth."

Shyly, she responded, "Thank you. I wasn't expecting to go anywhere other than to work this summer, so I had to buy something new. The only nice things I brought were for church, but that's about it for the summer. We don't usually go anywhere else besides work and sometimes to church. Most of our time is spent working at the club." "You said you go to church?" Greg interjected.

"Yeah. You don't?" she asked as if that was strange behavior.

"Not really. But you don't even live here," Greg answered in a puzzled tone.

"Since we're here for the summer, we go while we're here. What about you? You live here."

"Well, we usually only go sometimes, on special occasions or holidays... maybe. My parents aren't the religious type. I mean...we believe in God and all...but that's where it ends."

"Oh," Beth responded softly.

"Is something wrong?" Greg asked.

"Oh, no." she said quickly. "A lot of Christians don't go to church regularly. I'm sure there's nothing wrong with that. Greg, have you heard or read any reviews about this movie?" she said, trying to quickly divert the subject. Greg seemed to be getting a little defensive about the subject of church. Even though he brought up the topic in the first place, she got the impression that he got a little perturbed. She didn't want to ruin their commonalities that they had already discovered. And in no way wanted to cause their new friendship to end. Their conversations were always so interesting and full of laughter. "Why did I even have to say the word church?"

Responding to her question, he answered, "Yeah, just the other day my brother was telling me how great it was." He said, interrupting her thoughts. "He tried to persuade me to go with him and some friends of ours, but I knew that you and I would be going, so I turned him down."

"That was so nice of you. I know, I say those words all the time, but it's true."

"Beth, take it like this, I'm just being me… that's all. I guess I do seem like a freak of nature compared to some of those other guys. And being one of the nice guys does seem a bit strange. So then you must be a freak too just like me then because I think you're really nice." They both laughed and continued their conversation throughout the drive. Beth got a real chuckle when Greg told her how he had been practicing what to say to her father in the car and all the way up to the door, almost running into that hanging tree limb.

"I'm sorry, but I could just see the whole thing in my mind." Then more seriously, she said, "My mom has asked my dad a million times to cut that branch. He says he keeps forgetting."

"That's okay. It wasn't your fault. I should have been watching where I was going." He also admitted being somewhat frightened of her dad. She assured him that her father was as soft as butter. In between subjects, laughs, and pauses, she would point out some astonishing sights along the way.

They had practically reached their destination. The car had gone silent again. At this time, Greg felt an overwhelming sense of fear. He tried not to show his anxiety. He was beginning to get a flood of "what if" thoughts. What if he sees some of his friends? What if he sees friends of his parents, but worst of all, what if he sees his brother? He found some consolation in the distance that he was from his hometown and had armed himself with excuses that he had quickly thought of. It was Saturday, and the parking lot was just about full. As they drove around to the movie parking lot, he found a parking space and quickly got out of the car. What a spineless hypocrite he was, he thought, as he inconspicuously walked around the car to open the door for Beth. A couple was getting into their car as he was helping Beth out. It seemed as though the woman had given him a look of disgust when she glanced at him. He could imagine the letter "H" for hypocrite stamped on his forehead and quickly bent over to say something to Beth to avoid the woman's stare. "Let's hurry up. We have about fifteen minutes before the movie starts to get something to eat and get in our seats. We don't want to miss anything." Beth got out quickly and they both rushed inside. The food line was quite long.

Fortunately, he had already purchased the tickets by phone. "Do you want to get our seats first and I go out later to get the food?" he asked. This was one of the ways he thought of to conceal being with Beth.

"No, that's okay. I'll just wait here with you. I don't have to get anything. I can wait until dinner if you want to."

"Well, we can at least get something to drink," he responded. There were several lines and so many people. He scanned over the crowd to see if he knew anyone. He stood a couple of steps behind Beth. He bent over to tell her, "This must be a really popular movie. It's so crowded."

"Yeah, it must be." No one could tell that they actually knew each other until they spoke to one another. They had almost reached the cashier when a voice from behind called Greg's name. Beth turned to look at Greg. Greg didn't turn around. There are more Greg's in the world than just him, he thought. Suddenly, he felt a tap on his shoulder. Reluctant to look, he turned around anyway. A short, statured redheaded guy stood next to him. "Hey man. I thought that was you. You still look the same."

"Hey, how are you?" Greg responded with a puzzled gaze.

"You don't recognize me, do you? I'm C.J. We were in middle school together. One day in the cafeteria, you came to my rescue when a couple of bullies started knockin' me around."

"Oh, yeah, now I remember. How've you been?" asked Greg.

"I've been great. I'll be joining the Navy when I graduate next year. What about you? Hey, you by yourself? Maybe…" As C.J. was getting ready to delve into questioning Greg further, a female's voice called out from the other line.

"Hey C.J., you're going to lose your place."

"Okay, man, gotta go. Good seein' ya', man."

By this time, they had reached the counter. "Can I help you?" a tall, chubby cheeked teenager asked. He turned around once more towards C.J. who was now hustling over to the other line.

"Okay, C.J., great seeing you, too. Take it easy." The annoyed cashier was beginning to become a bit perturbed and asked again for Greg's order. Throughout the whole conversation, the line had been steadily moving. Beth had been slowly inching along in front of him, heading towards the counter. He then looked at Beth and asked in a monotone, "What would you like?"

"I'll take a soda."

"No, get something else," Greg insisted.

"Okay, a number three please."

"What kinda drink with your number three?"

"Coke."

"Will that be all?"

"I'd like the large cheesy fries and a large Coke," Greg butted in.

"Will that complete your order?"

"Yes, thank you." The annoyed cashier returned shortly with their order and his change. They had only minutes to get to their seats before the show began. Beth quickly gathered the napkins and straws. Just as they got into their seats, the lights went out.

Greg could hardly concentrate on the movie. His thoughts were on having seen C.J. What were the odds of that happening? It had been a few years ago that he had left that school and also he was so far from his home. This area was not even near his old neighborhood. Who else would he run into? He certainly didn't want to run into him again. He could see Beth's profile as the light from the movie shone on her face. She looked intensely at the screen as she ate her popcorn. She was really into it. She was so innocent of all that was going on around her. If she could read his mind, it would destroy her. He wished that he could apologize for his behavior. Truthfully, he was no better than his asinine brother, he thought. In reality, his thoughts and feelings were that he was desperately trying to conceal his feelings that he wanted to hide her and was ashamed of her. Still not sure of the truth he wondered. Was he ashamed of her? Or did he really want to protect her, or himself? "What have I become?" he thought to himself. "I'm not ready for this." He looked at her again. This time she saw him and smiled, then immediately turned back to watch the movie. "Somebody help me. I don't deserve her as a friend," he thought. Finally, he regained his composure and thoughts and began watching the movie. He needed to know what it was about because surely Beth was going to ask him what he thought about it. He touched her arm to get her attention, and then offered her some of his cheesy fries. He picked some up with his fork and tried to hand it to her. Her face shone as bright as the movie. She smiled and held her hand in a stop position and continued eating her popcorn and watching the movie. The light from the movie screen revealed the happiness on her face.

When the movie ended, the lights came on. Remembering the look on Beth's face, Greg decided that if he ran into C.J. again, so be it. Yes, Beth was indeed a friend from out of town, and he was showing her a good time. What's wrong with that? They gathered up their trash and started walking towards the receptacles. "Here, give it to me. I'll put it in." He reached for her trash and she blushed.

"Oh, thanks." Milling through the crowd, he pulled her by the hand and guided her towards the exit. During the mass exit from the theater, he didn't see C.J. or anyone else that he knew. This time he felt he was not hiding. They found the car and got in. There were several restaurants not far from the theater. While walking to the car, they discussed whether they were hungry enough to go to a restaurant, but decided to go according to plan and just have something light.

"What kind of food are you in the mood for?"

"Nothing in particular... I'll have whatever you choose."

"Well, when I was looking for a theater in the newspaper, I saw that there was a Japanese restaurant just down the street from the theater. It had great reviews. Do you want to try it?"

"Sure. I don't eat much Japanese food, so it'll be something different."

"Also, it's close enough that we can walk there," he added. "I hope it's not crowded. I guess we should have talked about this earlier and could have made reservations. I'm sorry. I guess I wasn't thinking."

"That's okay. Not a big deal. I don't mind waiting if we have to."

"Well, since we don't have to drive there, let's start walking." He came around to her side to open the car door. When he opened the door, she looked up at his kind, smiling face, thinking again that she still hadn't awakened from the dream that she never wanted to wake up from. They walked back onto Lafayette Street in front of the movie theater. Okay, it's this way." As they walked to the restaurant, Greg told her that he had read about the history of the Lafayette Theater. Then asked what she thought of his choice.

"I thought it was a great choice. Most movie theaters look like any other building, but this one actually looks like what it was originally built for. You could almost see the crowds as they were back in those days." She had done her own research after he told her about it.

"You know, I felt the same way. I'm glad those history buffs decided to preserve it." "Yeah,…and what about that organ? Was that awesome?" She even mentioned that her dad was very impressed with him for choosing this historical venue. His thoughtful idea gave her father a little more confidence that maybe he could be wrong about Greg, but was still not totally convinced and didn't absolve him from his infamous reputation. In just a little while, they were at the doors of the restaurant. He opened the door and Beth walked into a foyer. Just inside, there were two well-dressed women standing there getting ready to open the inner door to go in the restaurant. Greg quickly stepped in front and grabbed the handle. He smiled and opened the door, stepped aside, and motioned for them all to go in.

"Ladies..." "The women thanked him as they walked inside. Beth also expressed her gratitude, as all the women walked inside. She was waiting for him just inside the door. Again, she was impressed by Greg's chivalrous display of courtesy because she, too, had had some thoughts that maybe his astounding display of manners may have been a put-on, in order to deceive and only appear to be charming. With a new sense of liberty, he walked up to the desk where the hostess was taking names of patrons waiting to be seated. With Beth at his side, he asked for a table for two. Since they were not having the Hibachi, the hostess told him that there would be about a twenty-minute wait. Greg looked at Beth and waited for her response. "It's okay." There was one seat left in the waiting area. Persuading her to take it, he stood close out of the way of the bustling traffic. It seemed that everyone was in the mood for Japanese food that day. It was a huge restaurant and very crowded.

Beth sat thinking over her incredibly inconceivable day. She had pinched herself several times until her skin began to bruise, just to make sure that this was indeed happening to her. She couldn't even hear the normal noises of conversations going on about her, the cries of little babies, chattering voices of children, the laughing teens, and the clashing dishes in the distance. When they called out Greg's name, she hadn't even heard it. He stepped over to where she was sitting and tapped her on the shoulder. She never heard him call her name, nor did she feel the light tap on her shoulder. At the second tap, she lifted her head and there he was, standing there beside her, smiling.

"What were you doing praying? Just kidding," he said jokingly. She was so embarrassed and apologized for being so out of it. The hostess, who was a tall, lean bleached blond college-age girl, led them to a table for two that was situated near the rear of the restaurant. As they followed her, the lighting and décor of the restaurant drastically changed. There were huge fish tanks that were used as partitions all around the restaurant. Schools of fish that were of a variety of species adorned in their thrillingly, colorful beauty were swimming in unison from one side of the tank to the other. The walls were covered with Japanese art. The chefs, who were also Asian, were dressed in their cultural attire, tossing their meats and vegetables in the air and onto the Hibachi grill tables. Tall flames were spewing up from the grills as the succulent victuals sizzled loudly from all around the huge room, entertaining and captivating their guests who were in awe of their performances. When they reached their table, the hostess waited as he held the seat for her as she took her place. The hostess looked on and subtlety rolled her eyes upward as if she thought this was overkill. When he finally took his seat, she handed them the menus. "Your server will be with you shortly. Have a great evening," she said politely, but with a tone of insincerity. Because they were not having anything on the Hibachi menu, regular waiters would serve them. The flame from the tea lamp in the middle of the mahogany and white marble top table softly emitted light as it flickered against the shiny surface like a neon sign. They looked over their menus. "They really have a lot to choose from, don't they? I don't know where to start," Beth said. "It's quite amazing. I see here that your meal is prepared right at your table."

"No, I think that's only done at the Hibachi grill tables." Having convinced himself that he didn't want to sit with a crowd of strangers because of Beth's shyness, he told the hostess they didn't want the Hibachi grill seating.

"Well, I love seafood, so that narrows down my choices," he said.

"Wowww, they have sushi," she said in amazement.

"Oh, so you like sushi?"

"No. It just amazes me that people eat raw fish."

"It's not all made with raw fish. You can get vegetables only, with no meat at all, if you want. It's called the California sushi. Do you want to try some, since you haven't had it before?" Just as he asked Beth about Sushi, the server walked up to their table. He was a handsome, well-built male of medium height. He appeared to be of mixed race. His loosely curled, shoulder length sandy brown hair was pulled back in a ponytail, which rested on the back of his neck. The waiter introduced himself as Eric and said he would be serving them. Since they had their menus, he proceeded to ask, "If you like, I'll take your order for drinks while you decide what you'd like for dinner."

"Okay, Eric, that sounds great," Greg, responded as he looked over at Beth. She looked into Eric's grayish-green eyes and asked if they had peach tea.

He politely directed her to the list of favored teas on the menu. "We have an array of teas and other beverages on the second page of your menu."

"Oh, I'm sorry. I hadn't noticed."

"No problem," Eric answered with a smile.

"Okay, I'll have the raspberry tea."

"And you, sir? What would like to drink?"

Greg looked seriously at Eric and said, "Oh, I'll have a beer...just kidding." He chuckled when he saw Eric's eyebrows rise and his eyes widen. Beth's eyes grew wide too, just like the waiter's.

"Okay... I'll have a Coke," Greg answered facetiously and smiled.

"Okay, then I'll be right back with your drinks and if you've decided on your meal, I'll be happy to take your order then." He turned and walked towards the kitchen.

Greg laughed, "I really gave you a scare, didn't I? I know I gave ol' Eric a shock. Did you see his face?" laughing again.

She smiled and answered, "Yeah, I was a little shocked." Feeling somewhat nervous about all the events of the day she felt the need to get away to regain her composure.

"Greg, would you excuse me? I need to go to the ladies' room."

"Oh, sure. Are you okay?"

"Yes, I'll be right back."

"Okay, go right ahead. Do you know where it is?"

"Not really, but I'm sure I'll find it."

Greg stood up when Beth got up to leave. "This is too much," she thought. "This is almost overwhelming." She grabbed her pocketbook and walked towards the direction of the entrance, disappearing into the crowded room.

After getting directions from one of the waitresses, Beth finally found the ladies' room. When she walked in, there was a lounge area with a sofa and two armchairs with an Oriental floral design. She slowly sat on the sofa, put her head back and took a deep breath. Raising her head and looking over the room, then noticed the matching Oriental flare. Concentrating on how beautifully designed the room was, she tried to slow down the racing thoughts in her mind of all the activities of the week; the arguments with her father, the shopping, and the planning.

"I can't believe that all this is happening to me. This is so incredible," she thought. "I have to calm down." She took another deep breath and got up to look in the full-length mirror to make sure that her outfit was okay and her hair and makeup were still holding up. Refreshing her lipstick and putting a few strands of hair back in place, she then felt ready to go back. After washing her hands, she dabbed her forehead with a cold, wet paper towel. Slowly wading through, she found her way back to their table. Upon her approach, Greg stood again to hold her chair as she sat down. She smiled and thanked him. As soon as he sat back down, he asked, "Well? Do you want to try the Sushi?" leaning towards her waiting for an answer.

"Oh yeah, I'd forgotten all about your question when the waiter came. You know, I forgot. Yes, I have had it once, but only the all-veggie kind, though. In fact, it was in California. But that was a few years ago."

He burst out laughing. That's funny. Really...you had a California in California. He asked, still laughing.

"Yeah, my dad had to go there for a conference and my mom and I went with him. But I don't think I'm ready for raw fish," she answered with a giggle. "What about you?"

"Sure, I have."

"You have?" she asked, as if awed by the proclamation.

"Sure. I'm a guy."

"Is Sushi a guy thing?"

"No, not really. But it's a dare thing."

"That's right, 'the dare'", she said.

"Eating raw fish is a dare thing," he confirmed.

"So how did you like it?"

"It was okay. But truthfully, I don't know what the hype is. Have you found anything yet that you think you might like?"

Yes, I think I'm going to try… the-e-e chicken and shrimp Tempura."

"That sounds safe," he said jokingly and smiled.

"How about you?"

"I think I'll go with the Seafood Teriyaki."

"Boy, that's quite a lot of seafood according to the menu. But I'll bet it's good."

"I'll let you taste it to see if you like it."

"Okay, and you can taste mine as well." Just then, Eric came back with their drink orders.

"Oh, Eric, by the way, we've decided what we'd like for dinner."

After putting their drinks down in front of them, he placed the small tray under his muscular arm and pulled the order pad from his waist and amazingly, a pen seemed to magically appear right between his ginger-colored fingers. Greg gave the request for both of them.

"Thank you. Is there anything else that I can get for you right now?"

"No, thank you."

"All right, I'll be back soon with your meal."

While they waited, they talked about the movie and an array of other interests, which they seemed to have an uncanny commonality. Greg was having such a good time, he had completely forgotten all about his dilemma. Beth was so enchanted by his voice. Reveling and totally engrossed in their conversation, she was profoundly enveloped in the day. She took every opportunity to look into his eyes. They were so soft, yet penetrable. She was afraid that he might even be able to read her thoughts. Knowing she could never get any further with Greg, she enjoyed the moment and allowed herself to imagine the contrary. She even saw in her mind's eye being engulfed in his arms.

"So, Beth, what college are you planning to attend after graduation?"

"I'm not sure yet. I'll probably be offered scholarships from a few colleges. Anyway, that's what I've been told by my school counselors. I'll probably go with whoever is offering the most money. That would be a big relief for my parents. What about you? I'm sure you'll be able to go wherever you want."

"I know what you mean, but that's not always true," he answered, insinuating that he was just as ordinary as she was. "Some of those schools are very picky with who they let in. They want to maintain a good reputation and want to be represented by students who rank high in scholastics," he said in his defense. With a look of regret and embarrassment, Beth began to apologize.

"Oh, Greg, I'm sorry. I feel like an idiot. I wasn't trying to say that you weren't..." Greg cut off her apology.

"It's okay. Don't feel bad. I didn't take it that way. Most people think the same as you. They think if you have money, you can do whatever you want. Some of it is very true, but my dad is different. He wouldn't stand for that. We didn't always have money, you know. My dad has very high standards and values and he taught us those same values and standards. Although it seems as if my brother wasn't listening sometimes," he said with a laugh. She laughed with him, but wouldn't dare make a comment. Just then, Eric appeared with a huge round tray, which became a small table. Greg could feel the stimulation of his salivary glands. After neatly placing his napkin on his lap, he picked up his knife and fork and was about to thrust it into the lobster tail when he glanced up at Beth and saw that her head was bowed, and her hands and fingers clasped together. She was praying. Feeling awkward, he quietly placed his utensils down on the sides of his plate and waited for her to finish. The whole ritual was over in less than fifteen seconds.

Beth spoke as she placed her napkin across her lap. "How's your lobster?" Greg's eyes were still on Beth, wondering what she could have been saying, as he searched for his knife and fork without looking. Not finding the fork, he then looked down, picked it up and proceeded to cut a piece of his lobster.

"Oh, I was just about to try it." He put the piece of the butter-soaked lobster into his mouth. Shaking his head in the affirmative as he chewed with absolute delight, he finally said, "Man, this is great…uuummm…and so tender. You have to try it." He cut a piece, dipped it into the butter sauce and held it up to her mouth. Beth was astonished. Her eyes grew as did her disbelief.

"Here, try it," he insisted again, gesturing with his fork for her to open her mouth.

"Here's that dream again. Does he really want me to open my mouth? He wants me to get it from his own fork. "Ah oh, I'm getting woozy," she thought. After gathering her composure, she opened her mouth and grabbed the piece of lobster from Greg's fork with her teeth. Using the same affirmative gesture, she agreed while holding the napkin over her mouth. Finally, saying through her intermittently masticating chomps, "Yes, you're right. This is excellent. Would you like to try mine now?" She pointed to her plate. She wouldn't dare use her own fork as he did. She was not going to chance embarrassing herself. He reached over, cut a small piece of shrimp with the side of his fork, and ate it. "Ummm…that's good, too. Great choice," he commented. She shyly looked at him and smiled. Beth felt so strange. She was feeling awkwardly comfortable with Greg. Shy, but still comfortable. His amicable personality made her feel unusually relaxed. They both were enjoying each other's company. He still hadn't remembered his dilemma, so caught up in his enjoyment of being with her.

Throughout the meal, their conversation continued about school, college, the movie they had just seen, and parents, but mainly hers. Greg didn't want to talk about his mother, so he diverted the conversation from parents. Beth was very aware of the deflection and followed his lead. She hadn't seen his mother or father that she knew of. It was possible that they may have even been at the club. Even though she knew Greg's father was a participating member, as he had told her, she didn't know what he looked like.

"Is everything okay?" The waiter had been back a few times.

"Oh, everything's great," Greg answered.

"Is there anything else that I can get for you at this time? Dessert maybe?" This was the cue to leave the check or order dessert.

Greg looked at Beth. "Would you like something else, Beth?"

"No, not right now. I'm fine, thank you," she answered.

"Okay, then," Eric responded, and left the check.

"This seems to be a very popular restaurant. It's so crowded."

"Yeah, and I can understand why. The food is awesome. Would you like to get dessert?"

"Oh, my... I don't think I have any room. I may have to get a doggy bag. I can't eat another thing." Greg was about to scold her. If he were out with his parents, his mother would never allow their leftovers to be taken home. She wouldn't stand for it. That would have been an insult to her and the family.

"Would you like to order dessert and take it home then?" asked Greg.

"No, thank you, Greg. I'll take a rain check."

Just then reality struck. He remembered the task at hand. Why he was in this fix in the first place. This was going to be his debt paid in full. Greg's stomach began to quiver. Thoughts were rushing through his mind.

"Should I respond? Was she only joking? I can't do this again. So far, I've been lucky. I can't push my luck. She's a nice girl, but I can't do this again." Suddenly, he thought of a place nearby where they sold homemade ice cream that was not too far from where they were. He and some of his friends had gone there last summer, just for a change of scenery. All his friends had pools, but they wanted to get out to see different faces for a change and maybe meet new girls. He had planned to take Beth over to the Erskine Lakes after dinner to finalize the day anyway.

Changing the subject, Greg said, "Beth, have you ever been to the Natural Pool in the Highlands? It's not far from here. ...maybe not even a twenty-minute drive. It's very beautiful there. You'd love it. Do you want to go?"

"Do you think we have time?" she asked.

"Sure we do. I told your dad that I would get you back early and I will. But if you don't want to, it's okay. I'm not trying to force you to go. I just thought we could take a scenic walk before you go back home and maybe stop to get ice cream."

In actuality, Beth really didn't want the day to end. She still couldn't believe all that was happening to her and all in one day. She was even willing to defy her parents if she had to, to prolong her dream.

"Sure, I'd love to go," she said emphatically.

On that note, Greg started looking around the room for Eric.

Before paying the check, they both decided they were too full for dessert. Since she had most of her meal left, she asked for a doggy bag. Not being used to taking leftover food home, Greg left his uneaten portion for garbage, which was quite a bit.

"Aren't you going to take your leftovers, Greg?"

"No, I'm finished. I don't want anymore," he responded casually. "Are you ready?"

"Yes," she responded. Automatically, he ambled around to where she was seated, reaching out for her hand, he gingerly grasped it as she stood up. Presuming he was being watched, he glanced around, and at the table nearest them, spotted one of the patrons subtly pointing in his direction and then leaned over and whispered something to the person next to her. He studied their faces to be sure they didn't look familiar. Assured that they were not, he wondered why people could be so amazed to see a normal display of courtesy. Three other patrons alternately stopped to watch them prepare to leave. Beth noticed them also and wondered to herself why they were staring and pointing. He left a generous tip as they turned to walk towards the exit. As they walked along, she whispered to him, "Did you notice those people whispering and pointing?"

"Yeah, I did. I guess they're not use to seeing how a gentleman should treat a lady." "Aww, Greg, that's so sweet."

Walking to the car, they raved about how great the food was. "I can't believe you left that delicious food. It'll just to be thrown away. I know. Remember I work behind the scenes. Why didn't you get a doggy bag? You could have had it later on or even tomorrow."

"Are you kidding me? I was done. I didn't want anymore." He could envision the disdainful look on his mother's face if he brought leftover food into their house. She would be traumatized. They didn't need to save food. They were not "impoverished paupers." These would have been her words exactly. He wouldn't dare take that food, nor could he let Beth know the true reason why. He didn't want her to think that he was a pompous snob. He wouldn't have minded taking the food, but in truth, they didn't need it. He could get whatever he wanted, at any time, but was that his fault? Anyway, did it really matter other than keeping his mother happy? This way would surely render a better outcome. Changing the subject said, "I know you're going to like this place, Beth."

Making sure that she was securely in the car, he closed her door. After getting in, he turned on the radio. He enjoyed listening to soft rock music and apparently so did she. "School's Out" by Alice Cooper was playing. He could see Beth's head gently moving to the rhythm and heard bits and pieces of her singing and humming it softly.

"You really like this kind of music, huh?"

"Oh, yeah, I usually listen to this station when I'm here."

Turning the ignition and stepping on the gas, Greg proceeded into what he thought was "the end of the final chapter." Beth unwittingly gazed out the window in silence the entire ride. They turned off their exit to enter Ringwood, New Jersey. In a few minutes, the landscape changed vastly. There were tall trees throughout what seemed to touch the sky. Wild flowers decoratively bordered the roadway, edged by a multiplicity of types of foliage on either side, which lined the narrow two-way road. The green foliage seemed to be never-ending, blotched with exciting brightly colored flowers and scrubs. Beth looked at Greg with a huge smile and said, "This looks like…like the Land of Make Believe. It's so beautiful. How did you ever find this place?"

"I don't know … I guess just driving around one day … me and some of the fellas were looking for something to do. There was a sign that read, Erskine Lakes, so we decided to explore. Then we saw another sign that read, To the Natural Pool. That really stirred our curiosity."

"Well, I'm really glad you found it. I don't think my parents know about this place. Anyway, I've never heard them mention it before."

"There're lots of places to park if you want to get out of your car to go hiking or just take a nature walk. Do you want to take a walk?"

"Sure. That'll be fun. This way I can work off some of that food I just ate."

"Sure, like you need to," Greg responded with a chuckle. She really didn't need to lose a pound. Beth was tall and very thin, which added to her already low self-esteem. Her mother constantly tried to get her to eat a little more to put on a few pounds. Although she tried, but could never gain a pound, none that would stay on. Greg was only teasing, but noticed he had struck a tender spot. Trying to buffer the blow, he commented on how athletic she looked.

"But really, Beth, Do you play any sports at your school? You have very nicely built legs."

Her head turned quickly as she looked at him inquisitively. "What do you mean?" she asked.

"Beth, I'm only complimenting you on how athletically built you look. Do you run? You have the legs of an athlete. It's a compliment." He was lying. She was not muscular at all, but he had to somehow get his foot out of his mouth. "Well, not really. But I do walk to school every day because our house is so close to the school." Having been in the area many times, Greg knew they were close to the Natural Pool. "Do you want to go for a walk? There's a waterfall not far from here."

"Sure. If I can, I'd like to pick some of these beautiful flowers."

"I'm sure it's okay. I'm going to pull right over here in parking lot D."

"If I'd known we were coming to a place like this, I would have brought my sneakers."

"Aww, you'll be fine. The hiking paths aren't too bad. If it gets too rough, you can always hold onto me."

"Thank you." When he said that, she was virtually caught off guard. It was totally unexpected. She pinched her arm again. After coming around to her side to open the door again, they started their journey towards the pool. They crossed the roadway to get to the hiking path. Immediately there was an incline. Greg looked over at Beth, who was looking down as she walked.

"Are you okay?"

"So far I'm okay."

"…you sure? We don't have to go this way. We can drive there if you like."

"No. I'm okay."

"We're not so far that we can't turn back, you know," remembering her shoe comment.

"No really. I'm fine. I'd rather walk. It's more fun."

He smiled at her and took a glance at his watch to check the time. "Yeah, we'll get back in good time."

The path was very well carved out. It was wide enough that they could both walk side by side. It had obviously been trod down countless times by hordes of nature lovers. Beth's elongated stride still left her slightly behind Greg's stretch, as he stepped in clock-like cadence. She was tall, but his height was majestic. His stride was that of a monarch. Taking advantage of having fallen behind, she was able to capture the full beauty of her surroundings and him. His neatly fitted designer khaki shorts and golf shirt wore like camouflage along the brown and green path in the woods. Beth was becoming enamored by Greg's charm, looks, and kindness. "What am I thinking? What's happening to me? I have to stop pretending and pull myself together," she thought. Greg had been so amicable and treated her with such politeness and benevolence. She was beginning to feel a warm sensation inside. He turned around and saw how far ahead he was.

"Hey, what are you doing back there? Am I walking too fast?" he asked.

"Oh, nooo. I've just been admiring the beautiful, picturesque surroundings."

"Oh, such poetry," he jested.

To shake off this strange feeling she had, she began to step up her pace. Walking now right next to Greg, she began gabbing away about a range of topics. Asking questions and sometimes not even waiting for an answer. She started garrulously babbling nonstop. Greg looked at the profile of her face from his periphery with a look of uneasiness. "What's wrong with her?" he thought. "I wonder if she's having a reaction from the food, or a plant, or something. She did mention picking flowers."

He stopped dead in his tracks and grabbed her gently by her shoulders, looked her straight in the eyes, and asked, "Beth, are you okay?"

She immediately came to herself. "What's wrong? Why did we stop walking?"

"Beth, you have been babbling nonstop for the past five minutes. You never even gave me a chance to respond to anything you said. Do you feel okay? Do you have any food allergies or something? Which flowers or plants have you touched?" he asked nervously.

"Greg, I am so sorry. I didn't even realize it. I guess I'm feeling a little anxious. I do tend to rant when I get nervous."

"Hey, listen, we don't have to do this. If you're not feeling well, I can take you home right now…no problem," he said with great concern.

"No, Greg, please. I'm okay. I'd really like to see this Natural Pool. I did warn you though."

"Warn me about what?"

"That I'd never been on a date before. I guess maybe that's why I was rambling. I'm a little nervous," she continued.

"Listen, Beth, you don't have anything to be nervous about. You're in good hands. Now, before we go any farther, are you sure you're all right?"

"Yes, I promise."

"Okay, then let's go. We're almost at the waterfall, you know."

"Oh, wow! Just think… I almost missed this. This is going to be awesome." She looked into Greg's blue-gray eyes and smiled. He smiled back, thinking, "It's almost over and in two weeks she'll be back in New York, and I can get my old life back again." In his gut, he felt embarrassed, even a little guilty from that last thought. He felt that this whole ordeal had caused him to feel uncomfortable just being himself.

Chapter 9

Two weeks had gone by since that eventful movie date with Beth. Greg had delivered her home on time, safe and sound. He could remember the piercing eyes of her father when he opened the door. Even though she had a key, her father opened the door as soon as they reached the porch. Apparently, he had been watching and waiting for their return. She asked Greg if he wanted to come in for a while, but he declined. He made up a phony excuse, so they said their goodbyes. Greg thought as the door closed behind him, that this was the end of a very peculiar chapter of his life.

When Beth walked past her father, he tried to act as though he was truly excited about her date with Greg. She could tell that he was pretending to be enthused. She also noticed the restraint in his face when he opened the door, the way he had looked at Greg. He had a fake smile. She could see the contempt in his eyes. She knew her father well and his pretentious behavior was so obvious to her. Beth was sure that Greg noticed as well, and that was probably the reason he declined to come in.

"How was the movie?" her father asked.

"It was okay," she answered despondently as she walked pass him.

"What's the matter, Beth? Are you okay? What did he do? What happened?"

She turned around, looked straight in her father's eyes, and angrily said, "Nothing! Nothing happened. What did you expect to happen? I had a great time until I came back home!"

With all the yelling coming from the living room, Beth's mother raced in.

"Don, Beth, what's going on? What's all the yelling about?"

Beth walked hastily past her mother to her bedroom and slammed the door. Somberly walking away, Don headed towards the den.

"I don't know, Jan. I simply asked her how the movie was and she got upset and started screaming at me."

Jan looked at him as he proceeded to explain. He was obviously upset and bewildered over what had just happened.

"Don, why...?" she started to ask.

"I don't know," he interjected.

Then, thinking that Beth was also upset, turned to go and find out from her what had happened. She didn't know that Beth was home until she heard the shouting coming from the living room. Standing in front of Beth's door, she knocked and turned the knob. The door was locked.

"Beth?" her mother called softly. "Are you okay? Honey, why don't you open the door and tell me what happened."

"Mom, I don't want to talk right now," she said between sobs.

"Beth, this doesn't sound good, I'd like to talk to you, so please open the door," she said, her voice in a more austere tone.

The doorknob turned and the door opened. When she walked into the bedroom, Beth was lying across the bed sobbing. Her mother walked over and sat on the bed beside her. "Beth, what on earth happened between you and your father? Why are you so upset? I've never heard you yell like that, ever. Now sit up and tell me what happened." Beth wiped her eyes and sat up. She hung her head down as she spoke softly, her fingers intertwining. Now, looking into her mother's face, she began to replay the whole scene and explain. "Well, when Greg brought me home, I hadn't gotten a chance to even get to the door to turn the knob because Dad was right there to open it, as if he had been standing there waiting at the door."

"Sweetheart, what was wrong with him opening the door for you?"

"Mom, he evidently was watching and waiting at the door for me to come home. Plus, he looked at Greg with such anger in his eyes. I'm sure that was the reason why he didn't want to come in when I invited him. I could see it and I'm sure that Greg could too. Mom, Greg is the nicest guy I've ever known. He was such a gentleman the whole day. He opened and closed doors for me. He pulled out my chair at the restaurant and he even stood up when I got up to go to the ladies' room."

"That is very nice, and gentlemanly, I might add. I guess his parents raised him well. But honey, what started all the yelling?" her mother asked.

"Well, when Dad asked me how the movie was, I told him that it was all right. I admit that I didn't sound very excited, but that's because I was humiliated and angry that he was at the door. And because of that, he immediately thought Greg had done something to me and started asking me what had he done to me and what was wrong. Mom, when I thought about how wonderful this guy had treated me and how Dad had looked at him so angrily and even insinuating that he had done something to me, it really made me mad and that just took me over the top and I started yelling. I'm sorry, Mom, I just got so angry because Dad didn't want me to go out in the first place and then after having such a great time to come home to his unjustified, negative assumptions about Greg, I guess I kinda lost it." "Yes, you did," said her mother. "Don't you think you owe your father an apology for yelling at him?"

"No, Mom, I don't. He should apologize to me for jumping to conclusions for which he had no grounds. He never gave me a chance to tell him how nice a person Greg really is. Immediately, he assumed the worst. Mom, he treated Greg badly and he should know that."

"Well, I'll speak to your father about what you've told me and I think we all should come together and talk about this as a family. We can't let outside influences or people destroy us as a family. But still, he is your father, and you have to respect him as such. You need to apologize for raising your voice at him. That was very disrespectful."

"Okay, but he should also apologize because he provoked me. I remember in the Bible where it says that parents should not provoke their children to anger."

"That is true. You have him there." Her mother kissed her on the forehead and walked out. "I'll talk to him."

An entire week had gone by. Beth was hoping to get a call from Greg. She was still somewhat embarrassed by her father's behavior that fateful movie day and didn't want to initiate a call, not knowing how Greg really felt. She had a feeling that he noticed the look her father had given him, but didn't know for sure. Because she hadn't heard from him since that day, she guessed that was the reason. Every day at the club she looked for him, but never saw him. He never called.

It was the last week at the summer cottage. Beth's family had made amends and was back to their routine family life as before. They finished their work contract for the summer at the club and began packing to return home. Beth never called Greg, and he never called her. She was disappointed that he hadn't at least called to say goodbye. Her mother and father took note that she never heard from him again, but wouldn't dare bring up the subject. Her dad felt somewhat responsible for Greg's disappearance. After their family meeting, he admitted his dislike for him and admitted that it was unwarranted. She forgave her father and was satisfied with his apology, so all was forgiven. She, too, apologized for her behavior. She felt ashamed for her disrespect after realizing that he only acted out of love. Her father loved her dearly and would do anything he had to do to protect her and didn't want to see her hurt. Don thought that if he saw Greg at the club, he would have personally apologized for his conduct and mistreatment of him, but never got the chance because Greg never went back to the club for the rest of the summer.

The evening that Greg dropped Beth off at home after their movie date, he felt as though fifty pounds had been lifted from his shoulders. No more lying, sneaking, and hiding. Finally, he was free. He felt he paid his debt to society. With nothing to hide, he even began hanging out with his brother and the guys again. Jack had really missed being with his brother and he never caught on to what was really going on with Greg. With the strange way he had been acting, he thought there must have been a girl involved. His mother also noticed the change. She made a comment about him having "fixed the problem." She didn't pursue, and he didn't offer any explanations, no matter what she thought the problem was. All in all, Greg was relieved of this heavy burden, but strangely, for reasons unbeknownst to even him; he somewhat oddly, and inexplicably, missed Beth. He thought about the fun conversations they had, all the things they had in common and when she was dressed up, was to some degree a little cute. Beth would have been a most valuable, honest, trustworthy and kind friend. He thought many times that he should call her, especially their last week at the club, but felt it best to just leave well enough alone. Her father did make him feel a little uncomfortable and knowing how he felt about him and having to sever their relationship would only have confirmed his beliefs.

Greg found out from one of Jack's friends the actual day that Beth was leaving. It was D.J., one of the guys who was with them the day he first saw Beth. They had been hanging out around the pool. Stretched out on a lounge chaise, when out of the blue, he blurted, "Hey, remember that dorky girl that works at the club… yeah, they're leaving next Thursday. I heard they're from somewhere in upstate New York."

Greg said to him emphatically and directly in his face, "Why do you have to make fun of people? That girl could be the nicest person you ever met."

"Hey, chill, man. Don't get your panties in a bunch. Wow, you act like, maybe you know her personally, or something. Do you?"

"Look, man, I just don't like for people to be mistreated and made fun of, that's all," Greg said. Self-deprecating thoughts began flowing through his mind as he reflected on his own hypocritical behavior throughout their very brief relationship. "I have the audacity to slam him. I'm no better than he is. In fact, I'm worse. At least he's honest. I deceptively led the girl on, and then dropped her just like that. I'm such a hypocrite," Greg thought to himself. "I could have at least called to say goodbye. Now, after all this time, I wouldn't dare try. I'm such a coward," he thought, wallowing in guilt.

That Thursday, Greg got up early in the morning. He had no idea at what time they would be leaving. It was so early that it was still dark out. Trying to be as quiet as possible, he washed his face, put on his clothes, practically in the dark. Tiptoeing down the stairs, he quietly walked painstakingly down the long hallway and out the door. He started his car, hoping not to be heard and drove to Beth's house. Though inconspicuously parked, he had a clear view of the house. He had no idea why he was even doing this. It wasn't to say goodbye. How could he? What did he expect to happen, or to feel? Whatever it was, he just felt compelled to be there. Somehow he felt that it was the least he could do, that somehow he could be relieved of some of the heaviness and shame.

As the sun rose, crouched down he could see images coming and going to and from the house. It was a furnished house, so there was no furniture to haul. Into their van, they put numerous quantities of suitcases, shopping bags, and boxes of various sizes and shapes. In the dawn, he could see Beth's tall, lean figure, her hair in a ponytail, carrying things from the house to the van. "If I wasn't such a coward and a phony, I could have helped them." The task seemed to be laborious. He continued to watch as he was drowning in deep feelings of guilt. He could see them walking to and fro, their heads bobbing up and down in cadence with the back and forth movement of that bothersome tree branch which hung over the walkway.

"Obviously, her father never got around to cutting it," he thought. What a stupid, pointless thought. He felt like an idiot for even being there. In about an hour and a half, it appeared that they were done. He couldn't believe that he had been there for that long. The sun had begun to softly and slowly illuminate the eastern part of the sky. It had become light enough now that he could see their faces. Beth seemed to be staring in his direction, as if she saw something familiar. He slid down further in the seat so as not to be seen. He could hear a muffled masculine sound of Beth's name being called. Apparently, it was her father's voice, almost in a whisper, probably trying not to disturb the neighbors at that time of the morning. He was calling for her to get into the van. At that instant, Greg raised his head just in time to see Beth turn around and shrug her shoulders. She got into the van as they slowly, but deliberately, drove away.

"She was looking right at my car," he said out loud, yet in a whisper, feeling that he almost got caught.

"What would I have said? Why am I even here?" When he saw that their van was fully out of sight, he sat up, started his car and headed back home.

Chapter 10

Last summer's memories had been covered over by the beautiful vari-colored leaves of fall, the waters stilled and frozen by the icy temperatures of the northeastern winds. Spring semester had ended and preparation for finals had begun. Greg was looking forward to the prom and graduation. He had already been accepted at Georgetown University and several other colleges and universities, but his heart had been set on attending Georgetown ever since he was a young kid. Even though he accepted an invitation to visit Glasslane University in Pennsylvania the last week in June, Georgetown was his final choice. He thought it would be cool to get away alone for a week, away from home and get the feel of what it would be like on a college campus and away from parents. A couple of his friends from school had also received invitations. Excited about college, he already started making plans for moving to D.C., although when the letter came his mother had other ideas.

The day the letter came was one Saturday in April, when there was very little sound and movement in the Tyler household.

"Gre-eg!" his mother sang, standing underneath the huge crystal chandelier that hung from the cathedral ceiling at the foot of the curved steps of the balcony. Nancy had gotten up to get ready to prepare the morning meal for whenever the guys decided to come downstairs, as she had always done every Saturday and Sunday. She could see Jack's bedroom door from the angle where she stood, which was adjacent to the corridor along the balcony. "Aren't you coming down for breakfast?" she chimed. "You have a letter from Glasslane University. Remember the college that I told you about?" She had so wanted Greg to go there, the school that she had only dreamed of attending after her high school graduation. Nancy's parents could never have afforded such an expensive college. In her pathetic imagination for years, she had held this against them as the cause of the unsuccessfulness of her life. But they could only do what they could afford to do, which was the reality.

Her parents were both late bloomers, neither had ever been married before. They met at a pharmaceutical conference that was being held at the city's huge commercial conference center. Her father was a pharmacist and during the summer months when school ended her mother worked as an office manager at the office of one of the many pharmaceutical drug companies represented there. These represented companies from all over the country. At their stations, there were an assortment of pamphlets describing their products, their many achievements, and their products, some samples and gifts. While organizing some of the products at their display table, Nancy's dad, Carl, walked over to her, pretending to be interested in her company's wares. As soon as their eyes met, they were immediately attracted to one another and after a short chat, they got married, so said her mother whenever she told the story of how they met. She would tell that story in detail to anyone who would listen. She never failed to add how she couldn't believe why he was attracted to her. In only six months, after they met they got married. Both in their late thirties decided that they would start a family immediately. It took about two years before Nancy's mother would conceive. Carrie was thirty-nine when Nancy was born. Four years later, her brother was born, which was a shocking and unexpected surprise. After Nancy was born, her mother never went back to work. They both decided that it would be best for the children if she stayed at home. There were plenty of tough times, but they managed. Seldom was there ever enough money, much less to save, especially after her brother was born. They made the sacrificial choice to live in a better community and send the children to a private school, rather than have more money just to buy more things. When Nancy was a child, she could never understand why she couldn't have any, and every, new toy that she saw or every fashion that she wanted when she became a teen. Her desire for things was insatiable, and she was extremely materialistic. No matter what her parents tried to do to please her, she was never satisfied with anything. They tried with their modest income to get most of the things she wanted, but still, it was not enough. As she got older, she felt that the birth of her brother impinged upon what she could have gotten. Consequently, this selfishness caused her to never have a close relationship with him and avoided him as much as possible. The only thing that he had ever done to her was to be born. Incredibly, she still found it unnecessary to recover their relationship.

After graduation, Nancy's parents tried to convince her to work at least a year to save and at least try to help with the costs of her tuition to go to Glasslane, but Nancy argued that she should not have to work to put herself through college. Other kids at her school didn't have to postpone their lives to work for their college tuition, so why should she? As usual, her arguments were unfounded, selfish and unreasonable. The truth of the matter was many of those students at her school had studied painstakingly hard to acquire scholarships to go to those schools. But Nancy would never acknowledge that. She was only an average student, but never considered herself anything other than brilliant and never thought it necessary to study hard and would always blame the teachers' dislike for her average grades. She probably could have done better had she not always been so preoccupied with the lives of the more prominent students at her school, or so she thought. Most of Nancy's opinions about anybody came from her own childish, vivid and twisted overactive imagination, which resulted in a deep, destructive emotion, which was "envy". She had few friends, and those were whose personalities were similar to hers, who only gave credence and affirmation to her egotistical behavior. Always forgetting those minuscule paths, which was how she perceived the events of how her life played out, yet had ultimately led her to meeting her husband and the subsequent affluent lifestyle of which she so undeservingly enjoys, yet still left her void. Somehow, Nancy developed a sense of entitlement of which emanated to her sons by always reliving her warped childhood memory of what she thought she had been deprived of and vowing that they would never experience that heartbreak in their lives, as she had.

Hearing his mother's voice from downstairs, he yelled back to ask, "What, Mom? It's Saturday, for crying out loud. It's too early to get up," Greg yelled sleepily through his bedroom door.
"Early? What do you mean too early? It's one o'clock in the afternoon. Why don't you come down and open this letter," she pleaded. "It's from Glasslane."
"Can you wait until I take a shower first?"
"Oh, okay, sweetheart. ...see you in a little while," said Nancy and swished

back down the long marble paved hallway, smiling happily back to the kitchen. She was becoming increasingly anxious to find out what the letter could be about. Before her second trip to the stairs, John had come down and was now sitting at the table having brunch, the meal she had been preparing all morning. He had slept late as well until Nancy came upstairs and into the bedroom to awaken him. After being on the road for days at a time, and sometimes weeks, he always made the most of being home by lying in his own bed for as long as he felt like being there. Trips like those were not as frequent as they had been in the past and he would have to remind himself of that when traveling and feeling grumpy about it. Those thoughts of home and family are what kept him resolute, unyielding to concede, to persevere and now he can appreciate his effort.

Nancy had gotten up early to get the mail as always, and prepare the morning meal, which on weekends became brunch. But this particular morning, she had such anxiety in her voice that John couldn't just turn over and go back to sleep. Before she had awakened the boys, she had rushed upstairs, plopped on the bed, intentionally on John's pillow … almost on his head. "John", she said with excitement in her voice.

"What's going on, Nancy?" John said, sounding groggy and a bit irritated.

"Greg got a letter from my favorite college. Glasslane University, can you believe it? I didn't even know he had applied," said Nancy, clearly out of breath.

"What's the big deal? You know he's already chosen Georgetown," John moaned as he tried to turn over.

"Not so fast, John. This is a second letter; maybe he's changed his mind."

John gave up trying to sleep, got up and walked into the bathroom.

"Did you fix any breakfast yet?" he muffled through a mouthful of toothpaste.

"Yes, I did. In fact, by this time it's now brunch. Check your watch." He tried talking again, this time through mouthwash.

"John, just wait until you at least come out of the bathroom," Nancy pleaded, annoyingly.

"Well, stop talking to me then," he muffled again while wiping his mouth with his washcloth. When he walked out of the bathroom, she was standing across the room facing him. Losing patience, she headed towards him at a fast pace, letter in hand, to the closet and handed him the shirt that she had hung on the closet door. He looked it over and then put it on. The jeans were hanging there as well.

"I'll talk to you when I get downstairs," he told Nancy. She took the hint and as she was heading out of the bedroom, he smiled and pleaded with her on behalf of the boys, "Hey, I know you're excited, honey, but why don't you let the boys sleep a little while longer," She smiled back and left the bedroom, closing the door behind her.

Nancy hastily strode down the long winding stairs and down the hallway into the colossal kitchen. It was much larger than anything that she would ever need. If she and John were entertaining, she would hire chefs and servers and for any other special occasion to handle the whole affair. These were the only times that the kitchen would ever get its full use, especially since the boys had gotten older. Now, they would grab a bite at one of the fast food places with their friends or make a sandwich whenever they got home. It was very seldom that they sat down together as a family anymore for a meal, except on weekends and it was not until the boys were in middle school that they got to spend a little more time with their father than they had in the past. Since John had finally been able to be at home and work from the main office more often, Nancy would try some of the recipes that she had had at a luncheon or had read about in one of the Gourmet cooking magazines or books that she had subscribed to or purchased.

"Hey, Greg, what's all that yelling going on?" asked Jack, walking over to Greg's room. He had heard his mother when she called out for Greg from downstairs and got up to listen. Since he hadn't heard his name, he figured that whatever it was, he was in the clear.

"I don't know. Something about a letter from that college that she loves so much or something."

"Oh, wow… man. You know how mom feels about that place. Well, I'm gonna jump in the shower now. I'll see you downstairs.

Greg answered, "Yeah, okay… me too."

Chapter 11

Nancy was thrilled that Greg wanted to go for the week Glasslane University was offering to potential fall freshmen. "Greetings from Glasslane University of Pennsylvania," Greg began reading out loud. Nancy had insisted he read the letter out loud.

"This is an invitation for top ranking high school graduates and potential freshman for a week of getting to know the enriching opportunities and unique studies our college has to offer its students from freshman to senior year. Blah, blah, blah,…Dorms will be assigned upon registration on the day of arrival. Blah, blah, blah…."

"Come on, Greg. Read the words please," said his mother.

"Okay. Those persons bringing students are to leave the campus immediately after drop-off in order for students to register. Parents/guardians are invited to stay the day of the pickup, which is Saturday at 10 A.M. for a brief summation of the students' stay with a reception lunch to follow. Blah, blah, blah …"

"What? I can't believe that," Nancy said. Greg had read the letter out loud, and then handed it to his mother to read.

"Here, see for yourself. No parents." Receiving this invitation had given Nancy restored hope even though John had cautioned her not to have any expectations of Greg changing his mind about Georgetown. But she disregarded John's warning, especially when he mailed back the RSVP. She thought that if he would only visit the campus and spend time there, plus telling him and lamenting the story of her misfortune of not being able to attend years ago, he would somehow feel pity and would go, if just for her. Greg had heard that story so many times before and couldn't understand why she was so unhappy about it. What had she missed? She has everything. They have everything.

Spring had come and gone. Proms, parties, and graduations were over. Diplomas were in frames and trophies had been shelved. It was the second week of July. Anxiously awaiting this day to arrive, Greg's bags had been packed for weeks and were now was waiting for Matt to arrive. Since the letter stated that students were not permitted to have cars on campus during the stay, Matt's dad volunteered to drive the boys there and John rode along. Driving up before sunrise, they thought they would beat the crowd and arrive at the campus early, which would have been around six-thirty. The letter had also stated that students had to be there by 8 A.M. They thought for sure they would be too early to even get in line. But when they arrived, cars were everywhere and from everywhere. The parking lot looked to be almost full. There were license plates from as far north as Canada and North Dakota, from the south Florida and Texas, California and Washington from the west and from everywhere else in between and beyond. It was as though invitations had been sent to every high school senior in the United States and Canada. There were people from everywhere of all nations and nationalities, all ambling towards the buildings. It appeared as though this was a conference for the children of the members of the United Nations. They were in awe and overwhelmingly impressed at what they saw.
"Nancy would be thrilled if she was here," thought John, feeling a little guilty that she wasn't, but she didn't want to be the only female in a car filled with men. Finally, after finding a place to park and unloading their suitcases, both John and Matt's dad, Philip, took pictures of the boys and walked around for a little. Before they got too far, they were hurriedly directed by security to go back in the direction of the parking lot. They couldn't understand the necessity to clear the campus so quickly. Registration in itself would be an all day event and by the looks of the parking lot, leaving would be just as long.

It seemed the dorm rooms had been prearranged so that students were intentionally matched with students from different schools and areas. Matt and Greg both had been matched with roommates who were from different states. It was very disconcerting in the beginning, but in a day or so, they agreed it turned out to be a good experience for all of them. By the third day, they both had become friendly with quite a few students from many other states and other countries who had immigrated to the United States. They even invited their newfound friends to have meals with them and just hang out in the canteen, especially to meet the girls. They ate junk food and, listened to the loud music playing in the background. They met up with their new friends, who introduced them to other students. This gave them a great opportunity to learn about different cultures, traditions, and lifestyles. From this experience, they had a chance to meet so many different people whom they probably would have never met otherwise. Greg was having the time of his life. It was so much fun that he found himself beginning to have second thoughts about going to Georgetown. The school was not as dry as he had envisioned it to be.

Seated at the bar style food counter, he and a few of his new friends were having lunch. They opted to forego the free, more nutritional lunch in the cafeteria, for the greasy fried food with the music and a more party style atmosphere in the canteen. Greg was quite surprised to have seen so many gorgeous girls on a college campus. "Could they really be smart enough to have been selected to come to this school? Could they really have brains?" he thought. These ideas came from the influence of his mother, and he knew it. He wanted to slap himself for thinking this way. "What do looks have to do with intellect?" he reasoned. He started to brush his arms as if he was brushing something off. But the gesture was symbolic, of which he was not even aware of, whenever he did this. How unclean he felt when he thought like that, and would brush his arms as if to brush off those terrible thoughts. The friends on both sides of him simultaneously jumped off their stools.
"Hey man, what are you doing? Don't brush it on me," said Shane, who was from the Bronx. The friend and roommate from India, Kumar said in his deep Indian accent, "Yeah, man, not over here. What is it anyway?"
"Oh, I was only brushing my sleeves straight, that's all." They both looked at him strangely, as they mounted their stools again. He was wearing a short-sleeved shirt. All that jumping brought on a lot of stares from the other customers, and they began looking closely at their food. Poppy, the cook, didn't look so happy either, giving Greg the evil eye. Noticing how Poppy looked at him, apologized again, "Sorry, I was only straightening out my wrinkled sleeves." The cook stared and mumbled something as he turned away towards the grill.

It was Thursday, Greg and Matt had planned to meet at the library after Matt's last class. They sat out on the library steps and looked over their itinerary that they received during registration. The itinerary was specific for each potential student's major. Matt's major was science and Greg's was business. There were several sessions they had together, which gave the guys a chance to catch up on the happenings of the day, before they met for lunch. The sessions were comprised of watching films of the history of the career and its course of study, and how the college could, through teaching and today's technology, prepare and fulfill the requirements necessary for that particular career choice and potential future opportunities. Many of the sessions and classes were given by a guest speaker or one of the faculty members of the college. It seemed that four years of college was being crammed into a week of all-day sessions and classes. Classes began at 8 am with lunch in between and ended by 2:30 p.m. When everything was over, students could do whatever they wanted. It was time they could spend on their own. Most times, the school had planned activities after classes had ended. A couple of nights, ice cream cones were offered in the cafeteria. Another night, there were snowball huts there. Almost every day there was a movie showing after the 5 p.m. dinner. The game room was always available but only until 10 pm. The canteen stayed opened until 6 pm. In each dorm building, students had a place to hang out where there were sofas, magazine racks, vending machines, and a first-come, first-serve room with numerous pay phones along the walls. The last night of the stay, there would be held the most anticipated event of the week, the dance finale. They had known about it since first receiving the invitation. The ticket to the dance was enclosed in the invitation to insure that only the invited students could attend. There would be a D.J., dance contests, singing contests, food, and prize giveaways.

Matt and Greg met in front of Pop's place as they had decided to make plans for the dance. "Hey Matt, what time do you want to meet to go to the dance? Come on, let's go in and talk after we get a seat."
"Aw, Greg. I'm sorry, man, but I met this chick in one of my classes and she asked me if I would go with her to the dance."
"So Matt, why didn't you tell me? Had I known that maybe I would have made myself more available. There are a lot of hotties out here, you know."
"I know, but this just happened outta nowhere. I really just started talking to her today. I'd seen her and we spoke, but never a conversation until today. And anyway, she asked me. I couldn't hurt her feelings. Maybe you can go with Shane and Kumar. Knowing you, Greg, I'm sure you'll meet girls once you get there."

146

"I don't know. Do you think Kumar even goes out to parties?" asked Greg.

"I'm sure he does. He sure likes it hanging out here at the canteen," Matt said reassuringly.

"Okay, I'll see what the other guys are doing. Come on. Let's go in and order. We can talk inside." Matt just stood at the door, staring at Greg.

"All right, so what are we gonna do then? Just stand out here?"

Matt looked at Greg sheepishly.

"Don't tell me."

"But Greg, she asked me if I would have dinner with her tonight over at the cafeteria," he said in an explanatory tone.

"What?" Greg exclaimed. "The caf-e-teria? You? What is this? She must really be hot. I've got to meet this girl."

"You will tomorrow."

"Okay, I'll see you tomorrow then. Guess I'll just head over to the dorm," said Greg sarcastically.

"Okay. See you tomorrow." They did their man hand shake and headed in opposite directions. When Kumar came in the room, he was surprised to see Greg. He knew that Greg and Matt were friends from school and just the two of them would hang out sometimes. Obviously, they had more in common than their new friends, but he didn't mind.

"Hey, where's Matt, my friend?" he asked. "I thought you two were going to Pop's place."

"Can you believe he's out with a girl?"

"Yes, as a matter of fact, I can. There are quite a few beauties of all flavors here, you know. Do I hear a bit of jealousy, my friend?"

"I don't know. Maybe," Greg admitted.

"Ohhh, don't be jealous. You still have a chance at the party tomorrow."

"Kumar, are you going tomorrow?"

"Of course... I might have a chance of my own." They did the man hand shake that Matt and Greg had taught him and both laughed.

"Have you talked to Shane?"

"Yeah...he's coming too."

The week seemed to have dragged along, but now it was Friday and everybody was excited. Those who had received an invitation knew that the proper attire had to be worn to attend. No exceptions. On Friday, the dance was all that everyone was talking about, in the classes, walking across campus, in the canteen... everywhere. Greg and Shane had stopped by the canteen earlier that day to get a hamburger when somebody yelled out, "Hey Poppy, you need to close this joint down, cause nobody's gonna be here tonight." The whole place roared with laughter.

"So why don't you get out now so I can clean up then," Poppy responded in his deep southern accent. Everybody laughed again. Greg and Shane left to go to their dorms to get ready for the big dance. It turned out that some of their other newfound friends also had found dates for the night, as he found out when he called them. Only the canteen lunch buddies would be hanging out together that night, Shane, Greg, and Kumar.

On their way across campus, the three buddies attracted the attention of onlookers as they strutted to their destination in synchronic cadence. They even got a few whistles. When they reached the building, there was a long procession outside the entrance, barely moving. Standing in line, they saw people who they had met during the week and began chatting with them while waiting for the line to move. The music was bellowing seemingly through the walls. Finally, they got to the door along with a trail of other revved up partygoers. After handing over their tickets, they got a hand stamp to assure reentry. As they went into the fun filled room, it was filled with wild party animals moving to the rhythm of the music. The music had been blasting even before they got into the building. The room was gigantic and packed. The decorations resembled that of a dance club with rotating glass balls illuminated by multicolored lights oscillating back and forth across the ceiling. The light was clashing against the turning glass balls, reflecting a colorful display of brilliant sparkles that intermittently lightened the darkened room. All around the walls were long tables of food and drinks. There was a stage where the DJ played his music loud and noisy, coming from huge Dolby speakers. It was so loud the floor and walls seemed to vibrate. On the stage, the DJ, a tall, thin black man wearing large yellow star framed sunglasses with a huge Afro hairstyle. He was bouncing and dancing in place, singing, talking, and shaking his head to the beat as he scratched and played his humongous assortment of records and LP's. Greg thought as he looked around this dimly lit mammoth room and the size of the crowd that there was no way he would ever be able to find Matt, but he tried anyway. Shane had found a girl to dance with as Kumar went off to the food tables. Incomprehensible chatter and loud music absorbed all the other sounds.

"Man, this music is so loud, that the vibrations are making it impossible to hear anyone say anything, let alone hear your name," Greg thought to himself while piercing through the crowd still searching for Matt. More than anything, he was eager to see what Matt's date looked like. As Greg peered into the crowd when the light lit the area, he thought he saw someone who looked familiar. The lighting was dim despite the flashing lights, but he could see when the light shone into the crowd that this person was also looking at him. It was a girl from what he could see. Trying not to stare, he could see that she was not anyone he had met during the week. He slowly moved in a bit closer to get a better look, but not wanting to appear as if he was in pursuit. He did know her vaguely as he got a flashback, but couldn't remember from where. She even looked at him inquisitively. When their eyes finally met, she then started to move towards him. As she got a little closer, he remembered. His stomach sunk. It was Beth. It was too late to turn away. She knew that he had seen her and was moving in towards him. He couldn't run again. But what would he say? What could he say? He tried to read her face as she got within speaking distance. He decided that he would let her carry the conversation. Putting on a forged smile, he waited. She had gotten her haircut and in the dim light appeared to Greg to be quite attractive. With loud music drowning out her voice, she yelled, "Hi Greg. I couldn't believe it was you. What are you doing here? I thought you were going to Georgetown."

"I will be," he yelled, trying to speak over the loud music. "So, how's it going? You want to go outside. I can hardly understand you."

She shook her head in the affirmative. He took her hand and led her through the crowd towards the exit. The thrill of him taking her hand brought back memories of their first date. She hadn't gotten over him as she thought she had. As he held her hand, those feelings that had begun last summer were coming back. When they got outside, he said, "Hey, you want to get away from this noise?"

"Okay," she replied. He felt that now he had a chance to rectify the awful exit when she left to go home last summer. He thought it strange that he hadn't felt badly or even thought anything about it until he saw her. They walked away from the building until they were able to hear each other.

"So Greg, how have you been?" glancing at him, then bashfully looking down still intimidated by his good looks.

"I didn't get a chance to say goodbye to you before we left." She said to him while still looking down. Stealthily taking a glance over at his profile as they continued to walk, she wanted to see how he would respond. He knew that this was coming and was not ready. Scrambling for words, he fell right back into the same careless deceptive mode.

"I guess sometimes it's hard to say goodbye. I felt bad about not giving you at least a call, but I'm glad that I have the chance now to say it. I'm sorry Beth." He turned her face towards him, looked into her eyes, and said, "Can you forgive me?"

Looking into his eyes, she thought, "Why did I have to see him again?" She was falling weakly right back into his charm. She had planned not to go back to the club again next summer and was going to take summer classes at college instead. When he looked at her, she completely gave in. Trying to regain her composure said,

"That's okay. You really made last summer the most wonderful time ever in my whole life. I really didn't want it to be over."

"Come on, Beth. We only went to a movie and got something to eat."

"Yeah, but no guy had ever treated me so nicely before."

Wanting to divert the conversation, he asked, "So where are you staying?"

"Oh, my dorm is right over there." She pointed in the direction of the building to their right, which was close and in the direction of where they were already walking. "Do you want to go there?" he asked. "We can go sit and talk in peace and quiet and maybe catch up with what's been going on." The sounds from the dance were still audible. Hesitantly, but overcome by her desire to be with him, she consented.

There was some truth of not wanting to say good-bye. After spending time with her and their talks on the phone, she had become a special friend to him. He did have a special place in his heart for her, a place where she had to remain. There was no way their friendship could have gone any further or even been revealed, even if it was what he had wanted. His mother would never have accepted Beth, not even as a friend, and his brother, Jack would never have let him live it down, especially after finding out that she was the girl that he had been avoiding them for and had just about spent the whole summer with. For him, it was good that she was leaving. But being away from home this night made him feel free to be with her and with no apprehensions. His unconstrained spirit gave way to carelessness. There was no one there who knew her, not even Matt, who was off somewhere philandering with a girl of his own whom he had just met.

On their way to the dorm, they passed several couples strolling across the campus together, holding hands, stopping to kiss along the way. How she had hoped that some day she would be like them. They walked up the seemingly long walkway to her building. By this time, the noise had dissipated into the night air. Beth was apprehensive, but nevertheless wanted to go inside. Although her appearance showed otherwise, she was still very shy. Along with her new haircut, she wore a short skirt and more noticeable makeup. Greg thought she looked much better than when he had last seen her, the day they went to the movies. In the lobby of the dorm, there were a few couples sitting around on the sofas. Everyone else had either gone to the party or was just walking around the campus. Beth was overcome by a feeling of embarrassment and discomfort as they went up the stairs to her room. She felt as if they were being watched, and wondered what they might be thinking. Unlocking the door, she immediately switched on the lamp that was on her desk. The room was small, but neat. The furniture was not much different from the guys' rooms, Greg thought. There were two of everything, desks, chairs, and beds. Greg sat on the bed and Beth grabbed the desk chair. She was becoming seriously nervous. Never had she ever been in a situation like this before and her palms were becoming moist from sweat. "What's happening to me? I shouldn't even be here. Why are we here?" All these thoughts were going through her head as Greg was calmly asking her about her parents, the prom, and graduation.

"I'm sorry, Greg, what did you say?"

As he looked at her in the dim light, he began thinking about him and Beth... together. What would it be like to touch her? He wondered if she had been kissed since she left last summer. This new freedom caused his mind to go in an entirely different direction than he had ever thought about Beth before. "What's happening to me?" he thought. "I've never thought of her in this way." He had thought about her once or twice when she first left, but only wondered if she still thought of him as a nice guy after not even saying goodbye. He took her hand and gently tugged. "Why don't you sit here beside me Beth?" Her stomach sunk and her face flushed. She had only dreamed of being this close to Greg, with his arms around her he kissed her gently. But this was not a dream. Greg had pulled her to the bed next to him. Looking down at her hands folding and unfolding as she answered his questions about school and family, she never looked up until he turned her face toward his. Their faces were so close; she could feel the warmth of his breath. She stared into his ocean blue-green eyes as he leaned over and tenderly kissed her lips. Her eyes closed as she felt his soft lips against hers. She didn't want to stop him, but she knew that she should. Beth's fears became jubilation when she touched his skin. He began to slowly peel off her clothes. She didn't resist. Knowing she should stop him, but not wanting to disappoint him, she willfully and painfully submitted.

Realizing what they had allowed to happen, both feeling shame, they got up and said nothing. Unable to even look at each other, fumbling with the buttons on her blouse, she rushed into the bathroom. She looked in the mirror as tears rolled down her cheeks. With shame and remorse, she immediately turned her face away. She couldn't stand to look at herself. Sitting on the toilet, she wiped away the tears. What was she going to do? Nothing like this had ever happened to her. He hadn't raped her. She wanted him. When she wiped herself with tissue, she saw blood. At that moment, she felt dirty and filthy. She was no longer pure and untouched. Her affection for Greg had become disgusted.

"What have I done?" she asked herself.

She took so long to come out of the bathroom that he became worried and called quietly at the door, "Beth, are you okay?" She didn't answer. Soon, he looked down and saw the doorknob slowly turn. He stepped aside as she walked out and sat on the desk chair. For the first time, Greg held his head down in shame for what had happened and walked in the bathroom. He called himself every disgusting adjective he could think of. "What have I done to this girl? I can't just walk away now. I don't even want her to look at me." All of those thoughts of regret raced through his mind. When he came out of the bathroom, she was staring out of the window sitting on the desk chair where she had moved it.

"Beth," he said softly. She didn't answer. He called her name again but she wouldn't turn her head around. He tried to turn her face as he had done before, but this time she resisted. She turned her face from him, got up and walked away while wiping the tears with the toilet tissue that she had gotten from the bathroom.

"Beth, I am truly sorry. I guess I really did miss you."

"Is that what you do when you miss someone?" she said sharply.

He had never heard Beth speak in this tone before, which made him somewhat surprised and a bit perturbed. She was trying to put the full blame on him, he thought.

"Wait a minute, Beth, I did say that I was sorry. It was not my intention to go this far, but you can't blame me totally. You never resisted. I kissed you and you kissed me back. You could have stopped me if you really wanted to, but you didn't."

At that, she broke down sobbing uncontrollably. He went over to her, wrapped his arms around her and held her head against his chest to comfort her, pleading with her not to cry, explaining that he was not trying to hurt her. She regained her composure, pulled away and sat on the bed. "I guess I'm all grown up now. So now what do I do? Greg, why don't you just go back to the dance and look for your friends?"

"No, I'm not going to leave you like this."

"I'm fine. I'm okay, really."

"Beth, why don't you take a shower and get into bed? It's already one o'clock. Don't worry I won't look. I just don't want to leave you alone while you're so upset."

Saying nothing, she got up, went to the closet to get a towel and pajamas from the drawer inside and took them into the bathroom. He sat on the bed, listening to the water from the shower, replaying and regretting what had just taken place. The opening door cut off his reproachful thoughts. She came out with the damp towel wrapped around her already clothed body and slipped under the covers, never looking in his direction. He attempted to kiss her on her forehead, but she turned over. "Greg, if you don't mind, I don't want you here when my roommate gets in," she said softly.

"Okay, I'll leave as soon as you doze off." She allowed about a half-hour go by, and then pretended to be asleep. Thinking she had finally fallen asleep, he left and started back towards the party. By this time, people were beginning to leave the party, and the campus was becoming more crowded and noisy.

Chapter 12

Three weeks had passed since the week at Glasslane University. Greg had not seen or heard from Beth. Early the next morning after the dance, he had gone back to her dorm because she hadn't answered her phone. When he knocked on the door, a small Asian girl peered from around the partially opened door. "Yes, can I help you?" she said with an American accent. She was obviously born in America.

"Yes... ah, my name is Greg, I'm a friend of Beth's... ah... is she in?"

"No, I'm afraid not."

"Did she go to breakfast already?"

"No, she went home."

"Are you sure?"

"Yes. She packed her things and got a taxi to the bus station around four-thirty this morning. She told me that she wouldn't be staying for the farewell conference."

"Okay, thanks." Greg was petrified. He knew she was upset, but he didn't know what to do to comfort her. Later on that morning after the incident, he planned to go over early to talk to her again over breakfast. Now, she had left and he had no way to contact her. Immediately, he headed back to his dorm, wondering what he should do, or even could do. When he got back to the room, Kumar was in the bathroom brushing his teeth. Mumbling through his toothbrush, he asked, "Hey man, where did you go so early, my friend?"

Greg said, "Kumar, wait at least until you finish brushing your teeth, man. I can't understand a thing you're saying." Finally, when Kumar came out of the bathroom, he asked again, "Where did you go so early? I didn't see you at all last night. I saw your friend Matt. That girl… she was a real winner. He asked where you were. It was really hard to see anybody in that big crowd you know, but I had the most fun and…"

"Kumar," Greg interrupted, "I'm going over to Matt's dorm room. I'll see you in the cafeteria for breakfast."

"Okay, Greg. Hey, Greg, are you okay, my friend?"

"Yeah, sure, I'm fine. I'll hold you a seat."

"Okay, thanks, Greg."

Greg's mind was still racing with thoughts about Beth. He was so angry with himself for what had happened. It really was not his intention. Why did he always have to wind up feeling so miserable when it came to her? Yet, she always made him feel so relaxed. He always felt comfortable being himself, yet he was always under pressure. Greg was devastated that he hadn't worn a condom. What was he thinking? It was not his intention on having sex, so why would he even need one? This was the worst-case scenario. When those thoughts crossed his mind, he broke out into a cold sweat. What if she became pregnant? But maybe she wouldn't because he noticed that she had been a virgin, and he had heard from his friends that virgins couldn't get pregnant. But if she was, his life would be over. He had tried early that morning to call her, but with no success. He didn't have her home phone number. The only thing he could do now was wait to hear from her. Three weeks had passed and she hadn't called. After that, he had completely forgotten about the whole ordeal and hadn't given it another thought.

Registration had gone smoothly. Greg had already settled in at Georgetown and had begun his first week of classes when he got a frantic call on his dorm room phone.

"Hello?"

"Hello, Greg?"

"Beth?" He wondered how she got his dorm room number. "I haven't heard from you since Glasslane. When I went to your dorm, your roommate told me that you had left. I'd tried to call, but you didn't answer. So what's going on? How did you get my dorm number?"

"I called the school operator and told her there was a family emergency. Greg…" There was a pause.

"Yes?"

"I haven't had a period yet."

Greg's stomach dropped. He had gotten the most dreaded news.

"What are you telling me, Beth?"

"I don't know. I'm just letting you know."

"Have you been tested?"

"Oh, no," she quickly responded, as if it was something she wouldn't dare do.

"Why not? Did you say anything to your parents?"

"Oh dear God, no. What would I say to them? Greg, I'm scared. What do I do?" He could tell that she was crying.

"Where are you?"

"I'm at home."

"Didn't you register for school?"

"No."

"Why not? I thought you had gotten a scholarship for Glasslane."

"I did."

"So why didn't you go?"

"I can't go back there. I never want to go back there," she said with hostility.

"What did your parents say?"

"I don't know... they can't understand why I didn't want to go. They say that I'm acting strangely and just keep asking me what's wrong and what happened? They know something happened at the school because I came home so suddenly. They keep threatening to take me to see a doctor."

"Do they know that I was there?"

"No, I wouldn't dare mention your name."

"Beth, why are you acting so weird? I think you're jumping the gun. You haven't really told me anything, except you didn't have your period yet. It's probably nothing, just something normal."

"Greg, I just feel like something's wrong, like I could be pregnant. Now, I've said it." "Beth, you can't be. It was your first time."

"Well, I've been reading about this and being a virgin doesn't matter."

"Then, why don't you get one of those test kits and find out for sure. I heard that some drug stores sell them." Greg was talking as multiple thoughts and scenarios went through his mind. If she is, who could he go to? He wouldn't dare say anything to his family.

"Yeah, get one of those test kits and call me back and let me know the results. Listen, I gotta go. I have to get to my class and I'm running late. Call me back, okay?" Greg hung up the phone. All his thoughts of regret of that fateful night had begun to resurface. He couldn't seem to get this girl out of his life. And this was the worst thing that had ever happened to him… ever. His mother always warned them, even more than his father had, to always wear a condom. He felt stupid and scared.

Beth couldn't believe the manner in which he had spoken to her. He gave no words of comfort, had no compassion, nor encouragement. She felt abandoned. He sounded so different from the Greg that she had first met. The other Greg was such a sweet and gentle person. Even the night after their encounter in her dorm room, he tried to console her when he saw how upset she was, although she rejected him.

Beth didn't have many friends and surely, none that she could confide in to help in such a dreadful situation as this. Her mother had always been her best friend. Any concerns or problems she had, she could always talk to her about them, even things that she didn't want her father to know. But this was something that she could never bring herself to tell her mother. She had always thought so highly of her. Her parents taught her to always do what was right. They trusted her. They were a Christian family and tried to live accordingly. It would break their hearts if she was pregnant. She never wanted to do anything that would hurt them. How could she ever face them again? Feeling so much shame and remorse, she felt she couldn't even bring herself to even pray for help. This was truly a most horrible dilemma. One of which she felt there was no solution. She couldn't stay in her room forever. In order to decide what to do, she knew she had to buy a pregnancy test kit to find out for sure. Fifteen minutes after her conversation with Greg, her mother knocked on the door.

"Beth, honey, do you want something to eat?"

"No, Mom. I'm not hungry right now."

"Beth, you're going to have to eat something. You didn't eat breakfast and only a little something last night. You haven't been eating much of anything for weeks now. You really need to eat." Her mother turned the doorknob. The door was locked. "Beth, open the door please. We really need to talk."

"Mom, I don't have anything to talk about right now." Her mother was really getting frantic and knowing this she got up and unlocked the door. When her mother walked in, Beth was sitting at her desk, her back to her.

"Beth, why didn't you want to register for school? You were so excited about going and you worked so hard for those scholarships. What happened?"

"Mom, we've already talked about this. Nothing is wrong. I just changed my mind about going to school right now. I'm thinking that maybe I would work for a year, then go, but not there. I think I might want to go to a smaller college or something."

"Well, then why haven't you been eating? Your dad and I are very concerned about you and your health. We feel that you should see Dr. Barnes. You were going to have to get your physical anyway for school."

"No, Mom. I don't need to see Dr. Barnes and since I'm not going to school right now I don't need the physical yet."

"Well, something is wrong and we need to find out what it is. I'm going to make an appointment. You seem to be under a lot of stress for some reason, and you've also lost weight. Maybe he can give you something for it."

"I don't need any medicine, Mom. Maybe I'm just not ready to take such a big step yet. I just need a break."

"That could be, and only you would know that, but I'll feel better if you get checked out," her mother said as she walked out of the room.

Beth knew she had to work fast. She got the Yellow Pages phone book to find locations for pregnancy testing facilities and the locations of abortion clinics. She felt so guilty of the thought of destroying a living person, but she felt that there was no other way to keep from embarrassing herself and especially her family. She couldn't imagine having a baby, let alone caring for one. Adoption was out because she would have to be seen pregnant for nine months. She couldn't imagine living through the gossip and slander. Having an abortion would be her only alternative. She was too young to be a mother. They both were too young.

"He wouldn't marry me even if we were old enough, she thought. Who would?" These thoughts made her feel even worse. She still allowed her old self-deprecating habit to continue to uproot her self-esteem whenever problems would arise involving other people. She had found an abortion clinic that she would have to drive about twenty-five miles to get to if it came to that. Not wanting to be seen and fearful of someone seeing her who might know her or her family, she couldn't go anywhere nearby to buy a kit. Before she went to the facility, she first wanted to get the test kit. She thought hopefully that Greg could be right and her body was just playing a dirty trick on her, or maybe God was teaching her a lesson for losing her virginity because her periods were always on time. She got dressed in a nice outfit, mainly to impress her mother and went downstairs.

"Mom."

Her mother was startled. "Beth, you're downstairs."

"Can I borrow the keys? I don't want to eat anything here. I want to go out and get something to eat… probably a burger from one of the fast food places or something."

"Anything to get you to eat," her mother said smiling. "You need any money?"

"No thanks, I have some. Thanks, Mom."

Her mother got the keys from her purse and placed them directly in her hand. "Be careful driving."

"I will," responded Beth in a contrived cheerful tone, trying to mask her heartfelt agony.

Her mother was so heartbroken over the way her daughter had been acting ever since she came home from the college early and abruptly on the last day without any reasonable explanation. Something had happened and she was determined to find out what. Somebody had done something to her child and she was going to find out what, or who had caused her this misery. These thoughts went through her mind as she listened to her go slowly upstairs to her room that day. She had to contain herself that day to keep her husband calm. He had already planned to go to the school that very day when Beth arrived home early that morning in a taxi. It was that evening they were to meet her at the bus terminal. Filled with anger, he swore that before the farewell ceremony had concluded, he was going to be there, even though the college was about a three-hour drive away. He knew something was wrong and it had to do with the dance the letter mentioned would be held the last night. So angered about his daughter's strange mode and sudden return, he threatened to literally squash the throat of whoever he found had touched his daughter. Beth heard every word and was terrified. She knew how more enraged her dad would have become had he found out it was Greg. There was a possibility that his anger would render him irrational and there would be no telling where it could lead. He never cared for Greg and never trusted him in the beginning.

Driving to her destination, the anxiety started again. Ever since that fateful night, Beth's life had forever changed. She had never felt so frightened and alone in her entire life. She couldn't stand being in the presence of her parents, nor could she look them straight in the face. She felt disgustingly unclean and unworthy to have them as her parents. They were very upstanding, highly regarded people and raised her to be the same. She had been deceitful, dishonest, and evasive with them and now she was lying to hide her wretched ignominious act. When her period hadn't come, she panicked. She hadn't slept restfully since the night after the dance, envisioning the images of her and Greg on that bed in the dorm room. Her appetite had abated to all but a day's meal of a bottle of water and bits and pieces of the evening dinner. Her dwindling weight alarmed her mother, which was why she insisted that she see the doctor. She constantly urged her to eat, but Beth had lost the desire. She couldn't seem to rid herself of those thoughts of how such an amazing culmination of the week's events could wind up being the most devastating end to all her life's dreams in such a brief amount of time, due to a total disregard of the consequences of her actions. First the image of Greg removing her clothes, allowing him to touch her in the most forbidden and intimate places of her body, causing her such incredible pain and yet incomprehensible bliss. Those memories made her feel lecherous and cheap. It angered her. As the days came and went, irrepressible and distressing thoughts of the possibility of being pregnant whirled her into high anxiety and became overwhelmingly agonizing. The thought of the word "pregnant" launched her into extreme hysteria. Trying to suppress the thought, she still would often visualize herself sitting and wailing with a bulging abdomen as her parents scolded her and with pointing accusing fingers. She could see her mother grasping and covering her tearful face with both hands as she would walk away in disgust. Those thoughts and images became nightmares. From her dreams, she would awaken every time after seeing heads turning from her in disgust or sometimes just find that she had been sitting in her room wringing her hands as she watched in her mind's eye her disgraceful future. How could she ever tell them such a thing? How could she have been so stupid? Even though she was suffering, she wanted to protect her parents from being wounded by her iniquitous behavior, so she was not going to let those fears and nightmares become a reality, therefore, she devised a plan to cover it up before it surfaced. On the advertisement section of one of her mother's magazines, she found the names of the drugstore chain that carried the kit. It was located in the next county, on a side of town far enough not to run into anyone she knew. At least that is what she had hoped. Building up from within was even more anger towards Greg as she recalled his apathetic response to this dreadful dilemma. From this fury, she was developing a new sense of self-confidence. He had abandoned her to figure this whole thing out by herself.

"It was at least half his fault," she thought.

"Call me when you find out," she said aloud in the car mocking his very words. So clearly she could hear his voice in her memory of that phone conversation when she told him about their problem. She figured maybe her father was right about him after all. Had she listened to him, she wouldn't be in this terrible predicament.

As she drove to the pharmacy, so many scenarios and images were playing through her mind from every direction until she thought she was going to go crazy. Reaching the store's parking lot, she sat in the car for a while to regain her confidence and composure. Taking a deep breath, she got the courage to go in. Through the many isles, she pretended that she was diligently looking for something other than the item that she really had come for. She didn't want to go directly to the isle with the pregnancy kits because she didn't want anyone to see what she was looking for. Making sure that no one was there, she crept into the isle with those items. She would pick up something and then put it back quickly, pretending that it was a mistake. There were not that many brands to choose from and still she didn't know which to get. She had no idea of the difference if there was any at all or how if the kit even worked. One of the employees, a middle-aged woman about her height walked up from behind. "Can I help you, young lady?" Beth was startled. She turned and stared wide-eyed at the woman.
"N-n-n-no thanks." Seeing how red Beth had become and what was in her hand, the woman guessed that she probably was a girl in trouble and left the aisle so that she could pursue her search without fear or embarrassment. She quickly grabbed one of the kits and hurried up to the register. Unfortunately, by this time, there was a line and someone had walked up behind her. Trying to conceal the kit and making sure that the woman employee was not around, she waited her turn. Getting to the register, she was extremely embarrassed as she placed the kit on the counter, never even glancing at the cashier's face. Just doing his job, the young man didn't seem to care what was being purchased. He only told her the cost. She looked down and reached into her shoulder bag to get the money from her wallet. Barely raising her head, she placed the money in his hand. The cashier put the kit into a bag and handed it to her along with the change. Grabbing the items, she speedily stuffed the bag under her arm and left the store. She only wanted to get out of there as quickly as possible. Again, those thoughts crept up. Her resentment towards Greg grew as she thought of how he had gotten away unscathed not having to deal with the humiliation and embarrassment that she was going through. To put some truth to what she had told her mother, she drove into the parking lot of the first fast food place that she saw and bought a hamburger, fries and a soda, but

still was not hungry. Sitting in the car, she decided that she had better read the directions before she got home, so she stayed in the car opened the kit and read the directions. It appeared to be quite difficult to do. She took a couple bites of her sandwich, ate a few fries and sipped half of the soda. She put what she needed for the test along with the directions and placed it into the zipper compartment of her shoulder bag. Not wanting any more of the food, she put the rest of what was in the pregnancy kit into the food bag and threw everything into the garbage can. No way did she want her mother to see her walking in with any bags to arouse suspicion about anything.

Even though there were fast food restaurants near her house, she had already been gone for almost an hour. Along with the drug store location, she had also written down the location of a Planned Parenthood in that same area. Reconsidering how complicated the test appeared, she decided that maybe trying to do the test herself was not such a good idea. She didn't want to blow it. But she had to find out what her future was going to be. Although she didn't know how to perform the test, she did know that the test had to be done with the first morning's urine. Fortunately, for her it was early in the morning when she thought she would be able to catch Greg in his dorm room and hadn't even taken the time to go to the bathroom. After talking to him about a pregnancy kit, she was glad that she had held off from going and had been holding off ever since. Looking again at the address, she started the car and headed there. She was familiar with the area, but had never been near that building nor did she know that there was a Planned Parenthood location in the city. During that time of day, traffic was somewhat heavy. Walking up the long scale of steps and going through the heavy doors, she could see what appeared to be an information desk facing her at the end of the corridor. Looking all around, she slowly walked up to the large desk. The receptionist greeted her with a smile, and asked,

"May I help you, young lady?"

"Is this where somebody can get a pregnancy test done?" she asked softly, whispering. The woman could see that Beth was scared and tried to make her feel more at ease.

"Is the test for you, honey?"

"Yes," she said hesitantly.

"Don't worry, someone will take care of you, but I need you to fill out this form first. Okay? You can go right over there in that room."

With the clipboard and pen, she proceeded into the room. There were only three other women there. Sitting in the far corner, she scanned over the form. It was a medical questionnaire. Some of the questions were very personal and to her were quite embarrassing. Greg had been her only partner, but he was not her partner, she thought. Their relationship had been only platonic. She quickly filled out the form and took it back to the receptionist at the desk.

"Honey, I have to get a cup for you to take home. They're going to need a first morning sample of urine."

"But I thought I could do it today. I haven't been to the bathroom yet."

"You mean you haven't urinated since last night?" the woman asked in amazement.

"No ma'am. I knew I needed to hold it, so I did."

"Sweetheart, come with me. I know your bladder must be about to burst." The woman went into a room and came out with a plastic cup with a lid and a sticker.

"Here, go into this room and urinate in this cup. There should be a marker in there to write your name on the sticker. Now put the sticker on the cup and leave it on the ledge in the room."

Seeing the toilet was a thing of beauty. Beth was so happy to be able to empty her bladder. The fullness was becoming almost intolerable. It was most uncomfortable and beginning to be a bit painful. She wasn't sure for how much longer she would have been able to hold it. The receptionist left and had gone back to her desk.

Beth stopped at the desk.

"How long is this going to take?" she asked softly.

"It's going to take at least two hours, honey."

"Can I wait here for the results?"

"No sweetheart. Usually, we call or mail your results."

Beth panicked. "Oh no… please don't call my house." She began to cry. Through the sobs, Beth was stressing out, continuing to plead for anonymity. The woman came around from behind her desk to comfort her. Someone else who had watched this tearful and hysterical scene went to get someone to help. They took Beth to a room where there was more privacy. She was given a small box of tissues.

"Your name is Beth Tinsley?" the woman asked.

"Yes." Beth finally looked at the person who was asking her questions. Her voice was so gentle and consoling. Beth looked at her and thought of her roommate for the week at Glasslane. She was of Asian descent with an American accent just like her roommate.

"My name is Mrs. Taylor and I'm a nurse. Why are you visiting us today Beth?
"I wanted to get a pregnancy test done."
"How long has it been since your last period?"
"I don't know. I only know that I'm overdue… I want to find out if I'm…you know." She started to cry again.
"Beth, was this your first time with a boy?"
"Yes."
"Were you raped?"
"No."
"Okay, I just want to let you know that we offer birth control so that you won't have to worry about this again."
"I won't need any." Her responses were somewhat curt.
"Well, it's only to help you so that you won't even have to come here for this again."
"I won't go through this again."
"Are you okay? Do you want to talk about what happened to you?"
"No. I only want the results of my test. I don't want my parents to know that I've been here."
"Okay, you can sit in this room until we get your results."
Sitting in fear of the worst, she still couldn't bring herself to ask her anything about her alternative if the test was positive. She had made her decision. Alone she sat in the room thinking of all that she had been through. What was she going to tell her mom when she got back? What excuse would she have for being out for so long just to get a burger, which was only fifteen minutes away? As she contemplated this new dilemma, the nurse, Mrs. Taylor, walked back into the room. She hadn't even realized how much time had gone by. The nurse handed her the envelope with the results.
"This should make you feel better."
Beth smiled, but even so, wouldn't open it.
"I just want to let you know that we offer many other services for women here. We have doctors and other skilled nurses and counselors, so if you need us, we are here to help you."
"Thank you for everything… for helping me. I'm really sorry for the way I acted. I feel so stupid, but I was just so scared… and…" she rattled on. The nurse politely cut off explanation,
"Don't worry about it. I know you were." The nurse listened patted and rubbed her on the shoulder. Standing up, she said, "Well, you take care, Beth. Good-bye. And remember we're here to help."

She was thrilled as she sat in the car and read "negative" on the paper. Now, what explanation would she have for being out so long? She no longer wanted to lie to her mother, but she could never tell her where she had really been.

Her mother quietly watched her as she came into the house looking for signs of any kind to figure out what was happening to her child.
"Mom, I put your keys on the table by the door," Beth yelled from the top of the stairs. She went straight up the stairs and into her bedroom, and then locked the door.
"Okay, sweetie." Her mother answered from downstairs.
She had no explanation and her mother didn't ask for one. The look on her daughter's face somehow gave her a sense of relief.

Beth had held her bladder for hours while trying to figure out how to get the test done. She had saved some to try out the kit that she had purchased once she had gone to Planned Parenthood. She nervously went into the bathroom and locked the door. Hanging her shoulder bag on the hook on the door, she took out the instructions, the cartridge, and the small cup. Somehow, while she was at Planned Parenthood she maneuvered on the toilet and managed to get some urine into the cup from her own kit. More had gotten on her hand than in the cup. She frowned when she remembered how disgusting it was washing the urine off her hands with hot soapy water. Following the instructions exactly, she began the test. As the minutes ticked away, she felt relieved knowing what the result was going to be. She kneeled on the bathroom floor and said a prayer thanking God for the negative outcome of the test, asking for His forgiveness, and vowing never to do such a thing again until she was married. After the incident those weeks ago at Glasslane, she had stopped praying because she was so ashamed of her disobedience and didn't feel worthy to pray. Putting all that was in the kit into a small bag that she had found underneath the sink in the bathroom, she tied it up and hid it in the trashcan deep underneath the other trash that was already there.

Thinking about the test results, she was now worried that maybe something else could be wrong since she hadn't had her period. "Maybe I should see Dr. Barnes after all," she thought. "It could have been stress from that awful event at Glasslane… but I'm not going to think about that now, I'm going to call Greg," she said to herself in a low tone. Even though she was not pregnant, her feelings toward Greg hadn't changed. She even thought about waiting and letting him sweat it out for a while, but then realizing her blessing, thought that wouldn't be the right thing to do, so she dialed his number and waited for him to answer.

"Hello."

"Hello, Greg."

"Beth…is that you?"

"Yes, Greg, it's me."

"Did you get the kit?"

"Yes, I did."

"Well?" he said, sounding impatient and edgy.

"I didn't use the kit. I bought one, but I didn't use it."

"So what did you do?"

"That test was too complicated and I didn't want to do anything wrong and waste it so I went to Planned Parenthood and got the test done there. And it was negative," she said, crassly.

"Wow, what's wrong with you. You think that you'd be happy," he said, reciprocating her tone.

"Believe me, Greg, I am overwhelmed with joy and relief," she said coldly.

"Then why are you talking as if you're angry or something? This isn't like you," he said. He was unbelievably surprised at her.

"No, none of this behavior has been like me. You want to know why I'm talking like this." Answering her rhetorical question, not even giving him a chance to try to respond, she continued.

"It's because I am angry. No, I'm infuriated. When I told you that I thought I could be pregnant, you showed no concern. You didn't even try to console me, nor did you try to encourage me. You had no words to try to lift my spirits, or calm my fears. You told me to buy a pregnancy kit and call you with the results. Then you hurried me off the phone because you had a class, as if you were blameless. Because you abandoned me, I was left alone when I needed you most."

"Beth, I am so sorry. I didn't realize that I came off like that. I just didn't know what to say. I was caught off guard."

"Well, how do you think I felt? What if the test was positive, Greg? What would you have said then? Truthfully, I don't even want to imagine what you would have said, or how you would have reacted. I wouldn't be able to bare it."

There was dead silence. "Greg?"

"Yes," he answered sheepishly.

"When I met you, you had given me a new sense of hope in men… in people.

I guess my dad was right about you."

"Right about what?" he asked, being taken aback by her comment.

"It really doesn't matter now, but thank you for the confirming what I guess I always knew. Outside of family, nobody really cares. People are heartless, ruthless, and cruel. Goodbye, Greg. Have a nice life."

"Wait, Beth. Beth wait! I…" The connection on the phone ended. She had hung up and all he heard was a dial tone.

"This is the story of my life," he thought. "I try to avoid hurting people, only to wind up hurting them anyway." Although relieved that she was not pregnant, he thought about Beth's last question. What would he have said or done? He shuddered at the thought of having to confront his mother with news of an unwanted pregnancy. This left him with great anxiety and fear. Unbeknownst to each other, they both vowed to themselves never to utter a word to anyone of what had happened and what could have been.

Chapter 13

It had been a little over six months since Ally and Greg's first meeting at Huntington Beach. They were in daily contact with each other after that day. Even though the business and home for Greg were both on the east coast in New York and New Jersey, he visited Ally in California quite frequently, as much as time permitted. At least every third weekend, and sometimes during the week if he could manage to get there. She thoroughly enjoyed the many trips and generous gifts that Greg showered her with, but most of all she loved just being with him. He always treated her in a very special way. She tried not to let herself get too involved emotionally. It was very difficult not to, even though she knew it would be to no avail. Unbeknownst to her, she had become first in his life; a place that had been vacant for many years.

It was not long after they met that Greg took Ally to meet his parents in New Jersey. He had purchased her a plane ticket and set her up to stay in the guest room of his apartment. His love for Ally had heightened to the point that he was even contemplating marriage, but knew that she wouldn't meet with his mother's approval, as she was always finding fault in any one he showed interest in, but this time, he didn't care. After her usual inquiry about Ally, Nancy concluded that her background was not fitting with their social standards. She had always tried to encourage both her sons, all their life, to only get involved with those who were in the same socio-economic status as them. "It would be less complicated," she explained. She had even tried to encourage Greg and Jack to date the daughters of the heads of businesses who were associated with their company and those of bank executors who were or had been affiliated with their father. Many of whom they had been well acquainted with, since the beginning of the business. Their children had practically grown up together. Many times, she tried to use her overbearing influence on them to cajole them into going out with these girls. But she was always met with opposition, especially from Jack. He refused to be controlled by her or anyone else and handled his rejection of her choices in such a manner that she was totally oblivious. Neither of them wanted to get involved with their dad's associate's daughters, or anyone else associated with the company. Remembering his mother's domineering interference brought back to his remembrance a particular incident of her manipulation, and of her resistance to accept anyone of his choice. This particular incident Greg knew changed his whole future.

Some years before, Nancy had gone so far as to concoct a scheme that would resolve her little conundrum. Unbeknownst to Greg, for whom she had devised her devious plan, invited the daughter of one of the firms' presidents, along with her family to dinner one evening. She implied to the young lady's parents by suggestions and hints, that Greg was interested in their daughter, but explained that he was just too shy to approach her himself. On that particular evening, Greg had already made plans weeks prior to his mother's sneaky stunt and was in his room getting dressed for the occasion when he heard her knock and call to him at his bedroom door. He unlocked the door and opened it to a little crack to find out what was going on because of the urgency in her voice.

"May I come in? I need to speak to you." When she stepped over the threshold, she immediately proceeded to inform him of her prearranged dinner plans. Shocked and perturbed by her inconsiderate actions, he proceeded to tell her that he was going out with Janice and wouldn't be able to attend, but she only thwarted his reply. Greg was infuriated, but even so was urged by Nancy to change his plans to avoid causing any embarrassment to either family.

"Better start getting ready, dear, our guests have already agreed to come and will be arriving in a few hours, so dress appropriately. Everybody's expecting you, and Jack as well, since they're bringing their daughters." Her performance was cunning, but he knew. He had seen her exploits many times.

"How could you, Mother? Why would you tell me at the last minute that you made dinner plans? Not only that, why didn't you ask me first before you even invited them? How am I going to explain to Janice that our date is off?"

"You'll think of something… I'm sure," she said in a snide, sarcastic tone and walked out of his room. Greg was enraged at her arrogance and total disregard for anything other than what she wanted, but, even more so, was appalled with himself for allowing his mother to manipulate him in this way… still. He was a man now, not a boy anymore, and yet she seemed to still be able to commandeer his life.

At this time, Greg had only been going out with Janice for a few months. Nine months later, she would become his fiancée. Under duress, he managed to get enough courage to call and explain why he had to cancel their date. She completely understood having been told previously of how manipulative and narrow-minded his mother could be. Greg was still fuming about this abrupt dinner revelation and having to cancel his date. After calling Janice, he tromped down the long hallway outside his mother's bedroom where she was getting ready and again, he angrily confronted her for yet another intervention in his life.

He knocked, "Mom, why do you do these things? All you had to do was to let me know… no, you should have asked me. I do have a life aside from just what goes on in this family."

On this occasion, his father, who was also in the bedroom, even came to his defense, after finding out that he, too, had been hoodwinked and deluded into her deceitful scheme. John heard the two of them as they hashed it out in the hallway in front of the master bedroom. He thought about how he had only found out that she had invited Harry Forrester and his family over for dinner during a golf game a couple of days ago. Harry was a long time colleague and friend of the family with two very beautiful daughters. When Harry mentioned coming over for dinner, John not wanting to appear unaware of the plans, played along.

"Oh, yeah," John replied "…that's right. I almost forgot. Is that day okay with you…Saturday night around six thirty?" He was only speculating because he didn't even know the day of the affair.

"No, I thought it was Friday at six thirty. Anyway, that's what Karen told me," Harry answered with a tone of confusion in his reply.

"Oh, yeah, that's right. It is Friday. Sorry, Har, I got the days mixed up with something else, I guess. You're right." John was embarrassed and felt foolish. Apparently, Nancy had prearranged everything with Carol, Harry's wife. "Nancy Tyler strikes again." John thought to himself, irritated by her rash, inconsiderate and selfish behavior.

Greg was angry, but still being the empathic, softhearted person that he was, remained for dinner as planned by his mother. Harry and his family arrived on time. Everyone gathered before dinner in the garden where appetizers and drinks were being served. The young ladies and their family came that evening, having no idea of the immense altercation which had just transpired only a few hours before their arrival. The conversation remained general throughout the evening. He didn't want to give any impression to either daughter or her family of any romantic attraction or any interest of any kind other than that of being a family friend. The evening ended with laconic conversation, except for his dad, who seemed to be enjoying chatting with Harry, a man who was quite a hoot. Nancy and Carol were not close friends, but they were involved in some of the same social societies, so their conversation was mostly gossipy. Jack was mainly the entertainment for the girls. He could always get a laugh. Dessert and coffee were served following dinner as the evening came to a short close. The older young lady had become quite aware that Greg never attempted to involve himself, not even in the conversation. When everyone had gone, Greg reiterated to his mother his disappointment and inability to run his own life without her undesired intrusions.

"Oh, Greg, you're making a mountain out of mole hill. So, what do you think of Veronica?"

Greg was stunned and just stared at her for a moment in disbelief. Saying nothing, he continued down the hallway. He looked at Jack, who was standing on the steps heading up to his room, and just shook his head. Jack only grinned and continued up the stairs.

"What's funny?" Greg asked him.

"You... you're funny. Why do you let her get to you, man? It's your fault. She knows how you are and uses it manipulate you."

Greg only stared at Jack as he walked to the closet to get his jacket and quickly leave the house. He didn't even bother to change out of the suit he had worn for dinner. During the evening, he managed to slip away to call Janice to tell her that he would be over later. Thinking of the whole manipulated evening, Greg muttered to himself as he walked to his car. "She's unbelievable." "She'll never change. So, I'm going to have to," he thought to himself.

Driving to their destination brought back those unpleasant memories of bringing any of his female guests to family gatherings or just for a day of simply hanging out at the pool, or playing a game of tennis. Unlike with Jack, his mother almost always managed to find an excuse to show her presence whenever he brought a girl home. The frequency of those interruptions made him suspicious that it was intentional just to make them feel uncomfortable. Of course, she denied the accusation when confronted. She had the audacity to reverse the discussion as she being the victim of assault by humiliation for him even to have such a thought. Jack usually outsmarted his mother by bringing his girlfriends home when no one would be there. As he looked over at Ally sitting quietly staring out the window, he wondered what he was getting her into. She was blown away at the miles of copious land with its beautifully gated homes, which seemed to surround them as they rode to his house. She reminded him of a little kid, gleefully looking in amazement at the sights as at an amusement park. The homes around the area were those that she had only seen in magazines. Pointing to a huge stone house resembling a castle, she exclaimed, "Look at that one. Where's the moat?" she said, laughing at her own joke. She was fascinated at the sight of such opulence. When they turned onto the long driveway, Ally was speechless when she saw the tall manicured shrubs that outlined the landscape. Far off between the shrubs was an empty tennis court and a smaller house which was the beach house for the larger pool. The view was magnificent.

"Greg, we've been driving for quite a while now. Are you sure this is the right way? You did say this is the driveway, right?"

"Yes, and of course, this is the right way. I have been living here since high school, you know."

"Oh, Greg, I'm sorry. What was I thinking? Of course, you should know where you live. It's just that … it seems to be such… such a long way and we haven't gotten there yet."

"Okay, we're almost there," he interjected.

As soon as he said that, the colossal edifice had come into view. Ally was in awe. She was beginning to feel a bit uneasy as she began to grasp the full significance of what she was seeing. She had no idea that Greg's family was so rich. It never really crossed her mind. She knew that they owned a business, but didn't know the amount of wealth it had brought them. The house was a mansion. Amazement was quickly being replaced with feelings of regret. She became intimidated by the overwhelming display of such opulence. Seeing all this made her realize that she was definitely out of her league and didn't belong. Ever since they met, he never mentioned the extent of his business' success. Having never seen, or spoken to his parents before, she was becoming even more nervous and was now about to meet them face to face. She had no idea of what to expect because he always managed to change the conversation concerning parents, unless it was about hers. Whenever she would ask, somehow they wounded up talking about something else. In actuality, he didn't want to frighten her and possibly lose her before their relationship began. His mother had already ruined his relationship with Janice. Except for his evasiveness, their friendship was flawless. He couldn't believe that he could have met anyone as perfect as Ally yet, had thought the world of Janice. He had to really contain himself from the time he first laid eyes on her. Love at first sight was a manifestation he believed never happened except in fiction, but now had second thoughts. Other than an occasional date to quench his carnal appetite, he had no desire to ever involve himself seriously with any woman, especially after his wedding debacle.

Almost twenty-three, a year after getting his Bachelors degree, Greg decided to enroll in the Master's program at the University of Pennsylvania. He had been working a great deal at the company and wanted to become more skilled, especially in the area of international finance. It was around this time that he told his parents about his plans to marry Janice almost soon after graduation. She was also in school, completing her studies in business law. They thought with both their fields of study would be a great asset to the company. However, his mother was not in agreement with the planned union and was horrified at the announcement. During that time whenever she had the opportunity, she tried to convince Greg that he should wait, that he was too young, and really didn't know enough about her background or anything about her family. She even tried to coerce her husband, John, to reason with him because Greg had once threatened to elope if she didn't back off.

Greg tried his best to adhere to his mother's criteria for potential mates, but he could never fall in love with those types of girls. Why did he let his mother dictate to him, who and what was best for him anyway? There was no problem with her family; they adored him. His father was of no help. He continued to allow his wife to run everything except the business. Even now, she still made him feel guilty, because, as she put it "she had practically raised the boys alone." This caused him to resent his father even more sometimes. Knowing that she would never let him forget it, when she needed to, would put him on such a guilt trip that his dad would never stand up for himself. He could run his business with absolute precision, but knew nothing about being the head of the house. He knew even less about the necessity of a husband's role of leadership in the family, and to his children, especially sons to train to become men to someday become the head of their own household. This was necessary, for the family to function properly. He didn't know how he knew this, but this way seemed to be the right way things should be done in a family.

Greg was sure, but had no proof that his mother had been the cause of Janice no longer wanting to get married. Their wedding breakup sent him into a total emotional abyss that took years of counseling and therapy to recover. He was virtually left at the altar. It was days before the wedding, and after not being able to contact Janice, that he got a letter in the mail, telling him she was calling off the wedding. In the letter, she explained how regretful she was for all the time and trouble wasted, only to find out that she was not ready for such a huge change in her life and furthermore was not truly in love with him as she thought and could no longer pretend. Again and again, he played their times together over and over in his mind, picking and prodding to find the true reason why she would suddenly run away and how something so real could have never existed. He didn't believe it. He knew she loved him. Those feelings could not have been pretended or imagined. They loved each other. He tried searching for her, but her address and phone numbers had changed. She had moved with no forwarding address. It was as though she had never existed. Now, again he was faced with his mother's scrutiny. He knew Ally didn't meet her criteria as well. She wasn't rich, nor had she graduated from any university, or even college, for that matter. But he thought she was the most beautiful woman he had ever met, inside and out. Finding someone whose admirable personality and virtuous character like hers was of immense value to him, far greater than any other person he had ever met. And he was not going to let anyone come between them, not this time.

Ally's heart was about to jump out of her throat as Greg led her to the entrance and into the huge foyer of glossy white and gold marble, which extended the length of the hallway. She gazed upward and was in awe of the elaborate gold and crystal chandelier that hung from the high cathedral ceiling. Having a wild thought, she couldn't imagine how it could ever be cleaned. Quickly she tried to focus on what was now the matter at hand. Greg called out to his parents that they had arrived. Ally tried to regain her composure as she watched the images of John and Nancy increase as they approached them, coming down the seemingly endless hallway. Upon meeting his mother, this being the first time, she felt an expected chill of indifference. Before she had a chance to open her mouth, Ally could see that she would never have a chance at ever winning her favor as she watched how Nancy scanned her from head to toe, having barely stepped into the foyer. Greg also noticed and gave his mother a look that she had never seen before, but could read exactly what he was telling her. Nancy was not intimidated, but cooperated. He proceeded with the introductions. She extended her hand with a spurious smile, and said, "Nice to meet you, Ally. It is Ally, isn't it?"

"Yes. Nice meeting you as well, Mrs. Tyler. You have a lovely home."

"Thank you," she answered with a snide intonation. His father's response was a far cry from Nancy's bogus greeting. Ally could feel the warmth and see that his kindness was genuine. He walked over to her with a welcoming, authentic smile as he opened his home to her and was eager to accommodate. He urged Nancy to offer her whatever she wanted before dinner. "Nancy, see if Ally would like something before we have dinner…maybe something to drink?" he asked, as he guided them into the bar and game room. The over-sized room was lit by hanging glass lanterns, which hung in threes at each corner of the room. The walls and ceiling were of shiny cherry wood panels. Sitting on a large Oriental rug, was a huge luxurious mahogany wood pool table in the center of the room. Along one side of the wall was a glass and metal cabinet behind the bar. Ally sat on a stool at the bar, wondering how anyone could drink all that alcohol that was inside. There was a plethora of bottles of all shapes and sizes of alcoholic varieties and other beverages, which practically filled every space on the shelves.

"Oh, no thank you, sir… uh… Mr. Tyler."

"Call me, John."

"Okay. No, thank you, John. I'll just wait until dinner. She felt awkward calling his father, John.

"Greg told me how great a cook your wife is."

"She is pretty good at it I must say, when she does decide to cook."

Nancy had just gotten back from the kitchen and headed straight over to the bar to get him a drink. He always had Bourbon with Diet Coke about an hour before dinner to relax.

"I'm going back to see how dinner is coming along.

"Oh, is there anything that I could help you with Mrs. Tyler?"

"I don't think so," she responded with the same snobby tone. Catching herself, she added, "No, I wouldn't dare have my invited guest in the kitchen helping to cook the meal. You just relax dear. Everything's just about ready anyway."

Before she could turn away to go back towards the kitchen, she caught Greg's look. He had been following her every move and she could see that he was not happy. They continued with their getting acquainted palaver until Nancy interrupted them to announce dinner was ready.

Across the hallway, they paraded into another spacious room, which was more breathtaking than the other. All this affluence was disheartening to Ally. Feelings of inadequacy and inferiority were beginning to build as she saw over and over the profusion of wealth that this family had acquired. The grand piano, the famous paintings, which she had only seen in books, that hung on the wide eggshell colored walls and separated by gigantic arched windows made her feel out of place. His dad had managed to acquire several authentic paintings and a few sculptures at auctions. Greg smiled at her and took her by the hand to guide her to the dining table. It was a gesture of reassurance as he noticed the look on her face. He pulled out her chair, and as she looked into his eyes when he sat down beside her, she became more comfortable and self-assured.

Dinner had gone well. John proceeded to tell Ally the whole history of the business, of which she could tell that he was very proud. She was impressed with how he had persevered through all of those years of trials and disappointments, the rejections and denials, and sometimes failures, to establish such a large and still growing corporation from such humble beginnings. "Mr. Tyler, that is such a fascinating life story. Have you ever considered writing a book?"
"Ha…oh, no," he said laughing bashfully."
"Well, maybe you should. A lot could be learned from someone like you. There could be someone who may be thinking of going into business for themselves, but lack the confidence and self-motivation to start."
"Ally, that's very kind of you to say. But no,… not at this time. I'm still a little too busy right now. Maybe sometime in the future I might consider it."
Nancy patiently waited her turn. Her questions were more directed towards Ally's family. She could see Greg staring at her from the corner of her eye. She had to be careful how her questions were to be asked. She didn't want to appear as though she was interrogating her. Her questions were basic and concise. She asked about her parents, what they did for a living, and if she had any siblings. The conversation was kept very general. Afterwards, they had dessert. And at this time, Greg decided to drop a bomb.
He announced that he wanted, one day soon, to marry Ally. Both John and

Nancy were shocked, but most of all; Ally was dumbfounded. This was the first time she had ever heard Greg express any interest in getting married. They had only been seeing each other for about six months, and even so, never thought it was that serious. She tried to conceal her amazement, so as not to embarrass Greg. She liked him a lot, but didn't think he cared that much about her. They had gone out numerous times and spent a lot of time together, but it never crossed her mind that he would ever consider her for marriage, which didn't bother her because she enjoyed his company and was not looking for any kind of commitment anyway. She was both flattered and upset.

"So uh… are you making any plans?" asked John, looking at Greg and then at Ally. Greg was about to respond when Ally interjected and said, "No, nothing right now. That would probably be sometime later in the future," she said, as she looked at Greg. "Good," Nancy said. "That's a relief."

Greg's head snapped around, his eyes piercing towards his mother.

Noticing his stare, being polite, but in no way apprehensively, she added, "It would be good to know when, so you'd have time to plan and prepare for it properly, and well in advance. It's less stressful that way. Don't you think, Ally?"

That question was rhetorical. She continued, but wanted answers. "So, when did you two meet?" she asked, but actually already knew.

Greg knew what she was alluding to. At this point, he interjected. "We met about six months ago… remember Dad … when Jack and I were in Huntington Beach out in California?"

"Oh, yeah, you were meeting a couple of new clients there. Yeah…as I recall that meeting went quite well."

"Anyway, we met on the beach," he continued, while looking at Ally and smiling. She looked down at her lap to pick up the napkin to wipe her mouth as a means to cover her embarrassment.

Nancy listened and noticed that the two of them were expressionless.

"Would you like some coffee, dear?" Nancy asked to divert the conversation.

"Yes, thank you, Mrs. Tyler. I would love some."

"I'll have some too, Mom."

"Well, it looks like we all are having coffee then," said John, adding to the moment. Nancy got up to prepare a pot of coffee. She felt that she needed to leave that room in a hurry. "How dare that little "have-not" try to weasel her way into this family," she thought, as she hurried to the kitchen. "What does she have to offer my son?" She imagined how Ally must have been scantily dressed on the beach that day. She looks like a little kid. I know he's much older than she is. She's just like that other one … Janice. He thought that he was so in love with her too. Thoughts of detestation and displeasure raced through her mind and her choice words uttered under her breath were uncharacteristically raunchy as she grabbed pots and cups, going back and forth to the refrigerator, to the cabinets, to the sink and to the stove. She became so incensed and furious that her hands began to tremble uncontrollably. Juggling to hold onto the China cup that she tried desperately to cling to, she lost her grip, and it dropped from her hand, crashing to the floor.

While Nancy was gone, they had moved from the dining area to the living room and faintly heard the sound of the shattering cup. John got up to go to the kitchen to find out what was going on. In his absence, Ally asked Greg in a low tone, "Greg, why would you make such an announcement without at least letting me know first? You put me in a very awkward position. Your parents don't even know me. Remember this is the first time I've ever seen them. I was totally embarrassed. I didn't know what to say. That completely caught me off guard, let alone your parents."

"I'm sorry, Ally. It kind of just slipped out. When I looked at you, I thought of how much I loved you and I wanted them to know that I'm serious about you."

Ally was stunned. He had never said he loved her before.

"Greg, you never even told me how you felt about me. You never said that you cared that much for me. And please don't take this the wrong way, but it would have been better to let me know first how serious you were. We have never talked about marriage. We've only been seeing each other for a just few months."

"Are you telling me that you don't feel the same way about me?" he asked with fear of disappointment.

"No, I'm not saying that. I'm not saying anything. I don't know what I'm saying. Greg, this isn't the time, or the place, to talk about this. Let's talk about this later, okay?"

"Okay." Just as he finished his last word, John and Nancy were heading back to the living room with a tray of coffee and an assortment of flavored creamers. She placed the shimmering silver tray on the coffee table where there were also samplings of little cakes. Nancy handed them a beautifully embroidered edged napkin, and everyone helped themselves. Ally had completely lost her desire to eat anything since that sudden revelation, but wouldn't dare refuse Nancy's courtesy, no matter how pretentious it may have been.

The drive home was silent. Ally was staying at Greg's luxurious Glenwood apartment in downtown New York. He had flown her in for the weekend to meet his parents and do a little sightseeing and shopping. This was her first time in New York. When he first asked her to come, she was so excited and counted the days until they would be arriving. Before Greg dropped his bomb, everything had gone along just fine. She had even begun to adjust to his mother's snobby personality. Greg respected Ally's tacit request for a quiet drive back. She needed time to digest what had transpired during the evening of her first visit, which she was, above all, absolutely unprepared for. Greg pulled his midnight blue Audi sports car into the underground garage near his apartment. Since he lived on the tenth floor, he always tried to park close to the elevator; but, finding a parking space was harder to do. When he finally found a spot, he walked around to open her door. Opening the door, he saw her wipe a tear from her cheek with her finger as she attempted to get out of the car. Regret and disappointment had overtaken the night. He had apologized several times during the drive home. Looking up at him, she faked a half smile as she placed her hand into his already extended hand and proceeded to come to her feet. He hadn't moved back when she stood to her feet. They were so close she could feel his warm breath against her face. Since she didn't respond, he moved back to give her room.

"Ally, I see that you are still upset and rightly so."

"No, I'm not upset, just a little confused right now."

"Yeah, maybe you'll feel better in the morning. It is kind of late."

"Yeah, you're right. I just need to get a little sleep."

"We did have quite a lot to eat and drink for one evening," he added, not mentioning the bombshell that he blurted out about "love" and marriage."

Immediately she went to her room and after saying goodnight, she closed the door. She wasn't sleepy, but just needed to be alone to think. She was perplexed. In her moment of solitude she was both happy and in disbelief from Greg's unexpected revelation to his parents of him wanting to get married... to her. She had no idea that he was that serious about their relationship. Even though they spent a lot of time together whenever he could fly in, she still felt that he hardly knew her, hardly enough that marriage would be in anyone's thoughts. Finding out his intention was to marry her, and the thought of being his wife was virtually unbelievable. Their relationship began as fun, almost platonic, nothing that alluded to permanence. She always thought that he would be a great catch but she had nothing to offer him. They came from two entirely different worlds. Always such an enjoyable and fun person to be with and was someone who she could trust and not worry about being seduced or making sexual advances. Greg was a true gentleman…a knight. Whenever he came to visit her in California on many of their outings, he would invite her friends Toni and Jessica to hang out with them. Always surprised when he showed up, she still looked forward to seeing him, but had no idea that their relationship would go any further. She wanted to call Toni to tell her about the whole thing, but didn't want Greg to overhear her speaking to anyone. Both Toni and Jessica would always tease her that some day she and Greg were going to get married and she told them how crazy they were to even think such a thing. In his travels, she knew he had many occasions to meet other women and probably did. Telling her parents the news would have been complicated because she never mentioned Greg to them. Thinking that their involvement would never amount to anything serious, she thought there was no reason to mention him. It was just a fleeting moment in her life and his. So she never allowed her feelings to go any farther than a friendship and took everything at face value. Did she love him? How was she going to answer him? She didn't want to say anything to discourage him. Finally, she dozed off, and the next thing she knew was waking up to the smell of breakfast. She could smell bacon and coffee all the way in her room. Lying in her queen-sized bed under her soft plush royal blue comforter, she thought, "How could I not be? What have I been feeling this whole time? Now that I know he loves me, I can have the freedom to call it love." Ally had been attracted to Greg from the first time she met him. Her affections grew as they spent more time together, but her realization that their differences wouldn't allow a future together constrained her true emotions, she was content with what they had.

Almost a year had passed since that life-changing visit and that morning after breakfast discussion about possible marriage. They decided that they would wait at least a year to see if they still wanted to marry. As time passed, they continued as they always had and, talked more and more about marriage and even children. She couldn't believe that Greg had waited that long for her. Ally was a virgin and he knew that she wanted to save herself for her husband. It was very difficult when they were together, but Greg respected her views and wishes. As months went by during their relationship, his mother remained detached, but John continued to be his kind and gentle self towards Greg's relationship with Ally. Jack told him how stupid he was to wait for any woman until he was married to her to have sex.

"Man, you're crazy. What have you been doing for almost a year?" Jack would tease Greg about his celibacy all the time, but Greg blew him off. He didn't care about what anyone thought. He loved Ally and wanted to be faithful to her. There was no one else for him that he wanted to be with. But Ally had her own dilemma. Her concern was that she wouldn't be welcomed by his mother into their family as his wife, but Greg convinced her that what his family felt didn't matter in their relationship. He told her that she was marrying him and not his family. They loved each other very much and vowed even before the ceremonial vows that they wouldn't let anyone or anything come between them.

During his many visits to California within that year, Ally had never even told her parents that she was in a serious relationship. She had never brought anyone to meet them and never talked to them about anyone special that she had met. They had heard her mention Greg, but thought he was no more than a long distance friend. Initially, her reluctance was because she was not sure about the seriousness of their relationship. Also, during that time, he hadn't given her a ring, nor mentioned one and she wouldn't dare ask. Greg had emphasized to Ally that if their relationship was going to go further he should meet her parents. He told her facetiously that her parents couldn't be as bad as his. She knew it wasn't fair that he hadn't met them, so during one of his visits, she finally decided that now was time. There was no way that she could tell them of her impending engagement, especially since he still hadn't given her a ring. A few weeks later, Ally arranged with Greg for a day to meet them.

Many weeks had gone by and finally the day had come. She and her mother had gone the extra mile to make the house look more attractive and bought a tablecloth. Since they hardly entertained, the thought of buying something had never occurred until now. The set of China rarely had it been used. The silver set of flatware was cleaned and polished. The atmosphere was set and everything was ready. It was time for them to meet Ally's Greg. When Greg rang the doorbell, and her father let him in, both of her parents could see why their daughter fell for such a man. He was handsome, well groomed, and looked to be very well off. As impressive as Greg was to Ally, her parents were not impressed by his exterior. They both knew that what was on the inside was more valuable than on the outside. They greeted each other warmly, and had small talk while waiting for dinner. With everyone seated, Greg complimented her on the exquisite table setting. Both Ally and her mom looked at each other and smiled.

Throughout their conversation during dinner, her parents pointed out how they had raised their daughter to be a respectable Christian woman. Greg only smiled and concurred. Their difference in age was obvious to them. Ally knew that it would cause some feelings of mistrust and skepticism. Alone in the kitchen after dinner, her mother asked her if Greg had ever been married before since he was an older man. But more of a concern of her parents' than the age difference was whether Greg was a Christian. Their biggest issue with Greg was when they found out that he wasn't, that meant as they said, "…they would be unequally yoked." They felt that this difference would put a strain on the marriage in the future. Her parents throughout her life had indoctrinated this Biblical reference in her. They told her that she should always look for a Christian when choosing a mate. They emphatically discussed this when she finally divulged to them of Greg's background. But, from what she had told them and from their observation of him, they felt that he seemed to have all the virtues of a Christian but had no interest in becoming one. In their years of wisdom, they foresaw that this could be a problem. But the reality, which they knew, was that only Ally could make the final choice.

The time had come when Greg and Ally seriously decided to get married. He had finally gotten a chance to meet her parents over dinner and told Ally that he now wanted to join them again to formally ask them for her hand in marriage. Soon after that discussion, Ally arranged with her parents to invite him to meet them again. Two weeks later, he flew out to California to meet with them as planned. Again, he met with them by virtue of a dinner invitation. During the meal, they reiterated their values and high moral standards. They prattled on and on about her growing up by modest means, and being thankful for everything that God had given them. It was almost verbatim from his first meeting them. But he respectfully and patiently listened and affirmed what they said as he ate the very modest, but tasty meal. "Sir, ma'am, I don't go to church, but I do believe in God. And I totally agree with everything that you said. This is why I fell in love with your daughter. She is rich in character and has great integrity, and this is why I would like to ask you if I could have her hand in marriage." Greg continued to explain how and why he agreed with them and supported their principles and standards. He expressed his unconditional love for their daughter and vowed to take care of her as they had done. Even after their conversation, Ally's parents were not thrilled with the fact that Greg was nearly ten years older and not going to church. But he appeared to be respectable, kind, and was a successful man, aptly and quite capable of taking care of their daughter. Acknowledging that he was her choice of which they could do nothing, conceded and gave their blessing to the marriage, but also wondered where the engagement ring was.

And so did Ally. She just knew since he wanted to ask her parents formally, that a ring would surely be produced as proof of his proposal. Again, she wouldn't dare ask.

Greg and Ally had long discussions over this issue of faith. He had no objections to children allowed to be raised Christian, if ever there would be any from their union. Ally was satisfied. She knew this was the convincing factor in her parents giving their blessing. She hoped and prayed that as time goes on, he would change and someday come into the faith. Even though she wanted her parents' blessing in her decision to marry Greg, they knew how they felt would not have prevented her from going through with the marriage. She had fallen deeply in love, and nothing else mattered.

It was on this visit that Greg had arranged for them to spend the weekend at Huntington Beach at the Hyatt Regency where they had first met. This would be their last time there as singles. He had contacted Toni and Jessica months before to tell them about his plan to surprise Ally. Greg wanted his proposal to be extra special. For this exceptional occasion, he wanted Jessica and Toni to be there and this time they all would be staying as guests at the Hyatt Regency. He wanted to replay as close as possible that summer evening almost one and a half years ago when they first met. Toni was not too happy about Jessica coming though, but Greg didn't think that it would be the same without her. He assured Toni that his brother Jack wouldn't be there.
"Good," said Toni. "Maybe we won't have to look for her this time." He laughed, remembering that whole fiasco, but even now, Toni didn't think it was so funny, recalling what she and Ally had gone through. Greg wanted this to be a huge surprise for Ally. This time he was going to ask her to marry him right there in the same dining room at the resort. He wanted the same place where they came for dinner when they first met on the beach. It would be only the three of them this time for dinner.

The whole occasion was like déjà vu. They packed their bags with swim gear, outfits for the weekend, and dresses for the big occasion. Ally had no idea about Greg's plans. She just knew that he was flying in to speak with her parents to ask them formally for her hand in marriage, but had no idea that he was going to propose to her that weekend. Along with her friends, the plan was to convince her of how nice it would be for she and her two friends to spend the weekend together again at Huntington Beach, but this time in style. Of course, she had objections, but knew that if the girls found out they would never have let her live it down, plus, he insisted. He also told her that he wanted to have dinner with the three of them Saturday evening like they had done before. Unbeknownst to her, the girls knew all about their stay and dinner with her and Greg.

Since they had the whole weekend paid for, they took full advantage of it beginning with a huge breakfast at the hotel. Their whole day was spent between the dining room, the exercise room, the pool, and the spa, being pampered, groomed, and fed. During their activities, they decided to go back to the room early to rest up before their dinner that evening. Looking around at their suite, they oooed and ahhhed about the lives of the rich. Greg had gotten them a plush suite unlike anything any of them had ever had before. Through the doors was a huge balcony with a view that was breathtaking. They couldn't imagine living a life like this. Stretched out on the lavish gold colored sofa and following Ally with her eyes as she walked across the room on her way to the balcony, Jessica commented,

"Just think Ally, you're going to be one of them."

"What are you talking about, Jessica? What do you mean, 'one of them'… one of whom?"

"I mean, you're going have lots of jewelry, designer clothes, and, of course, money, like them…the rich," saying the last two words in a dialect as if she was a snobbish old English woman.

"Money doesn't mean anything to me, Jessica."

"Oh, come on, Ally. Don't tell me that you're going to keep on living and dressing the same way you do now. Are you going to refuse to live that life style?"

"Oh, Jessica, leave her alone," Toni interjected. She could hear Jessica's interrogation going on from the bathroom where she had been putting on nail polish even through the noise of the hair dryer that she was using to dry her nails. She stepped out into the room where they were.

"What…so what if Greg has money? Is that a bad thing? What has all his money made him? He's a real down-to-earth person. Besides, you're here at the Hyatt Regency, aren't you? …and for free, I must add," said Toni, snapping her fingers in the air.

Jessica didn't say another word. She only turned over and eventually fell off to sleep. Ally looked at Toni and smiled. After her nails were dried, she went into her room to try to rest up as well before the evening began. But Ally couldn't sleep. She was too excited and scared. What Jessica had said made her wonder just what lay ahead for her in this family. Would she be able to adapt? She had already met one obstacle… his mother.

The entire evening was like a dream. They walked to the entrance of the dining room. It was the same setting with classical music playing in the background. When everyone was seated, Ally looked across at Greg, but in her mind's eye, she replayed that entire day nearly a year and a half ago beginning with the first time she looked up and saw him standing with the backdrop of the sunlight surrounding him and that night at the restaurant in this very room. To think that that same guy wanted to marry her had to be a dream. It was truly a Cinderella story. "Somebody, anybody, wake me up," she thought. "Ally, Ally… "Slightly raising her voice with a melodic tune, Jessica chimed, "Oh Aaally, where arrre you?"

"Oh, I'm sorry. I was thinking about the first time we came here. Shortly after they had been seated and the waiter walked to the table to take their orders, he soon came back with their meals. During the meal, they were reminiscing about everything that had happened that evening, intentionally leaving out Jessica's shenanigans changing the subject each time she tried to bring it up. They asked about the other people who had been with them that night, making innocent jokes, laughing, and poking fun. As they were finishing up their meal, Greg asked if anyone wanted dessert.

"Oh no. None for me, I'm stuffed," Ally said.

"Oh, come on," Toni urged. "I'm going to get something."

"Yeah, come on, Ally. I'm going to get something too. You have to at least taste it. I asked them to make this special dessert just for you to remember when we first met," Greg said smiling.

"Okay, but I really don't remember ordering dessert that night. I certainly won't be able to finish it all. You guys will have to share it with me."

"No," Greg said, "It's especially made for you."

Jessica blurted, "We're getting our own."

The waiter came with four silver covered trays. Greg had arranged for the dessert to be brought in on covered dishes after dinner. The waiter first placed Jessica's dish in front of her then proceeded with the others. Ally was last to be served. When they each removed their cover there was some type of fancy dessert dish. But Ally hesitated. "Come on, Ally. Let's see what's so special about your dessert," Toni said. When she lifted the cover she almost screamed, but caught herself and covered her mouth with her hands after a tiny noise escaped from a wide-open mouth, but not before the patrons nearby looked to find out what was going on. She stared at the uncovered dish. What she thought was dessert was a huge diamond engagement ring. Feeling light-headed, her hands were grasping the sides of the chair to gain her balance as she stared at the diamond ring that was lying on a china plate. She was totally shocked. She had no idea that Greg would be proposing marriage there.

"How could you guys not tell me?" she said softly through tears of joy.

"Why would we tell you? It was supposed to be a surprise, silly," said Toni.

Greg took the ring from the plate, got on one knee and looked right into Ally's eyes. "Will you marry me, Ally?"

At this time, other patrons and employees who had stopped eating to see what the commotion was about.

"Yes.., yes…, yes," Ally exclaimed in a crescendo. He took her hand and placed the ring on her left ring finger. She reached out and hugged Greg around his neck then kissed him gently on the lips. Jessica and Toni were snapping pictures of the whole event. The patrons all started to clap and some came over to congratulate her and to see the ring. It was indeed beautiful and large. The bright white gold band sparkled with smaller diamonds embedded and continued surrounding a brilliant pear shaped five-carat diamond that sat in the center.

Jessica looked at the ring as she turned to Greg and said, "Now, where's my surprise?" "What are you talking about, Jessica?"

"Didn't Jack come?"

"Sorry, I'm afraid not," Greg responded.

"Why not? He was here that day."

"Look Jessica, it's not about you, okay," Toni said being quite irritated over her behavior. "This night is for Ally. Jessica, you are incorrigible."

"I'm sorry, Ally. Congratulations. So when's the wedding?" Jessica asked Greg.

"We haven't gotten that far yet. You'll have to ask Ally about that," Greg answered.

"I don't know, Jessica. I just found out tonight myself," Ally said while holding her hand out gazing at her ring and smiling. They all laughed.

"Well, keep me posted," said Jessica.

"Of course, I will."

Although Ally lived in California during their engagement, she never went back until after they were married, except for weeklong visits to see her parents, or sometimes for special occasions, some weekends or when Greg could get time away from the business. After they were married, Greg would fly as often as he could, but would pay many times for her parents to visit them in New

Jersey.

     Greg didn't want to wait so; they were married within the year. The wedding was small, with about seventy-five guests. Ally wanted the wedding to be in California to be closer to her parents, relatives, and friends who would then be able to attend. Most of the guests were neighbors, former classmates, coworkers, some of her close relatives, and members of their church. There were not too many out-of-town guests, except for Greg's parents and a few of their friends. Jack, being the brother and the best man was, of course, there, along with his uncle and aunt, Nancy's estranged brother and his wife were surprisingly there. Never feeling welcomed by their aunt, his sons, her nephews, declined the invitation, but sent a card expressing their best wishes. Greg insisted and paid for his uncle and his wife's flight and hotel expenses. Both Greg and his dad were adamant about inviting them, even though it was against his mother's unreasonable protests. Greg wanted them to be there and John supported him. John could never understand the detached relationship between Nancy and her brother, and usually stayed out of that family conflict unless it became too unreasonable. And this time, it was irrational. Her brother never quite understood either why their relationship was estranged.

     Throughout the wedding plans, Nancy hadn't been very cooperative. Fortunately, Ally was in California, far enough away that Nancy was not able to sabotage the wedding. Sure that these were the same tactics she used with Janice, Ally wouldn't give in to her threats, nor could she be bought. She never let Greg know what was going on between her and his mother, until she threatened not to attend. Ally thought that she had better let Greg know about this new contrary move. Greg told his father about her bold reluctance to attend the wedding. Hearing about this nonsensical standoff, John became infuriated about Nancy's behavior. To abate the immensity of his anger, he decided to wait awhile before approaching her so as not to have an all out quarrel. After dinner the following day, he decided that the issue needed to be addressed. When she tried to justify her actions, he again became fervent, remembering what his son had gone through after the sudden debacle of his first marriage attempt. John displayed emotions contrary to his character and behavior. This time he didn't turn away, but intervened even though Greg, after urging her diplomatically, yet acrimoniously, left the choice up to her. This time he compelled her to attend in a tone of voice totally unfamiliar to her. He looked directly into her eyes,

"Look, Nancy, you've been interfering in the lives of those boys all their life. And no, I wasn't able to be there for them many times throughout their childhood like I wanted to, but I was looking out for their future and ours and with your help, I was able to build that future... for all of us. But they are men now. We've taught them all we can and have given them the tools they'll need to shape their own destiny. It's time to let go and allow them to use those tools we've given them to decide their own future and if they make a mistake, they can blame no one except themselves. So, get over it. You will be there."

Stunned and speechless, she could only stare at him in amazement, then turned on the balls of her feet and whisked herself away, appalled. Her anger was so intense that her thoughts seemed as though they could have been heard. She was outraged. Almost thinking out loud, she couldn't believe that John would speak to her in this manner. He had never accused her of meddling in their sons' lives before. Had this "gold digger" influenced her husband too? She had already noticed the changes in Greg since he had met her. What did he know about their sons... her sons? He was never there. What does he know about hard work? This was the hard work, trying to raise two children alone. "He doesn't know them. They don't even know themselves," she thought. As she thought about what John had said, she decided to cooperate. She would at least be cordial. "I'll go to the wedding and act the part of the gleeful mother-in-law," she thought, "...but, I will never recognize that 'opportunist' as a member of this family," she vowed under her breath.

A week later, the wedding took place at Ally's church in California. Everything went perfectly. Greg insisted on paying for the entire wedding and reception. Her parents could contribute very little. His mother was furious. It only confirmed her reasons for Greg not to marry Ally. Her family didn't even have enough money to pay for their own daughter's wedding. They broke all the rules of wedding etiquette. Keeping her vow, Nancy was unwillingly cooperative and spuriously courteous to everyone throughout the day. She and John danced and laughed as everyone in the wedding party told their anecdotes and toasted to well wishes, for many years of bliss, and good fortune for the newly wedded couple. The whole day and into the evening, Nancy's pretentiousness of joy went practically unnoticed, except by Greg. Toni was the maid of honor and caught the bouquet after much scrambling with the other wishful marriage seekers. When the garter was thrown, Jack had scurried off pretending to be preoccupied in a conversation at the bar. Nancy caught his antics but was pleased as her face lit up with an insidious grin. Nevertheless, totally oblivious to any deviance, Ally was flying high in her dream come true. Greg had done so much to make everything happen; she was very much grateful for it all. The food was superb, the decorations were awesome, and the photographer was a true professional, taking pictures from beginning to end. Her fairytale story had come true. Jack, who was best man, had given the first toast of the evening to the bride and groom, but later after the traditional reception order of service was completed, he disappeared with Jessica, who was one of the bridesmaids.

Ally and Greg had arranged to go on their honeymoon immediately after the reception. After the reception, there were more pictures taken, hugs, and well wishes from relatives, friends, and guests. Gradually, they all began to leave the small ballroom. Nancy didn't want to stay any longer than necessary, so she had John get the return flight tickets for the same day of the wedding to leave directly after the reception ended. Ally's parents offered their home for them to stay overnight, knowing that they could afford much more than what they had to offer, but their gesture was sincere.

"Thank you, but we have to get back to New York tonight. I have to prepare for a meeting on Monday about a fundraising event," Nancy responded with such mendacity. Nancy couldn't imagine being crammed into their tiny little home, let alone a bedroom.

"Well, I know we live so far away from each other, so I don't know when we will see you again…maybe at the baby shower."

Ally's mother chuckled, but Nancy didn't find her comment even remotely amusing, but managed to conjure up a smile.

"Well, we have to go," she said urgently. "It was nice to have seen you both again."

"Yes, although the time we really got to know each other was short, I feel as though we've been friends for years," said Ally's mother. Nancy looked at her with a forged smile and no comment. John and Ally's dad shook hands and hugged her mother. "You're welcomed to come to our home anytime. Just give us a call so we'll know when you're coming," said Ally's mother as they got into the airport taxi.

Greg had the limousine take Ally's parents back to their house along with all of the many gifts that her friends had so graciously packed into the vehicle. Her parents were exhausted after such a long day and finally got a chance to sit down in the kitchen to relax with a cup of coffee. "You know,

Dad…" Ally's mom started calling her husband "Dad" after Ally was born. "…Greg's mother isn't very friendly, is she? And she doesn't seem too happy about this marriage either."

"Yeah, Mar, I noticed that too even from the start. Poor Ally, we have to pray hard for her. She may have some tough times ahead."

Chapter 14

Right after the wedding, Ally and Greg headed directly as planned to the airport to fly to Hawaii for their honeymoon. Coming back, they flew straight into New York to begin their lives as husband and wife. Ally shuddered at the thought as they rode in the taxi to the apartment. The honeymoon was like a two-week long date, but being a wife felt strange. Leaving California behind, she felt as though her former life had come to an abrupt halt, only to take off again and land in totally unfamiliar territory. Looking out the huge picture window but missing the awesome view from their 10th floor apartment only saw images through her mind's eye accompanied by a flood of questions that also swept through. "How do you begin being married?" she asked herself. "Should I ask Greg?" She thought of their bedroom. How awkward and strange it felt lying there next to him when he held onto her on their honeymoon. "Oh God,…the bedroom. Isn't this supposed to be natural? What's wrong with me?" She even thought of the possibility that he might be disappointed with her body or her lovemaking, or lack thereof. She felt so stupid. They never actually stayed together before; except for the time she had come to meet his parents. She stayed at his apartment, but now she would be sleeping in his bed… with him. She still felt embarrassed at the thought of having to take her clothes off in front of him even though she tried during the honeymoon, but wound up undressing in the bathroom throughout the entire honeymoon. Greg tried to convince her to relax knowing that he was the very first to explore this untouched and pristine territory that he had acquired. Again, she wondered if she really knew what to do to make love and was embarrassed at the thought. She had never been intimate with a man before, only going as far as kissing before their honeymoon and wondered how disappointed he must have felt with the same during the honeymoon. Greg had been terribly patient with her all during that whole time, occupying their time and exhausting themselves with all sorts of activities, tours, and exploring the beautiful sights that Hawaii had to offer them. Even after the wedding, he agreed to give her more time, but was suffering inside. He loved her so much and wanted to wholly experience the true love that he had for her. She wouldn't dare ask if he was okay with waiting for fear of finding out his true frustration. They still hadn't yet consummated the marriage, even after several days back from their honeymoon. All these questions were causing angst and apprehension, so she tried to blot them from her mind for now, but knew she would have to get used to undressing in front of him and performing her role as a wife with intimacy eventually. Another thing that bothered her was what would she do while he was at work? She thought about trying to make a plan for her first day as a wife. Having quit her job because of the move left her somewhat empty as far as how she would spend her time. They had discussed before they were married that there was no need for her to work. He wanted his wife to take care of the home and help him if need be. Coming back to the moment, she realized that she had lapsed into a daydream. She looked at Greg who had walked over and stood looking out of the window. She wondered, but didn't ask what he was thinking. She had grown to love him more than she had ever thought possible and he loved her in return. She was going to do whatever it took to be a good wife and hopefully, someday be a mother. As the weeks went by, Ally became more affectionate and eventually more passionate in her lovemaking. Greg could feel this change and was very responsive to her. Their love for one another grew immensely. He couldn't wait to start a family, but Ally felt they should wait to get to know each other more before having to give their attention to someone else.

It was exactly a year later that Ally announced to Greg that she was pregnant. Even though secretly she would rather have waited at least another year, but he kept reminding her that he was getting older and wanted to be able to enjoy growing up with his children. When she told him, he practically leaped off the floor. He was elated, grabbing her and kissing her all over her face and neck. He couldn't wait to tell his parents that they were going to be grandparents. Neither of them knew how his mother would take the news, but Ally's intuition about her mother-in-law was correct. She knew that even this wouldn't change her. Whenever the subject came up, her responses were always negative. She would often try to discourage them by suggesting that they should wait and not rush into such a daunting task of parenting. Adding further in her efforts to thwart any plans to add yet another undesired addition to this family was her warning that this would only add enormous responsibility and stress to their unfamiliar lives as newlyweds. She was still not accepting to this already intolerable mistake of marriage. Further, in her insincere act of concern, she explained emphatically in detail, that marriage was already demanding in itself and required much time to adjust. It galled her, the thought of the two of them being married. Subsequently, her advice and concerns had only malicious intent and said those things only hoping to cause some chance of their undesired union to shatter. Privately, she would try to persuade Greg to wait and make sure that their relationship was going to last before bringing a child into the picture. Greg never responded to her admonitions, convinced that his mother would never change and just accepted how things were with her. He did love his mother in spite of her ways, but as long as he had Ally, nothing else mattered.

Eight and a half months later, Ally gave birth to a little girl who they decided to name Sage. She was born a few weeks earlier than her scheduled date of arrival. All the family went to the hospital, even Jack, who had never had any interest in children or family life …not one of his own, anyway. Nancy reluctantly went simply to make a showing so as not to expose her true feelings of discontent. Sage was a beautiful, adorable happy baby. Even at birth, she appeared to be smiling. Because she was premature, she had to stay in the hospital longer than the normal stay, for observations but was doing well and soon went home.

Several months before Sage was born, Ally and Greg had moved into a four bedroom colonial in a plush community outside New Jersey, not far from his parents. Five years later, they had an addition to the family. Unfortunately, to their devastation, two years prior there had been a miscarriage. Nancy was secretly overjoyed, but of course, expressed her insincere sympathy and regret, only hoping that the loss would be the last effort to try for another. In her deviant mind, she thought by adding children, Ally was only trying to secure her position in their family. It was not their intention to wait so long, but after the miscarriage, Ally had had problems conceiving. The doctors felt that it was probably due to anxiety and told her to relax and concentrate on taking care of the other child. She was young and had no need to rush. But soon after his advice, she conceived and the new baby was a boy and after much discussion, it was decided to name him, Casey. Casey was Greg's grandfather's name. His dad was very proud and honored by their decision. Nancy, feigning thoughtfulness and fairness, tried to persuade Ally to name the baby after her own dad. She tried to convince her that since she was an only child, it may have been her only chance to give such an honor to her own father who had no sons. Her concern was only selfishness. She didn't want any acknowledgement that Ally's children were her grandchildren and never showed any love or tenderheartedness towards them. In fact, she could barely bring herself to touch them. Whenever she saw them, she would stroke their cheeks with the back of her hand or maybe give a light peck on their foreheads, as a show of affection, of which there was none.

Primarily, holidays were spent at Greg's parents' home largely because Nancy would never have allowed Greg and Ally to host any of the family holiday functions, or any other function, for that matter, for she loved entertaining out of sheer selfishness and pride. She had never accepted their marriage and rarely would she visit their home. The only time she would go anywhere near their home was for the children's birthday parties. On those occasions, Ally would appeal to Greg to speak to her about having their own children's parties in their own home, (she had even tried to take those occasions) other than that, her interaction with her grandchildren were limited to concerts, recitals, sporting events, or when there was a school event, which she would attend only to make the appearance of the "adoring grandmother." Secretly, Ally had hoped that once there were grandchildren, Nancy would warm up to her, but she didn't. As the children grew older, they could sense her apathy especially Sage. She never wanted to visit them, but she was crazy about her grandfather, John. She adored Ally's parents and would often ask why they couldn't live closer to them. Ally's parents were not able to visit as much as they would have liked, but they stayed in touch often by phone. For the children's birthdays, Greg would pay for their flight to New Jersey and for other special occasions. For at least a week they would stay which gave them more time to spend with their grandchildren. Nancy insisted on hosting almost every other special event. This routine went on until the children got older, at which time they no longer wanted to go to their fraternal grandparents' home unless coerced by their parents.

Before Sage was ten years old, the marriage had begun to become strained. Constantly, mulling over their situation, Ally thought back to the early days of their marriage to the present to try to figure out if there were any signs of a breakdown. The business was doing well, but the traveling that he and Jack had to do caused him to be away from home often and sometimes for long periods of time, especially if it entailed being out of the country. Before any children, Ally would travel with him. Even then, he had conferences, spoke at seminars, met potential clients, and attended meetings. Sometimes those lasted well into the evening, which depleted much of their time together. Occasionally, she would mention to him how lonely she felt when he was away. He would apologize, but still could not understand why this was such a problem. While in meetings, she had the whole day to do whatever she wanted to do. And it was she, who had insisted on coming with him in the first place, was his response.

During those times before there were children, she got a chance to visit other states, cities, and countries. Places she would never have had a chance to see had it not been for her marriage to Greg. There would be sightseeing tours, museums, shopping and exploring the history of each place they visited. She was able to do whatever she pleased and she loved it…that is, in the beginning. At first, he allowed her to spend as much as she wanted and she began to love shopping. Finding dresses, shoes, and jewelry that she bought from other countries, especially from Paris, to wear to dinner parties, social events, and family affairs would make her the envy of the other wives. But that was then. Many times, he reminded her of the opportunities she had that many other women only dreamed of having. That was true, but how many dresses and pairs of shoes could she buy, and seeing the same sites became a bit boring. Loneliness had become her companion. During those early times, when they were childless, he urged her to change her thrifty spending habits and not be such a penny pincher. "Go ahead and buy what you want. We can afford it. I want you to look good and have nice things," he would say. But Nancy had begun to chide him and cautioned him about her spending. Telling him how she had become careless and needed to be watched more carefully with her wastefulness, as she called it, and to curb her freedom to spend so much. Contrary to what Nancy thought, money was never the reason Ally married Greg. She didn't care about having the liberty to shop or spend and verbally denied the desire to do so. Shopping for her was only done as a pastime…to help fill the empty time when she was alone. Money was meaningless to her.

Her parents had taught her how to be content with little. She only did those things to occupy her time and he had even encouraged her.

"Greg, that was then. I don't do those things anymore. In fact, we hardly do anything anymore. Even then, it was hard being alone. I know that you have to help with the business, but whatever happened to the days when we were dating?" she asked during one of their seemingly now regular spats.

"Remember when you would come all the way to California just to see me, and you came many times. Back then, we were together more and you still managed to accomplish your obligations to the business. Greg, I need you. Not only do I need you, but our children need their father." Even now, he couldn't understand her frustration.

"Yes, but we were dating then. That's what people do when they're dating they go on dates. That was then, and this is now. Now we're married," Greg responded harshly.

"Then …then what about the kids, Greg? Sage will be ten years in a couple of years, and Casey needs a father figure…you. He's only three, for God's sake."

"Where have I heard this story before?" he asked rhetorically and with sarcasm. "Oh yes, my mother. That's all I heard all my life was her whining about my dad not being home enough."

"Why can't Jack pick up a little more of the traveling responsibility?" she asked. "He's not married. Or maybe train some other senior employee to handle more."

"Oh, so now you're trying to tell me how the business should be run?" He responded with a sneer in his voice. These arguments had begun to happen with more frequency. As they drifted farther apart, the altercations became more intensified until he gradually became so desensitized and apathetic to the situation, that he barely spoke a word or responded to anything she would say. With his money and good looks, he didn't have to deal with her. There was always some other woman willing to hold out her "compassionate and understanding arms" for him to fall into if necessary and with no ties. At first, there were a few which were of no consequence, but only someone with whom to vent. Then there was one. In the beginning, he felt guilty, but after some consolation and advice from his mother, he decided that maybe they should not waste anymore of each other's time and suggested that maybe they should consider getting a divorce. This revelation was devastating to her. As much as she didn't want to, especially since her parents had warned her, she knew that she eventually had to call them. Ally waited for weeks and hadn't told them because she thought there was a chance her situation would improve, hoping that maybe it was a passing phase. Besides, knowing that they were up in age and living so far away, they wouldn't be able to help anyway. As their relationship grew worse, Ally felt that she had no other choice but to tell them. They were deeply distraught as was expected by this dreadful news, but never rebuked her for not listening to their warning and not following what she knew was right and was "out of God's will". They felt extremely frustrated and utterly helpless having no means of giving her anything except consolation. The only solution they had to offer was for her to come back home with the children, but Ally didn't want to take the children so far away from their father. Often they called to try to comfort and support her with their prayers and encouragement, but felt powerless that they could do nothing else to rectify their only child's plummeting life. "Ally, we love you and please don't stop praying," they would say at the end of every conversation. Ally would only give an affirmation in her response, but thought her dilemma seemed to be hopeless in spite of her intense prayers.

Constantly she prayed day and night that her marriage to be reconciled and strengthened. But now, prayer to her seemed useless, so they only ceased, and eventually so did her Sundays at church. Other than her parents and Toni, she had no one else to talk to. Since she had not worked, there was no real possibility to have met anyone with whom she could be friends with, except for members of the society groups that Nancy had encouraged her to join. They had only snubbed her from the first introduction, of which Nancy knew, would happen. Some of those same people were her neighbors and the parents of the children at the most prestigious school where her own children attended and were even friends. There was virtually no chance to have made any true friends with whom she could confide. They were only associates and acquaintances, and there were plenty, but no one that she could trust enough to call a friend. Her only true friend still lived back in California, Toni.

When she left, throughout the years they continued to stay in contact either by phone or by mail. Toni was the only person to whom she trusted and confided in. They hardly ever got to see one another except on occasion when she and the kids went to visit her parents. Sometimes even Greg was able to go. Toni had gotten married herself and eventually had children of her own. Upon hearing the news about Ally's impending divorce, she was devastated. Seeing from the beginning, the great love that Ally and Greg had had for each other, and now this calamity was unfathomable. Never, ever had she thought that Ally and Greg would ever speak about getting a divorce. It was incredible to believe that they even argued.

"Oh, Ally, I'm so sorry to hear this. I can't believe this is happening to you and Greg."

"I can't believe it either."

"I feel so badly that I'm not there to be with you."

"I know. I wish you were here too."

"Did you try going to a marriage counselor?"

"Oh, yes. I begged him to go, but he was dead set against it."

"I can't believe this." Toni was crushed at all that she was hearing. "Look, I'm going to keep in touch even more than I have before. Believe me; you are often in my thoughts, more often than you know. We just get so busy and caught up in our own lives that we don't take the time to call our friends. But Ally, please don't hesitate to let me know if I can do anything to help you… even if it's just to talk." Toni was overcome with hurt for her friend.

"I will Toni and thanks for being there for me." They both hung up with eyes filled with tears.

"How did we get to this point?" She would ask herself day after day. The thought of she and Greg not being together never entered her mind when they married. They both vowed, "… 'til death do we part" and meant it, or so she thought. At least she did. All she had ever wanted was for them to be together and have a family. That was all she had ever asked for. She didn't want a divorce and did everything she could to avert the subject. Often she prayed that God would not allow this union to end. Not wanting to upset the children, they both tried to keep their discussions and conversations as normal as possible in front them. But even so, Sage knew that something had gone wrong when she overheard them bickering one day in their bedroom. She felt a foreboding of losing her dad and not ever being able to see him again. Even though they were confident that the kids were unaware of what was going on, Ally could see changes in Casey's behavior that maybe he was troubled, and Sage did not seem to be the zesty "tween" that she had been. Bringing these observations to Greg's attention, she tried to convince him that they go to family counseling again and again, but he refused and denied that there were any signs that indicated that anything was affecting the children. Because of this badgering, as he described it, eventually he moved into one of the guest bedrooms to avoid any more confrontations and would come in from work well after the children had gone to bed.

In just a few months, Ally felt that her whole life was crashing down around her. There was no place to go for help. There was only one last resort and that was to go see his parents. She called John first who had always been more caring. He promised to speak to Greg and try to talk some sense into him even though knowing it would probably be pointless. Out of absolute desperation, she went to plead with Nancy face to face to convince Greg to stay in the marriage. Nancy opened the door and pretended to be pleasantly surprised.

"Oh, hi Ally. This is a surprise. How are the kids?" She asked after turning away and walking down the long hallway with Ally trailing behind.

"They're fine," Ally answered curtly. She knew that Nancy was only sweet-talking. "Come on in. I was in the kitchen when I heard the door. Can I get you something?" "Come on, Nancy. Let's cut to the chase."

Nancy stopped and turned around with a look of surprise.

"What on earth are you talking about?"

"I know that you know about what's going on with Greg and me."

"Look, Ally, I try to stay out of other…"

"Nancy, would you please just speak to Greg." Ally had cut off her phony attempt to respond. "Nancy, I love Greg! We need to be together to raise our children. Can't you just help us…please." she implored.

"Ally, I'll try, but Greg is a grown man. He's not going to listen to his mother. I know you wanted to have kids, but you may have to start thinking about what you might have to do without Greg. I know it's too late now, but I've always felt that you got married before you and Greg really got to know each other that well. Then you decided to have kids and…."

Ally cut off her rambling.

"What are you saying, Nancy? We both loved each other very much, and we knew each other very well. And we both wanted children…. Oh why did I even come to you anyway?" she said, turning away, walking back down the long hallway towards the door. Ally stopped and turned around looking at Nancy, who had turned and was now pacing close behind. She had come to a screeching halt and was looking right at Ally's angry face.

"I know you've never accepted our marriage or the children, but I thought at least you would encourage your son to stay for his children's sake. Even if you don't want them, they are here and do need a father." Ally turned again and proceeded to head toward the door again.

"That's not true, Ally. How could you say something like that? I've always tried to involve myself in their lives. Did I ever miss anything you ever had for those children? We both came. John and I both went to games, their birthday parties, the graduations, the recitals… we were always there."

Nancy had finally caught up with her again, as she again turned around. Ally's face twisted with rage as she said bitterly, "That's right… you and John. I'm sure that John was your only motivation. I'm also convinced that you had something to do with why our marriage is falling apart."

"Ally, that is not true," Nancy said weakly, defending herself.

"Well, you certainly have the ability to help if you wanted to, but you won't. You know that he'll listen to you. You've always controlled him. So now you're finally getting what you've always wanted."

Nancy said nothing as she watched Ally walk out the door and down the path to the driveway.

Later that same day, John immediately confronted Nancy when he got in from work about what should be done about Greg and Ally's marriage crisis.

"I don't know what's gotten into Greg. I tried talking to him, but he doesn't want to say what happened or what's going on."

"Well, I can't blame him, John. It isn't our business."

"What do you mean, not our business? Don't you care about our grandchildren?"

"Of course I do. But what can we do?" she asked feigning innocence.

"Well, he's not listening to me. But maybe he'll listen to you. You've always had more influence over both of them … much more than I ever had. Or maybe you don't want to help them. You've never really liked Ally anyway. You think I never noticed how you treated her and the kids. It's a wonder she didn't leave him years ago because of you." John had blurted out feelings that he had held in for years. She looked at him in amazement, "John, you mean…are you…? Oh, no, I can't believe that are you accusing me of breaking them up. Look, John, don't get angry with me because Greg's marriage is falling apart. I didn't have anything to do with it," she said defensively.

"Didn't you?" John walked away to the bar, poured himself a drink, went into his office and slammed the door behind him.

Chapter 15

Greg had been saying for a while that he was going to move into one of the guest rooms since he made his final decision to go through with the divorce. Ally gave up trying to persuade him to try any solution to salvage their marriage. Sage had become more introverted. She mainly stayed in her room to herself. No longer did she ask if her friends could come over and Ally noticed that Casey no longer asked to go out to play with friends or even go over for sleepovers. She insisted that the children continue with their after school activities and sports commitments, although Sage constantly made excuses not to go. She began to worry about how detached Sage had become. She also noticed that calls for Sage had started to abate. Quiet and withdrawn, Sage would only retreat to her room saying that she needed to study and do some reading. One day Ally noticed that she was unusually somber and went to her room to talk to her. Gently knocking on the door, she then turned the knob and slowly opened it. "Sage, honey, are you okay?" She was lying across her bed.

"Yes, Mom, I'm fine," she said in a monotone.

"Sage, I can tell that you're upset about something. Is anything wrong? Did something happen at school? I know something's wrong. I'm not leaving this room until you tell me what it is. You know you can always come to me about anything, so what's bothering you?" Finally, she sat up holding onto the pillow that she had balled up under her head. Clutching it, she told her mother about a discussion that she had had with a friend from school. "Mom, do I have to leave my school and are you and Dad going to get a divorce?" Sage asked, sadly looking straight into her mother's eyes.

"Who told you that?"

"One of my friends at school heard her mom talking to someone on the phone. She said that I might have to leave the school because you and dad are getting a divorce. Is that true mom?"

"Well, Sage, I was going to talk to you about your dad and me. But first, I wanted to make sure that it was the final decision. No, you are not leaving that school. And I'm so sorry that you had to hear it from someone else." Ally grabbed Sage and hugged her tightly. Their faces were streaming with tears.

"Nosey people... They're always gossiping about other people's lives," she muttered to herself.

Sage pulled out of her mother's grasp.

"Are you and Dad getting a divorce?"

"Yes. And I'm so sorry. I should have told you what was going on."

Sage fell backwards on the bed, grasping her pillow and weeping into it profusely holding it over her face.

"Sage, honey, please don't cry. Everything will be okay. We'll be fine. Please don't cry. I don't want Casey to get upset." She tried to grab her daughter and hold her, but Sage clung to her tear soaked pillow. "Sweetie, please, you'll make yourself sick. We will be fine. I promise."

"I don't want to go to that school anymore Mom," Sage muttered through the pillow.

Greg was never there for the tears and sorrow. He would get home well after the children were in bed and asleep. On some weekends, if he was there they might have breakfast together, but he would be sure to leave well before anyone got a chance to ask him any questions. But one morning Casey did manage to ask a question before he could scurry out of the door. Greg had poured the last of his coffee into the sink and said, "Well, gotta go." Casey was still sitting at the table when his dad was walking away towards the door.

"Dad, are you coming to my soccer game today?" Everyone's eyes were fixed on him waiting for a response.

"Well, Casey, I didn't know that you had a game today."

"Dad we have a game every Saturday. You used to come."

"Casey, I'm not sure, but I will certainly try. I'll try to leave the office early."

"Do you really have to go today?"

"Yes, son. I'm meeting a special client who could only meet me today."

With a look of disgust, Sage got up from the table, went to her room and slammed the door. Grabbing his keys from the ledge, he then walked out. Casey looked at his mom with tears in his eyes. She went over and hugged him.

"Casey, Sage and I will be there. I'll even give your granddad a call. I'm sure he'll come. And if your dad can close his meeting early, I'm sure that he'll be there too." Ally was so tired of defending and making excuses for Greg. She couldn't believe that he was the same person that she had met that eventful day on that beautiful California beach. No one could pretend to be that kind. Maybe this was the fear that her parents had of marrying someone out of her faith. It was as if he had no conscience.

It had been two weeks after the argument that Greg told Ally that he would be moving out of the house. He told her that the next night would be the last time he would be staying in the house. That night she had been waiting in the living room on the sofa when he finally got in. This particular night she hadn't had the glass of wine that she started to drink every night to help her to sleep. The depression from the continuous thoughts of a broken marriage and the loss of her most beloved husband caused her to have many nights of insomnia. She was going to ask that night, but fearing what the answer would be, decided to wait until the following morning to ask him to stay with her in their bed since it would be his last day in their home. She still loved him as much as she ever had even though his treatment towards her was the contrary. He agreed, but warned her that nothing would change. The following night, she wore a white see-through negligee beneath a white silk long robe. He sat on the king sized bed and watched her disrobe. He had had a drink or two, but wasn't drunk. When she got into the bed asked, "Aren't you coming to bed? You did say that you would spend your last night with me." He took his clothes off down to his underwear and got into the bed on the other side. She turned off the light of the frosted glass globe lamp on her night table and proceeded to try to entice him by touching and kissing his body gently. He tried to respond, but finally apologized and turned over as if she was a stranger. She laid there staring in the dark at the ceiling that she knew was there, but couldn't see until the sunset pierced around the sides of the closed silver colored vertical shades. With tears still flowing down the temples of her head onto the pillow, she knew that it was over. All through the night, the song by Bonnie Raitt that she loved so much played over and over in her head, "I Can't Make You Love Me." She would always feel sadness and wonder who that song was written for, after last night she knew it was written for her.

In the beginning, after they had separated, Greg managed to squeeze the kids in on some of his free time and Casey so looked forward to those times. In fact, this is how Ally found out that he was dating. She knew that he had already started seeing other women, even when they were still living together, but she never believed that any were serious. Even after some years had passed, after accepting their heartbreaking demise, whenever she thought about him with someone else, she knew that none of his relationships was serious. Nancy would never have allowed it. She never knew Greg as this person. It was as if he had no feelings for anyone other than himself. Greg had become Jack.

Chapter 16

Nearly five years had passed since Ally and Greg were divorced. The house had been sold three years prior right after their divorce and they went their separate ways. Sage no longer had to make excuses for not going out with her dad when they had made plans because he never showed up. Eventually, he never bothered to even call. She was fourteen now and started hanging out with kids that she had met at the new school where she had been transferred. The separation brought on times where his visits had become less and less. A year after the divorce, contact with their father had totally ended. The children were placed in public schools. Although John had offered to continue paying for their private school education, Ally refused. Nancy could not believe Ally's decision when Greg told them what had happened at the divorce proceedings. Although in the decree Ally had stated that she did not want anything, the judge gave her a chance for reconsideration,; she declined. Nancy's suspicions were debunked by Ally's humility. She almost felt guilty.

Ally was so distraught and devastated over the divorce that she refused to accept any alimony or any other financial help that her in-laws had offered, especially since for some reason they had severed Greg's affiliation with the company. This act had surreptitiously been done apparently well before the divorce was finalized. She figured it was probably done out of fear of ever being sued, especially when she heard that Greg had even left the company and was now working for the competition. Still, Nancy would not acknowledge

Ally's good character. Greg continued to pay child support, but the amount decreased over time after he left the family company. Due to lower wages paid at his new employment, the support checks no longer came. Gradually, any contact with the children had dwindled, along with the support. Ally hadn't married Greg for his wealth so she never sued for child support. She had lived in mediocrity before and felt no real need to have more now. When she was single, she had no desire for more than what was necessary. But even in her current situation, she was still determined to do whatever she had to do to make it and make the children happy without their handouts. She knew it was not going to be easy, especially since the kids were so used to a higher standard of living. But what drove her more was the need to get as far away from Greg as she could. For as much as she had been through and even after all the time that had passed, she was still in love with him and hated herself for it. He obviously had started a new life and was living it.

With the money from the sale of the house, they were able to move into a very chic apartment in an upscale part of town, but it was nothing compared to what they once had. Greg had allowed her to have the house, keep all of the elegant furniture they had acquired through the years, the car, and whatever else she wanted after the divorce settlement. She also had thousands of dollars worth of jewelry and for now no place to wear it. Except for a few pieces that she took to the apartment, the rest was kept in the bank safe. At that time, they had enough money and she didn't have to work and planned not to look for a job until Casey was at least in middle school. Some years after the divorce and now in their new residence on some evenings out of loneliness she would get dressed and go out to one of the classy bar and restaurant style establishments downtown. After the kids had gone to bed, as a means of detachment from her very convoluted and unsocial life she would go out to have a drink or two. Her style of dress had changed to be more outgoing and her makeup was made to emphasize her more attractive features. Sage now a teenager and was now old enough to look after her brother Casey if she was out. At first, she felt uncomfortable about leaving them alone even for a little while and only did her drinking at home. Needing to get out, she would always leave a note on her bed if ever they might awaken and look for her while she was out or if they needed to get in touch in case of an emergency.

It was on one of her outings on an extremely hot summer night in that she met someone while sitting alone at the bar, which became her usual spot.

Feeling that she was being watched, out of the corner of her eye, she noticed a man sitting at the end of the bar having a drink. Before long, he got up and boldly sat down right beside her. After introducing himself, he offered to buy her a drink. Later in their conversation, he mentioned that he had seen her at the bar several times before and thought he recognized her. It turned out that at one time he was an employee at Greg's family's company and remembered her as being Greg's wife. Colin Jacobs, he told her was his name. He had once been a program developer for the company. A fairly nice looking man, not as tall, and a bit younger than, but still not as attractive as Greg, she thought. As would be her tendency, she would always size up the men that she would notice or meet and compare them with Greg. Colin was a very loquacious fellow, which she liked because she didn't have to answer a lot of questions, especially since he was talking so much about himself. He talked about how he had moved up in the company. Learning more about his skill and being more creative, he eventually was promoted to a management position he told her, chattering seemingly nonstop. She also learned that Colin was divorced and thought that it was fortunate for him that there were no children out of the marriage. His wife had left him for another man after only two years of marriage. Of course, she was saddened and empathetic since their situations were quite similar. Their almost identical circumstances did seem to her a bit ironic, but he appeared to be harmless, so they exchanged phone numbers and eventually began meeting at the same restaurant and talking on the phone quite often.

Because Colin started calling regularly and she was going out more frequently, Ally thought the kids should be told about her newfound friend… a man. They were not too excited about the news, especially Sage, who was quite upset. Casey seemed indifferent. He didn't care one way or the other, but Sage was really not happy about her mother's new male friend. They both would rather have seen their father come back into their lives. Eventually, they met him one evening when Ally had invited him over for dinner. He thought when he told them how well he knew their dad and had once worked with him that would make an impression on them. He soon found out that his words didn't make any difference to them. They were both aloof toward him, to his conversation and his presence. Immediately after dinner, they retreated straight to their rooms. He could tell that he definitely was not a hit. Ally tried to cheer him up by reminding him that they had just met for the first time, but later felt the need to reassure the kids that he was just a friend.

They continued going out off and on for months. Ally had begun to like Colin a lot and thoroughly enjoyed his company. He was someone who she could talk to and was fun to be with, plus he took her mind off Greg who still had a place in her heart. Talking to him gave her a feeling that there was still some hope that she could start enjoying her life again. She started dressing even more differently than before. The hems became shorter and the neckline lower exposing more cleavage, which she thought would make her more attractive, especially to the male species. Once he invited her over for dinner at his apartment. From the looks of his place, it was much less than the upward progression of his life that he had boasted so much about and had caused his career and salary to soar. Rather, it was a small barely furnished one-bedroom apartment, although he did live alone and really didn't have the need for anything larger. The furniture was old and worn, and he could have used cleaner and better-looking curtains at the windows. He tried to make excuses to explain its appearance and told her that his ex-wife had gotten the better end of the deal and this place was only temporary, and decided to hold off buying anything new until he found a better place to live. She never questioned him about it, but figured that his explanations were because he may have noticed the strange expressions on her face. She did feel a bit creepy and uncomfortable, constantly looking around to see if at any time something would go racing across the floor or crawling on the walls. For their future meetings, she preferred that he come to her place. He had been invited over for dinner many times and a couple of occasions had taken the kids out with them. The restaurants were always one of the family style chains, either for pizza or hamburgers. The children were not very interested and would rather not have gone out with them at all.

Very late one night, Colin called Ally sounding very distressed. He asked if he could come over because he needed to talk to her. She had decided to go to bed early that night and was already in bed when he called. It had been almost three months by now that they had begun seeing each other more often. Sounding desperate, he told her that there had been problems at work, which made his day almost unbearable, and desperately needed someone to talk to. He told her that he had thought about going out and getting drunk, but decided to call her instead. Sounding very much distressed, she acceded and allowed him to come over just to talk. Before that night, they had only spoken on the phone, gone out on movie or dinner dates, many times he had come to her place for dinner, after which, they would part ways. He knew exactly what time the kids went to bed so that there would not be any problem with him being there at this time. In fifteen minutes, there was a gentle knock at the door. She looked through the peephole and opened the door. Apparently, he was nearby when he called. His face was sullen, and his hair was disheveled. Stepping quickly over the threshold as if being chased, he asked for a glass of wine so that he could try to relax. Looking at him curiously, she went to the bar cabinet to get a glass and poured him a glass of wine. When she walked back, he had gone into the living room and had taken a seat on the sofa. Coming back with the wine and wineglass, he asked her where her glass was and said that he didn't want to drink alone. She hadn't expected any company that night and was not really in the mood for any alcohol, but she did anyway. Since she and Colin had been seeing each other, her desire for alcohol had greatly diminished. Only when she felt herself delving back into the past did she try relaxing with a glass of wine. A daily glass of wine or some other alcoholic beverage became Ally's only way of coping with her failing marriage, loss of sleep, and the loss of her most beloved husband. At first it was one glass to help her to relax and sleep, then her drinking had become more frequent to the point of drunkenness, which had begun to affect the children, especially Sage.

Colin, as he had always done since he first came to visit or while waiting for Ally to complete her final touch ups before leaving out on a date, looked around the living room desirously admiring all of the pictures and valuable paintings that almost filled the rich Caribbean sand colored walls, and all the other opulent ornaments that were strategically positioned around the huge elegantly designed sunken room. He would imagine himself living this kind of lifestyle with no financial worries, being able to fulfill all his wants and desires. He also loved her Mercedes sedan even though it was an older model, but compared to his car he thought his was just an old jalopy. Often he would ask if they could use her car whenever they would go out, admitting how embarrassed he felt driving her in his own car. He would further feed his fantasy of being rich sitting behind the steering wheel of her Mercedes. Because of his ongoing divorce responsibilities, he was unable to do much as far as an upgrade in his life, as he would always explain was the reason for his shortcomings.

Finally, she sat down on the opposite side of the olive green plush soft Italian leather sofa which brought him back to the issue at hand. He motioned for her to sit a little closer and with the sign of his finger to his lips let her know that he wanted to keep the conversation at a low tone. She complied by moving over nearer to him. Taking a sip of her wine, she placed it down on a leather coaster on the glass top stone bottom coffee table. With her elbow on her knee and leaning on her fist, she looked at him and asked what had happened to get him so upset, as she stared into his eyes. He leaned over as if to speak to her close up and quickly he kissed her on the lips. In a state of shock, she quickly straightened up and at first was speechless. All that time, their relationship had only been one of friendship. Seeing how surprised and puzzled she looked, he began to quickly apologize. She was completely caught off guard. Trying to remain as quiet as possible, she asked, "What's going on Colin? What's this all about?"

"I'm sorry, Ally, but I can no longer go on as if I just want to be your friend. I've really grown to like you a great deal and yes, there were troubles at work. The troubles came from the constant thoughts of you... you kept me from doing my job. I can't stop thinking about you. So if you don't want our relationship to go any further than where it is, I can no longer do this. I can't keep seeing you and treat you as if you're just a buddy or a pal. I need for you to tell me now because I don't want to waste anymore of your time or mine."

She had no idea that she would be thinking or talking about a romantic relationship that night or any night. Before this time, to her, their relationship had been one that was simply platonic. He had never shown any inclination toward anything other than that. She had not thought of being in any romantic encounter at all since the divorce. It was not something that she felt the need to have. Feelings of loneliness would creep up at times; especially when she would see couples together at the mall or strolling around in the park, but those feelings would soon pass until the next time. Thinking about her encounters with Colin were quite pleasant, though. They both seemed to enjoy one another's company, although he continued to talk a lot, it was okay and he was quite a handsome man. Not that looks had anything to do with whether a person would be acceptable or not. Beauty was only skin-deep. She could hear the voice of her mother saying when she was growing up back home in California. Being deep in thought the sound of his voice brought her back to the present. "Well, what's it going to be Ally? Do you even like me at all?" he said sadly.

"Of course, I do. I like you a lot," she said as she grabbed his hand. "You never talked about having a relationship or showed any signs that I was anything other than a pal. I enjoy your company and hadn't thought about not having you around. You have to remember, Colin, this is all new to me. I guess you weren't listening to me when I told you that I hadn't gone out with anyone since my divorce."

"Are you kidding me? No, I don't remember you saying that. I would think that guys would be beating your door down and ringing your phone off the hook."

"Well, I hadn't really made myself available. Since I met you, I've really gotten out of the rut that I guess I put myself in."

"So, do you think we can give it a try?" he asked with a plea.

"Colin that sounds so weird. I've never heard of planning to have a relationship. Let's just continue seeing each other and see where it goes. How about that?"

"That sounds okay, but can I kiss you?"

She didn't answer, but grabbed his face with both hands and brought his face to hers. He embraced her gently bringing her body close to his. She wrapped her arms around his broad shoulders in response.

It didn't take Colin and Ally long to see that their relationship had burgeoned into a romantic, and more intimate, union. She even called Toni, her friend in California, to tell her about her new interest. Toni was thrilled that she finally let someone else into her life. They had been together for a little over six months now as a couple and it was becoming very difficult to find alone time when desires became passionate. Ally couldn't believe how comfortable and willing she had become sexually. While she was married to Greg, she had become the aggressive one. Her sexual desires became more wanton and sometimes overwhelming. Greg was about eight years older than she was and not always up to the challenge. Anyway, that was his excuse for rolling over to the other side of the bed leaving her very disappointed and unfulfilled. This was not an issue with Colin. With the kids always around and not much time or the place for any privacy, it became a real strain on their relationship. Colin felt that getting married would be a great solution to their problem. He could then move in with them as her husband. Truthfully, Ally had never given marriage a thought. She didn't think that she would have to break that kind of news to the kids, not yet anyway. That solution was problematic. Their feelings toward him had not really changed. They still had a loyalty to their father, and to them, Colin was only an inanimate object. In their eyes, he was no more than one of the statues in their living room. Ally could see how they felt by the way they interacted with him and didn't know how they might treat him if he was to become a permanent member of the family. Toni also had apprehensions of her going this far so quickly. When she called Toni to share her great news, her friend cautioned her on acting so hastily into such a commitment. Ever since she and Colin started seeing each other, her thoughts about Greg had begun to wane. And she wanted to get her life back.

"Ally, I think it's wonderful that you've found a friend, but you really haven't given yourself enough time to get to know him well enough yet to get into such a binding commitment as a marriage. Give this a lot of thought first. There's no need to rush. You have a lot of time. Did you talk to your parents about this yet?"

"I did, and they said the same thing that you said. Of course, they told me to pray about it."

"That's not a bad idea, you know. Well, call me if you need me. You know I'll be here for you no matter what."

"Thanks again, Toni. I'll be in touch."

Colin had put a spark into her life and she wanted to go forward and wanted him to be a part of it. In spite of everyone's opinions, it didn't matter what they said she knew how she felt. Convincing herself that she had begun to fall in love with him and dreading their displeasure, she knew that eventually she had to reveal her possible intentions of marriage to the kids. Thoughts of what she was going to say and how she would tell them began to run through her mind. They had to someday finally realize that she and Greg would never be together again. Ally and Colin had discussed whether he should be there when they were told. She even thought it would be better for them not to see him around the apartment for a while, after being told, at least until they had gotten accustomed to the idea.

Two weeks had gone by and Ally hadn't yet told the kids about her intentions of getting married again. One evening when the three of them were having dinner, she felt that this would be just the right setting to break the news. She had fixed their favorite meal and even made a special dessert that she told them about earlier that day. Near the end of the meal, she began asking them questions about Colin.

"Seems like Colin has been around quite a lot, huh? He's a nice guy, don't you think?"

"Yeah, he's okay," Casey answered.

Sage was looking down at her plate. "Well, Sage, what do you think? Do you think he's an okay guy?"

"He's all right. Why are you asking us these questions?" Sage asked. She was becoming suspicious and wondered what her mother was up to.

"Well, I know he's here a lot. I was wondering how you felt about that."

"He's not in my way. When he's here, I'm in my room."

"And I'm watching TV," Casey chimed in.

"A lot of times he's not even here because you go out with him. Why? What's going on?" Sage asked with raised curiosity.

"Well, what if he was here more?"

"Come on, Mom, what do you mean? What are you asking?" Sage asked.

"Do you guys want that special dessert I made?" Ally asked in a bubbly and excited tone to divert the conversation. She got up and walked briskly into the kitchen. Sage was getting angry. She knew that her mother was up to something and she wanted to know what it was. She came back with the delightful dessert that she promised and placed it on the table.

"Uummm, doesn't that look good?" She asked smiling. She knew that Sage was watching her every move, waiting for the answer to her question.

"Yaaay, I want a piece," said Casey cheerfully. He had paid no attention to their conversation and didn't know what they had been talking about.

"Okay, Casey, do you want a big piece or a small piece?"

"Big," Casey shouted.

"What about you, Sage?"

"Is he moving in here?" Sage shouted sharply.

"No, he's not moving in. Not yet anyway," She sat down and was eating a piece of the dessert.

"What do you mean, not yet? Why don't you tell us what's going on? We have a right to know."

"Okay, I'll come right out and tell you then. Colin and I are going to get married. When we do, he'll be moving in with us."

"What do you want to marry him for? What about Dad?"

"Yeah, what about Dad?" Casey echoed.

"What about dad?" Ally asked. "Have you seen him around here lately? When's the last time he even tried to call you? Casey, whose been going to your games? I haven't seen your dad at the games, have you? But I've seen Colin there."

"I don't care. He'll never be my dad," Sage said loudly.

"He doesn't want to be your dad, sweetie."

"I'm going to my room," Sage said angrily.

"Don't you want some dessert?"

"No!" she said harshly.

"Okay, we'll talk another time," Ally said, as Sage walked away. Casey was still eating his dessert.

"Well, Casey, do you mind if Colin moves in?"

"I don't care. But he'd better not come in my room."

She pat him on the top of his head, "Awww, you don't have to worry about that."

Three months after the kids were told about their mother's intentions of marriage, Colin and Ally went to the courthouse to have their matrimonial ceremony performed. Getting married in a courthouse was of no consequence to either of them because both had decided they didn't have to, nor wanted to be married in a church. She had long since separated herself from any church affiliation and had never asked Colin about any kind of religious faith he was, if any. It didn't matter to her because religion was no longer a part of her life.

It was a sunny day in April. She donned a beige satin cocktail dress that she had not worn in years. Because it was sleeveless, to cover her shoulders she wore her very short gray fox fur jacket that was bought in Paris. He wore a pair of black dress slacks, white shirt, bow tie, and a sports jacket. The unattended ceremony proceeded with the declaration of vows and exchanging of rings. They exchanged rings. Together they had gone to the jewelers to pick out their set. Ally wound up paying most of the cost, which was no surprise to her. He told her then how embarrassed he felt that he couldn't even afford to pay even half of the cost. Earlier, when they first met, he had explained to her about the debt that he had incurred before his divorce from his wife's insatiable need to spend. She consoled him about the rings, and told him that the cost didn't matter because they had each other. Even so, he promised to reimburse her for at least half. When she told her parents of her decision to go through with the marriage, she offered to bring them over for the occasion, but they declined. They knew she really could no longer afford to keep spending her money unnecessarily. Toni couldn't afford the flight, but mailed a gift.

Ally rented a small room at the restaurant where she and Colin had first met to have a very small reception. Since she had become a frequent customer, the owner gave her a bargain to rent a room with catering for the occasion. He also threw in a congratulatory bottle of champagne. The attendance was very small. There was seating for about twenty-five people, but they had only invited twenty. He had no parents to invite. Since the age of five, he hadn't seen his birth parents. It was after their engagement that he confessed that he had been raised in several different foster homes until he was old enough to be on his own and had no ties to any of them. Colin didn't have many guests. Ally had not befriended many people except the ones that she met at the restaurant and a couple of neighbors in her apartment complex who were all very happy to attend. The kids adamantly opted not to attend. When she walked around to the tables to thank all her guests for coming, two people introduced themselves as employees at the family's business whom she didn't know, nor could she recognize. A few days before the reception, she had gotten a surprising call from them and proceeded to tell her that they had heard she was getting married and wanted to congratulate her. She had no idea how they could have found out or how they had even gotten her phone number. Even though a bit suspicious, she invited them anyway. When she told Colin about the call, he swore that he had not contacted anyone from there, so they both presumed because of his past connection with the company, somehow the news must have gotten out, especially since the bride-to-be was Greg's ex-wife. It was okay with her, besides, this way Greg could find out that she too was going on with life.

Colin didn't have much money to contribute which he told her when they first started making wedding plans. She knew that he could never give her what Greg had, but having and buying expensive things was never something that she aspired to have or do anyway. All she wanted was to have someone who would love her for who she was and she wanted to return that love. For the ceremony, she got to wear one of her fancy designer dresses that she had bought when she and Greg had gone to Rome many years before. The memories came back, but she managed to suppress them because this was going to be the beginning of a new life for her. Earlier that day when she was getting dressed to go to the courthouse, she called out to Sage to ask if she could help zip up her dress. "How do I look?" she asked. Looking in the full-length mirror in her bedroom, she was surprised that she could still get into it. Sage quickly zipped her up, told her that she looked nice and sadly walked back to her room. She knew that Sage still was not pleased about her going through with her wedding plans. She thought when Colin moved in, she wouldn't have to ask for Sage's help. Still not able to slough off her early life of Biblical teachings, she could not allow Colin to move in until they were married. "What a hypocrite!" she thought, looking in the mirror. "We had already been sleeping together. But that's fixed now." She also had gone to the bank to get the diamond bracelet with matching earrings that she had in the safe.

At the reception, Colin gave her a great compliment on her outfit. His eyes were fixated on the glittering jewelry that she had not worn to the courthouse. He was amazed at how someone had such things at their disposal. He had never seen those things before except in a jewelry store and wondered what else she had. Everyone was having a good time. One of Colin's friends stopped everyone and offered a toast with the champagne that the owner had contributed. Everyone continued to eat, dance, and drink until her agreed time was up. Not wanting to appear like a total schmuck, Colin had gotten a room at an expensive hotel for the night. Before they went to the hotel, she wanted to go home to make sure that the kids were okay and to get her overnight suitcase. Sage was old enough and very capable of being alone with Casey for at least one night. Colin had given them the contact numbers in case they needed her. Both had gotten in their beds by the time she was ready to leave. Casey had fallen off to sleep. She kissed him softly on his forehead. Sage was watching TV when Ally knocked on her door and went over to her bedside.

"Are you going to be okay?" She could tell that her mother had been drinking a lot. "Sure, I'm fine. What time will you be home?"

"Probably around nine o'clock. Checkout time is ten."

"Okay, I'll see you in the morning," Sage said. She reluctantly allowed her mother to kiss her on her forehead. She could smell the stench of alcohol on her breath. As Ally was walking out of her room, she said, "…and I'm not changing my name."

"Oh, Sage, sweetie, don't worry. You will always be a Tyler," She assured her, and then proceeded to her bedroom to get her overnight suitcase. While in there, she took off her diamond bracelet and earrings and placed them way in back in the drawer of her nightstand. Although she knew that she had had a lot to drink, she also knew what she was doing. She wanted to make sure her jewelry was safely put away before she went to the hotel for fear of any hotel thief.

Ally closed the door of the apartment and was on her way to the car where Colin was impatiently waiting. He got out of the car and met her at the walkway to get the suitcase and put it in the trunk of the car. Thinking that he was the more sober of the two, told her that he would drive. Truthfully, she didn't mind because she had no idea at which hotel they would be staying. He wanted to surprise her. Feeling inadequate about finances and almost always appearing to have a sad story about money, he really wanted to impress her. When they finally reached their destination, she looked out the window and saw Hyatt Regency. Tears began to roll down her face. At first, he thought something was wrong. Then he thought that she must be so overwhelmed with joy and realized that he was trying to make her happy by picking this elaborate place to spend their wedding night.

"Are you okay, Ally? I did this just for you, you know. Why are you crying?"

"Oh Colin, thank you. I'm just so happy. I'll get myself together. I'm sorry. Don't worry. I'm okay." She tried to hold back the tears. She didn't want him to ask her any more questions about why she was crying or why she seemed so upset. Truthfully, inside she was so overcome with grief and heartache. Memories and flashbacks were coming to mind about the first day she and Greg met on the beach, the dinner that night, and then the proposal the following year. She truly thought Greg was out of her system, but the occasion and the name of the hotel brought back those memories of how happy she once had been. She knew that she had to get herself together and forget about what was and what will never be again. She was just married and needed to enjoy her new husband who she felt loved her. She decided that he needed her and wanted her. Assuring him that she was fine, he proceeded to get her suitcase from the trunk then open the door for her to get out. After getting the keys, they walked to the elevator to go up to their suite. Grasping the reality of the moment, she looked at him and smiled. Since they didn't have a cake at their reception, he had preordered a small cake to be delivered to their room with a bottle of champagne. He really wanted to make a good impression. He wanted her to believe that he could live up to her expectations, but she had already accepted him as he was. Ally wanted no more from him except what was expected from him as her husband. Deeply moved by his planning of their wedding night, she was overcome with gratitude and told him so. When the cake was delivered, she was stirred with delight and felt that his act was most thoughtful, charming, and with love. This time her tears were truly tears of happiness. Her compliments made him proud and pleased when she told him. She kissed him affectionately and with passion. The table was draped with a white satin tablecloth where the waiter had placed the cake and the champagne. In the center of the table was a candle that Colin lit. They sat and had a slice of the wedding cake, and toasted to having many years of happiness together. He had even brought a couple of tapes to listen to while they enjoyed their first night together as husband and wife. The couple had almost drunk half the bottle of champagne as they danced and enjoyed being, not lovers, but husband and wife. Not long after they made their way to the bedroom. Their great intoxication and the bliss of being married made them enjoy a night of passionate lovemaking. They both dissolved in each other's affections until awaking early the next morning, wrapped in each other's arms and again found themselves unwilling to let go.

Ally wanted to make sure that she would be home by the time Sage and Casey woke up. She wanted to be there to prepare breakfast for them and wanted Colin there as part of their new family. With great angst, Colin went into this new life anticipating antipathy and indifference. He knew that the kids didn't care for him. Nothing that he tried could break the ice between them. All he expected from them now was for them to respect him as their mother's husband; he knew that they would never accept him as their stepfather, or for that matter not even as part of their family. Never had he ever tried to, nor wanted to replace their father, even though their father was not there. When they walked in, the apartment was still and quiet. Usually by this time on a Saturday morning, Casey would have been up and watching the television in the kitchen waiting for his mom to walk in and begin making breakfast. Before starting breakfast, Ally wanted to unpack her bag and change. She had already showered before they left the hotel. She too was a bit uneasy about their new family situation and didn't know how the kids would react to Colin being there as a part of their family.

Since no one had come out of their rooms, Ally went in to see what the holdup was. First, she went into Casey's room.
"Good morning. How are you?"
"I'm okay," he said while sitting with his eyes still staring at the television.
"Hey, don't I get a hug?" she asked, standing beside him at the bed.
Casey turned around and smiled. "Hi, Mom."
She bent over and hugged him tightly.
"You ready for some breakfast sleepy head?"
"I'm not sleepy."
"Well, I thought that you would be in the kitchen waiting for me."
"I was, but Sage told me not…"
Ally quickly cut off his response. She did not want to hear anything that

would change her positive state of mind.

"Okay, then. Have you washed your face and brushed your teeth?" He shook his head "No."

"You haven't? Well, let's get you into that bathroom and get you ready for a nice breakfast."

He playfully jumped off the bed and ran into the bathroom as she patted him gently on his buttocks, laughing as he darted by. Her laughing turned quickly into hesitation. She knew that she had to go to Sage's room next. How would she approach her? What would she say? She was against her mother getting married when she was first approached about it. Sage never really liked Colin, even from the beginning. She distrusted him and she let her mother know it. Ally tried many times to point out to them some of the things that she thought were good about Colin, being mindfully selective in her choices. He went to Casey's games when Ally would ask him to accompany her. He took them out to eat, but always let Ally pay the tip when she offered. When they went out usually, he had borrowed the money, but paid it back. She never let them know that he had borrowed the money from her, though. Helping with the drop-offs and pickups of the kids was always very helpful when he offered, with Ally's car of course. He even offered to wash the clothes right along with his own when he had laundry to do. Who was she trying to convince? Was she trying to prove something? If so, to whom was she thinking of? She had long since gotten over Greg until her temporary relapse at the hotel. He seemed to have gotten over her and his children pretty well. Still young, had a great life ahead and was going to live it to the fullest. "The children would just have to get use to their new family," was her bold thought.

Bracing herself, Ally got up enough nerve to go into Sage's room. First, she knocked and waited for a response. After three tries, she slowly turned the knob. Peeking around the door, she saw Sage lying in bed with the covers up to her neck staring at the television.

"Good morning, Sage." There was no response. "Are you all right?" she asked, still standing at the door.

Sage looked at her without turning her head. "Morning." she said, sounding downtrodden and somber.

"Sage, what's the matter?" Ally knew what was wrong. Not knowing what response she would get and how she was going to handle it, waited to hear.

"Nothing."

"Then why are you still in bed?"

"Because it's Saturday and there's no school." She said in a monotone.
"Did you want to get ready for breakfast?"
"No."
"Why not? We usually eat breakfast together on Saturday mornings."
"I'm not hungry this morning."
"Would you like for me…"
"Mom, I'll get something later, okay?" she said emphatically.
"Okay, but …"
"Mom, can I just lay here for a while?"
"All right." Ally closed the door. She got the reaction that she so fearfully anticipated. Now, how would she deal with it? She had no idea and no one to ask for any advice. All of her allies had been against her going through with this marriage so quickly, anyway. They all thought that she had not given herself, or the children, enough time to get to know him better. Having only been seeing each other for a few months, they were already talking about marriage and going through with it a few months later. Her parents could not believe how reckless their daughter had become. Her defense of him and declaration of confidence in her decision could not assuage their fears. She had evidently not learned from her first marriage debacle. They could not believe that he was the answer to her prayers, as she had told them. Toni, her best friend, had already cautioned her. Because of her refusal to heed to their advice, she was now left alone to resolve her own problems.

Seeing the expression on Ally's face, Colin could see that Sage would not be joining them. Casey had gotten washed up and was now ready for breakfast. He was already sitting at the table with Colin and chatting away when Ally came in to join them. Casey already knew what breakfast would be…his favorite. Every weekend this was the usual breakfast they all had. Ally quietly made the batter and proceeded to pour it onto the hot griddle making spheres of all sizes and funny shapes. She asked Colin if he could make a pot of coffee and give Casey a glass of orange juice. One way to be a part of the family was to get involved. He took the initiative to get the plates and the cups for their coffee and plates for the pancakes. When the food was on the plates, Casey wanted to say the blessing. Even though Ally had stopped praying, she never discouraged the children and urged them always to be thankful for what they had. Colin cooperated, but was still baffled by the formality.
"Are you going to live here with us, Colin?"
"Yes."

"So where are you going to sleep?" He and Ally were both embarrassed and caught off guard.

"I guess I'll be sleeping in your mom's bedroom," he sheepishly confessed, not knowing what the response would be since Casey was so outspoken.

"Oh. I guess that's okay since you and Mommy are married now." They both looked at each other with a sigh of relief. Now the real challenge would be Sage.

Colin had taken a week off for their honeymoon. Not being able to leave the kids alone for any length of time, they only took little day trips that were short distances away. They did a lot of sightseeing, finding places they discovered that neither of them had ever been before, even though they both had lived in the same state for as long as they had. They took a lot of pictures of each other and often found someone willing to take pictures of them together, overjoyed that they were newlyweds. Stopping for a refreshing ice cream cone, going to little Ma and Pa restaurants for lunch was so much fun. Ally had not been this happy in years. Getting back in time to fix dinner, she tried to always have something to surprise the kids with. Buying weird souvenirs that supposedly represented the state, but had "Made in China" stickers on the bottom they both found to be amusing. Some had so much dust on them that they seemed to have been on the shelves for years and probably were. Still too chilly to get in the water, they strolled along the beach collecting shells and while hiking they found odd looking rocks for Casey. Some days they would stop for homemade ice cream and try to get it back for the kids before it melted. Each day was planned so that they could have as much fun as possible. The last day they offered to take the kids with them, but Sage declined and went to school. Casey was more than willing to go. The three of them had a wonderful day together. Ally was sure that Casey's indifference to Colin had been due to Sage's influence.

After their weeklong honeymoon ended, the couple began to adjust to their new life of living together without the fun-filled activities of leisure. Ally continued with her daily routine. She resumed her volunteer work at Casey's school two to three days a week, and at home, tutoring the kids with their homework mainly with Casey. It seemed after the wedding, Sage no longer needed her mother's help with questions in preparation for upcoming tests, or calling out vocabulary words to spell and give the meaning. This bothered her, but thought that eventually Sage would adapt to their new family. Cleaning up around the apartment was a continuous chore, but she didn't mind since she still managed to be able to remain a stay-at-home mom.

For the first time since the wedding, while cleaning up in the bedroom, she finally got a chance to get the jewelry that she had placed in the night table drawer before they left for the hotel that night. She wanted to put it back into the safety deposit box at the bank. Somehow, she had not even opened that drawer since their wedding night. Reaching one hand in and searching around for it, but it wasn't there. She knew that she had had a lot to drink that night, but clearly remembered putting it in the back of the drawer because she didn't want to take it to the hotel. There was no way that she could have lost it. Ally had been continually and carefully watching her bank account as she had after the divorce and needed to keep up with her finances. She always knew that her jewelry could easily be liquidated if she got into a bind and needed money. For now, there was enough money in the bank from the sale of the house. There was no need to sell anything. Not finding this jewelry was becoming a troubling mystery to her. That diamond set was worth thousands of dollars. She still wanted to continue being at home and not have to start a job yet if she didn't need to. Not that she felt Colin should take on the care of her children, but now that he had become a part of the family, she felt certain that with the portion of his income it would certainly help with the continuing costs of running a household. Not wanting to panic, she decided to wait until another time to see if she could remember if she could have possibly placed it somewhere else.

Months had gone by, but Ally had not seen much in the addition of funds from Colin to help with the expenses. They had never really discussed his salary even when they planned to get married. She didn't want him to think that what she was looking for was money from him. For this reason, the subject of financial obligations was never brought up. He never spent much when they were dating, and she never questioned it since he had already explained his apparent inept purchasing power which at that time she willingly accepted. But even so, she had expected more in the way of cooperation in terms of his share of the responsibility towards the running a household, since they were now married. He had moved in from his apartment after they were married and no longer would have had to pay rent. In spurts, he would give her money to pay for the utilities, buy food or contribute a little something towards the rent. Other times, he gave absolutely nothing at all. This lack of financial participation and responsibility became very problematic in their relationship. Not only did he not help with the bills, but he also thought that it was not his duty to help with the upkeep of the apartment and had the audacity to utter that sentiment. He felt the children should be doing more of the chores rather than him. They already had chores to perform according to their ages and these had been given to them as soon as their mother felt their age permitted that type of responsibility. Ally was beginning to feel as though she was taking care of three children, rather than two. His behavior was nothing like she had ever seen or expected, when they first met, or as they became closer in their relationship. As time went by, his uncooperative stance was now causing her to question, and even regret, her abrupt and hasty decision to marry him. She didn't want to admit that her parents' and best friend's advice was right. And to have to concede that her children were more cognizant of her untenable decision than she had been, was truly a hard pill to swallow. She never revealed the truth to her parents or Toni about her crumbling situation. In spite of the children's plea to put him out, she talked to them with importunity to give him more time just for her sake, reiterating that in spite of everything she still thought that he was worth giving another chance by trying to point out some of the fun things that they had done together, and how helpful he had been to them. Therefore, she endured the consequences of his willful negligence, hoping that things would turn around once he got back to work.

It didn't take a year to see that the marriage was not going to work. To confirm even more, after a year, Colin had been through at least five different jobs and continued to give as little as she would accept. It had taken him months before he confessed that he had lost the job he had when they first met. After a brief stay at another place of employment, he didn't seem to be very interested in looking to find another. Consequently, Ally found herself spending much more than she had to before. Claiming the necessity to have money in order to find a job, he began borrowing money more often now. He convinced her that once he began working again this would enable him to pay her back and to help out more as if he had been contributing any. This constant mooching, followed by more of his bogus promises of repayment was becoming intolerable. Avowing after each interview that this was sure to be the one job that he would be hired was now cliché. At one point when she reminded him of already not repaying what he had already borrowed, he snidely reminded her that they were married and everything that she had was legally half his anyway and he did not have to repay her. His arrogant and abrasive remark took her by surprise. Fortunately, she had only added him to one small bank account and never gave him a key or an inkling of her having any other of the safety deposit boxes, or accounts. Even in his unwillingness to cooperate, she still continued to withdraw money from a different account that she knew he had no access to pay for his expenses. His car was old and needed repairs which she paid for because she no longer allowed him to drive hers. To avoid any other legal issues that could affect her financial status, she had even given him money for his alimony as well. With bills mounting, she found herself having to sell or pawn much of her jewelry. With his constant lies, the drinking, the arguments about money, the kids always upset, along with his staying out late hours she began drinking heavily again to try to cope with her horrendous situation, just as she had when Greg left. After a year and a half, this was the beginning of the end. She finally admitted that the marriage had dwindled along with her affections. Their intimacy had become less and less. Disdain for him had replaced her desire. His touch was almost detestable. As the weeks and months went by, she was horrified by something that she found out about Colin that he had secretly kept hidden from her. She deduced later that maybe that was the reason he was unable to keep a steady job and even wondered if he ever had a one.

One night while waiting for him to come home, she decided to watch him this time rather than approach him as soon as he would come into the bedroom as she had done so many times in the past. Usually, she waited for him to come to bed to approach him about his inconsiderate behavior, but this night she watched for him because she was not going to even allow him to enter the bedroom this night. What she saw profoundly shocking. Coming into the apartment, she watched him walk down into the living room where the glass top coffee table was and all of the other lavish possessions were. Finally he sat down on the sofa after standing in front of each item, looking and touching each one very gently, the small carved statues, the picture frames, and crystal carvings on the sofa table. Stepping quietly out and away from the bedroom door to get a better view, she saw him take something from his pocket. He started tapping something onto the table. Getting onto his knees on the floor, he bent down and began sniffing a white substance through a straw from the glass top table. Her stomach sunk and her heart began to race. Not wanting to wake the children, she quietly rushed into the living room. He was still on his knees and looked up at her with some of this powder still under his nose. Her face was gnarled by anger. Whispering angrily through her teeth she confronted him with what she had just witnessed. She told him that night that he had to leave. Her body trembling with outrage, she asked very low but with fury in her voice, "Colin, what are you doing? Are you doing drugs…in my house?" With tears streaming down her face, she pushed him and he fell backward. On his back, still looking up at her… his eyes wide with surprise and guilt, she exclaimed, "Get out! Get out, I said! You need to go right now… tonight," she snarled out slowly. "And I'll be filing for divorce immediately!"

In a stupor, he denied the accusation. She threatened to call the police if he did not leave. "I said get out!" she kicked his leg. Not wanting to be arrested, he wiped the table off with his sleeve and left. Bemoaning this scandalous revelation, she silently cried as she pulled out and packed up everything that he owned that night, which was not much except for what she had bought for him. She was nervously trembling, upset, and unable to sleep. Lying on her side on the king size bed, in her mind, she played that ghastly scene over and over, again and again. Not being able to tolerate it anymore, hearing the verbal foreboding fears of her parents and her dear friend shouting in her mind, the inevitable condemnation that she would have to face, she went to the liquor cabinet and got a bottle of vodka. She took it into the bedroom where she drank herself to sleep.

Late the next morning, the phone rang. She sleepily and with a hangover reached out to answer it. It was Colin. "Hey, honey. Did I wake you?" The voice alone awakened her out of her hangover and returned her to the fury of the night before.

"Why are you calling me, Colin?" she angrily asked. "We no longer have anything to talk about."

"But Ally, I love you! I want to come back home."

"I don't care. I don't want you here. Not around me and not around my children anymore. They were very unhappy with you around and now I can see why. Sage and Casey have wanted you to leave for a while and I begged them to give you more time. Now I find out that you are using drugs. I had no idea that you were into this kind of thing."

"But Ally, I don't do drugs. It was just a onetime thing. A friend of mine had given me that little bit and asked me to try it."

"I don't believe you. I'm sure that that is the very reason why you couldn't keep a job." "That's not true. Nobody is hiring right now."

"Come on, Colin. You weren't even looking for a job. Half the time you didn't even get out of bed until I woke you. All you've had were excuses for why you hadn't been looking or why you weren't hired. First, it was your car. Then it was money and then it was your car and money. I no longer want you in my house and I'm filing for divorce. Don't worry, I won't ask for any alimony like your first wife did. But really…were you ever even married? Maybe that was another lie that you told to get more money from me. And the next time you have something to say to me… don't call me, call my lawyer. Oh…and one more thing, now I know what happened to my jewelry. Good bye, Colin."

"Ally! Ally! I didn't take your jewelry. Please don't hang up."

She slammed down the phone, then picked it up and immediately called her lawyer. She didn't bother to confront him with the little plastic packet of white powder that had fallen from his underwear drawer when she dumped the contents on the bed. While she waited for her lawyer to answer, she picked up the glass and sipped down the last bit of vodka that was still on the night table, wondering what other chicanery he may have been into. It was just ten-thirty in the morning.

After she spoke to her lawyer that morning, she called her parents and Toni to confess that she had made a dreadful mistake about Colin and that they were right and was immediately filing for a divorce. None of them condemned her as she had expected, but tried to lift her spirits with encouragement. Toni did pick up a slur in her speech and questioned her about it. "Ally, I know that you are hurting, but I hope you're not drinking to solve your problems, honey. Things will only get worse if you resort to that. I'm so sorry that I'm so far away. I wish you would consider coming back here."

"No, Toni. I don't want to take the children that far away from their family. And no, I'm not drinking to help me cope, but I did have a drink last night because I found out something really awful. I'm only going to tell you but please promise me you won't tell my parents or anybody else." She began telling Toni about the whole ordeal. Toni was horrified. She couldn't believe what was happening to her most dear and longtime friend. It seemed that her love life that had begun like a fairytale had now become a terrible nightmare. Ally realized her parents were getting older, but through Toni, she learned that they were not doing well, especially her father. There was no way that she wanted them to see her as she was. She hated even looking at herself. She felt that their worrying about her was probably the cause of their waning health. Ally asked Toni if she would continue to look out for them in her absence and that she would soon try to get out to California to visit them. Toni was so deeply saddened about her friend's pathetic life that she cried as if mourning over her death.

Chapter 17

The money was depleting quickly. Getting the divorce from Colin had costs and Ally had a tremendous amount of lawyer's fees, which was also emotionally distressing. Because he tried to get half of her possessions, it took more time and money to contest his claims. Within two years, the marriage had taken a toll on Ally and the children. The relationship between them had become even more strained. She found out later that the children knew more about the failing marriage than she thought. Sage was older and only accepted her mother's choice by staying as far away from them as she possibly could while living in the same residence. She mostly stayed in her room or would go out to a friend's house when she couldn't tolerate any of his insincere affection towards them. Even Casey had watched Colin's sometimes quirky behavior when he would pick him up occasionally from school; he now began to confess as they sat around on the large living room sofa. It was also revealed to her why they would sometimes be so late getting home from school when he had gone to pick Casey up, or from his games when Ally was unable to attend and why Sage no longer would ride alone with him. She had begun to refuse to go anywhere with him without her mother or Casey. He told her that Colin would on occasion drive to someone's house while he was left in the car waiting for him.

"Mom, Colin always made me promise not to tell you where we went," said Casey, feeling guilty that he had not told his mother. "Mom, I was scared."

"Ohhh, my poor baby. What have I done?" I promise I won't let that happen to you ever again. Okay?" She hugged him tightly and kissed his forehead, while Sage with her arms folded was now standing and looking on at this mushy scene with contempt.

"While we're making confessions, I caught him standing at my bedroom door some nights. He'd walk away when I would look around and catch him standing there."

"Why didn't you tell me, Sage?"

"For what? What would you have done? You'd only make excuses for him like you always did or even question why I would accuse him of 'such a thing', like you said about the jewelry that you couldn't find." She walked away and went to her bedroom. She was so disappointed with her mother. She had heard and watched them from her room many times when they would argue; ready to intervene if it became violent, although it never did. She even saw that last blowout about the drugs. Often, she would take Casey into her room and turn the volume up on the TV so that neither of them could hear their tumultuous altercations. Casey would confess to her that he didn't even like Colin and wished that their mother would make him leave. Whenever their spats were outside of the bedroom, it was because their drinking had taken them there. They were totally unaware of anything during those times. Sage was old enough to see the transformation of her mother and hated what she had become. She also hated her father, as well, for leaving them. She could not figure out who she hated most. Her rebelliousness was becoming more apparent to Ally every day.

Between the rent, food, clothing, and outside activities, Ally knew that she was going to have to get a job soon. They had already moved a couple of times because the rent was too much. But before they had to move this time, she and the kids took a flight to California to visit her parents. She really could not afford it, but the trip was well overdue. They were not able to visit as often as they had when she was married to Greg. The kids missed their grandparents so much.

When their plane landed, Ally had gotten a rental car for their weeklong visit. Her parents were overjoyed when they saw Ally and the children pull up in the driveway, but seeing how beaten their beautiful daughter looked now crushed them immensely. It was more hurtful because there was nothing that they could do to help her. They thought they had prepared her for bad times when life takes a toll and turns down the wrong path. They wondered what had happened as they looked at her with pity in their hearts. The children thoroughly enjoyed every moment they had with their grandparents. Seeing them gave them such tremendously cheerful hope. It had been nearly five years since they had last seen them. Ally had cautioned them not to discuss their home situation with their grandparents because they were elderly and she did not want them to worry. The children truly missed the love and affection that they knew grandparents have for their grandchildren, something that they never experienced from Greg's parents, especially Nancy, their grandmother. For a week, they were able to literally feel how much grandparents could love and cherish them and get all the hugs and kisses that they had so sorely missed all those years, the physical affection they never could have gotten from telephone conversations.

She got a chance to visit Toni and her family and even some of her former coworkers who were still working at her old job on one of the days that she and Toni met for lunch. Some of them hardly recognized her and even told her so. Embarrassed, she made excuses with self-deprecating jokes. Toni felt so sorry for her and contradicted their inconsiderate remarks. But she could see for herself that drinking had taken its toll. Before the week ended, she and Toni had been able to have dinner together twice. One evening they all were invited to Toni's house, including her parents. They had such a wonderful time together that the evening lasted longer than expected. Toni and her husband had to get up early the next morning for work. It was difficult for Toni to keep the thought out of her mind of how all of Ally's troubles first began; however, she never spoke a word about it. The kids had a great time dancing around and playing video games with Toni's kids. Ally couldn't remember the last time that she had seen her kids laughing and having so much fun. She was overjoyed about that, yet also sad. Her selfishness had deprived them of a happy childhood. Knowing the burden that she was carrying, Toni wanted to have a chance to speak to her alone before they had to leave, therefore, she thought by going out to dinner, just the two of them, it would give her that chance.

Toni asked Ally to meet her at the restaurant as a precaution, rather than ride together, just in case things got heated. She didn't know how the evening would go or what she would say. Ally agreed and met her there. They got a booth away from any other tables. The scene was an unpleasant reminder of the place where she had first met Colin. This too, was an upscale restaurant and bar with booths near the rear for privacy. She hated that she had to live with those memories. What a life. What had she done to deserve such a life? Was God punishing her? If so, then why? What had she done that was so wrong? Were her sins that much greater than anyone else's? Why was it that Greg was not suffering? ...or his evil mother? All these thoughts raced through her mind as they both sat quietly after being seated. Toni opened the conversation when the waiter came over to ask what they wanted to drink. Toni ordered a Coke. Ally ordered gin and tonic. Toni gave her a look of disapproval. Ally had already noticed her expression. When the waiter left, she made a comment about Ally's choice of drink. "Ally, do you think you should be drinking and driving?" Looking up from the menu, she responded,

"Toni,... really? Please don't lecture me. It's only one drink."

"Okay," she said in a relenting tone. Ally was apparently vexed by Toni's accusing question. She apologized.

"Listen, Ally, it's just that I'm concerned and worried about you and the children."

"I know, and I'm sorry. You're really the only true friend I have. And I know that I can come to you for anything and tell you anything. You're the only person that I can really trust."

"Thank you for saying that, and it's all true. You can trust me... and I do want you to come to me for anything. I pray for you all the time. I know that somehow God is going to work everything out for you."

"Come on, Toni. Don't give me that God stuff, okay?" her tone was tart.

"Ally, what are you saying?" Toni asked with surprise. "You're the person that kept me straight. You were always so ... so..."

"So what? ...religious?" Ally interjected with a sneer.

"Oh Ally. What have those people done to you? My God, they've stolen your innocence." She looked at Ally, engulfed with sadness as tears from both eyes rolled down her cheeks. Ally handed Toni a napkin and patted her hand.

"Toni, please don't cry." By this time, the waiter had come back with their drinks and asked if they were ready to order. They both asked for a little more time.

"I guess we'd better look at the menu," Ally said smiling. Looking down at the menu, Ally began to confess.

"You know, ...I can't even cry anymore. I think I've used up all my tears. So don't worry about me." Looking up at Toni, who was wiping away her last tear, smiled and said to her, "What I need now is a job. With that last divorce, I had to use most of my money in attorney's fees and the settlement. Can you believe that that thief tried to claim half of my possessions? He brought absolutely nothing to the table. I know that I didn't when I married Greg, but I didn't ask for anything either. What I have, he willfully gave to me." This was the first time that she had mentioned Greg's name.

"Well, I'll try to help as much as I can…."

"Toni, Toni… your friendship is enough. Money can't buy real friends, so please, just be my friend."

"Ally, you're still so sweet. You're still young. There's still a chance for you to meet a nice guy."

"No, no more marriages for me."

"I didn't say marriage."

"No, Toni. It seems that my heart has been replaced with a stone. I will never be able to get involved with anyone again."

"But, Ally, God will…"

Before Toni could get another word out, Ally interrupted her. "There you go with the God thing again. Look Toni, I went to God when Greg and I were having problems. I prayed and pleaded for God to save my marriage. I fasted and prayed and what did I get? I got a divorce and a big hole in my heart. That's what I got for praying to God. So please don't tell me about what God will do."

Toni was astounded. The little religious girl that she met so many years ago had lost her faith and hope in the God that she had believed in and loved.

When the waiter came back to ask if they were ready to order, they were ready. For the rest of the evening Toni brought Ally up to date about the job. She told her who had left and who had gotten married or divorced. Ally asked Toni about Jessica. She wondered why she hadn't come along with the other coworkers for lunch that day. "Wow, I thought you knew."

"Knew what?"

"…that Jessica moved to New York."

"Really? She did? You never told me that."

"Oh, that was years ago. Truthfully, I didn't think you'd want to know."

"That is true. But, why did she move so far away from home? Did she get married too?" she sarcastically asked.

"No. She told me that she was going to New York to be near Jack."

"You mean 'his' brother? Are you serious? Why? He never even liked her."

"Well, she thought he did. She thought that she had a better chance with him if she lived closer."

"Did she really tell you that?"

"Yeah, she really went crazy over him. And never stopped talking about him."

"Wow, I thought she was just flirting around with him that night. Well, the whole time I was married I never saw her. Is she still there?"

"As far as I know, she is."

"Does she keep in touch with you?"

"Not really. But she did give me her phone number and address when she first got there."

"Have you talked to her lately?"

"No, not lately. I've only spoken to her a couple times since she's been there. Why don't I give it to you in case you want to get in touch with her? Hopefully, it hasn't changed. Do you want it? I know she always got on your nerves when you were around her."

"Not really. She got on everybody's nerves when anybody was around her, but I'll take it." They really got a good laugh about that, but neither would dare bring up Huntington Beach. Toni insisted on paying. She knew that her friend had to be in dire financial straits after what she had gone through. Since this was the last day that they would have a chance to see each other, they said their goodbyes in the parking lot of the restaurant. Both promised to stay in touch, and Ally promised to take better care of herself by drinking juice and water rather than alcohol. Ally also promised to call her as soon as they arrived back home. She was too embarrassed to tell her friend that she would be moving again.

Chapter 18

Most of the jewelry that she had aquired through the years as gifts from Greg had already been sold or pawned. During the time she traveled with her husband in the early years of their marriage, she had bought several pieces while shopping out of sheer boredom. The pictures and other art had to be sold as well. Having to move to a smaller, more affordable place, there was no need to keep all of the expensive furniture, or even the type of furniture that she had. She had sold several other items before the previous move because they needed the money. Not wanting that type of furniture anymore was only an excuse for selling it. In the settlement, Colin had gotten quite a few pieces of the art and furniture, as well as money. As before, Ally could see what a toll this was having on her children. Sage was becoming more disrespectful and rebellious. Casey, having to get used to yet another school, made him very angry the day he learned that they would be moving again. She expected Sage's hurtful, acrimonious remarks. But Casey never expressed any feelings of ire until this particular day, when he erupted with unexpected, but apparently stored, anger.

"Why do we have to move again? Why can't we stay in one place? Why can't I stay with my dad? Why did he really stop coming over? I know why! He can't find us because we keep moving, that's why. Or maybe he doesn't like us anymore because you married that stupid Colin. What did you do to Dad? I hate my life!" he ranted and ran into his room. Ally went after him.

"Oh, Casey. I'm so sorry, honey. I wish I could explain it so you could understand." He started pounding his fist on his pillow. She tried her best to comfort him. When he finally calmed down, it seemed to her that he cried for hours until he laid across the bed and fell asleep. He was ten now; yet, he was still her baby and was crushed by his outburst.

Whenever they had to move, she was always thoughtful enough to try to hold out until the school term was over if not being forced out. She thought it would give them time to become acclimated to their newest environment. It was during these times that she fell into deep depression and condemned herself for ruining their young lives. She believed not being able to find a decent job to live and raise her children in a better environment was in itself incriminating. Now having to apply for unemployment with all the other responsibilities became so stressful that she began drinking even more. The fact of the matter was that she realized that her drinking started when her first marriage began to take a downturn. The glass of wine she had while waiting for Greg to get home from having to work late, she did to quell her anxiety. Or was she trying to convince herself? As time passed, it had become a sedative. After the kids were in bed, she felt a little glass of wine before bed would help her sleep. In the beginning, she would never have let them see her drink any alcohol at all, but as her life spiraled downward out of control, she got to a point where she didn't care whether they saw her or not. Watching her marriage crumble into extinction became unbearable. And after she and Colin divorced, her drinking had unquestionably gotten even more out of control.

Sage was sixteen, and now more rebellious by the time they moved this time. She began to hate her mother even more. She had taken them from the comfort and security of wealth to abject poverty and she resented her for it. Then she had the nerve to try to escape in drunkenness. Sage would look at her mother with disgust and anger. Ally noticed that Sage's look showed rancor and would feel even more of a failure and regret that she was even their mother. Drowned in self-pity, she realized she had driven her child to this extreme hostility. "What kind of a mother am I?" she would think. "I'm not worthy to have the title of mother." And many times Sage would even tell her so. Is this where pride had taken her? Her pride had deprived them of living a decent life. To prove to Greg's parents that she did not want their money, that she had not married him for money in the first place, then later, refused to accept alimony or even pursue Greg for child support when he stopped paying. Had she proved or made her point? Had her pride gotten in the way of common sense? Had she let pride cause her to refuse her children a private school education? Was it this same pride that had convinced her to marry someone that she hardly even knew? Or maybe she didn't want to know who he was. Surely, had she known, she never would have married him. Was it for revenge? What was she trying to prove and to whom? Murmuring this self-deprecating soliloquy was as constant as the drinking, she continued to get drunk daily with part of the money she was getting from her checks.

The reason for the quick move this time was because they were under threat of eviction. There wasn't a lot of time or money to find a better place where they could move this time, or one she could really afford. This was even worse than the dump that they had lived in before, as Sage described it, situated well into the inner city. It was low-to-no income housing. As the social worker was describing their next place of dwelling, she told her that they were small apartments within the high-rise buildings. She figured just as before there would be the usual two bedrooms, hardly large enough for a bed and a dresser. The kitchen was probably large enough for a dinette set. Of course, it had one bathroom, and hopefully enough room that could be made into another bedroom. She knew that she had to get a job. It was so depressing to see where her choices in life had taken them. They were living from one unemployment check to another by this time, and the stress of it all had reached beyond her ability to humanly endure.

The drive there was very quiet. The deplorable scene on the way was one of boarded up homes, of treeless and trashy streets, littered with empty potato chip bags and candy wrappers, tread on plastic soda bottles, crushed beer cans, broken and empty bottles of alcohol still in the brown paper bags, only deepened Ally's depression and intensified Sage's feelings of anger and disgust. Pedestrians peered into their old car with a look of suspicion and overt displeasure. Ally could see the disappointment on the faces of her children when she looked at them in the rearview mirror of her old rundown clunker that she somehow had managed to buy. Looking over at Casey, Sage thought about her promise to her brother as she had made many times to get them out of their miserable situation. She promised him that when she graduated from college she would get a good paying job and get them both away from their mother, who had been the cause of them having to experience all of these awful living conditions. In spite of their mother's seemingly uncaring and unloving behavior, Casey loved his sister and his mother dearly, but would not tell her that he would never leave his mother. Not even to get out of this latest dump. As they got closer to their building, there was an abrupt change in the appearance of the neighborhood. It looked as if it was out of place, as if it did not belong there. There were three buildings of this type. The contrast was surreal. They were like flowers in the midst of weeds. The buildings were only three stories high. The entrances had double doors of glass with an awning over the top. There were women and teens out sweeping the sidewalk and gutters, urging the little children out playing to pick up their trash and place it into one of several trash receptacles they had seen at the curbs and at the steps near the entrance of each building in this area. Ally was impressed.

"There's our building, right over there. It doesn't look too bad. What do you guys think?" she said, hoping that they felt the same as she.

"I think it looks nice, Mom." Casey had become a bit more cheerful and conjured up a wide smile as he saw the improvement when they drove closer to their destination. Sage only looked out in silence. She was not pleased because she felt that this whole situation should never have been anyway. Thinking back to how things used to be, she thought of Colin. Things were okay until she married that loser. He always gazed at her with a strange wanton stare. She never liked him, even when she first met him, nor trusted him, which was why after the first time that she rode with him she would never get into the car with him alone again. She didn't want to imagine what lay ahead for them at this place or who her mother would subject them to this time.

Ally's drinking kept her from making rational decisions, subsequently causing her to act with no sense of caution and would mindlessly trust anyone when she was drunk. She would invite a perfect stranger or some drinking buddy that she had met that same night to come home with her when the bars closed to continue their night of gaiety and fun. Her actions were a huge embarrassment and disappointment to her children. But unknown to her children, underneath all the laughter and playfulness was just one miserable, lonely, heartbroken soul.

Inside the apartment building, as they were moving their boxes into their apartment, a neighbor who introduced herself as Sharon had come from across the hallway with her five-year-old son to welcome them to the neighborhood. "Hi, my name is Sharon… Sharon Ames. This is my son Benjamin. We call him Ben. Welcome to the neighborhood."

"Oh, hi, thank you, My name is Ally. Nice to meet you, Sharon."

Sharon reached out to shake her hand. "Where are you from? I see that you have a daughter and a son."

Caught off guard, she began to stammer out explanations.

"Well,…uh… I used to live, uh…on the other side of town, see and …uh… I got a divorce and lost my job… and huh, I could…" Why did she have to lie, she thought to herself? She had not had a job in years, but needed one really badly.

"Honey, I don't need to know your business. I'm just runnin' my mouth. You know, I have a daughter about your daughter's age. What… is she about fifteen? My daughter's fifteen also sixteen."

"Sage is seventeen… or soon will be."

"Okay, okay. Look, if you need anything, just walk across the hallway and ask. Do you have a church, Ally? If you don't have a church home, you should come with me to my church. My pastor speaks the truth. So if you're looking' for the truth, come to my church."

"Okay. Thanks, Sharon. I'll keep that in mind."

Turning back around as she had started walking away, she asked, "Do you need any help? I can send my son over if you do. He's eleven, but he's a big boy."

"Oh, no, but thanks for asking."

"I have some chocolate cake, she said in a melodic, enticing tone. "And it's homemade, too. I just baked it Sunday and today is only Monday. So, why don't you and the kids come over later and have some?" She continued gabbing. Casey was smiling; Sage only listened. Ally chuckled at her persistence. "Okay, maybe later after we've unpacked. We'll see," she responded.

"Okay, then." She turned and went into her apartment across the hall. With sadness, she wondered what on earth had happened to that poor family that could have brought them to this neighborhood.

Ally and the kids continued bringing in the rest of their boxes and bags from the old dilapidated Chevy that she bought after selling the Mercedes. By this time, a few teenagers had gathered around the entrance of the building, nosing around, watching in silence as the newcomers moved in their neighborhood. The community was busy with people and cars going in one direction or another. There were kids riding their bikes. Mothers were pushing strollers and yelling at their other little ones who were running in between those who were tugging along with their heavy shopping bags of groceries. The dog walkers seemed to command the sidewalks as fearful pedestrians moved cautiously aside. The move was finally finished when Sage brought in the last worn plastic shopping bag, reminding her of their numerous treks through the city searching for shelter that they could afford. Sage, looking back through the glass doors at the onlookers who were still standing around the steps, rolled her eyes, and then walked on towards the elevators.

Without a word, Sage unpacked her belongings. As bad as she knew things had gotten, she could no longer cry. Her depression had changed to total hatred and resentment. She had envisioned retribution many times over for what her mother had subjected them to. She wanted her to suffer in some atrocious manner as payback, even if by her own hands. Soon to be seventeen and in the twelfth grade, she only waited for the day to have a chance to get out of this life forever and never look back. Running away had crossed her mind many times since she was twelve, but all that she could think of was her little brother being left behind with a drunk for a mother and the unforeseen circumstances that she might put him through. For this, she felt trapped. Was this supposed to be the life a child? Why should children have to suffer for the bad choices of their parents? Was there any way that there could be someone… or some way, to make parents be good parents or accountable and responsible to at least do their job as parents? Her childhood had been taken away. It was she, who had to look out for the welfare of her brother when her mother was too inebriated to function. She had long ago realized that she felt only disdain for her father and his mother. For as long as she could remember, she had no recollection of her as being a loving and affectionate grandmother. She could not remember his mother ever smiling whenever she saw them or recall ever receiving any big hugs because she was happy to see them. She never showed any affection toward her and her brother, unlike her maternal grandparents in California. All that she could remember about any encounter with Nancy, whenever they went for a visit was to turn around and go back home. But her grandfather was different. He was very likable and she was very fond of him. Once she had even thought of calling him when her dad first left and had stopped coming to see them. Somehow she thought that maybe he could talk to her dad and persuade him to come back home, but then decided against it for fear that her grandmother would answer the phone. Giving the whole plan some thought she realized that if he really wanted to see them, no one would have to ask him to come. That idea never crossed her mind again, nor did she long to see him as she had wanted to before. Resentment began to fill that space in her heart. As she continued to settle in, she thought about the lady across the hall that they had just met. She appeared to be a very nice person. Nobody at those other shabby places had ever welcomed them before. In fact, they were very tight-lipped and cagey. She never trusted any of them. Later that evening, Ally and Casey walked across the hallway to Sharon's apartment and knocked. Casey had begged her to go for the chocolate cake. First looking through the peephole, Sharon opened the door. "Oh, hey, come on in." They walked in and Ally thought that her apartment was a real contrast to the looks of the neighborhood they had just moved into. Everything looked so new and beautiful, although in their part of the development, the area was well kept and the buildings were new and modern. Her apartment was much larger than theirs. Driving in, no one would ever imagine that these apartment buildings were even in this part of town.

The aroma coming from the kitchen was sublime. "Have a seat."
"I hope I didn't interrupt you or anything," Ally apologized.
"No, in fact, you came just in time for dinner."
"Oh, no. I don't want to impose on you and your family."
"Honey, there is always enough for more around here. You haven't seen my other son, have you? Well, you'll see why. That boy can eat. I know he's going to play football some day. They'll be in here in a minute. Where's your daughter? Tell her to come on over too and have dinner with us."
"I'll ask her, but I don't know if she will. She's sort of shy." Ally went back over to the apartment and begged Sage to come. She told her that the woman was reaching out to them in kindness and that it would be rude and impolite not to accept her offer. She also as an enticement reminded her that the woman had a daughter around her age that could show her around and maybe introduce her to some of the other kids her age.
"It's always good to know someone, Sage. She seems like such a nice person. She reminds me so much of my friend Toni. Please, Sage. Don't disappoint her." Reluctantly, Sage gave in and went over. When they went over everyone had already taken their seats at the table. Sharon had introduced her children to Casey, who seemed to have gotten quite comfortable with his new neighbors. She told them to go and wash their hands in the kitchen sink, this time. The boys crammed over at the sink, playfully shoving and giggling until Sharon asked them to finish and have a seat so they could get on with dinner. When they sat down at the table, she then introduced her daughter and her other son to Sage and Ally. He was kind of big for his age, Ally thought. He

was a tall, stocky, friendly-faced kid. He smiled and gave the motion of a wave with his four fingers. Her daughter Elesha was a tall, thin pretty teen of very light complexion. She had long reddish wavy hair pulled back with a colorful ponytail holder. She smiled and greeted Ally and Sage when they were introduced. Ally noticed how polite they all were. Since her children were all so fair-skinned, Ally surmised that the father had to be very light, or maybe a foreigner, or even white. It didn't make a difference to her, though and she felt quite ashamed of the thought afterwards. But she did wonder where her husband was, since she wore a wedding ring on her left ring finger and no adult male had come to the table. But she didn't dare ask.

"Okay, since everybody's here, let's say the grace." She proceeded with the blessing and even asked a blessing for their new neighbors. Ally bowed her head out of respect and felt her mentioning them in her prayer was caring and kind. She was also thankful herself to have met such a nice family. After they ate, her older son, David, invited Casey to come back to his room to play video games. After pleading with his mother, she gave in.

"Do you want to hear my new CD?" Elesha asked Sage.

"Okay," she responded.

"Well, Sharon, let me help you with the cleanup."

"Oh, no. You don't have to. I'm so used to doing this. I do it every day unless I tell Elesha to do it, and since she has company, I won't."

"Sharon let me help, or else I won't feel right about you feeding me and my children."

"Girl, that's okay. I told you I had plenty to share. Now you just sit down and relax yourself. Do you want to try my chocolate cake now?"

"Okay, but just a small piece."

When the boys heard the word 'cake' nobody could figure out how, but they both ran back into the kitchen to get a slice.

"Okay, boys, now go wash your hands, again," Sharon, told them. They sighed and complained, this time they had to go the bathroom. Ben, the smallest child, was still sitting at the table. He had just about finished his meal. He knew that he had to finish eating before he could have any dessert.

"Ben, you've been so quiet," Ally said to him, playfully.

"Don't you have any little kids that I can play with?" he asked Ally.

"Oh, no, sweetheart. I'm sorry. I only have Sage and Casey."

"Oh, please. There're so many little kids around here, it's not funny," Sharon said, laughing about her son's concern. She reminded him of all his other little friends that he had. Eating his cake now, he seemed to be quite satisfied with his mother's solution. She laughed as she put the other boys' slices of cake on the table in front of them. "Mommy, this cake is really good, isn't it?"

"It sure is, Casey."

"Oh, thank you, Casey and Ally. Now, if you want more, don't be ashamed to ask." "Okay," said Casey with enthusiasm.

"Oh, Casey…" said Ally, feeling embarrassed.

"Girl, he is just fine. Let him enjoy himself."

After their cake, Ally thought they should leave. She didn't want to wear out their welcome. Gathering her children and walking towards the door, she thanked everybody for allowing them to come to their home for dinner.

"You were no bother to us," Sharon corrected her comment. "We enjoyed having you over."

They went back over to their own apartment, back to their own routine. Sharon could see that that was a troubled family. She could see the lines of unhappiness in Ally's face, the dark circles under her eyes from depression and the coarseness in her voice from what years of alcohol consumption had done. That family really needed help, she lamented. But most of all, she felt sorry for the children, especially when she first saw Sage's incensed expression as they were moving in. She knew then they were a family in turmoil.

That Monday morning, Ally got up early to go to the Unemployment Office. It was almost the end of summer, and the kids had not yet started school. She found out from Sharon the schools that were in the area and knew that they had to register soon. But finding a job had the most priority. Because she didn't have a long work history, her unemployment funds would soon run out. At eighteen, her first real job was in California at the law office where she met Toni. It had initially been her intention to work there for a couple of years to save up enough money to go to the community college in her hometown. She had worked there for nearly two years when she met Greg. If only she had listened to her parents, she thought, as she drove to the unemployment office. She hadn't worked since California. Since her second failed catastrophic marriage had left her in more debt than before, she desperately needed a job. With her parents ailing and aging, to be able to keep in touch with them made the necessity for a phone indispensable. Toni continued to look after them as she had promised and kept Ally up to date with their progress and was immensely grateful. Being too embarrassed and ashamed about her inconsequential life, she felt inadequate to go back there to care for them herself. Her own life was so botched up, how could she care for anyone else?

There were so many people at the Employment Office when she arrived. She thought by getting there early, she would manage to beat the crowd. There was hardly any place to sit and the lines had already begun to form. The walls were patchy where spackle had been applied to cover the holes, resembling images on a canvas. The color of the peeling paint on those walls was a shade of 'depression' blue, which conveyed the looks of everyone there. Some walls were partly covered with wood and cork note boards filled with tacked pieces of paper with instructions of the 'do's and don'ts' required documents and forms, lists of proper ID, and other requirements along with updated announcements. The floors were grayish white speckled tile, worn and discolored by constant walking and shuffling around through years of misfortune, hard luck, and wrong decisions. It was nothing close to its original color. The almost crowded space was as dreary as its occupants. After speaking to the receptionist in the information line, Ally was given a form and a number and was directed to fill it out and wait to be called.

She had left a note as usual for the children and was out and on her way before eight o'clock that morning. When they went back to their apartment after leaving Sharon's the night before, it was very difficult to refrain from taking a drink. In three days, she had not had a drink since they left the old apartment. Sage had been watching her every move that day as they were putting their bags and boxes in the car. The movers had already taken the little furniture they had, so there was nowhere for her to hide anything except a small miniature bottle of vodka that she had managed to keep hidden in her pocketbook. Back to her old habit, she gulped that down when she lied about having to go back in to check the cabinets to make sure that nothing was left behind. That had been her last taste of alcohol since then. Any smell of alcohol on her breath, she knew could be incriminating and possibly the demise of her family, and could jeopardize her qualifications for any monetary assistance. This also could possibly launch an investigation into a questionable competence of parenting. But in her deceptively warped mind, her drinking was medicinal. She only drank to alleviate the stress that she has had to endure, having been left to raise her children alone and dealing with the consequences of two failed marriages. Even to the point of groveling, she surrendered her integrity to keep her first marriage together. It was a shameful thought. Being miles away from home and having no trustworthy person around to talk to or confide in, led her to resort to alcohol. Her small daily consumption had helped to quell her emotional state during her diminishing marriage to Greg and had calmed her nerves after finding out about Colin's duplicitous life. Her intoxicated mind sometimes suppressed, if not obliterated, any knowledge of the calamity that had been, and still was going on around her. She felt her prayers had made no difference at all. Where was the God that she had once trusted? The God that teaches you to ask for whatever you want and He will give it to you? She had always been a faithful and obedient Christian. Her parents were so proud of how good their daughter had turned out. She was never influenced by her peers and was not ashamed to express her love for God to anyone. But it seemed those requests had fallen on His deaf ears… that He had abandoned her because of her life…God's promised life, had not come. She felt her only way to deal with the life that she was dealt, with all its misfortune, disappointments, and misgivings, was to have a drink to calm her nerves and forget about everything else. It had helped her before and it continued to give her tranquility and peace to survive in this wretched life.

Sitting there indulged in reminiscences about her seemingly irreparable past, she almost missed her turn. The interviewer asked her questions while reviewing her application. She noticed the number of previous addresses and declination of the areas of residences in which she didn't ask about. She also didn't mention the noticeably large gap in her places of employment that she had stated on the form. Ally explained to the interviewer about her work history and failed marriages. For this, she qualified for temporary financial aid while job hunting and was given a few places of possible employment. Seeing so many such cases and applicants, the interviewer was very sympathetic. As Ally was leaving, she wished her good luck and told her to be careful. Ally could not understand her last statement, but thanked her for her help.

Her next stop was to go to the schools. First, she went to the middle school that Casey would be attending. She stood at the long tall counter that separated office personnel from visitors waiting to get someone's attention. There was part of a body that could be seen sitting there in front of a computer screen. After Ally called out to get her attention, the secretary's round heavily made-up face peered around the computer screen and looked at her as if annoyed for being disturbed. Her hair was gelled so that no strand could possibly escape, and a huge braided, twisted bun that sat right on top of her head captured all of it.
"Yes, can I help you?" she said, sounding somewhat irritated.

"Yes, uh…uh my son will be attending this school in September and…uh…"
The bothered secretary cut her off as she tried to explain.

"What grade?" she asked in a monotone.

"Seventh."

"Miss, you are at the wrong school. This is the elementary school. You need to go to the middle school."

"Oh, I thought this was the middle school. I'm sorry for disturbing you."

"Oh, no bother," Rolling her eyes, she went right back to her computer.

Embarrassed, Ally left the building. She got back into the car and checked for the address again. She would not dare ask that rude secretary for the correct address. She decided to call the school to get directions and felt foolish for not calling there first. Hours had gone by, attending to all of her tasks for the day. Finishing at the high school which was the last 'to-do' on her list and she was now hot and hungry. Since they didn't have much food, she decided to go to the grocery store before going home. Famished and sweating, she couldn't wait until she got home to eat; she decided to stop at a little bar and grill nearby to get a sandwich. It was indeed a small tavern with barely enough room to even offer eat-in meals, but they did. They sold hot and cold sandwiches and a small selection of alcoholic beverages. She sat down and ordered a sandwich and a beer. It was hot today and she felt that it would cool her off. After she finished the sandwich, she ordered two more beers. Feeling a little better about how her day had gone, she left a small tip and proceeded home. On the way she saw a bar and carryout and decided to stop in and get something to take home. First, she sat at the bar and ordered a gin and tonic which after a time became three. By the time she got home, the milk and cheese that she had bought earlier had lost its chill. Barely finding the keyhole, she finally opened the door. The children could see that their mother was wasted. Even in her drunkenness, she could see that Sage was angry.

"I bought you guys something for breakfast tomorrow and you can fix sandwiches for lunch," she slurred.

"Lunch? Do you know what time it is, Mother? Lunch was over hours ago."

"How can that be? I only stopped to get a sandwich."

"Oh, you got a sandwich? Well, what about us? What were we supposed to eat?" Sage said, bitterly.

"I'm sorry, I just didn't realize how late it was," she garbled out. Grabbing a kitchen chair, she sat down on it and began to cry. Casey went over to his mother and hugged her.

"Mommy, don't cry. Sharon fixed us lunch."

"She did?" muttering her slurred words through her whimpering voice, as she wiped at her tearful face with her hands. "That was so nice of her."
Sage rolled her eyes and walked away to her room. Sharon had watched Ally through the peephole when she staggered to her apartment. She wondered what had driven that poor woman to this point. Feeling pity for them, she felt that she would have to try to help them in any way that she could.

The next morning Ally had such a hangover that she couldn't even raise her head. The kids had gotten up and fixed their own breakfast, as they had had to do many times through the years. Leaving the kitchen empty, Casey had gone back to watching television and Sage was now in her room looking over listings of colleges and universities that she may be interested in attending. Her counselor at the last school was very impressed with her grades and always encouraged her to continue with her education. He was sure that Sage would be a candidate for some scholarships if she applied herself and kept her grades up. After looking over the curriculum that each one offered, her next interest was the location, which she wanted to be as far away from home as possible. Not wanting to leave Casey too far behind was a concern, but she knew that he was close to their mother. In Casey's young mind, he felt that he needed to be there to watch out for her and take care of her. He loved his mother dearly and knew that she loved him and even Sage. He knew that her problem was from drinking too much. Sometimes he would find her bottles and would move them to another place, hoping that she would forget where she had hidden them. Whenever he did that, she would just go out and get more. Most times, he would try to distract her from her drinking, and keep her attention by talking and asking questions or trying to get her to play games with him or pretending that he needed help with his homework. As the weeks went by, he would try to get her to visit Sharon's apartment and every time she would always welcome them in. After watching her mother drag herself out of bed those few days after moving in, Sage started hanging out on the front steps of the apartment building with some of the other neighborhood kids that she had become acquainted with.

It had been a couple of weeks and Sage had met quite a few of the kids in the area. Just hanging out on the front steps, doing much of nothing had become quite boring. She soon managed to get a job at the neighborhood grocery store about a block from where they lived. One day she walked in and asked the man there if she could speak to the manager, who actually was the manager, Mr. Melmann. She had been there a few times buying things and her face had become familiar to him. Since he had not recognized Sage, he figured that she was new to the neighborhood.

His grocery store had been there for over twenty years. Many of the residents in the community did not drive, so he thought it would be a convenient place for the community, especially for the elderly. His kindness and generosity gained him the stature of 'friend' to his customers and neighbors. During hard times, he was always there to help. He allowed customers to purchase on loan if they didn't have the money right away to pay and would allow them to pay back whenever they could. Because of his benevolence and his generosity, the 'wannabe gangsters' in the neighborhood protected him and his store. Those were the kids who needed to have a bad reputation to have status, recognition, and respect, because some were the ones who had been bullied themselves when they were little kids. Mr. Melmann had known some when they were mere babies in their mother's arms. "I'm the manager," he said, in answer to her question. As a newcomer, she did not know him that well, but saw that he was a kind and gentle man. One day when alone there, she told him how she'd noticed the shelves were not always full around the store, there were unopened boxes that sometimes sat for days without being unpacked and since there appeared to be no one except him manning the store, boldly told him that he probably could use some help to straighten his store out and that she was available. He was so impressed by her self-confidence, boldness and desire to work that he hired her right on the spot. She let him know that when school started, she could only work part-time, which he agreed.

Working at the grocery store, Sage became familiar with many more of the other youth and adults in the surrounding neighborhoods, besides those in her building. Because she was young and new, the little ones would try to sneak a piece of candy when they thought she wasn't looking, but would eagerly put it back when she would threaten to tell their parents. She had seen a few scolded right in the store by their parents if they were caught and even a few had been brought back to the store with the goods to apologize for their little heist. The older kids also found out that only her looks were soft. They found her to be 'a force to be reckoned with' if crossed and therefore, they respected her. Even the 'wannabe gangsters' treated her with courtesy. She learned how much the neighbors really appreciated and respected Mr. Melmann and she did as well. For his empathy and kindness, he and his store were well protected. What she didn't know was that he even knew about her family. He never told her, but on a few occasions, he had seen her mother drunk in his store after having been at the bar across the street. Fortunately, those were days when Sage was not working. He knew that had she been there, she would have been terribly embarrassed and angry. For the remainder of the summer, Sage worked at the store. A few of the male teens tried to flirt with her when she was working. Some of the guys she would allow to walk her home when she got off from work. There was one guy in particular, a twelfth grader who she really got to know well and liked a lot. He was a skinny, redheaded, an exceptionally tall, pale kid, named Mark. He played on the high school basketball team. His family had moved into the area a few years earlier. Some of the kids became jealous when they saw that she paid more attention to him. Having someone near to talk to considerably helped her cope a little better with her situation. The tone of his voice emanated such a sense of calmness that she became very comfortable talking to him. She got to know him well enough to trust him and began telling him about her family skeletons and derelict mother.

It had been such a load off her shoulders to have someone to trust and really understand how she felt, and share her burdens. Mark's situation, as she learned, had been just as bad. His mother had to leave his father because of the physical abuse inflicted on her and the verbal abuse that the children had endured. He had two younger siblings. Mark had not seen his father in five years and didn't know where he was, nor did he care. The day he punched his father to defend his mother in one of their many tirades that often resorted to physical, she decided they had to leave. She told Mark's father that she did not want her only son in jail over a worthless wife beater. His father was of no help anyway; he was always too drunk to keep a job. Mark told Sage that he also had a job. He worked at the mall in one of the athletic stores in Secaucus New Jersey. It seemed that the whole community was a mishmash of dysfunctional families. Many of their circumstances were initiated by unexpected misfortune and others by consciously making wrong choices with children having no control over neither. Both Sage and Mark had a defiant nature. They were fighting back to rise above their circumstances. He was fortunate to have a talent and a supportive mother, but Sage's anger and vengeful spirit were her enforcers.

Ally's alcoholism had caused her to lose several jobs. She never got past the first interview in her first attempt for employment because she reeked of alcohol. The interviewer was exasperated by her condition, and she was quickly, but politely, shown the door. This failed attempt only sent her to the nearest bar to immerse in self-pity and become even more intoxicated. When Sage got in from work, she knew what had happened. Ally was sprawled out on the sofa with one shoe on the couch and the other on the floor. Her head was dangling off to the side of the sofa. The television was blasting from the opposite side of the room in front of her. Casey was in his room. He had been at Sharon's apartment, which is where he went every day while Ally looked for work, but had come home when he heard their apartment door slam. Sage blasted her with every insulting word that she could think of for being a drunken, unfit, and unworthy mother. The next week after being so badly berated, she managed to stay sober enough to get past several interviews and was hired by one of those employers. After the second paycheck, she missed a day. Using her children as an excuse for not showing up, she was given another chance, but with a final warning. Sage wondered and was very suspicious that she already had earned a day off since she had just started working. By the end of the third week at work, Ally was fired. This time, instead of going to the bar, she went straight to Sharon's apartment because she knew that Sage was going to be irate. Sharon had watched and heard Ally staggering to her door many times from her peephole and could hear the frequent arguments, the yelling, and screaming coming from their apartment. So when Ally knocked on her door, Sharon immediately opened the door. She had never come alone and sensed that something must have been wrong this time.

Ever since they first met, Sharon had invited Ally and the kids over many times. It was Sharon, who had offered to let Casey come over and stay with her while Ally looked for work and while Sage was at her job at Mr. Melmann's grocery store. Most of the time, Ally would decline. She truly appreciated Sharon's kindness and generosity but didn't want to be caught in a position to have to explain anything to her about what was going on or anything about her life. Just like her best friend Toni, she knew that Sharon thought she had a problem with alcohol, even though she never mentioned anything to her about it. But she could tell from their short conversations that she, just like Toni, had some suspicion that alcohol was an issue. Sharon tried to talk to Ally without any accusations, or insinuations, by talking about her own situation. This was the first time she had a chance to speak to her alone without any children around. Sharon had been married for nineteen years at one time, but her husband had died about three years ago from an accident that happened at his job. There had been a fire at the chemical plant where he had worked for many years. He knew the company was cutting corners with safety because of costs, but he thought since he had already been there for so many years, only had about nine more years to go before retirement. He was offered an early retirement but opted to stay in hopes that things would change, especially after a government inspection found there was some negligence. Even so, their findings were in dispute with the company. She knew that it was dangerous as well, and wanted him to leave, but it was a well-paying job and with his income, she could be a stay-at-home mom, which he preferred, and loved. One day the inevitable happened again; there was a fire at the plant. However, this time it had gotten out of control and her husband was badly burned. He was burned over seventy percent of his body. After many surgeries, skin grafts, multiple infections, months and months of being hospitalized, and years in rehabilitation, he was able to come home. They had to sell their beautiful home in the suburbs of New Jersey, because of the multiple medical bills they had incurred. The chemical plant went out of business after having to pay all the lawsuits and medical expenses for all those employees who had been injured or killed. Since there was no more insurance to cover his medical bills, they had to use all their savings for his care, as well as what they had received from the lawsuit so far. The lawsuit was still in litigation, but she had not heard anything in two years. The place that he had to come home to was the apartment that they were in now, which they managed to obtain due to hardship. The three new buildings had just been opened two years before they arrived when they first applied for assistance. The applicants for those apartments were checked very stringently and had to qualify by strict guidelines. The federal government regulated the buildings. They were conducting a study. On every application, there was a consent portion if you wished to participate, which contained an agreement to abide by the rules and regulations stated on the agreement. It was orally explained as well to every applicant because most applicants didn't read the agreement or the terms on the consent form. The only thing that most interested the applicants was signing the papers to live in these fresh, new apartments. They would have agreed to anything. Sharon felt so blessed to have been able to bring her husband to a nice new place to live after losing the home that he had worked so hard to have, and especially after they had exhausted their savings due to the overwhelming medical bills. Since the government would have had to provide for his care in a facility, it would be more feasible and less costly for his wife to stay at home to be his caregiver. He needed twenty-four hour a day care. It had been excruciating for the children to see their disfigured father, who had once been so handsome and virile before, lying in the bed or sitting in a wheelchair. Because they loved their father so much, they were very good to him and eager about helping their mother with his care. When Sharon's husband passed away, it was sad but a relief for him and the family. Sharon told Ally how she cried more while he lived than when he died. He had suffered in pain and regret. She also told her how angry she had become because she knew that her husband's injuries and death, along with all the others in that dreadful accident, could have been prevented had the company complied with the government's safety regulations, for which she was still waiting for in retributions. Admitting that the only thing that kept her from doing something drastic was her faith and her devotion to her children, that choice of what she could have done still haunted her. In the courtroom, she had envisioned a plan of somehow inflicting much deserved agony to all those rich executives sitting there who had ignored the warnings, and had not lost one penny for their deliberate disregard for human life. What they had done was reprehensible and she wanted to hurt them as they had hurt her and her husband, but she knew that her family needed her. She told Ally how her obedience through faith had kept her straight. The company owners and board members walked away with millions of dollars while the workers who made the company rich were left penniless with nothing but heartache and grief. She tried to encourage Ally to come to church with her and to pray as she had done. As Ally listened to what had happened to Sharon's family, she was deeply grieved and held back her tears. Looking at Sharon, no one would believe the tremendous tragedy she had endured. She felt so sorry for the children, especially the little one who had been just a baby when this happened to them. Thinking of her own situation, she wondered which was worse… a father who is alive but did not even want to see his children, or not having a father at all. The thought only infuriated her more, because her life didn't have to be this way. To hear about praying and God, only resurfaced the anger which dwelt inside her. She did not want to discuss with Sharon about her unanswered prayers. Whenever Sharon brought up the subject of church or praying, she would only shake her head in agreement and make up an excuse to leave. She never got into real depth about how, or why, her two marriages failed, nor the destruction they had caused in her life. She never told her about her resolve for her heartache, which was never to marry again, but to have as much fun in life as possible, and not try to get her problems fixed in the church, which she found, was a waste. Whenever they talked, she would talk about former coworkers or her ailing parents and her desire to visit them. "You know Sharon, you remind me so much of my friend, Toni, who lives in California. She is such a great friend. She even keeps an eye on my parents while I'm here. I miss her so much. We talk about once a week, or so."

"It's so good to have a friend like that, Ally. Why don't you think of me as a good friend like Toni? You can come to me for anything… I mean anything. Okay?"

"Awww, Sharon, you're so sweet. You are a friend. Now I have two very good friends. Thanks for everything you do for me… for us, really."

"Well, what are friends for?" Sharon said, as they chuckled.

Ally wanted to leave, but this time she needed her help. She had to confess to Sharon that she had lost her job.

"What happened?" Sharon asked her in disbelief. She knew that Ally only had the job for three weeks. "Can't you ask them to reconsider?"

"No. I can't. They already gave me a second chance when I missed a day last week. I wasn't able to call to let them know and..." She told the same lie to Sharon that she had told her employer the first time for not showing up for work. But this time she made up a different lie for being late. Sharon knew why Ally had trouble finding work. She knew Ally was an alcoholic.

"If I have to tell the kids, Sage is going to be so angry. I don't know what she might do."

"Don't worry. I'll talk to Sage. I have to start looking for a job myself, you know. I want to be able to get out of this subsidized housing some day. When Dave died, I wanted to start looking then, but I didn't know anyone well enough around here that I could trust to watch, Ben, my youngest. Now that he's five, he'll be going to kindergarten and they stay all day at this elementary school. Okay, I'm going to tell Sage that you and I are going job hunting together."

"Thank you, Sharon. I'm going to keep the next job I get. I promise. You wait and see." They both got up from the kitchen table and were walking towards the door.

"Ally, I never wanted to bring this up but…." Ally stopped and turned around, interrupting Sharon mid sentence.

"Uh oh, here it comes. Whatever it is, it's not true."

"I'm not so sure, Ally. The residents in this building are coming to me about you being drunk all the time."

"Drunk? Drunk? I don't know what they're talking about. They don't know anything about me. I know that I might have a drink now and then, and I will admit sometimes I might've had more than I should have sometimes, but…"

Sharon interrupted her bantering.

"Look, Ally, I'm just letting you know so that you'll be aware of what's going on. I guess they know that you and I talk, so they came to me. I guess they're just worried about any trouble as far as reports getting back to the main office. The residents… actually, we all are being monitored for that study and they just want to abide by the rules."

"Study? What study?"

"Didn't they explain it to you when you applied for housing?"

"I don't know. I guess they did. I was so desperate to find a place to stay I just signed the paper."

"Didn't you notice those other high rise buildings when you drove in?"

"Yeah."

"Well, that's why you're not in one. Look, Ally, just be careful. You have great kids, and they need to live in these homes. And one day you and I both are going to get out of these government run homes."

"Okay, Sharon thanks for the heads up." Ally hugged her and went across the hall to her apartment.

"Maybe you should go back and read those papers," Sharon smiled and said, as she closed the door.

Later that evening, looking through the peephole, Sharon saw Sage getting ready to unlock the door to their apartment. She wanted to catch her before she went in. It was 6 o'clock. Mark and Sage strolled along talking and laughing on the way home from her job up to the steps where he usually ended the walk and continued home to his building across the street. When Sharon opened the door, she asked Sage if she could stop in for a minute. Sage became nervous, thinking maybe something had happened.

Seeing the look of anxiety as she walked towards Sharon's door, she quickly calmed her. "Sage, let me just assure you that everything and everybody are just fine."

Sage breathed a sigh of relief.

"So, what's going on?" she asked, as she walked over looking straight at Sharon's face.

Her anxiety now had become curiosity.

"Come in and have a seat. Have you had anything to eat? Can I get you something to eat or drink?"

"No thanks, Sharon. What's this all about?"

"Well, your mom came over today and was very upset."

"Why? I thought you said everything was okay."

"Well, it is. It's just that your mom lost her job."

"Oh, another one?" Sage asked sarcastically.

"Come on, Sage. Your mom is really trying."

"Trying to do what? Trying to see how many jobs she can lose in a week?"

"Sage, I'm not stupid, deaf, or blind. I know your mom has a drinking problem. And I know it must be hard on you guys, but whatever has driven her to this point can't be helped as long as you treat her this way. She loves you kids more than you can ever imagine. I know it doesn't seem that way, but she does. So, please, let's try to help her. Don't condemn her this time. In fact, she and I both are going out job-hunting… together. Ben will be in kindergarten this year, and I'll be able to work. As I told your mom, when I was taking care of my husband, I wasn't able to work because he couldn't be left alone. But now I'm going to be out there looking myself."

"I'll try like you said, but Sharon you don't know what my brother and I are going through or what we've already been through. This hurts us, too. We have to deal with the embarrassment of her being drunk around our friends, the teasing, and laughing behind our backs. All this she has caused. We've had to move so many times, you wouldn't believe… and…"

Sharon hugged her. "Sweetheart, don't worry. Everything will be okay. Just trust in God and He will work everything out. You'll see. You should come to church with us some Sundays, you and your brother…and your mother." Now holding her by the shoulders and looking straight into her eyes, said,

"Now, don't you worry. If you ever need anything or need to talk to someone, I'm right across the hall. Okay?"

"Okay. Thanks, Sharon. Goodnight."

"Goodnight, sweetie." She hugged her again.

Sage walked in their apartment past the used sofa, the floral design faded from sunlight and years of wear and tear. Stopping in the kitchen, she glanced in the sink, checking for dirty dishes. Casey and Ally were sitting on the small loveseat watching TV.

"Oh, hi, Sage," Ally said. Casey also chimed in.

Ally had heard the door open and close. "Do you want something to eat?" yelling again from the small den at the rear part of the apartment. "I fixed some barbeque chicken, mashed potatoes, and green beans. Would you like for me to fix you a plate?"

"No, thanks."

"Casey and I already ate. How was work?" She was still yelling from the den. Ally was afraid of talking to her face to face for fear of seeing her angry look and hearing the rebuke that always followed. When she asked that question, it took everything she could muster up to keep from blurting out a nasty remark. She had the audacity to ask that question knowing she had just lost yet another job. Sage was enraged. Everything she and Sharon had just talked about went right out the window in steam. She went to her room and cried. How could a mother who cares, act as though nothing had ever happened? No apologies, no expressions of regret or remorse.

Chapter 19

Summer was over and school had begun. The kids settled in and adjusted well in their new schools. Over the summer, they had already gotten a chance to meet many of their soon-to-be classmates. Sage and Mark decided to catch the bus together since they had become such good friends. They continued to be each other's support system. She often had some new and more astonishing fiasco to tell him, which helped to dismantle her ever-building burden of anguish. Sage knew time had run out for her ever having any semblance of a carefree childhood for whatever was left of it. It had been stolen years ago by her parents' selfishness and pride. Her main concern now was to try to help her brother. Talking to Mark enabled her to formulate her plan more effectively and rationally. With his input and advice, she could see the future without the veil of hatred distorting her vision.

After losing yet another job as a receptionist at a doctor's office, Ally finally found a job at the restaurant bar near the subway where she had been a frequent patron downtown in New York some years before. The manager remembered her and after hearing about her hardship hired her as a barmaid. The location was perfect, but the type of job was not. But this place, with the noises, loud music, and bustling activity was where she could forget about her problems. With her car failing, she conveniently was able to catch the subway and from where they lived, the subway was a bus ride away. This eliminated the need to drive, which helped her on those days when she would have had too many freebies, courtesy of her generous customers, or was unable to get the car started. Sharon offered her help by making sure the kids were home safe from school and also made sure they got something to eat since Ally would be on her way to work by the time the kids were getting out of school. Sage was perfectly capable of looking after her brother, but she wanted to continue working at Mr. Melmann's store after school. Sharon agreed to let Casey stay at her apartment so that he could get his homework done and not have to be alone. Sharon had landed a job as well at a nursing home. It brought back sad memories, but she wanted to work.

Sage was not pleased with the type of job her mother had gotten, but had reached the point where she no longer cared. Her only goal was to someday get as far away from her as she could and was not going to let anything or anybody get in her way of the chance to escape from this almost destitute life. Every chance she got, she studied to get the highest grades necessary to get a scholarship. Fortunately, their private school education helped them both. She was very much prepared for the curriculum required. If she could keep her grades high enough, she felt this would be advantageous for a chance of receiving at least one of the scholarships that most likely were going to be offered to the honor seniors at her school. Her mother's drinking problem continued to engulf her, no matter how much she tried to ignore it and her job was not enough to help squelch from her mind their distressing home life.

Sage worried about her brother and was so thankful they had been lucky enough to have a neighbor like Sharon who cared about their family. Sharon was a very empathetic person who tried to give guidance to all the children she knew and virtually offered to help anyone she encountered who needed it. Everyone who knew her liked her. But trying to talk to Ally was a daunting task. Whatever she said only seemed to fall on deaf ears, even in spite of the warnings of the residents' concerns and displeasure about her thoughtless behavior. Even though Casey did not seem affected by his mother's actions, Sharon could see the signs of changes in his behavior. Sometimes during play, he would become short-tempered and was easily startled at the slightest noise. She was sure this behavior was a result of his mother's fractured parenting, without doctrinal influence and discipline, along with his fear of the consequences of her reckless drinking. Because of this, she constantly prayed for this heartbroken and broken-spirited family.

In spite of everything, Ally continued to come home drunk and staggering right up to her door. Sometimes she was seen bringing other people with her, especially on weekends. Sharon was becoming very worried and decided she was going to have to speak to her yet again about this matter. One day she caught her just stepping out of her apartment when she was leaving for work. "Look, Sharon, I know you're concerned, but can't I have a friend or two over sometimes? Besides, I think it's impolite when a friend gives you a ride home that you can't even invite them in for coffee or something as a thank you. What's wrong with that? Usually, the kids are asleep anyway and in their rooms. I get lonely sometimes. Can't you understand that?"
"I do understand that, Ally, but you have to be careful. You can't trust everybody you meet."
"Are you looking through your peephole again, Sharon?" she asked, feeling annoyed at that fact, which was heard in her voice.
"Why would you ask that?"
"Look, I have friends. Just because you haven't seen them doesn't mean they're strangers. These are people I know."
"I'm sorry. I'm just concerned about you and the kids. That's all. I pray for you all the time. You are a grown woman, but I told you before, people are talking and watching."
"You know what, Sharon, let 'em watch all they want. I'm not doing anything to them. Look, I've got to get to work. My ride is downstairs waiting. By the way, while you're praying, pray for my dad. I just got a call that he's very sick."
"I will. I'm so sorry to hear that," Sharon said with deep concern.

Ally continued with her wild and careless behavior. She didn't have men over all the time, but she had her fair share and continued to let them stay over from time to time which caused Sage to feel very troubled. This brought back horrible memories. At this point, she had thought maybe this part of her mother's bad behavior was over. She had been through this before with that loser Colin and had hoped that her mother had learned her lesson. After that time in their lives, she and her mother had very little to say to each other. They had had nothing much to talk about ever since her dad moved out of their home and stopped coming over for visits. After they moved into their first apartment, he was totally out of their lives. Her mother hadn't asked her about school with any sincerity since she left the private school. She was so engrossed in her own unhappiness she started drinking to cope. And still, all she cared about was getting her next drink, Sage thought. That is why she was surprised when her mother told her their grandfather was very sick; it was so unexpected when she came to her room to talk to her. Fortunately, she had already found out from Toni that her grandfather had begun to slow down more, so she was somewhat prepared, but not for news as drastic as this. Toni, not wanting to reveal any more before her mother had said no more. She tried to stay out of their family affairs, but only did what she had to as far as keeping an eye on Ally's parents since their daughter was so far away. Soon after Sage started working, she was able to buy a phone through her mother's service plan and paid her own portion of the bill. She hated having to go to her about anything, but had no choice since she was under age. Toni was stunned the first time she received a call from Sage. Like Sharon, she was also concerned about them. It had been several weeks since Sage had last heard from Toni, after their initial conversation about her grandparent's progress.

One Monday evening when Sage had gotten home from work, she was angered to see her mother sitting in the kitchen crying with Casey by her side. Sage thought the inevitable had happened again. She certainly was not in the mood to hear anything about how her mother had gotten drunk again and was now fired yet from another job.

"What's wrong with her?" Sage asked harshly, looking directly at Casey.

"It's Granddad."

"What's wrong with Granddad?" she asked anxiously and with dread.

"He died," Ally said softly.

"Nooooo. It can't be," she screamed and ran into her room. She immediately called Toni, who affirmed the news.

"What happened? And where's Grandma?"

"Don't worry, Sage. She's here with me."

"How could this happen?"

"Sage, your grandfather was getting up in age. He hasn't been well for a long time now."

"I knew he wasn't well, but I thought he was just slowing down from getting old. What did my mom say?"

"She knows she has to come."

"So what about us,...me and Casey?"

"That, you'll have to discuss with your mother."

"Well, we're coming. I have to come."

"Oh, God, I didn't say that you couldn't come."

"No, it's okay. I'm okay. Thanks, Toni. I'll see you soon." She hung up before

Toni could say another word. Sage got herself together and went back out to talk to her mother. She sat down at the table across from Ally, but was not going to mention her conversation she had just had with Toni.

"When are you going?"

"I don't know."

"What do you mean you don't know? Have you talked to Grandma?"

"I don't have enough money to fly to California. And yes, I've spoken to Grandma. She said the funeral is next Monday."

"That's your father, and he has to be buried and we need to be there."

"I know, Sage. Please don't start. I'm just too upset to talk or think right now. I've got to figure out where I'm going to get the money," she said sobbing.

The same evening after they found out about Ally's dad, Sage told Casey to start getting some things ready for the trip. Today was Monday, and the following Monday would be the day of the funeral. They only had by the end of the week to get there. Ally had gone to her room and was sitting on the side of the bed with her hands in her lap, holding the same tissue she had been using to wipe her tear filled face, trying to figure out how she would be able to come up with the money. Several people had already been scratched from the already short list.

Ally had spoken to her mother several times a day concerning her plans since her father's passing. By Wednesday, she had not mentioned anything else about going to the funeral. That evening, Sage knocked on her bedroom door. She stepped just inside and closed the door. She began to pressure her again about their necessity to be in California as soon as possible.

"You can't let Toni do everything for you. She has a family of her own. It's your mother and your father. You need to be there to help your own mother, my grandmother." She was very upset and practically in tears.

"Sage, we've already talked about this. I've already talked to Toni. She told me she is helping Mom get her papers together. She took her to the church to speak with the minister."

"No, you need to be there. She's your mother and your responsibility. You should be thankful you have a friend like Toni."

"I am thankful, Sage. I thank her every time I talk to her."

"We shouldn't even be living here. We should have moved back to California years ago."

"Sage, I'm not going to think about what I should have done...not right now anyway. Anyway, it's too late."

"Well, not for me," Sage said softly, as she turned to leave to go back to her room thinking about her plan when she would finally leave for good.

"And don't worry, Sage. I haven't lost my job. I'm on bereavement leave."

Sage just looked back at her with disgust and closed the door. At that time, Ally had no idea where she was going to get the money for herself, let alone for them to go, too.

Sage couldn't even feel pity for her own mother. She knew her grandparents were terribly worried about them, which was probably why her grandfather's health declined so quickly, she thought. One day during their last visit, she had overheard them talking about how her mother's demeanor had changed and even her looks. They should have gone back to California to live, Sage thought, remembering their conversation. Maybe they would have been better off and even better. Maybe her grandfather would still be alive. But no, her mother wanted to stay in New York, hoping for her dream to come true. Her dream had become a nightmare for all of them. Their dad no longer wanted to be a dad or a husband. They had lost him years ago. The only person in that family she had been in contact with was her playboy uncle, Jack. After all these years, he was still a bachelor and with no regrets. But at least he cared enough to get in touch with her every now and then. How he found them through their years of migration, she never knew, because she never asked him, nor told him, anything. Most of those times, she wouldn't even know until days before that he wanted to meet with her. He always asked her if she needed anything and her response was always, no. She vowed never to take anything from that family. What they needed, he could never give them anyway. He always asked her not to tell anyone they had talked or met. Evidently, the two brothers were still influenced by their conniving, overbearing mother. She thought, how pathetic that kind of life must be.

Remembering their last trip to California, Ally frantically searched around for the piece of paper she had written that phone number on. She had not looked at it, nor did she think that she would ever want to look at it. But now out of desperation she had to find it. This could be the one person, who could loan her the money to get to California. She knew it had to be there somewhere because she had not thrown anything away that she had in her possession from their trip. Sitting on the bed, she thought about the outfit she had last worn and the purse she carried when she and Toni had gone out to dinner the last week of her visit. After searching every crevice and slot in that pocketbook, she realized it was not in there. It wasn't in the wallet either. Every piece of paper she had was taken out of every compartment of the two purses that she had taken with her and carefully unfolded and straightened out to examine. Exasperated, she went back to the wallet. There was no other place she would have stashed such a small piece of paper. Then, removing every expired credit card from each slot, there it was neatly folded in one of the empty credit card compartments. She wondered why she even carried those cards since they were no longer of any use. Jessica Bensen. She never thought she would ever be happy to see that name again. Now she had to figure out how to ask her for a loan. How could she? How would she react? She hadn't seen or spoken to Jessica since she got married. She wasn't someone Ally would characterize as a friend. But who else could she ask? Sharon had just started working. Feeling hopeless and helpless over her woeful dilemma, she began to cry again. What kind of life is it when you don't have any way to get to your own father's funeral? She took the bottle of vodka from the floor in the back of the closet where she had hidden it for safekeeping for a time such as this and poured a bit into a small glass she kept in the back of the drawer of her small, wobbly night table. She didn't want to replay any memories of any events, faces, or places that had initiated the crumbling of her once innocent life. This was the one thing that helped her cope with such a despicable existence. It was a tall fifth bottle and only less than half was left. She continued drinking until she had drunk it all. The drink began to take effect as she lay back on the bed feeling tipsy and thinking she would give Jessica a call later in the evening, hoping the number hadn't been changed. It was only noon and Jessica was probably at work anyway.

Even though Sharon didn't have the amount of money that Ally needed, she offered what she had. She was so deeply saddened by the news of her father's death and wanted so badly to help out in any way she could. Ally's boss was also sympathetic and allowed her a longer time off since she had to travel so far for the funeral. Her coworkers even pitched in for a donation. They really liked her at this job, because she was a lot of fun and could always make the patrons laugh. Sage and Casey continued to go to school until a day before their day of travel. Although Mr. Melmann told Sage she didn't have to come to work because of the death in her family, she insisted on going anyway, confessing to him that she wasn't really sure if she would have enough money to even be able to get there, and wanted to make as much as she could to help with her plane fare. He knew about the hard times she was going through for he knew about all of the families' problems in the neighborhood that came into his store to buy groceries. Sage had become special to him, though. He really liked her because he saw that she had great potential if given the chance. She was resilient and bold, had integrity and perseverance.

After sleeping off the aftermath of her excessive drinking and intoxication, Ally dragged herself off the bed and went into the bathroom to wash her face. She always tried to avoid looking in the mirror because she didn't want to see the harsh lines that life had put there. She didn't want to see herself because mirrors reflected more than just images. They also reflected wrong choices and bad judgment, which brought on feelings of guilt and shame. Therefore, she spent very little time looking at herself. The cool water brought her back to herself and reawakened the problems at hand. In her foggy memory, the thought that she needed to contact Jessica came back to her mind. After making a sandwich for Casey and filling a plastic cup with juice, she went back into her bedroom and got the paper with the phone number. Surely, by this time she should be at home. It was ten minutes after 6:00. Nervously, she dialed the number. As it rang, she practiced what she would say. "Hello." The voice sounded somewhat raspy and coarse.

"Hello, Jessica?" she said cheerfully.

"Yes. Who is this?" she asked suspiciously and with caution not recognizing the voice.

"Jessica, it's me, Ally."

"Ally who?"

"It's Ally, your ol' friend from California."

"Ally? I haven't seen or heard from you in eons."

"Yeah. I only found out you were here about a month ago. Yeah, when I went home to visit my parents. So, how are you?"

"I'm fine. How are you?"

"I'm okay. Hey, Jessica, how about I come over and pay you a visit? We haven't seen each other in such a long time; it would be nice to get together again. How about tomorrow?"

"Oh… okay." She was surprised at how pushy she was. Her request was so unexpected that she agreed without thinking. Regaining her senses, she thought it might be fun to see an old buddy from the past. "Okay, so tomorrow evening it will be. Remember my spaghetti? I'm going to fix that for you for dinner. Are you coming alone?"

"Yes,… just me. I remember your spaghetti. As I recall, it was pretty good," she said, pretending to be delighted.

Jessica gave her the address and at the same time, wondered what she really wanted after all these years. There had to be some reason for her to call after all this time. But what could it be? What could she know? What could a rich person need with her? They had never really been friends. Besides, she hadn't heard from either her or Toni in years…not since her wedding. And why did she want to come to her place and not meet out for dinner at a fancy restaurant or something? She certainly could afford it. What was she trying to hide? All these questions bounced through her mind. She recalled years ago phoning Toni when she first arrived in New York to give her the address and phone number. But after that, she would only hear from Toni only if she had initiated the call. Subsequently, she stopped trying to contact her at all and hadn't heard from either of them again… until now. Jessica was suspicious yet curious for this sudden desire to get reacquainted.

On Thursday, the following evening Ally got dressed after quickly jumping in the shower to get to Jessica's by 6:00, hoping her finicky old car would start. Sharon told her that Casey could come to her place for dinner and wait there until Sage got home from work. She had given her a quick synopsis explaining her relationship with Jessica, that began in California and who might be able to loan her the money needed for their airfare. Sharon felt so sorry for Ally. She had moved so far away from her family and had no relatives close by to turn to in time of need. Finding out she had a long time friend nearby who she could call for help alleviated some of the guilt and helplessness she felt.

It was a laborious drive especially in that old clunker of a car. The distance was not far, only thirty minutes away, but the anxiety was high and her car was not totally reliable. She became nervous again thinking how she was going to ask her for a loan. She was sure by now Jessica would have heard that her marriage had ended in divorce and would not have to get into having to explain what had gone wrong with that. Even now, the memory caused her great anguish. So worried about her current situation, she had not even thought to ask Jessica anything about her own life. She could be married by now. There could even be children, although she couldn't imagine Jessica with children…married maybe, but no children. It had been quite a long time ago and she could have met someone here. The Tyler men couldn't have been the only available bachelors in New York. She became irritated at the thought. Thinking back, she was hoping that through the years, all of the misunderstandings, the slurs, and the typical female spats had all been forgotten. Jessica at this point was her only hope. Colin had destroyed her financially. She could have tried again, but had already been rejected from getting a loan from several banks. Somehow, she had to find a way to get the money, because she didn't want the kids to blame her for them not being able to attend their own grandfather's funeral for the rest of her life. Overwhelming thoughts of her inability as a provider was sending her again into thoughts of self-destruction. Through these trying years, in her bouts of self-pity, she had sometimes contemplated ending it all. She had no one close by with words of encouragement or a shoulder she could cry on. Of course, her friends, the two she had, would be right by her side if called who would listen empathetically, but the pain still remained. For now, she had to think about her mother who had lost her dearest companion and friend and will from now on be alone. They had all enjoyed so many happy times together, the celebrations of birthdays, their many anniversaries, graduations, church picnics, amusement parks and fairs, even her first paycheck. She could not remember one unhappy time in their home. At least her mother will have all those many happy memories of the love they shared and the commitment shown to her from someone who truly loved and adored her throughout their many years of marriage. Drifting into the happy memories of the past she experienced back home with her parents, she was about to miss the street where Jessica lived. As she walked along, she admired the elite structures that stood regally guarded by huge trees. Some of their branches stretched across to meet the ones on the other side. The neighborhood was a series of beautiful three-story Brownstones. The steps were many and steep to get to the elevated entrance of each residence. At the top of each dwelling were large, heavy looking doors of several different architectural designs. A few were arch-shaped structures resembling the entrance to a Roman Catholic Church, and some entrances were double doors, fashioned with metal, glass, and wood. Always there to contradict the beauty was the ugliness of life. On each house, covering mainly the lower and first floor windows were black wrought iron security bars, but designed to try to preserve the architectural artistry. As she made her way to Jessica's place, she saw that some of the steps were decoratively lined with heavy ceramic flowerpots, from bottom to top filled with colorful varieties of flowers and greenery. This was an old neighborhood but had such extraordinary charm. She looked around while at the top of the steps before she rang the bell thinking how picturesque and awesome this neighborhood of old houses were and all the history within the walls of each one. Standing there at the top of the steps, she also began to have second thoughts and just wanted to turn around and leave. Before she touched the bell, she had contemplated three times to head back down the steps. But desperation gave her courage and taking a deep breath, she reached out with sweaty palms and rang the doorbell. As a last minute gesture, she had stopped on the way to buy a bouquet of flowers thinking this would be the proper and appropriate thing to do when visiting someone for the first time and in a long time. In spite of how she was now and how her life had turned out, there was instilled in her proper etiquette and behavior that she had been taught as a child and always practiced whenever the situation presented itself. The flowers could also appeal to her softer side if she had ever through these years developed one. From an intercom, she heard a loud voice. "Who is it?"

"Hi, it's me, Ally."

The buzzer sounded indicating the door was unlocked. She then pushed open the door and walked in.

Jessica's place was on the second floor judging by the numbers on the first door she saw when she stepped inside. The inside was just as gorgeous as the outside. The hardwood floors were waxed and shiny. Looking ahead of her she saw there were more steps. She took a deep breath and began the long, arduous haul to the top. As she had just about reached her goal, she looked down from where she had started and wondered how on earth Jessica could make this climb every day. Reaching the door of her apartment, she hesitated several times again at each attempt to knock. Her fist raised again and again just inches from the door. Once more, she dropped her hand. What was she doing here? She asked herself. But it was too late to turn around. After all, she had already rung the bell and told her she was there. Finally, she mustered up the courage to knock. Jessica opened the door. With a jaw drop expression on her face, she moved to the side and let Ally walk in. "God, what happened to her? Wow and that outfit…that skirt is almost up to her butt cheeks as old as she is," she thought in disbelief. Ally could see how she looked at her and tried to rationalize her apparent shock. Gathering her senses, the words finally accommodated the opened mouth to greet her.

"Hi, Ally. Come on in."

Ally handed her the bouquet of flowers.

"I guess you hardly recognized me, huh? It's been almost twenty years, that we last saw each other, you know," extrapolating the years. But Jessica had hardly changed, but for a few years in the corners of her eyes and around her mouth, she looked like the Jessica from years ago. Maybe the hair dye helped with that, she thought. Ally was amazed remembering Jessica's flippant and irresponsible behavior, especially with men. How their lives had changed… even reversed.

"Oh, thank you for the flowers. Welcome to my little ol' place. I'm sure this is small compared to what you're used to."

"Oh, come on, Jessica. Your place is beautiful and judging from the outside, quite large." Walking over to the huge dual picture windows, she looked outside. From there she could see her old car down the street, next to the BMW she had parked behind. "I was admiring the neighborhood. It's very nice around here."

"It's okay. It's nothing compared to what I'd planned on having. We never know how life will turn out …do we?" she said, thinking about her failed plan to marry Jack. "But it's not bad. It's something that I can afford."

"No, really Jessica…your place is gorgeous."

"Well, thanks, anyway. Here, have a seat." She directed her to the oversized walnut trimmed, chenille covered sofa. Arranged opposite the sofa was a matching chair. A large area rug lay in front of both, emphasizing the shiny hard wood floors around the periphery. Ally walked to the plush sofa and sat down. "Her taste has changed and so far so has her attitude," she thought smiling as she sat.

"Would you like a glass of wine… no, I'm sorry. I mean tea. I have some tea if you like." She said, almost apologetically. Ally's salivary glands began to react. She could not resist.

"Maybe one glass just to calm my nerves," she thought. "Thanks, I'll have a glass of wine," Jessica was stunned. She almost took a double take. Ally was never one to drink alcohol.

"Probably living around all those rich people all those years, with their cocktails at every chance, changed her," Jessica thought, chuckling to herself. Towards the kitchen was a small bar. Behind it were shelves that stored all types and sizes of glasses and several bottles of alcoholic beverages. Also behind the bar was a small refrigerator where she had chilled a bottle of Pinot Noir just before Ally was to arrive. At that time, she thought the wine would be only for herself.

"Is this Pinot Noir okay?" she asked.

"That will be fine, thank you."

Walking back with the two glasses and bottle of wine, she placed hers on the glass top coffee table while she walked over to hand a glass to Ally and began to pour. "Is this enough? Say when…"

Filling it almost to the top, Ally said,

"Okay, thank you, Jessica." She took a large gulp as if she was dying of thirst. Again, Jessica was amazed and couldn't believe her eyes. She had changed and not only in looks, she thought. She sat down on the chair in front of Ally after pouring herself a glass and took a sip. "Actually, dinner's ready, but let's sit here for a little while and catch up on old times. "So what made you think of me after all these years?"

Ally had been trying to think of some kind of explanation, but still was unprepared.

"Well, as I told you over the phone, I went… actually my children and I went to visit my parents at the end of the summer and…"

"Oh, you have kids."

"Yeah, I have two. My daughter will be graduating from high school at the end of this school year and my son is middle school."

"It has been a long time. I haven't heard one thing about you since I've been here."

Finding an escape, Ally turned the subject around.

"So, when did you come to New York?" Ally took only a sip this time, but never put her glass down. "I never knew you'd come here until my trip home."

"I don't know why not. I called Toni as soon as I found a place as you said, almost twenty years ago and a few times after that. You mean to tell me that you haven't talked to her until your trip a few months ago?"

Not wanting to make Jessica feel that she had been abandoned, she said,

"I've only talked to Toni briefly from time to time. I guess with raising a family, we didn't have a lot of time to talk." Trying to divert the attention from herself said, "So, why did you come here...to New York? That's quite a ways away from everyone."

"Well, I didn't have anything holding me there. I was single, no family per say, no commitments, so why not get a fresh start somewhere else?"

"That's as good a reason as any," Ally remarked.

"So, Toni never told you, huh."

"Told me what?"

"That I'd moved to New York."

"No, not until I went home this summer to see my parents. How's that dinner coming? I can smell something really good coming from over there. Are you baking Italian bread, or something?" trying to avert her questioning.

"Yes, oh my gosh. I completely forgot about it." She jumped up and swiftly rushed into the kitchen. In a little while, she walked back to the living room and told Ally to come into the dining room for dinner. "I'm glad you said something. I got there in time. It hadn't burned, but it was ready to come out of the oven. Let's eat now before something does go wrong."

Ally had picked up her empty wine glass and brought it with her to the table. "Why don't you sit here?" All the food had been placed in the center of the table. The bread was hot and the butter was chilled. The elegant ivory linen tablecloth was designed with a botanical pattern that hung so perfectly with only the corners of the mahogany dining table showing. The place setting was flawless. Recalling her instructions by her mother-in-law, Nancy, she saw that every item was properly and perfectly in place, from the napkin to the glassware. Thinking back to the last spaghetti dinner at Jessica's back in California, this was quite a difference. Probably, she learned this to try to impress Jack. She was sure he had been here.
"Ally, I never asked you about Greg. How's he doing?"
"He's okay. The business is keeping him busy."
"Oh, yeah, do I remember the business," sounding a bit annoyed by the thought. "That business came before everything and anybody." Jessica continued as she got up from the table carrying on, ranting and raving, describing Jack's insensitivity towards her and his total disregard for her feelings and the sacrifice she had made to be with him. She told her how he had treated her and used her for his own convenience and pleasure. "He never really cared for me, Ally," she said sadly, as Ally continued eating and listening as she watched her pace back and forth in front of her. She went on so with her garrulous rants that Ally could not even utter a word of affirmation if she wanted to. She knew Jack only used Jessica from the first time they met. What did she expect? The minute she saw the guy she went after him like a dog in heat, Ally thought. She poured another glass of wine before she sat down to take another sip. Her grievances and bitter rants continued with more details about how Jack took advantage of her knowing she loved him and played with her like a toy until he had had enough and then tossed her aside like a worn out rug that had been tread on for years.
"Lucky for you... you got the better one and married him." Finally, she made her way back to her seat and looking across the table at Ally sternly. A sudden termination of her tirade, she asked Ally, "Do you want some more wine?"
"Sure, I'll take some more. It's very good." As soon as Jessica got up and filled

her glass, she watched how Ally gulped that full glass of wine down without even stopping to take a breath. This gesture broke her train of thought from Jack and was more puzzled about Ally's drinking. She wanted to find out what was really going on. Why was she here anyway? She didn't look at all like the beautiful young lady she had known years before. Yes, it had been a long time, but she was so thin, her eyes were sunken with dark rings, and she had a look of such despair. Something was wrong. But what did she want with her? How could she help her?

Ally noticed it had gotten very quiet. She could tell that Jack had evidently left a sore spot with Jessica. To break the silence and quell the charged atmosphere she tried to change the direction of the conversation.

"You know my daughter, Sage, was inducted into the honor society at her school. She may even get a scholarship for college."

"That's nice," Jessica responded with disinterest. Then she began talking about her trip home. She talked about how she had visited their former employer and how Toni had gotten some of her old coworkers to go out for lunch with her. Many things had changed since they both left and so had the people. A few had retired, some had even been promoted, and like her, some had gone on to seek employment elsewhere. Jessica asked about her old boss that everybody thought she was sleeping with. She bragged about the money he had spent on her. She talked and laughed about her outings with him and that she had even met him at a few swanky hotels before. Knowing the old man was married didn't matter to her, she told Ally. He asked her out and what did she care he was buying. But even now, after all these years, she would still not admit that something more serious was going on between the two of them, but Ally didn't challenge her. Jessica finally brought up that long ago weekend trip to the beach. Ally didn't want to talk about that part of her life, even though that time had been the happiest time in her life. But it became the beginning of the end for her. She certainly didn't want to share that with Jessica. She never cared about anybody except herself anyway, and it was apparent she had not changed. From their conversation, it was clear that she still didn't have anyone even here that she could call a real friend. Those were her very words during her bellyaching about Jack. When they finished eating, Ally asked if she could have another refill of wine. Holding up the bottle and noticing it was empty, Jessica went behind the bar to get another bottle. First stopping to open it at her own seat, she filled her glass and then walked over to fill Ally's.

Standing next to her and pouring the wine, she said, "You said people have changed? You certainly have."

"What do you mean? I'm older, so I know I look a little older."

"Nooo… I mean you can put it away, girl. I remember when you would never drink any kind of alcohol. How many glasses have you had now?"

"I don't know. Are you counting? It has a taste like a really good wine, that's all." Having had a few glasses herself, she stepped back and said sarcastically, "So now you've become a real wine connoisseur."

"Well, I did have to entertain clients for the business," Ally responded.

Strutting around Ally, holding her glass, blurted out in a snobbish English vernacular, "Yes, and go to all those social functions that you rich people go to and have your dinner parties and invite all of your rich friends," she said tauntingly.

As Ally looked down to scoop up another helping, she said,

"Come on, Jessica. I thought I'd come over to see you since it's been such a long time, and…" Looking up to see that Jessica was now standing directly over her, face to face, she stopped her speech. So close, Ally thought, that she could smell the pasta and wine on her breath.

"Yeah, and that's another thing. You know what? I think you're lying." Jessica blared out with slurred speech.

"Lying about what?" Ally asked, surprised by the accusation.

"You didn't come here to see me. It's been almost twenty years, for God's sake," she yelled. Walking away, she asked, "What do you really want from me? I've been trying to figure this thing out ever since you called. It can't be money. That family's got more money than they know what to do with." Turning around again, she asked, "So what do you want from me, Ally?"

Ally stood up and very calmly spoke.

"Okay. I'm going to be honest." Beginning with the death of her father, she confessed that she did not have enough money to buy the plane tickets for her family to get there for the funeral that was the following week and how desperate she was to get the money, and thought about her.

"And you thought about me? Why would you come to me? You should have enough money. What about your rich family? What is the truth, Ally? You're still not telling me what's really going on. Are you on drugs or something?"

"No. Absolutely not!" she said emphatically.

"Then why can't you get the money from your husband? And why aren't you going as a family?"

"Look, I was hoping not to have to get into this, but Greg and I are divorced. I thought Jack would have told you."

"Divorced? When? I don't believe it. Greg treated you as if you were some

271

goddess or queen, or something. Now look at you. When did you get a divorce?"

"It's been over ten years now."

"Ten years? …God! Where's your alimony and child support?"

"I was so distraught over the divorce, that I…I didn't want anything from him,"

"Well, that was stupid. What about your children? Then again, that sounds like something you would do. I would have taken him for everything that he wasn't even entitled to. Even if you took the money, that family wouldn't even miss a penny. They have so much."

"Jessica, you just don't know what went on, or what was said about me and what they thought about me," she tried to explain. "It's too involved to explain, plus, it's no use talking about it now anyway. I already made my choice."

"You certainly did. And it was a dumb one. Now you have to live with it. Look at where you are now. You're here begging me for money and they have more than they will ever need. Did I hear you say you thought Jack would have told me about your divorce? So, you did know I was here. You liar," she said harshly. "I'm sure your friend, Toni, told you. That's the only way you could have known I was here, and why I came. I know she told you I came to New York to be closer to Jack."

"No, that's not true."

"Oh, shut up. You're just a liar," she shouted.

"No, Jessica, please listen to me. That's not true."

"That Toni, she never cared for me anyway. Nobody did."

"Look, Jessica, Toni told me you were in New York, but she never told me until a few months ago…this summer. It was only then that I found out you were here."

Mumbling to herself, "I'm sure it wasn't Greg… it couldn't have been Greg…" Again, she began to rant, "Jack wouldn't have told anyone about me. He hardly gave me the time of day. I saw him for about a month after I moved in and after that, he disappeared. It doesn't matter now anyway."

They both were intoxicated at this point.

"I'm so sorry. I knew you fell for him when you met that weekend, but I thought it was just a weekend fling. You must have fallen in love with him. I'm sorry. In all honesty, I only found out this summer that you were here, otherwise I'd probably would have contacted you well before now." They both had calmed down, until Ally asked, "So, do you think you can loan me the money? I really need it so my family and I can get to my father's funeral."

Jessica became angry and started berating Ally in a nasty and harsh tone. "You have the nerve to come here pretending to be a friend, knowing that your real motive was to get money. How do I know your father died? I don't believe you. I knew you were up to something the minute I saw you. You looked like you'd been through the mill, plus, you drink like a fish! And you thought you were so much better than me. You were so self-righteous with your Bible quotes…everybody thought you were so sweet. In your eyes, I was just a rude and selfish whore. Did you think I didn't hear and see you and Toni making gestures to each other at that dinner table that night we first met Greg? I was nothing in your eyes. To you and Toni, I was nothing but a foul-mouthed slut. Now who's the whore? Look at you. Now you come to me begging for money like you're on drugs or something. Even if you're not on drugs, you're an alcoholic, for sure. Where's your God now? Why didn't you ask Him for the money? How could you stoop so low? You know what… I want you to leave. Get out of my house."

So intoxicated and barely able to walk a straight line herself, she staggered over to open the door. Grabbing her purse from the sofa, with her head hanging down, Ally wobbled towards the door.

"I don't ever want to see you again."

"I can't believe that you don't believe me, Jessica," Ally said softly and pitifully. "The only thing I believe about what you told me is that you're divorced. That's all I believe. You need to get some help. You obviously have a substance abuse problem."

Ally was crestfallen. She was so deeply hurt over how she was chided and scorned. Why Jessica didn't believe her, she just couldn't understand. How could Jessica think she could be a drug addict or even an alcoholic? She had always admitted that she liked to drink sometimes and maybe have a little more than she should, but she enjoyed it. It was not something that she needed and it made her relax. She was not doing anyone any harm. But all of her friends felt the same way. They had told her to cut back on the drinking. She silently and tearfully walked down the steep carpeted stairway holding tightly to the banister, stepping slowly and very carefully.

Chapter 20

Ally left Jessica's apartment, despondent and catapulted into utter hopelessness. What was she going to tell Sage and Casey? Once she told Jessica the reason for the loan, she just knew her problem would be solved. Having known her for years, she thought she would be more than willing to help her out since she was in such a bind. In all these years, she thought maybe Jessica had changed for the better. But obviously, nothing had changed about her. She was still the jealous, selfish, erratic person that she met almost 20 years ago. And how could she have thought those awful things about her? She could not believe what had just happened.

There was no way she could go straight home, at least not without an explanation. Trying to think of someplace to go where she could be alone to think, she saw a little neighborhood pub not too close, but in the vicinity of where she worked. She had never noticed it before in all the time she had been working at Matthews Place, the restaurant bar and grill where she now was working. It was close to her job and very close to the subway as well. She needed to clear her head and figure out what to do. Hopefully, no one she knew would be in there. There was no time to waste. Jessica had gotten her so upset she needed something to calm her nerves. It was around seven-thirty, so it was quite easy to find a parking space on the street. When she walked in, she scanned the place to see that none of her friends or coworkers were there. After the dinner fiasco, she felt the need to be alone to sort things out and get over the contentious verbal assault by Jessica. The place was comfortably small. The lighting was dim. She decided to sit at the far corner of the bar where there was only enough space for one stool. The bartender was very kind and greeted her immediately. She ordered a whiskey and soda. Having only been there for about thirty minutes, ordered another. Beginning to feel a little better, she thought she would have one more then leave, even though she still had not figured out an alternative plan. Another half hour had passed, and the place was getting more crowded and noisier. Thinking she had better get ready to leave, she slowly and unsteadily maneuvered herself off the stool. When she looked up a man with a very pleasant smile was staring right at her face.

It was strange that she had not noticed him sitting there before. With his mouth closed, he smiled at her again and then sipped his drink. "My, he has the most beautiful smile," she thought. Thinking he was such a friendly looking middle-aged gentleman, she smiled back. He then turned and motioned the bartender to come to him. He said something to the bartender when he leaned over and in a few minutes, the bartender was walking in her direction with a drink. Placing the glass in front of her, he said, "Compliments of the gentleman over there." She had been drinking the same drink. Looking at the man, she mouthed 'thank you.' He bowed his head, smiled, and continued sipping on his one drink. She thought that that was such nice gesture from a complete stranger, just at a time when she was feeling so abandoned. She sat down again for another twenty minutes to finish the kind stranger's gift. By this time, she was quite tipsy. As she got herself together, she thought she would go to the generous patron and verbally thank him for his generosity. There were customers standing in the aisle close to the bar chatting with friends, waitresses carrying trays of food and drinks to the tables as she laboriously made her way through the crowd towards the exit. When she finally got to his stool, his back was turned. She tapped him on the shoulder and he swiveled around to acknowledge whoever had tapped him. She looked at his face and was stunned. This man could not have been who was just sitting on that stool. This man looked as though he was a hundred years old with deep wrinkles all over his face. His eyes were sunken down in the sockets, what should have been white was yellow. His pupils appeared to be slits, like those of a cat and their color was neon green, which flashed through his straw-like strands of hair over his forehead. His smile became a grin revealing sharp yellow rotting teeth. It seemed to her that she was frozen there, staring for an eternity. Her heart was pounding as she tried to turn away from the ugly sight and shove her way through the crowded pub to get away from it. Her body seemed not to be moving. Her feet were heavy, stuck to the floor. The whole scene was playing in slow motion as she glided towards the red exit sign.

Suddenly, she felt something cold touch her arm. He was trying to grab her as she practically fell running for the door. People looked at her in puzzlement as she went by. "Get off me!" she yelled.

"What's wrong with her?" she heard someone say.

"She looks like she's seen a ghost."

"What's going on?" another said.

"Let me go!" she cried out.

She thought she heard someone call her by name. She turned slightly, and it was him. Was this a nightmare? Was she dreaming? Maybe it was her imagination. No one else seemed frightened. Couldn't they see what she was seeing? Couldn't they see that heinous monster chasing after her? It was grotesque … something not human. The monstrous thing continued to ask her to wait, calling her by name. She kept pacing towards the exit sign, which seemed to be getting farther away. When she finally got to the door, the thing had caught up with her just as she pushed it open. Before she could step outside, he gently held her arm. She began to tremble and shake. Finally caught, with her eyes closed and petrified by fear, she gave up and surrendered. She heard a kind voice say, "Miss, you left your purse."

Still frightened out of her wits, she opened her eyes and turned around to look at him. It was the handsome gentleman who had bought her the drink. "Ma'am, I'm so sorry I frightened you. I had no choice but to grab you before you got away." Stepping outside, he continued to explain his pursuit. "You left your purse on the counter where you were sitting." With an outstretched arm, he handed it to her.

"Oh, jeez. I am so embarrassed," she confessed.

"Yeah, the bartender handed it to me so I could catch up with you to give it to you before you got too far away."

She took the purse and tucked it under her arm.

"Thank you so much. Again, I'm so sorry for running and making such a scene. But when you started chasing me, I got scared."

"That's okay. I'd be scared too if a stranger was chasing and grabbing at me."

"Do you know me by any chance?" she asked.

Puzzled by her question, he responded in wonderment. "No. I've never seen you before today. When I sat down and saw you sitting alone in the back of the bar …well, you looked so sad, I thought I'd cheer you up by sending you a drink."

"No,... well,...ah... I thought I heard you call my name when you were trying to catch up with me."

"No ma'am, I don't know your name," humbly, he moved back as he responded.

"Mister, I'm sorry about all this. I guess you think I'm crazy. I never even got a chance to thank you, so thank you for the drink... and my purse."

"Yeah, you looked at me and took off running like you had just seen a monster or something. I didn't think I was that bad looking."

"Ohhh... no, I'm sorry. Sorry, I know I keep saying I'm sorry, but I am truly sorry. No really. In fact, I think you're quite handsome. It's just that I suddenly realized the time and I had to get out of there in a hurry... and then you started chasing me..." she answered, with such a glib lie.

The man looked at her oddly again. "I guess you'd better be going then," he said, hurrying her along.

"Thanks again."

"Okay, and Miss, you take care of yourself and be careful," he said and went back into the pub.

The comment stunned her. That was the second time a stranger had told her 'to take care of herself and be careful.' "What did they mean?" she wondered.

When she got to the car, she just sat there for a while. She had not been this sober in years. That episode scared her nearly out of her mind. Was she out of her mind? It was so real. She clearly saw that gruesome face. What about the cold touch? She knew exactly where it had touched her because she could still feel it. What was happening to her? She thought she had better not tell this to anyone... ever...not yet, anyway. When she arrived home, she wanted to evade the subject of the loan she hadn't gotten from Jessica. Casey and Sage were sitting in the den watching television when she walked in.

Casey heard her come in and came in the living room to meet her. "Hi, Mom."

"Hi, sweetie, did you eat dinner?"

"Yeah, Sage made something for us."

"Oh, yeah. What did she fix?"

"We had spaghetti and hamburgers."

"Hey, that's funny. I had spaghetti too. Where's Sage?"

"She's back here in the den. We're watching a movie."

"Did she go to work today?"

"Yes, but she came home early."

Shielding her feelings of anxiety and despair, she thought she had no alternative but to confess to them the outcome and get it over with. The only other option she could think of was to ask Toni if she would loan her the money, if just for her ticket, and with regret, borrow the rest from her mother. She knew Sage would be upset, but there was no other way. Already, she felt like such a deadbeat for having to even borrow any money at all, so to ask for more than that would be a total disgrace. It was times like these that she regretted having let her pride blind her common sense during the divorce settlement. Jessica was right. She allowed her anger, her broken heart, and her disappointment to obstruct and deny what was in the best interest of even her children and allowed the sin of pride to result in self-pity and destroy her sense of reason.

"Sage, could you please come in the kitchen for a minute? I need to talk to you and Casey," she said soberly. Sage walked in and plopped down on the chair opposite her mother. By the look on her mother's face, she could see that she had been drinking. Not wanting to look at her, she turned her head and listened.

"It's not good what I have to tell you. Well, the longtime friend I told you about… who I thought I'd probably be able to borrow the money from, well, she wasn't able to loan it to me. I'm so sorry, but I can only afford for me to go next week unless I can borrow the rest from…" Hesitating, while the tears flowed down her cheeks, she looked at her silent, but attentive children. These pangs of hopelessness and helplessness were crushing her. She had never felt this low before. Having to tell her children they couldn't be present at their grandfather's funeral was almost unbearable.

Out of the silence, she heard Sage's voice. "We can go," she said in a tone of indifference.

"What did you say?"

"I said we can all go."

"Sage, please don't."

"Please don't what?"

"This isn't a time to be rebellious."

"I'm not being rebellious. The tickets are already paid for. My boss Mr. Melmann is loaning us… well, me, the money."

"He did?" she exclaimed in disbelief.

"Yeah, he told me today, just before he let me leave early. He said I can pay him back by working without pay."

"No, Sage, that's not fair to you."

"Don't worry. This isn't all on me. You have to pay as well. Together, we are going to pay him back as soon as possible."

Ally got up, went over to Sage and gave her a hug, but Sage did not respond, her hands still in her lap. She only cringed from her touch.

"Of course, we're going to pay him back." Smelling the seemingly forever odor of alcohol, Sage turned her head as her mother spoke. Finding out about the dilemma they were in, Mr. Melmann had asked Sage to tell him the details of their plane trip, and he would purchase their tickets and have them waiting at the airport. Stepping back and with a big grin on her face, she said, "That is so wonderful. That is so generous and so very kind of him to do that. I'll have to thank him myself." Ally was elated and joyful. That seemingly insurmountable obstacle had been removed.

"I already did," Sage said sternly.

"I know you did, but I would like to thank him personally to express my appreciation for helping us out. I've heard stories about how generous and kind he is. Plus, I don't want him to think I'm sending my children out to solve our family problems." Ally could see that Sage was not happy with her response. She also knew Sage was never pleased about anything she did. If only she had known this before she went to Jessica's. All the humiliation, her obvious contempt and vicious venom could have been avoided. So many years had gone by, and Jessica's callousness had not changed.

"Let's get packed and be ready to leave by tomorrow morning. Is that okay with you?" "I'll be ready," Sage said sharply, heading to her room. "Besides, I started packing as soon as I got the news."

Even though it was late and she was tired, her emotions were still frazzled from the evenings' unanticipated and startling events. Ally wanted to take a walk just about a block away to the local bar to be alone and try again to relax with maybe just a beer this time. It was a weekday night and the place was just about empty. That was very pleasing to her since she was not in the mood to have any kind of conversation with anyone anyway, which on some days was not easy to avoid. Most of the patrons were the neighbors, the locals in the community, who knew each other's deep secrets, but most times, were some fabricated, depressing story about some poor soul in the neighborhood. She never discussed her issues with any of them, nor participated in any gossiping and would always decline to give any input in their debates. Sitting there, she would overhear someone else's personal affairs being analyzed and criticized. The victim's life was sliced and diced by this panel of uninformed, unqualified locals who always had the perfect solution for the selected person's issue of the day.

Nate, the bartender, with his sleeves always rolled up to the elbow and his big glowing smile showing through his heavy mustache, greeted her as always when she walked in. She had become familiar with him from all her many visits to his little establishment. She ordered a beer and sat quietly sipping it wondering if sometimes in her absence if her life had been the 'topic of the day.' But that thought with all she was going through was the least of her worries and quickly dismissed the notion. Regressing to the thought of how her once hopeless problem had remarkably been resolved by a real life 'Good Samaritan' gave her a rare feeling of tranquility. Soon she noticed the bar had become a bit crowded. All the jabber that was going on in her mind was suddenly interrupted. She could hear one of those community discussions beginning to organize over at one of the tables nearby. About five people had gathered there at first. The fifth person who looked over her way was standing. She was almost finished with her drink and was ready to leave when the only clear word she heard in the almost deafening chatter in the whole place was her name. They were talking about her. They saw her sitting there. "How could that inconsiderate bunch of losers be so bold?" she thought. She had sometimes spent a good amount of her paycheck buying some of them rounds of drinks, which was part of the reason she stayed behind in her bills, including the rent. Another person who had joined the crowd looked her way. It was a familiar face, but she couldn't remember the name or from where she had seen her before. Getting a little ticked off about their audaciousness to talk about her right in her presence, she felt was a bit much. Gulping the last of her beer, she boldly walked over to their table and barged her way through. Just as she was about to open her mouth to give them a piece of her mind, she was shocked at who she saw facing her. It was Jessica. She could not believe that she was sitting there. What was she doing in this part of town? In her state of shock, not one word uttered out of her mouth. Time seemed to have stopped, and all she could do was stare. The only thing in her sight was her face. An eerie darkness seemed to be slowly pouring over and stilled the room. That face… that same angry face that had been embedded in her mind since she left her apartment. It was that same angry person who had gone on that slanderous tirade against her, kicking her out, and even slamming the door behind her. Suddenly, Jessica opened her mouth as if to start another vitriolic attack when her mouth began to twist, her face contorted and turned abnormally distorted. Ally was bewildered and terrified as she watched this horrifying transformation of her face occurring right before her eyes. She was slowly beginning to age. Wrinkles were forming rapidly and deeply. Her skin began to droop, appearing to be melting. The eyes began to sink deep into their sockets. And her skin darkened as the wrinkles became deeper. Onto the table her hair started to fall from her head over her face. She had become the ugly, wrinkled, half-bald, grotesque face of that male creature she had seen at that bar earlier that evening. In fear, she turned to run. Her strides were weak as she was heading towards the exit sign down a very narrow way to the door. It was happening again. What was going on? Could this be real or her imagination again? From the creature, she could hear those same berating abuses that Jessica had vehemently ranted at her and now had gotten up and was chasing right behind her. The more she ran, the farther the neon exit light appeared. She could feel the cold touch of his long boney fingers touching and grabbing at her shoulder. She tried to scream, but could only utter a grunt out of her mouth. It grabbed her shoulder again. Struggling forcefully to get away, the horrible figure, nevertheless, held his grasp even when she pushed the tavern door open. As she tore through the door, she was looking directly into the eyes of a dark, tall bearded man, standing in front of her wearing a military jacket, who had jumped back just in time before they collided. She noticed a very large dog with him, who had already leaped at her pursuer as he let her go and seemed to have vanished. Still running down the street, she heard a familiar voice calling her. She looked around, side to side, as she proceeded to try to find a safe place to hide, not being sure where the creature might be. She heard that familiar voice again. Stopping in her tracks to look for the voice, she heard, "Mom. Mom."

It was Casey. She sat up in her bed. She had been kicking and tossing the covers until they practically wrapped around her legs. Her heart was pounding and her breathing was hard. Casey was standing by her bed. "Mom, you must have been having a nightmare. Are you okay? I tapped your shoulder, but you kept kicking. I heard you yell for someone to let you go, so I started shaking you to wake you up." She grabbed Casey and hugged him. "Oh Casey, that was you grabbing me…awww. Then I was dreaming," she said, as she held onto him. With a sigh of relief, she spoke to him to assure him that she was okay.

"Oh yeah, I was having a terrible nightmare. But don't worry. I'm okay. You go on now and get some sleep. I'll be fine. We've got to get up and be ready to leave tomorrow morning, so make sure you have everything you want to take."

"Okay, Mom. Goodnight."

"Goodnight." She kissed him on the forehead and he left. Until then, she didn't realize how much her young son worried about her.

That whole ordeal had been a dream… a nightmare. What was going on with her? Relieved that it was only a dream, she got up to wash the sweat from her face. She didn't want to go to bed now. That dream seemed too real. What about earlier today? That was no dream. She was wide awake. What was happening to her? Was she losing her mind? Afraid, and not wanting to go back to sleep, she remembered her replacement stash of vodka in the back of her closet. She reached in to find it exactly where she had put it just the other day. Sitting on the side of the bed, she noticed her hands were shaking as she reached to get a glass from the drawer in the nightstand. "I guess I'm still nervous from that dream," she thought. She managed to calm the shaking and poured a little into the glass quickly downing its contents, rationalizing that this would calm her nerves and hopefully stop the shaking. She poured a second and drank several more glasses until it was practically gone. Opening her suitcase she had almost finished packing, she put the remainder of her bottle between her nightgown and robe for safekeeping. Remembering the reason she was packing brought back tears to her eyes. Her dear loving father was gone. Except for Toni's help, her poor, elderly mother was alone to take care of the final arrangements of her husband and her best friend. She felt so worthless, selfish, and ashamed for not being there in her time of need. Being an only child, the one child that her parents had to rely on in their golden years, but that was not so. She was utterly incapable of giving them the help they needed, as they were growing older. When she married Greg, she never thought being there for them would ever be an issue. Being able to get to them at a moment's notice would never have been a problem as he had promised her. He assured her of this because he knew this was her biggest concern when she agreed to marry him being she was their only child, and would be moving so far away from them. But that was when they were together. She never thought once that she would not have a life without Greg… something else he had assured her of. They had loved each other so much that there was no doubt they would always be together. How naive she had been, even at such a young age, she should have known better. How could she have believed that the "haves-nots" could ever survive, or be accepted by the "haves"? But she believed him when he told her that none of that mattered. Her tears were so profuse that they began to dampen the clothes she was packing in the suitcase. As she thought about her past and began making excuses for her mistakes and inadequacies, a suppressed thought of shame burst through from her subconscious mind. She was deeply ashamed. How could she cope with being there knowing she was going to be in the presence of her mother, the church members, the neighbors, and her friends? She was ashamed of having had two failed marriages and the awful life she was now living that she had subjected to her children. What she had become was not who her parents had raised and taught her to be from a small child. Shame was the real reason she could never move back home. It had nothing to do with keeping the children near their father. That was obvious. Quickly, she suppressed those thoughts and began blaming Greg and his family for the horrible life she was living. It was his fault and his weakness that had brought all the hardship they were going through. His mother was the 'thrown wrench', the troublemaker who was a hard-hearted, hateful phony, of who he was too cowardly to stand up to, to save his own family. She thought about Janice, his first fiancée. She was certain her life was one of blissfulness. The vodka was taking effect, as she sat down on the side of the bed remembering her poignant past. She did not want to lie down because she was still afraid that she would fall asleep. Now fully bashed, she just fell back on the bed and passed out into a deep dreamless unconscious sleep.

Chapter 21

"Aren't you going to your ex-father-in-law's funeral?"

"I don't know," Greg answered, sounding a bit annoyed. Jack had found out from Jessica that Ally's father had passed away and called his brother to make sure he knew about it. Even when Nancy gave her insensitive opinion discouraging Greg to attend, Jack stood his ground. He told her it was the right thing to do.

"I don't know, Jack. The kids probably hate me. I haven't seen them in so many years. What would I say to them?"

"Okay, then you figure it out. Now you know why I never got married. It's less complicated." Jack decided he would not say another word or ask anymore about the matter. It was Greg's decision to make. Jack had already bought his ticket to California, after speaking to Toni to get the details about the arrangements. He had gotten her phone number from Jessica. Not trusting Jessica, he called Toni to find out for sure if what she claimed about Ally's father was true. Since his brother's, not so mutual, divorce, Jack did not want to speak directly to Ally's mom because he didn't know how they felt towards his family. From what he had gotten from Greg, it appeared that all ties had been severed.

He could not believe that woman after all these years still had his phone number. After their last encounter when she moved to New York, he had told Jessica they wouldn't be seeing each other anymore, not that he saw that much of her anyway, but remembered how upset she became. The tantrums, the begging, and pleading made him quite irritated. Having no explanation to give her for his decision, he left her sprawled out sobbing noisily on the living room floor, as he last remembered. How she got the idea that he cared for her, he could never understand. So, why she would call now after that scene caused some suspicion and was reluctant, but somewhat curious to find out what she wanted, so he decided to call her back when he heard her voice message on the answering machine. After the affable exchange of greetings, she described the whole dinner scene with Ally. She also told him that she didn't believe a word she had told her and asked if Ally and Greg were truly divorced. Jack had already known for years what was going on with Ally and the kids, even before the divorce, something that he was not going to reveal to her, though. Admitting their divorce didn't bother him. It was already old news that everybody knew about, except her apparently.

Jack had not talked to Sage for a while and didn't know about her grandfather's passing until Jessica's call. She never contacted him to let him know, but as soon as he found out, he called her immediately to find out if they needed any money to help with the arrangements or transportation since Jessica had told him that money was the reason Ally had come to her in the first place. He never let on to her who had told him or why he offered money. Sage told her uncle that everything had been taken care of thanked him for his offer. She was so glad that Mr. Melmann had offered to help because she didn't want any help from that family. They had done without them all these years, but under these circumstances, if they hadn't come up with the money, she wondered what her answer might have been.

Going through another one of Sage's castigating tantrums after that horrible dream, Ally wanted to really go out this time and not in a dream, but she knew Sage would pitch a fit if she found out, knowing they had to pack and be ready for tomorrow's flight to California. She had come in to make sure her mother had packed. Sometimes Sage could make Ally feel so incompetent and unfit as a mother that she wanted to end it all. As she gathered all her things to take to California, she was bombarded with thoughts of unworthiness. What did they need her for anyway? She was a useless, a poor excuse for a mother who was probably one foul-up closer to losing custody of them than she had ever been. Sharon tried so hard to help her; she appreciated everything she had done, and was doing, to help her to maintain her family. There was very little means of paying back any of the favors she had already done. She also knew Sharon was not looking to be paid back for anything. She was the very epitome of a Christian…a loving, generous, caring, and sacrificing individual. She even managed to keep the residents at bay when they wanted to report her to the office for her undesirable and rebellious behavior. In return, Ally told Sharon she was going to someday visit her church that she bragged so much about. Whether she meant it or not was yet to be seen. Casey and Sage had gone with Sharon and her family many times. Ally thought it was good that they were able to find the way to live and get better guidance, admitting that they surely were not getting it from her. She didn't want to get in the way of the Bible's influence in their lives. Although it had done nothing for her, maybe it might work for them. In all the years that she had been a Christian, she felt she had gotten nothing out of the deal when she needed it most. And Sharon, what had she gotten? What had God done in her life? Sharon's life had been worse than her own and she got nothing but a dead husband and lost everything that they had worked so hard to get. Certainly, this was not by choice. So, why was she so happy and what did she have to be so thankful for. These thoughts only brought on more bitterness and resentment.

The next morning, with all the bags packed, they called a cab and went to the airport. Sage had been watching Ally's every move, and she knew it. Her bereavement leave was until the following Monday, but Mr. Melmann had given Sage as much time as she needed. The work was falling behind and Sage had decided that as soon as they returned she would get right back to it. When they landed at the airport, Toni was there to pick them up. Sage could tell by the look on Toni's face when she first glanced at her friend that she was not pleased with what she saw, but even so, she could see that she was truly happy to see all of them. Ally's mother Mary, wanted to stay back at the house to have it ready for them when they arrived. When they went in to greet her, everyone cried many tears of joy. The hugs and kisses were non-stop. Everyone's eyes were filled with tears, even Casey's. He dearly loved his grandfather, as did Sage. Their faces stayed wet with more happy tears and of the sadness of the occasion. Ally tried at all cost to avoid letting her mother get a good look at her face. She had enough to deal with. She knew that her face had changed. Her whole physical appearance had changed. The years and stresses of life had taken its toll. Toni helped Ally's mother prepare a light meal for them when they got to the house and then went home.

When Mary arrived home earlier that day from Toni's house, she saw all the monetary gifts and food donations which had begun to pour in from neighbors, friends, church members, and even from Ally's former coworkers. Toni had taken up a collection at her job. There was such a glut of food that much of it had to be taken to Toni's house. Mary was overwhelmed by the show of loving kindness and generosity from everyone that she could do nothing but sit on the sofa and cry. Some even stayed to help around the house. They knew that she had not been home and was staying with her daughter's best friend. Ever since her husband had been rushed to the hospital that fateful day, she had not been back home to stay until now. The house was very sullen. It felt as though it was no longer a home. Grandpa was not there, and the void could be felt. Everyone could feel it and it showed on all their faces. Guilt and grief poured out of Ally as she thought about all the time missed when she could no longer visit her parents as often as she had when she and Greg were married.

Later on that afternoon after they arrived, they all got dressed and went directly to the funeral home to see Ally's father. It was incomprehensible to even be there for such an occasion. They stopped at the door and looked around at the many flowers and sprays that had been sent and placed near the casket and around the room. Slowly, they stepped up to the casket holding hands. Looking down where their most beloved and once vivacious remains lay clad in a navy blue suit, white shirt and matching print tie, the tears began to flow. By now, she was over the initial stage of the realization of her loss; Mary saw how hard it was for the children and tried to comfort them. Watching as they wept brought back memories of how they had clung to their grandfather more than they did her. He always had some story to tell them about when he was growing up, a fun place to go where they had never been, or a not so palatable, but helpful lesson that he had learned along the way of life's beaten path that he wanted to pass on to them.

"He looks like he's only sleeping," Casey said, which mysteriously gave him an inkling of relief.

"Yeah, he does," Sage responded putting her arms around his shoulders.

Ally had to walk away. Seeing her dad lying there, still and not breathing, gave her such a rush of grief that she turned away and swiftly walked out into the hallway, swallowed up in guilt and tears of sorrow. She began to feel that she had deserted him. Her calls were so infrequent. She could have at least called. Why didn't she even call? Her mother went to her side to try to console her.

"Mom, I didn't even call like I should have."

"Sweetheart, don't get yourself upset. We understood that you had a family to take care of…and doing everything all alone. Just think, God gave you a chance to see him one last time before He called him home. That was a blessing."

Back home and deep in their thoughts both Sage and Ally regretted all the lost time they felt had been wasted when they should have been there. Casey went into the kitchen where his grandmother was preparing something for them eat. The day had somehow gone by quickly. She had a sweet treat for him as she always did when they came to visit. He sat at the table and asked many more questions about his grandfather.

Since it was late and everybody was suffering from jet lag, they decided to go straight to bed. Ally was somewhat reluctant to sleep because of her fear of having that awful dream again but took her chances anyway. She never told anybody about the dreams, not even Toni. She constantly reminded herself that it was only just a dream, as real as it may have seemed. Something like that could not have been real. What human being could look like that and be alive? "I'm not going to think about it," she told herself.

When they retired for bed, Sage went to her mother's room to warn her not to do anything that might hurt or embarrass her grandmother. They had already had visits from a few people in the neighborhood that day after they had gotten back from the funeral home. So far, she managed to get through the day unscathed.

"Come on, Sage. I don't want to hurt my own mother."

"Oh, really? You could have fooled me," she said with bite in her voice. Through the years, the neighbors had heard that Ally's marriage had ended. They had seen how infrequent their visits had become and in those years, they avoided any reference to her private life whenever they came to express their condolences and sympathy. They only had words of hope and encouragement for them all and assured them that they were going to look out for her mother and grandmother while they were so far away.

Saturday, the following morning, Sage had gotten up very early and made breakfast. Everyone could smell the aroma of breakfast. They had had a good night's sleep, even Ally. She always felt comfortable and safe in her old place of abode. Everyone had gotten up and came down to have breakfast. They all thanked Sage, and Mary said the blessing as everyone held hands around the table. It was something that the kids had not heard or done in a while as a family at their home. After breakfast, Mary and Ally remained seated at the dining room table to go over the funeral arrangements and write the obituary and the program for the funeral. By this time, they only had one more day to get things completed in order to have copies printed in time to be delivered to the church. They found a nice picture for the obituary cover. When Toni showed Ally the picture they had selected, she was very pleased. She would have selected the same one had she been home and was embarrassed by the fact that she wasn't. Although she knew that Toni was trying to help in her absence, she still felt a little jealous that she was not there to help with the arrangements for her own father. She was relieved to learn that her dad had everything in order and had paid for the plot years before, even her mother's. Ally was so happy to learn that their life insurance would take care of her mom and she would not have any worries because she had no means of caring for her financially or otherwise.

As they sat going over the finalities, her mother looked at her with weary eyes, and asked,

"Ally, are you okay, dear?"

"Mom, why are you asking me that? Of course, I am. I'm just fine. Since I've been on my own, I've had to work, but we're okay. And stop worrying about me. Now, how are you?"

"I'm doing okay. You know me and your father had been together for many years."

"Yes, I know."

"I'm really going to miss him, but you know what? We knew that eventually one day, one of us would have to go. And we knew where we were going. So I'm not worried, Ally.

Your dad is with God now, and one day I'll be with both of them."

"Oh, Mom, don't say that."

"It's true. Everybody will someday. Just be sure you wind up in the right place."

Sage was in the kitchen washing the breakfast dishes but had gotten close enough to hear part of their conversation. She just didn't trust her mother anymore. She had become so deceitful that she could put no trust in anything she said. She heard her lying about how well they were doing. Maybe she didn't want her mother to worry, but her whole life was still a mess and just one big lie.

Noticing that her hands continued to shake at times ever since that encounter at the bar, she convinced herself that having a small glass of wine or some type of alcoholic beverage would help. While preparing for bed that night her hands again began to shake. Probably the shaking was due to her nerves and knew for sure that she could calm them easily if she could only relax with even a small glass of wine or even the vodka she had brought with her. She didn't know how or what Sage would do if she found out that she even had it with her, so it was very early in the morning that she decided she would just finish the bottle off and get rid of it before anybody found out. She could never understand how much of this helped and no one knew she had this problem or so she thought. Ever since it started, she had been trying to conceal this new phenomenon. Knowing how to make it stop, avoided any interrogation or suspicion from Sage. It was about 3:00 in the morning, when she thought it would be a safe time to retrieve her little secret. Placing her suitcase on the bed, she went to get the bottle that she had safely placed in the zippered compartment after unpacking her clothes. What? It was gone. She was beside herself. She wanted to scream. Filled with anger that someone had sneaked into her suitcase and took what belonged to her was outrageous. Who had even been in her room without her permission? Was it Sage, or Casey? She knew that Casey would sometimes find her stash and put it somewhere else, hoping she would forget that she even had it. But from Sage's threatening warning, she thought that maybe she could be the culprit. The bottom line was that it was gone, but she wouldn't dare ask anybody about it. Her hands began to tremble and shake even more. For the rest of that early morning, her mind raced with angry thoughts, embarrassment, and guilt. Around 5:00, she decided that she could no longer lie in bed and think about it anymore, so she chose to get up and fix breakfast for everybody. Her intent was to figure out who the sneak could have been. Moving around in the kitchen brought on a sense of nostalgia. She envisioned herself many years before when she was a little girl helping her mother in the kitchen and the years that followed growing up. These thoughts had a soothing and calming effect and noticed that the shaking had even lessened. Those were the days when she didn't have a care in the world. Everything she touched in that kitchen had a meaning and brought back to her remembrance some of the happy events and interesting conversations discussed at their old-fashioned kitchen table.

Standing at the sink, she could see the Lewis' house across the street. They had all of those rose bushes of so many colors and the various annuals she planted every year. They were still living there. Next door to them were Mr. and Mrs. Winston and their three big dogs. Through the years, they always had three.

"Hey, what's that smell?" her mother pleasantly asked, startling her out of her daydream as she walked into the kitchen. Everyone else trickled in one by one behind her, raving about the titillating aroma coming from the kitchen. Casey and his grandmother were thrilled to be having such lavish feasts now twice in a row. Sage was silent. She slumped in her seat. Her thoughts were only of never having a hot breakfast at their house in years unless she fixed it herself for herself and Casey, while Ally was usually still in bed recovering from a hangover. Her mother's seemingly thoughtful gesture only aroused the resentment that had been building up within her.

"Sage would you like an egg?" Knowing that Casey didn't like eggs, she didn't ask him, but had prepared his favorite which was waffles that he always wanted to have, but most times didn't get.

"No, thank you," she said in a monotone. Not being able to hold back her feelings any longer, she asked, "Why are you up so early fixing breakfast?" She tried very hard to say her words without anger in her tone, but wanted her mother to know what she meant. Ally only looked at her.

"Bingo. There's the culprit," Ally thought. Seeing what was happening, her grandmother interjected.

"Oh, I think it was nice of your mom to have gotten up so early to make such a lovely meal for everybody. I appreciate everything that all of you are doing... including Casey. He's been right by my side, keeping me company." Casey just smiled. She sensed there was some friction between Ally and Sage ever since they had visited during the summer. She and her husband spoke about it. He was very grieved about what was happening in his daughter's life, but she never mentioned that to anyone.

Ally turned to the stove and began serving everyone.

"Casey, look. I have your favorite."

"Man, this is great. Thanks, Mom."

As she was placing a waffle on his plate, her hands started to tremble. She tried to control it so as not to be noticed, but the waffle fell on the side of the plate.

"Oh Casey, I'm sorry. I guess I didn't have a good grip on the platter."

He picked it up with his fingers and put it on his plate. "It's okay, Mom. It only fell on the table."

"Do you want another one?"

"No, not right now." He noticed, as did Sage, who had been watching her every move. Casey didn't want his mother to have another accident. He saw how her hands began to shake and also noticed how intensely Sage was staring at her. He lived with their constant feuding and Sage's animosity towards her. He didn't know for sure why his mother's hands shook, but thought she may have been nervous because of Sage's stares and attitude about fixing breakfast. But no, this was something new, and he was concerned, especially after witnessing her very frightening episode the other night.

Sunday after breakfast, they decided to stay home and rest. Friday had been quite an emotionally depressing ordeal for everyone and Saturday was busy with visitors. Also, they felt they would probably have more visitors who would come over after church service and wanted to be ready for them. After breakfast, Ally retreated to her room to relax and put on something more appropriate to receive any mourners if anyone should drop by. Sage, Casey, and Mary stayed in the kitchen to prepare some food and beverages in case anyone was hungry. They had been receiving almost daily a ration of some type of food or dessert from neighbors and friends.

It had been a couple of days and Ally's hands were beginning to shake more than they had before. She wondered if anyone had noticed her trembling hands that she experienced in the kitchen. She tried her best to control them and conceal what was happening to her. Sage's antagonistic attitude did not help the matter any either, she thought, getting a little perturbed about her mood. There was one way that she knew how to control it, and that was with a small drink of any alcoholic beverage, which would of course, be for medicinal purposes only. Sometimes it was socially she had to admit, but especially now was serious and she needed to control these shakes until she could get to a doctor and find out what was causing this to happen, although her suspicions were that it was simply from stress and her nerves. After becoming the victim of two unexpected failed marriages, something was bound to happen. All she ever wanted was to love and to be loved from both of her husbands, but rather she got nothing but heartache and emotional drain, which led to a life of financial debt, social depletion, parental ineptitude, and depression. But the prevailing problem now was to find a way to get out of the house to get something to fix this current health issue. Had that sneaky person not gone into her suitcase and taken what she had brought with her, there would be no problem. Her parents never kept alcohol in the house, so she had no other alternative except to go out and buy it. What excuse could she give them?

It would be easy to convince her mother that she needed to go out alone for reasons of getting her emotions together, which in all honesty she felt was the truth. Her mother knew how sorrowful and troubled she was about her father's passing. At this point, she didn't care about what Sage thought. So she proceeded to fine-tune her little plan. Although everything was true, they surely would not agree that her medicinal method would be the best choice for a remedy for her problem. When the kids went to their room to unwind, she found her chance to speak to her mother alone. Half willfully, she agreed that it would be okay for her to go out alone. Knowing how she would respond, she called Toni to tell her that she wanted to come over. Of course, Toni would agree to have her over. In fact, Toni was delighted for her to come and this she repeated verbatim to her mother. Her mother was thrilled as well. Mary loved Toni ever since they met her many years ago when she and Ally became friends at the law firm. Toni had become their second daughter, especially when Ally got married and moved away. When the taxi came, her first stop would be at a tavern or some liquor store that was open on Sundays. The driver looked in his rearview mirror at her very strangely at her request. This was a time when she regretted that her parents had ever sold their truck, that way she could have been able to move about more freely and privately. By this time, it was afternoon, so she did have that in her favor, she thought. Trying to deny the feeling of desire that was building up as she contrived in her mind of how her problem would be fulfilled, no, her problem would be solved and her health issue could be temporarily treated. The driver pulled over in front of the liquor store. Getting in quickly, she opened the bottle and took two large gulps. The feeling was almost climactic. When she sighed, she saw that the cabbie had watched her. She tightened the cap and stashed the bottle into her shoulder bag. He quickly stared straight ahead and kept driving until he reached Toni's house. When she paid him and got out, he thanked her and told her to be careful as she was entering the walkway. She did a double take as the taxi was driving away. What... again? Now she was getting an eerie feeling. Was this some foreboding message, an omen?

She knocked on the door softly and then rang the doorbell. Toni's husband opened the door and asked her to come in, hugged her then asked her to have a seat in the living room.

"Toni will be down shortly. How are you, Ally?"

"Well, you know…as well as can be expected, due to the circumstances."

"Yeah, I understand. Can I get you anything to eat or a soda or tea or something?" He thought he smelled a slight whiff of alcohol when she walked in. Toni had told him all about her drinking problem and everything about how her dear disheartened friend's wonderful fairytale life had come crashing down all around her. Toni had suffered right along with her longtime friend, and there was nothing she could do to help. All she had to offer was being there for her if, or when, she ever needed someone. Several times, she wanted to visit her since they moved from the first apartment after the house was sold, but Ally never gave her the address. She somehow would always manage to evade the subject. After noticing how she never offered that information, she never pursued the matter again. Entering the living room, Toni walked over and hugged her friend who had stood up to hug her as well. She could smell the alcohol on her breath, but it didn't matter. They were very close and both cherished their friendship. Ally knew with Toni there would not be any condemnation, but maybe a little chiding, of which she always expected. Toni's husband had gotten Ally a glass of tea which she had asked for that she was sipping on as she waited.

"Do you want to go out on the patio? No one's out there if you want to talk."

"Okay, that'll be better."

Sipping on her tea, she confessed the guilt she felt for not having been able to visit her parents more often and barely having the funds to bring the children to the funeral. She told her that Sage's boss had loaned them the money but she was going to pay him back as soon as she could. They also talked about Sage's cantankerous behavior. Toni's responses were very consoling in all of her lamentations.

"So, how are you doing with the cocktails?" Toni asked, putting the issue mildly.

"Well, I have cut back, but remember, I work as a bartender, and sometimes the customers want to buy me drinks every now and then out of kindness. But I do try to refuse without insulting them." Her lie was so blatant that she felt disgraceful. She even stammered as she spoke. Toni knew she was lying, but this was the only way that she thought could get her to face the truth about herself. She knew that deep within, there had been truths and morals instilled in her that could not be removed. While she was there, her mother called to make sure she was okay. Assuring her that all was well, she decided maybe she should head back to help and greet some of the visitors that her mother had told her might be coming. Toni wanted to drive her back, but Ally insisted on calling a cab. She wanted one last time to get a couple more drinks in before she reached home. This scheme Toni was completely unaware of. When the taxi arrived, they hugged and did not see each other again until the funeral. As soon as she got in the car, she immediately took out the bottle and drank more than before. She didn't want to get wasted, but drank just enough to satisfy. This time she slumped a little in the seat directly behind the driver so as not to be seen. After her last swig, she carefully put the bottle deep into her bag and was already planning where she would hide it so that no one would be able to find it this time. While she was at the liquor store, she also purchased a small bag of peppermints. Before she arrived at her destination, she had already consumed almost a quarter of the bag to try to stifle any hint of an alcoholic smell.

By the time she left Toni's and had gotten back, the last visitor had just left. First apologizing to her mom for not being there, she scurried immediately to her room to unload the new reserve. It was not long after she had gotten past the threshold that Sage came knocking.

"Yes Sage," she answered through the door.

"Can I speak to you for a minute?"

She was certainly not in the mood for her brash threats or cutting comments. "Give me a minute, please. I just walked in and I want to change into something more comfortable." Scrambling around to hide the bottle quickly, but could not think of a place fast enough. She didn't want to arouse any suspicions so she hastily placed it back into her shoulder bag and hung it on the closet door. By this time, she had taken off her dress and put a robe on.

"Come in, I just wanted to take my dress off," she said, as Sage walked in. "I'd like to get in the shower after I get a sandwich or something. So what did you want to talk to me about?"

"Where did you go?"

"What?"

"I asked you, where did you go?"

"Excuse me, but you are not my mother. My mother is out there, and she hasn't asked me anything. Sage, what do you want from me?"

"I just wanted to remind you about what we talked about before."

"Look, Sage, my father is dead, and my mother is out there and all alone now in mourning, as we all are. I don't want to hurt my mother any more than I've already hurt them by not being available for them when they needed me most. I'm suffering enough, so I don't need you to make me feel worse than I already do. And if you really must know, I went to visit my friend Toni. I needed a friend to talk to, that's all. So, if you don't mind, I'm just going to stay in my room. I'm not even hungry anymore."

"Well, that's your choice," She said coldly while walking out. Just before she closed the door, she stared back in at her mother, her face stern and emotionless. The following days their encounters were seldom and cold.

Chapter 22

It was the morning of the funeral. The funeral director had given instructions for arrival times to the house and to the church. Everyone was dressed and ready to go. Wrapped in an air of solemnity that filled the house, they quietly clung to each other for comfort. The families were quite small on both sides, and only a few of them who were not of the immediate family had come to the house to ride behind the family's limousines to the church. Uncle Ted, Mary's brother-law, had come along with his wife, Maggie, her sister and their daughter, Margaret, and her husband. Uncle Ted was Ally's father's younger brother. He was married with children well before his older brother, Jefferson, Ally's father. Consequently, Margaret, her first cousin was much older than Ally and did not have a close relationship with her. Ally's father's elder sister was living in a nursing home. No one could ever understand why she never married. She was such a beautiful woman in her youth and adored by everyone. Looking around at her relatives, Ally realized just how old everyone had gotten. She offered all who had come to the house something to eat or drink before it was time to leave. All that time that had passed seemed to have simply melted away. She hardly recognized any of them since it had been so long that she had seen any of them and was certain they thought the same way about her.

It was a slow, gloomy ride to the church. The hearse was already parked in front of the church when they arrived; the casket was already in place. The church was half full. Most of her dad's friends and former coworkers were older men and women. The once younger ones were now approaching retirement age, if not retired already. A few of his coworkers had even passed on before him. Many neighbors were there as were former coworkers from Ally's job, and even friends from high school. The choir sang beautifully, and the eulogy was well fitting for her father. He was spoken of as a man of immense integrity and a man of God. He had been titled as a loving husband, a wonderful father, the greatest grandfather and everybody's friend.

Ally sat on the front row next to her mom. She felt uncomfortably strange sitting in church. She felt so uneasy that she wanted to get up and run out. The church was not the place for her anymore. Sitting there only rekindled her feelings of abandonment, undesirable memories and reignited the anger and heartache that she thought had been put to rest. The faith she once had only brought a life of anguish and suffering. Her belief in the power of prayer was no more. It had only taken away her life's hopes and dreams. But now she had to play the part if just for her mother, who had no idea of her faithlessness in the church. Her mother would be absolutely devastated if she knew. She would be crushed to find out that her daughter had lost her belief. She looked up at the cross hanging in the background behind the minister with abhorrence. As they walked out following the casket, she could see the sunlight shining through the stained glass windows depicting the disciples and Mary holding the baby Jesus. They were still very beautiful to her, but at one time, those had true meaning for her. At one time in her life, she loved Christmas and Easter and what those holidays stood for and represented. But now she wanted nothing to do with any of it. She went through those holidays only for the sake of the children.

After the service, everyone went to his or her respective limousines and cars for the final ride to the cemetery. Quite a few cars had followed the hearse and the family for the graveside service. She looked around at the crowd thinking of how grateful she was for all the people who had thought so much of her father to come and share in her family's time of sorrow. She saw her friend Toni, who had sat with the family but now stood in the crowd. Next to her was another very familiar face. She saw Toni speaking to this very tall, handsome gentleman, and then he turned around and went back towards the cars. She didn't even know which car he was riding in. She couldn't wait to get the chance to ask Toni who he was. The service went very quickly. Distracted by the man, she was trying to figure out who he could have been. Apparently, he knew someone in the family since he was there, and Toni.

Quite a few people had come to the house for the repast. There was more than enough food and a plethora of desserts for everyone who was there. Ally and the kids got a chance to meet some of their relatives they had never seen before. Mary had done so well in the days prior to this, but the finality of it all broke her strength and ability to hold back her grief any longer. Ally and her sisters encouraged her to lie down and not worry about mingling with and greeting the visitors. After Ally had gotten back from helping her mother settle down, she saw Toni finally sitting down. This was her chance to find out who that stranger was who had been at the graveside service.

"Toni, who was that tall man standing next to you that you were talking to at the cemetery?"

"Wait...what tall man...at the cemetery?"

"Yeah, he was quite handsome. He looked very familiar."

"Oohh... that was Jack. You mean you didn't recognize him?"

"Jack? Jack was there? Wow. He came all the way from New York. What were you two talking about?"

"Nothing really. He told me that he was leaving, that's all. He said that he had been in town for a couple of days."

"Was he at the church?"

"Yeah, he sat in the back. As a matter of fact, he gave me a card to give to you."

"A card? Wow, that was so nice of him. I haven't seen him in years. Was Greg there?"

"If he was, I didn't see him."

"Toni, did you know Jack was coming?"

"All I know is that he called me to get the information about the funeral. I happened to see him as I was entering the church. That's when he gave me the card to give to you.

Evidently, he was waiting by the door to catch me going in."

"I guess he didn't want to come to the house, huh?"

"I don't know. I guess not. He may have thought that it was inappropriate or something."

"Yeah, that could be. You know everybody thought he was the bad guy... including me. Now look... he's the only one who cared enough show up."

"Thanks, Toni. I'm going to put this in my room right now. I'll look at it later."

Ally went to her room to put the card in her suitcase zipper compartment. She thought about getting a little swig of her stash while she was there, but decided not to. The time was not right. Her hands were not shaking, but she had felt a little tingling in her fingers that she had noticed at the church. When she returned to the sofa, Toni had gotten up and was again going about trying to accommodate the visitors.

Casey and Sage both lost their appetite, especially when they saw their grandmother crying. No one could convince them to take a bite of anything. They preferred to sit out on the porch. Their grandmother had not cried once since they had been there. She had been such a great encouragement to them. They sat talking about how alone she was going to be and they were very concerned.

"Sage, what's going to happen to Grandma?"

"I don't know. I guess she'll stay here at the house."

"But she'll be all alone."

"I know, but I'm sure she'll be fine. We could come visit sometimes... especially in the summer."

"I wish we could stay here."

"Yeah, me too. That would be nice. Would you stay here without Mom? I don't think she wants to live in California anymore."

"Well, I don't want to leave Mom all alone either. When you go away to school, I'll be the only one there with her."

"Like she really cares," Sage thought to herself. She knew that her mother was not the mother that she should be, and had not been for years. They were practically running the apartment themselves. Ally had hardly done anything in that apartment since they had been there. Sure, she may have washed the dishes occasionally, but most of the time she was either too drunk or sleeping off a hangover to do anything. Sage was deeply concerned about leaving her brother in the care of their unfit mother, but she had to get out of that way of life or die. All that she could think of was graduating from high school and leaving for college. Her plan was to come back for him, if he wanted to come with her after graduating from college, and then finding a job.

Sage's thoughts went to Sharon. She had been a godsend and such a wonderful friend to all of them. Sage could see how she tried to encourage her mother to be more attentive to her family. She tried to give her advice, like not staying out too late and helping with homework on her days off. Where her mother left off, Sharon picked up. More often than not, she rescued Casey by allowing him to stay at her apartment when she and her mother were not at home. If she didn't think that she and her brother would be taken away, she would have called Social Services herself, thinking her mother didn't deserve to have children. Remembering years ago how loving and caring she had been to them and how she loved her so, but because their dad left and no longer wanted to be a dad didn't mean that she shouldn't be their mom. Somehow, probably through time, they managed to get over their dad. Why wasn't she able to get over him? Now she preferred just to get drunk to solve her problems. She no longer cared about them, only herself. She only thought about herself when she married that drug addict, Colin. It galled her just to think about him. Not wanting to remember, but did, how he had looked at her even when her mother was there. He looked at her in a wanton manner. This made her sometimes afraid to go to sleep. She couldn't go to her mother about it; she knew that she would never believe her. The night that she finally kicked him out, she was thrilled but angry that it took so long for her to realize that he was nothing but a shyster and a thief.

After a while, some of the people started to leave and were coming out onto the porch where she and her brother had been sitting. They hugged and assured them that they would be readily available for their grandmother if needed. Ally had gone a few times to check on her mother who was still napping. In a few hours, everyone had left. Toni left as well, leaving only the family behind to try to cope with what had brought them all together. By Thursday evening, Ally and the kids had boarded the plane and in several hours made their way back home. Toni had brought Mary to the airport to see them off. Ally vowed to visit and call more often. She still managed to avoid giving Toni her address. In no uncertain terms did she want her mother and Toni to make a surprise visit and see where and how they had been living. Her lifestyle was no longer what it used to be. Her friends were no longer the type of people they would consider acceptable. They wouldn't understand and she didn't want to have to explain. When the plane arrived, they caught a taxi and went back to their dysfunctional way of life.

Ally told the kids they should try to relax from their ordeal to be ready to go back to school the following week. Sage was stunned at such insightful advice, but not impressed. She had already started drinking while on the plane with the excuse that she needed to relax her nerves with a drink from the pain and grief of the sudden loss of her father, which is also what she told the flight attendant. Sage, filled with rancor and disgust to hear how her mother used the death of her father as an excuse to have a drink. She sat quietly during the entire flight and ride home. As soon as they got in the apartment, she went straight to her room while her mother uttered her heedful advice. Giving her some time to let off steam, Casey went to see about her; he could see how upset she was.

"Are you okay?" he asked her.

"Yeah, I'm okay?"

"You still upset over Grandpa?"

"Yeah," was her single response. She didn't want him to know the real reason why she was fuming. She didn't want him to get upset. Eventually, he bought into her lie and left, although deep down he knew their mother probably had something to do with her silence. He hated to see their angry faces as they would bitterly and loudly get into their heated spats. Those incidents made him very upset. He loved both of them, but when they argued, he felt compelled to side with his mother since she was in a more fragile state and would always wind up in tears. During these times, he had to abandon his sister who was the stronger of the two. Sage understood and always assured him that she was okay. She spoke to her mother very harshly in those arguments, which was why she would windup in tears. "Go ahead, take your shower and go on to bed. It's late. I'll help you unpack tomorrow," Sage told him.

"Okay. I'm kinda sleepy anyway."

Going to her room, Ally immediately went for the bottle she had brought back from California. Her hands started to shake, but this time, it was from the anxiety that she had felt looking for her bottled prize. She was glad to be back where she could have the freedom to drink as much as she wanted and when she wanted. Deep in her subconscious mind, she knew that something was wrong with her life, her actions, her thinking, wants and desires. She knew that she was not heading in the right direction and did little to lead and guide her children toward having a successful life of their own. Their accomplishments were of their own volition. Sure, she congratulated and praised them for their achievements, but she had nothing to do with it and deep down she knew it. Sinking back into self-pity, she asked how could she have done any better? She had been abandoned… twice. And since then, it had been only her to make things work. Even with Colin, it was only her, as things turned out. She was busy trying to make sure that they had a place to live, food on the table, and clothes to wear. She was doing the best for her family that she could under the circumstances. But what circumstances, a voice inside her whispered? The circumstances that were brought on by bad choices, self-pity, pride, and selfishness that same voice answered. But she couldn't listen, wouldn't listen, wherein, she continued to indulge herself in discouragement and excuses, blaming everyone except herself for her world continuing to spin out of control... even blaming God, who she felt had turned His back on her. She reached into her night table drawer and got the glass that she kept there and poured herself a nice glass of vodka and drowned herself in self-pity, self-delusion, and self-destruction with the intoxication of strong drink where she could escape...even if just for a little while.

The next morning was Friday, Sage and Casey had gotten up and had breakfast. She thought she would surprise her brother with the same kind of breakfast that they had at their grandmother's house. Excited when he smelled bacon cooking, he hurried in the kitchen but was dreadfully disappointed to see that it was Sage and not his mom who was fixing breakfast. She could tell by his expression what was wrong, although he quickly tried to cover the emotional blow. Sage knew what he was feeling. She had seen it many times through the years and every time felt his heartache. She felt it before him, but after a while had built a wall between her emotions and her mother. Bricks of hatred and resentment built this wall, and there was nothing that her mother could do to knock them down.

"Hey...morning, are you okay?"

"Oh, I'm fine. I see you're cooking my favorite breakfast. Just like the ones at Grandma's. Too bad we don't have a waffle iron."

"Yeah, that would have been nice, but this is great. Thanks. Where's Mom? Is she coming?"

"I don't know. You know how she likes to stay in bed late when she's not working."

"I'm going to ask her anyway. She might if she sees this kind of breakfast." He went to Ally's room and knocked on the door. He turned the knob and only peeked in. He could smell the scent of alcohol and morning breath coming from her room. Seeing her sprawled over the bed still with the clothes on that she had worn the day before, he just closed the door. He tried to hide his disappointment when he went back to the kitchen.

"She's still asleep. Well, she's going to miss a good breakfast."

Sage did not respond. She knew what he was feeling. After breakfast, he went into the den to pretend to watch TV. Holding one of the small pillows on the sofa, he tried to hide his face as he wiped away the tears. He was so disappointed.

When they were in California, he had not seen his mother sober for so many days in a row in so long that he could not even remember the last time. Those few days had built up such hope, until this morning. He thought maybe he would once again have the mother that he remembered when he was a little boy. He did not even mention how he felt to Sage. She was so negative and would only get angry if he talked about her, so he had to keep his hopeful feelings to himself. Deeply saddened over his grandfather's death, but seeing his mother's continuous sobriety helped him cope with the sudden loss. His grandmother also eased his sorrow. She told him so many things about his grandfather that he had never heard before like when he had been a young man. Finding out these new revelations about his grandfather made him love and respect him even more. And he missed his grandmother too, already. Since his mother did so well there, maybe living there would bring her back to the mother he once knew. If only he could convince her to move back home with his grandmother. She was going to be all alone now and he and his mother could live with her. Sage would be going away to college anyway, and they could live in California. It was nicer there than where they are now living, although this place is much better than the run-down apartments where they had been before, he thought. As soon as she gets up, he decided that he would ask her. The thoughts made him feel contentment just thinking about it and gave him a sense of newfound hope.

Sage called Mr. Melmann and told him they were back home. She wanted to return to work that afternoon. He gave her the option to start on her regular Saturday, but could use her help. She was eager to get back anyway to start repaying the money that he so graciously loaned them for their airfare. It was also in her plans to stop by to see Sharon to let her know they were back but she probably already knew from the peephole. She only smiled at the thought. Since it was a school day and she would be going in to work, she told Casey that if he wanted to, she was sure that Sharon would be happy to have him over later on when her children got home from school, especially since it was Friday. She always brought something special for dinner and would always ask them to come over and join them. Sharon was such a nice lady. Sage thought fondly of her all the time. Secretly, she wished her mother was like her. Standing at the kitchen sink, called out,

"Casey, how about helping me with the cleanup."
"All right," he answered, in a reluctant tone and pulled himself away from the television and his thoughts.

After they had cleaned up the kitchen, Sage went to her room to finish unpacking. Sage usually washed their clothes. They did their own laundry now, but her mother had just about dropped the ball on everything else that was her responsibility as a parent. She dreaded even thinking about what her brother had in store when she leaves for college. If she kept thinking about it, she probably wouldn't go to college. But he would be almost thirteen by then and she had been trying to show him how to be more independent. Casey could make sandwiches; wash his clothes, and even iron if he needed. She was even hoping that Mr. Melmann would let him work a few hours when she goes away. At least he would have money in case he needed something or wanted to go to a movie or do something with his friends. He was getting older and their mother didn't seem to have much to give. She always whined about barely having enough money to pay the bills. Granted, she still had the debt because of Colin and was still paying some of it, she would complain. Desperately she needed to get the car fixed but opted to get the subway or hitch a ride with a friend or coworker to and from work. Other than work, she really didn't go anywhere except maybe to a friend's house which was rare, or to the local bar up the street, which is where she squandered a lot of her pay. She would never go to Sharon's anymore, which was right across the hall, for fear of hearing Sharon's considerate and most needed advice and have nowhere to hide from feelings of guilt and remorse. This was never Sharon's intent.. She had only tried in the most caring way to inspire her to be more responsible and to be aware of the effects of her way of living for those around her, mainly her family. Occasionally, after having run into Sharon, Ally would come in mumbling to herself, almost incomprehensibly, bits and pieces of her rants such as, "…nosy," "…busy body," fragments of "…mind her own business," or "…not bothering anybody," revealed just what had happened. Beginning to feel annoyed, she tried to blot out those wandering thoughts.

Since there was so little time left to do the laundry before going to work, Sage decided to get Casey to go with her to help.
"What about mom's clothes?"
"You know she usually does her own. Anyway, she's still in bed and, I want to get this done."

Back from the laundry, they returned to see their mother sitting at the kitchen table eating the leftovers from the morning meal. She looked as if she had not bothered to go to the bathroom to even comb her hair.

"Hi, mom."

"Hi, sweetie. I just woke up. So you guys had another big breakfast, huh?"

"Yeah, Sage fixed it."

"That was very nice of her." She talked as if Sage was not even in the room. She could see by the look on her face not to say anything directly to her. She had come to recognize that look for quite a while now. For years, she had been deeply distressed over their relationship and longed to have the closeness again that she still enjoys having with her own mother. It seemed they could never have a normal conversation no matter how innocently it began. The times that she had tried, they would only windup into a full-blown knockdown, drag out brawl, hurling insults and derogatory name-calling. Sage had lost all respect for her mother.

"Casey, I'm going to my room and get my clothes ready to go to work tomorrow, okay?"

"Okay, Mom." This was only an excuse to get away. She tried to avoid having much contact with Sage, so on the days they were in the apartment together, they both resorted to their respective bedrooms or Ally would get dressed and go out. Tomorrow would be her first day back since the passing of her father. Still recovering from the hangover the night before, she was glad to be off work and did not have to return from her leave until then. Sage was leaving for work early because they had not yet returned to school.

"If you get hungry later, you can fix yourself a peanut butter and jelly sandwich, okay?" Sage said to Casey as she was leaving the kitchen. When Sage left, Casey went to his mother's bedroom door and knocked softly.

"Can I come in?"

"Sure you can."

"Mom, are you okay?"

"Yeah, I'm okay. Why do you ask?"

"I don't know. You look kind of tired. Did you have another nightmare?"

"No, thank goodness. That was a horrible dream I had that night."

"I know. I could tell it scared you."

"Well, no more dreams. I see you and Sage went to wash clothes."

"Yeah, she wanted to get it done before the crowd got there, but since it's Friday, it wasn't crowded at all, plus, she had to go to work today."

"I thought she didn't have to go in until tomorrow."

"Well, she didn't have to, but since we're out of school, she asked Mr. Melmann if she could come back early today." He could smell the overnight stench of alcohol as she breathed and knew the reason for her unkempt appearance.

"Do you want to watch a movie with me?" He wanted to keep her occupied to keep her from the drink. Often he would use this diversion tactic to distract her from drinking or going out when she was off.

"Okay, but first I'm going to take a shower and get some clothes on. You know, I don't think we have any bread for your sandwich. I heard Sage tell you what to fix for lunch. I really need to go out to the grocery store and get a few things like milk and eggs...and bread," she added with emphasis.

"Can I go with you?"

"Well, I'm not going to get a lot, so why don't you just stay here until I get back. I shouldn't be long. Then we could watch that movie. But first I have to wash up and get some clothes on."

There went his plan. He knew by now what the consequences would be. Feeling the hurt and disappointment, he just walked out and went to the den, holding onto the pillow that he always clutched and held onto whenever he felt depressed.

When Ally started to unpack some of her clothes the night before, she came across the card that Jack had given Toni for her. She had forgotten all about it until now. Feelings of happiness and gratitude came over her as she held the envelope staring at the name blankly. Before opening it, with pleasant thoughts of how he had cared enough to come that far, opened the envelope and read the card: "*Ally, I was so sorry to hear of your father's passing. I wanted to let you and your family know that I am thinking of you as you endure your loss. Sincerely, Jack Tyler.*"

Inside, there was a check for two thousand dollars. She was totally stunned. "Two thousand dollars," she said it over and over, whispering softly through her almost closed lips. She could not believe it. It was so generous and kind of him. She also thought about how at one time she thought he was such a jerk, but now he seemed like the better of the two siblings after all. While she was going out, she decided to stop by the bank to cash it. Now she will have something to start paying Mr. Melmann back with, or maybe just pay it off, she thought, and possibly even have enough to get the car fixed.

An hour had lapsed by the time Ally showered and got her clothes on. She wore a pair of jeans and a brown turtleneck sweater. "Casey, I'm getting ready to go to the store now, okay?" she yelled.

"Okay," he answered unenthusiastically.

"I might be running a little late because I have to stop at the bank." Usually she would go to the bank near her job in New York, but decided to go to the one nearest the grocery store, which was two bus stops away from where they lived. She could have gotten what she needed from Mr. Melmann's store, but since she had to go to the bank anyway, decided to 'kill two birds with one stone' and go to the store closest to the bank. It was a little brisk and chilly on this bright October day. The weather was naturally changing in its eastern seasonal order. The warmer weather was another thing that she missed about leaving California, but gradually she had gotten used to the change. As she rode the bus, she gazed out the window at the people and the scenery. Not that she had not seen these same streets before, she saw them practically every day since riding the bus and subway, but there always seemed to be something different going on. The one thing she did not like about riding the bus was the many stops to pick up passengers. The subway was better because it was faster and did not have to make as many stops. Looking out noticing that her exit would be coming up next, she happened to see a familiar face as the bus rode by. At first, she could not remember from where she knew this person or had seen him. The jacket, she remembered seeing him in that same jacket. It looked as though he was headed for the subway. As the bus drove by, he continued walking and she looked right at his face. He glanced up at the bus and kept walking. A frightening chill came over her. She thought her face must have turned as white as a ghost. It was the bearded man that was in her dream, wearing that army jacket with the big dog. How could this be? How could she dream about someone she had never seen before? The first time she had ever seen him was in her dream, not on the street, certainly not from the bus. She became so nervous that she started shaking. She could never forget that face. In her dream, she had almost collided into him as she was running out of that bar. But there was no dog with him. His hands were in his pockets and there was no dog anywhere around. Had she seen him somewhere, maybe not wearing the jacket, and just never paid attention? That could be the only explanation. He didn't seem to recognize her. Maybe he didn't see her or recognize her. She couldn't shake from her mind what she had just seen. She could hardly concentrate. This was incredibly weird. Almost missing her stop, she saw the bank building that reminded her and raced to get off. She had not even realized how long she had been lost in concentration wondering who this man could be. This strange sighting got her so upset, she almost forgot what she had to do.

The bank was conveniently located right across the street from the bus stop. When she walked in, there was a security guard standing at the door. He was of medium height whose stern look was to show the public that he meant business. His eyes were shifting side to side as he greeted and watched patrons entering and leaving the bank. Looking around, she saw there were only a small number of people there. Four tellers and the lines were not long. She walked over to the tall table by the wall to get the check from her purse to sign it. Her hands were shaking so badly that she had to pause several times to try to get them stilled. A small elderly lady with slightly bent shoulders, wearing a heavy winter coat, was standing next to her. She could barely get her whole arm onto the counter. She kept looking at Ally's trembling hands and then looked up in her face.

"Are you okay, Miss?"

"Yes, Ma'am. I'm fine. Thank you." This made Ally feel a bit self-conscious, so she looked away. The lady left to get in the line. After pausing a few seconds, her hands settled down enough to hold the pen. She finished signing the check and quickly got in line to wait for the next teller. Over and over in her mind, she tried to think of an explanation of what she had just seen. "Next person in line, please," called out in a tone, which sounded like a little girl's voice. It was Ally's turn.

"I'd like to cash this check, please." She had not had that much money since the divorce from Colin. Almost giddy at having it, but knew it was practically gone already with her having to pay back the loan from Mr. Melmann. It would have been truly disgraceful for Sage to have to pay anything to help pay that loan. Whether she deserved the role or not, she was still the mother, she thought. It was bad enough that she had nothing to help send her to college.

"No, wait. I'd like a cashier's check." She gave the exact amount she needed to pay off Mr. Melmamm. She barely had enough to keep the account open. The teller carefully counted out the rest of the money to Ally, placed it in an envelope, and handed it to her.

"Thank you and be careful, Ma'am."

Ally thanked her as well, but thought about those words, 'Be careful.' Maybe this time she said it because of all the money that she was carrying in cash. Before she left the bank, she went to the table again to separate the money and put it in her jean pockets, the cashier's check in her purse.

The grocery store was midway down the block. These were the times she missed not having her car. That old car barely made it to Jessica's and back. Not wanting to have to lug so much around being so far away from home, especially while riding the bus, she kept her purchase at a minimum. She thought of her neighbor Sharon. She had practically kept her children nourished with meals that she cooked herself. Trying to rid herself of the guilt of her poor motherhood reputation, she knew that Sharon understood her work situation and how difficult it was to do all those motherly things when her work hours were not regular hours. And Sage, who had always been such a precocious child, especially behaviorally did so much of what she herself should have been doing. Not remembering the last time that she had bought fruit, she grabbed a bag of apples. She bought a shopping bag to carry her groceries. While waiting for the bus, her mind went back to the bearded man in the military jacket that she had seen earlier. The thought bothered her all the way back home. She was so afraid, she took one of the aisle seats. Thinking about what she had to do while riding home, she decided to stop by Nate's place to get something to calm her nerves. She needed to shake this feeling of anxiety. It was almost three o'clock and the place had quite a few people, but it was Friday and for many, it was payday. She knew, because at her job, this was the pattern for the weekends, starting on Friday with happy hour after work.

There was Nate with his rolled up sleeves pouring drinks. "Hey, Ally, whuz hapnin' babydoll?"

"Hi, Nate. I just got back from my father's funeral yesterday."

"Oh, yeah, that's right. I was sorry to hear about your dad, Ally."

"Thanks, Nate."

"You want your regular?"

"Yeah, I'm going to sit down over here for a little while. Can you put my shopping bag behind the counter for me please?"

"Sure, han' it here."

"Thanks Nate."

"Go on and sit down, I'll send it over."

Ally put her pocketbook on the seat beside her in the booth. She picked a different place to sit other than the one in her dream and pinched herself to make sure that she was not dreaming this time. Doris, the barmaid, brought her drink over. Doris was a short, stocky woman. She wore short skirts that hugged her wide hips with knit tops that were way too small, that always exposed too much of what should have been more in than out.

"Ally honey, I am so sorry about your dad," she said as she wiped the table and placed the glass down on top of the small white paper napkin.

"Thanks, Doris. Doris, can you bring me another one please?"

"Sure can, honey. I'll be right back."

It was noisy and the discussions of the day had started. This time it was about something they were watching on a television show. Watching the debate and looking around at her surroundings, her eyes were beginning to fill up with tears. Doris placed the drink on the table and saw that Ally was crying.

"Go head girl. Git it out. Don't be ashamed to cry. Everything's gonna be okay." From another table, she grabbed some table napkins and put them in front of her. "Here you go, sweetie." Ally picked one up and put it to her face. She was sad about her father, but what she was really crying about was her life's situation. She had been somebody at one time. She had the best of what life had to offer. Now here she sits in a neighborhood bar, almost penniless, working for practically minimum wage, a handout from a rich ex-brother-in-law, while living in the projects in a small city in New Jersey, one foot away from being homeless. There was only one person that she could think of who was to blame for this entire dreadful curse and calamity in her life, and that person was Greg.

He had lured her away from her plans of going to college and persuaded her to marry him with his convincing confessions of eternal love and happiness for her. He assured her that she would never have to worry about anything. How she had relentlessly begged and pleaded for him to stay... to be a husband to her and a father to his two young children, but he chose not to, but wanted out of the marriage. The more she thought about it, the more the tears came, and her hatred for him and his mother festered. After consuming three more glasses, she went to pick up the glass to down the last swallow, but could not feel the glass in her hand. The glass was there, she could see it and her hand around it, but could not feel it, nor could she raise it up. She tried with the other hand, but the feeling was gone from that hand as well. She started rubbing her hands together. Maybe the circulation of blood was slow getting to her hands she thought. It was kind of chilly, but not enough to have caused the loss of feeling. She had been there for about an hour. Getting nervous and scared, she just wanted to finish her last drink and go home, so she kept rubbing her hands together and finally began to feel them again. On the way out, she paid for the drinks and bought a bottle to take home. Eager to leave, she almost forgot the grocery bag that Nate had put away for her. He put her bottle in a bag and added that to the grocery bag.

"Thanks Nate."

"No problem. Are you okay?"

"Yeah, I'm fine. I've just been through a lot this week."

"Yeah, I understand. Okay now."

She left with her shopping bag. Her steps were a bit wobbly. She even staggered a little as she made her way down the street. Sage looked out across the street just as her mother stepped out the door. She could see her through the colorful lettering on the glass window of the store. Her eyes were fixed and she did not move. Mr. Melmann looked out to see what had suddenly caught her eye. It was her mother that she was watching. He could see how anger was beginning to transform her lovely, girly face and the intensity of her rage, which caused the redness on her neck. It was distressing for him to watch. "Sage," he called her name boldly, "Could you go in the back and see if we have anymore cans of corn."

When she heard her name, she immediately turned around. He was trying to distract her from watching. She said nothing and proceeded to follow his request to go to the back in the storeroom. He felt such pity for her... and her mother... actually for the whole family. "What could have happened to have changed a mother into such a pitiful drunkard?" he thought.

Chapter 23

It was Saturday morning. Ally again drank so much that she had to stay in bed to sleep it off once she got home the evening before. Sage worked full eight-hour days on Saturdays and had already gone to work. When Ally went to the kitchen, she could see Casey sitting there watching television. Before she got started, she went to the den to say "hi" and kissed him on the forehead. "How are you, sweetie?"

"I'm okay," he said, sounding depressed.

"What's wrong, honey?"

"Nothing."

"Then why do you sound so sad? You know it's going to take a while to get used to the idea of Granddad not being around anymore."

"I know. But that's not what's wrong. I'm not sad."

"Then what's wrong?"

"I guess I'm just kinda bored. There's not much to do around here except watch TV, or go over to Sharon's to play video games. Since I don't have my own."

"What about the one that you already have?"

"That system is too old."

"Well, I'm going to try to fix that. But I thought you liked hanging out with Dave."

"I do, but sometimes I want to just stay home in my own place."

"You never said anything before. Did you guys have a fight?"

"Oh, no, Dave is a nice guy and my friend. He lets me play on his system anytime I want to. But sometimes I just wish I could be able to stay in my own room and play video games."

"Well, we'll see. Maybe you will be able to do just that." How many times had he heard such promises?

"I have to go to work today, remember? It's my first day back. Did you eat anything?" she asked, as she headed back to the kitchen. She heard him answer as she continued walking away. She had completely forgotten about yesterday's promise.

Maneuvering around the kitchen trying to find something quick to eat, the thought came back to her of the episode of the loss of feeling in her hands. She was concerned, because of her job. She needed to be able to use her hands. The thought of losing her job was terrifying. She needed to work because she still had children to care for and care for herself. Sage would be leaving for college soon and would not be there to help her out if she needed her, nor would she be willing to be there. She knew that Sage hated her and wanted to leave. The thought of being disabled terrified her. She would not be able to feed or bathe herself. Such awful things were happening to her. Why? She had never done anything to anybody, yet she was suffering, as if it was some kind of Karma, she thought. Not only had her life unraveled, now it was her health. Maybe it was time to get checked by a doctor. She had not been to a doctor since her divorce from Greg. With her low income, her situation qualified them for state healthcare, at least for the children. Health insurance was an option at her job, but she couldn't afford it. She only hoped that she would remain relatively healthy until she could do better. Thinking about her hands shaking and now the numbness, she regretted her decision to decline the insurance. But if it got terribly bad, her only option would be to go to the emergency room at the hospital. Not to get stressed out, she blanked it all out of her mind. Instead, she thought about going in Mr. Melmann's store on her way to work to pay back the loan and thank him personally for helping them. She also wanted to thank Sharon for all she had done as well. Sharon only worked one weekend a month and was most likely at home this weekend. Managing to fix herself a cup of coffee and a slice of buttered toast without a problem made her almost forget that anything had ever happened. As she sipped on her coffee, she thought about how many friends had come by to pay their respects to her father who were there to support her when they were in California. And the thought still amazed her that Jack was there. Her ex-brother-in-law, the wild one had come all the way to California to attend her father's funeral. Although he could afford it, nevertheless, he thought about them and took the time to come, which showed how much he cared, not to mention the much needed monetary gift. She would have liked to have thanked him face to face; however, she was just happy that she got to see him at all. It was soon time for her to get dressed and ready to leave for work. Starting earlier than usual, she wanted to leave before her normal time so she could stop by Mr. Melmann's grocery store. Finally, she got up from the kitchen table and made her way to the bedroom after washing her cup and making sure to clean up behind herself. Sage had ranted on before about her sloppiness in the kitchen and leaving a mess behind for somebody else to have to clean.

The mirror... how she desperately hated having to look in that mirror. She hated the image that looked back at her so accusingly and unfamiliar. Was that really her? The answer was depressing. She quickly put on her makeup and got her hair in place for the customers. At least they never knew what she had looked like before... but, she did. She had taken the money out of her pockets and put it away on the top shelf in the closet in a peanut can. From her pocketbook, she took out the cashier's check, looked at it front and back before putting it back in the envelope. She sealed it and placed it deep into her shoulder bag. By now, it was time for her to go. She gave Casey the usual instructions in case of any emergency that hopefully would never happen and left. He knew how to prepare something to eat if he was hungry and always had the option to go to Sharon's, where she was now headed.

Stepping across the hallway, she knocked on the door. This time it was not Sharon who had peeped through the hole, but Elesha, her eldest. She opened the door and yelled, "It's Miss Ally." Sharon came from the kitchen, drying her hands with a paper towel. "Oh, Ally, how are you?" She hugged her gently as if she might hurt her. "How are the kids? I wanted to come over, but I thought I'd let you have more time to yourselves. I know you all have been through a lot. I'm still so sorry that I didn't have enough money to help you when you needed it most, but God made a way, didn't He?"
"Yeah, we got the money."
"Just like He always does... and on time, too."
Getting away from Sharon's religious declarations, Ally hurriedly thanked her. "Sharon, I came over to thank you for everything that you did for us, or

wished that you could. What you do is always more than enough. We made it through and now we're back. So, thanks again. I have to get to work. That's where I'm on my way to right now. I'll see you later. Bye, Elesha."

"Bye, Miss Ally."

Rushing down the hall and onto a crowded elevator, she greeted the people who were already on there. It was a band of children of all ages, probably headed out to play. She returned the greeting. When the elevator doors opened on the first floor, the kids burst out as if there had been an explosion and raced to the glass double doors, where she was also headed.

Ally walked briskly up the street heading to the grocery store. Her time was quickly running out before having to catch the bus for the next subway train to get to work on time. Mr. Melmann was standing behind the register when she stepped inside. She walked up and asked if she could speak to him privately after first introducing herself. She was surprised to find that he already knew who she was. Coming from behind the register, he led her to his office in the back. It was only a large desk situated just inside the storeroom, surrounded by boxes and crates of goods. The desk had file drawers on both sides with a phone and a desk lamp setting on the desktop where papers were scattered all across. There was also a safe, but it was barely visible just inside another room adjacent to the storage room. He offered her a seat, which was his own office chair, but she declined. "How may I help you, Mrs. Tyler?"

She had introduced herself as Ally Tyler, Sage's mother, simply to make the connection with her daughter. "Mr. Melmann I just wanted to come by to thank you personally for your help during our desperate time of need."

"Oh, you're so very welcome. I was glad that I was able to help."

She took the envelope from her purse and reached out to hand him the check. "This should cover our loan. You can see it's a cashier's check for the exact amount."

"Oh, Mrs. Tyler, there was no rush to pay it back so soon. Times are hard these days and I underst..."

"That's okay. I received another generous gift. It was enough to pay you back," she interjected. "So thanks again. We all appreciate you and what you do for the whole community."

"Why, thank you, Mrs. Tyler. I try to, when I can," he said modestly.

"Well, I guess I'd better get going. I'm on my way to work. And please, call me Ally."

"You know, Ally, you have a wonderful, kind and sweet daughter. She has helped me out a lot around here. I don't know how I ever kept anything together before she started working for me. I don't know what I'm going to do when she goes away to college."

"I'm sure you'll find somebody."

"Well, it was nice to finally meet you," he said, as he reached out to shake her hand. "Yes, it was nice to meet you too."

When she walked out from the storeroom, Sage was placing cans of string beans on the shelf on the other side of the aisle. She was suddenly surprised when she thought she heard a familiar voice and quickly stooped down. Standing up just enough to get a look, she dropped down again. It was who she thought. She saw her mother when she was walking back from the storeroom. When Ally walked in the store, Sage had been in the storeroom where the freezers were and had not seen her walking behind Mr. Melmann. Apparently, she had walked right by them holding a large box to carry out into the store area and had not seen them because of the high stack of boxes that incased his desk. She was so embarrassed and galled to find that her mother was there and had apparently spoken to her boss. What did he think of her? How would he judge her now? She had already thanked him, so why did she have to repeat what was already done? Stooping down again so as not to let her mother see her, she stayed there until she heard the door open and close. When she stood up, she caught Mr. Melmann's eye.

"Oh, there you are. I was wondering where you were. Your mother was just here." "Okay," she said as if waiting to hear the rest of his comment.

"Yes, she dropped by on her way to work to pay back the loan. I told her there was no rush, but she insisted. You know, she seems to be a nice person."

"I guess you can say that." Sage didn't want to talk about her mother anymore, so she changed the subject and started asking where he wanted certain products to be placed and replaced. He knew that she was being evasive and wanted to avoid talking about her mother, but he did manage to let her know that she had come to pay off the loan. Exhilarated by the news that she was no longer in debt, she was still curious and wondered where her mother had gotten that amount of money to pay back the loan so quickly. Even though her curiosity nettled her, she was not going to ask. She wanted to have as minimal contact as possible with her. Standing and watching out through the large store window, she could see people getting on the bus across the street up from Nate's Tavern, probably headed to the subway. One of them was her mother.

Chapter 24

Sitting on the bus, waiting to get off to catch the subway train to her job, Ally thought about how relieved she felt being able to pay back the loan as quickly as she had. In her mind, she thanked Jack over and over again and wanted to send him a thank you note, but decided not to try since there was no return address on the envelope or any means of contact inside the card. When she had met the generous grocer, she could see why everyone cared so much for him. He was respectful and courteous to her. She remembered seeing him on occasion looking out from his store's large picture window when she was sober enough after leaving Nate's place. He had seen her several times, as she laboriously made her way down the street coming from that very tavern. Most times if she had gotten too bad, Nate would send someone with her to make sure she got home okay. Other times when she would start hounding the customers to buy her drinks or was getting too rowdy, Nate himself would put a stop to her outrageous behavior by making her leave and other times when he saw she was getting too drunk, would put a stop to her orders, at such times he would send her home, again with an escort. From his store window, Mr. Melmann could see the damage that alcohol was doing in the lives of people old and young. Mothers and fathers were destroying their future and their children's future by consuming that foul tasting deadly toxin. He saw children peeping in the entrance of the bar looking for a parent or parents who had not yet come home to feed them. Sometimes they would even come into the store and ask him if he had seen their parent go into the infamous establishment and felt heartsick when he knew that indeed they had gone in. There had even been fistfights and altercations on that very corner when a spouse or companion found their mate had been there and spent most of their paycheck on the rancid beverage before paying the bills or buying food. But he never got involved except to make a small loan of food to tie them over until another payday.

Nothing had changed about Ally since the death of her father. Her first evening back at work an occasional thought would cross her mind of the shaky hands, the numbness, and the nightmares, but as the music played and the loud laughing bellowed throughout the night, she jubilantly absorbed herself into her noisy environment. She continued to drink as much as before, if not more and continued to invite people in who had been kind enough to give her a ride home. Anyway, that was always the excuse when questioned about her inebriated cohorts. They would stay longer than they should have and most of time would get boisterously noisy. This behavior added more strife between her and Sage, who had no problem expressing her harsh sentiment about their dysfunctional family. But all of her complaints and denigration only fell on deaf ears, as Ally continued with her reckless behavior. One episode had almost come to blows, if not for Casey, who dashed across the hall to get Sharon, who managed to quell the heated atmosphere. After that, Sage tried her best not to cross paths with her mother and only prayed harder for graduation day to come soon.

Contact with her mother did not improve, as promised. Ally would only call her occasionally, so Mary would then make the call. She, like her husband worried about her only child and her grandchildren. She could not help but think about the "what ifs" when she thought about how her once levelheaded and well-disciplined daughter had changed. Her compromised decision to trust in the material things in life had resulted in her having a completely different and disastrous life. When her mind tended to wander and dwell on what could have been, she would pray for them and for herself to have some peace in her heart. Both she and her husband were always sorry that they had not expressed more opposition to her marrying someone who was so much older and of no faith. It was not the age as much as it was that he was not a believer. How could a marriage survive without a Biblical foundation? They had nothing and no one to get them through the hard times. Her mother wanted to visit, but Ally always made up excuses as to why she should not travel alone at such a distance at her age and with her work schedule, it would be almost impossible to have time to spend with her. She never told her mother the truth about what she was doing for a living. Toni knew but vowed never to tell anyone, as Ally had made her promise.

The end of the school year was quickly approaching. Spring had come, and in spite of the dreadfully cold winter and their circumstances, along with a dismal-looking future, Casey and Sage continued to do well in school. Casey had been on the Principal's list throughout each term and was inducted into the honor society. He was so proud of himself; and so was Ally. The day for the award ceremony, which was to be the last celebration for the honor society was going to be held that evening. He never told his mother about the celebration day, because he shamefully did not want her to come and take a chance on being humiliated and embarrassed if she showed up drunk. There was no way that he was going to allow his teachers to meet her, which is why she was never told about any PTA meetings either, so he asked Sage to come instead. He felt terrible for being so deceptive, but he had already heard that some of the kids had been gossiping and laughing about his mother being a lush, as they mockingly called her. He was crushed and ashamed. Some of those very kids, he thought, were his friends, and in reality, some of those very scoffers were hiding family secrets of their own. His sister was upset that he found out. After talking to Sage, he felt much better. She reminded him of the similar circumstances of practically everybody in that school and encouraged him to disregard their teasing and continue to do well, to go to college like she was going to do, and get out of this way of life they had been hurled into. She told him that it was not worth fighting about, because they were probably just jealous of his accomplishments anyway, but when any of them came in the store, she warned them to back off of her brother and reminded them of their own pathetic circumstances.

As the weather began to get a little warmer, Sage started thinking about her prom, which reminded her that she was approaching her final days of school and the beginning of a new life. Several guys had already approached her to be their prom date, but her mind was already made up. Mark had been such a good friend ever since they met and was more trustworthy than some of the other guys. Most of them had only a one-track mind when it came to girls, and she was not interested and had no problem letting them know. She had seen the consequences of those gullible little, boy-crazy, romance neophytes who had fallen for their duplicitous confessions of love, only to leave them all alone with the product of their short-lived passionate, fatuous affair, and was still free to go hunting for their next victim. Some of these girls thoughtlessly and carelessly had repeated the same mistake. Their future changed before it could even begin. Mark was different; he was not like the rest of the boys she knew. On the weekends that they did not have to work, Sage and Mark would go to a movie or go downtown to a restaurant. Sometimes they would take Casey and Mark's younger sister. Sage never did anything to mislead him, and all that he expected was her friendship. Being together most of the time, he subsequently developed stronger feelings toward her, but he knew that at this point in her life, she was not interested in having anything other than a platonic relationship. Her main objective was to go to college and that in itself would probably sever their ties. Many colleges offered him full basketball scholarships, none of which were any that she had mentioned attending had approached him. She had already applied to several colleges. Some were offering scholarships, but they were only partial, even if the requirements were met. Being hopeful, she still waited to find out if she would receive any awards or scholarships through her high school because the counselor had assured her that she would most likely receive some type of reward for her academic achievement.

The relationship between Ally and Sage still had not changed. She loved her daughter dearly and thought of the days when she had cradled and cuddled her baby in her arms so lovingly, but now they merely shared the same living space and talked only when necessary. Deep within Ally knew, but suppressed the thought that she had let her children down and tried to forget about their miserable existence that she had subjected them to. She only drank more to rid herself of the thought. But even in her drunkenness, she knew her abuse of alcohol had been to enable her to use without guilt, this mendacious excuse and defend her actions by drowning out the reality with self-deception and the deception that her use of alcohol was simply for medicinal purposes… to "calm her nerves." In all honesty, she wanted so much to be happy just once again in her life. She wanted to be loved and to be cared for without having to succumb to any kind of romantic relationships. She thought by surrounding herself with her coworkers and friends that she acquainted herself with at work would ease the deep pain of loneliness that she so often felt. Toni tried her best to keep in touch, but most of the time Ally was at work and other times not in any condition to talk to anyone. Whenever Sage saw her rowdy friends in their apartment after coming home from a date with Mark, fuming at the sight, she would head straight to her bedroom and close the door. She tried her best to drown out the noisy times by turning the volume up on the television or putting her pillow over her head, but the bold shameless audacity of her mother to selfishly disregard the presence of her own children was even worse to bear. Again, Sharon had to remind Ally to try to keep the noise down especially with the bumbling around and loud whispers in the hallway when she and friends would be on their way to or from her apartment. Because their last encounter was on the verge of becoming violent, to avoid another "near miss" with her mother, Sage asked Sharon to speak to her about her disorderly companions. At one time, her mother's behavior would have been embarrassing to her, but now the time was closing in on just having to endure this degenerative way of life a little while longer.

The night had arrived for the senior prom. She felt the need to talk to her mother to remind her of the event and didn't plead, but expected her to refrain from her drinking for this one night, at least until she left for the prom. Ally was insulted by her demands, but to keep the peace between the two, she cooperated. Everybody in the building was full of excitement. There were several other seniors who lived in their building, who were also going to the prom. That night many relatives and friends came from everywhere to witness the glitz and glamour of this most anticipated affair of the school year. Sharon and her children had come over as she moved all around, following the star of the evening, taking pictures from every angle possible. Everyone was waiting anxiously for her prom date, Mark, to arrive. This was the first time he had come this close to their apartment. When he got there after knocking ever so softly, he stood shyly at the opened door. Everyone was watching and waiting for him to step in after Casey opened the door. He stood tall and stiff, clutching the corsage. Everything was quiet as he stepped in. Realizing what he was holding, suddenly reached with an outstretched hand to give it to Sage when she walked over to him with a big smile. The scene appeared to be dramatic, yet was so funny that everybody started laughing, breaking the silence of the whole event. This was the first time Ally had met Mark. She stepped over and gently whispered to him that he had to pin it on her gown himself, but after nervously trying for a while, she politely took over and pinned the decorative, floral ornament to her dress. The moment was awkward for both of them, but Ally felt blissful to be so close to her daughter, a closeness that she hadn't been allowed in years.

Sage hadn't seen Mark as anything other than a school chum and a good friend. Except for this night, something was different about him. This night she could see he was quite a handsome young man. The whole entourage followed them all the way to the waiting limousine with flashing camera lights all the way. Into the warm, beautiful night the limousine took off with the waving hands, bids of well wishes, and goodbyes left behind.

Some weeks after the prom, Ally with great determination managed to stay sober. She even lasted some time after the graduation. Her boss let her have off to attend. Sage told her Uncle Jack when she was graduating the last time they met one day downtown over lunch and was extremely happy that he agreed to come. At the graduation, before the ceremony, Ally stayed clear when she saw them talking. She didn't want him to see her, although she knew that he had gotten a glimpse of her at her father's funeral. At one time, she thought she could face him, but now she looked nothing like the person who was once his sister-in-law, so she kept her distance. What she didn't realize was that he always understood what she had gone through. He knew how she had so unjustly been treated and so had the children when his brother and she were divorced. From a distance, when she saw that he was there, it hadn't surprised her. As expected, if there was any one of the Tyler family who would attend, it would be Jack, as he had so nobly demonstrated before. Later during the awards portion of the ceremony, they were shocked and watched the astonished look on Sage's face when it was announced that she had gotten a full, four-year scholarship from Glasslane University in Pennsylvania. She hadn't even applied there, in fact, she had never heard of it, but was certainly not going to turn it down. There were many awards and scholarships given and the competitors had been tough contenders throughout the school year, but she was satisfied with what she got. Jack was stunned when he heard the announcement. He dared not tell her that it was her grandmother's most cherished university. If she had known that, she probably would decline the offer. He even wondered if his mother may have somehow secretly had something to do with the scholarship that had been awarded to her. But in reality, that notion was a long stretch and totally out of character for her.

Chapter 25

What Jack had handed Sage was a checkbook for a bank account, which he had opened on her behalf as her graduation gift, starting with a fifteen hundred dollar balance. He told her it was to help with any expenses she might incur while living on campus and would be more than happy to keep it replenished for as long as she needed. Reluctantly, she accepted. He also told her not to hesitate to let him know if she needed more before then. This was the first gift that she had ever accepted from him.

Before the fall semester began, Sage wanted to visit Glasslane University to see the campus where she would be spending the next four years of her life. She was glad that it wasn't too far from home so that she would be able to visit her brother without any real transportation problems. Breaking her short-lived conquest, Ally slid back into her life of overindulging in alcohol. And again, Sage asked her if she could sober up enough to go with her to the college for a tour of the campus.

"Of course, I want to go with you. We can get the bus or the train. Just let me know when you want to go so I can ask off from work."

"Thanks," Sage said dryly and with doubt. There was no trust in her mother anymore. This seed of doubt had been planted years ago with empty promises and worsening acts of disregard from her mother. She could be off the drink for a while, then right back on the wagon again. For her sake, her mother managed to come through a couple of days before their travel date. They went to the open house. All in all, she was pleased and could not wait to begin her new life away from home. On the way back, there was complete silence. Inside the apartment, Ally finally broke the dead air between them. "Well, how did you like your new college?" hoping to start a conversation with her distant and uncommunicative daughter, especially now that it was coming down to the last lap of living with her. Sage answered affirmatively, but she didn't expound. The next day everything was back to the same torturous routine.

Mark had gotten many offers from many colleges, but had gotten the best offer from Florida State and took them up on it. He promised to keep in touch with Sage as they said their goodbyes before he left in the airport taxi, right outside of his apartment building. All his friends, neighbors, and high school team buddies were there to see him off. He was shocked when Sage leaned in and kissed him on the lips just before they pulled off, and it was not just a peck. It was rather intense. He was so stunned by her passion that he couldn't even enjoy it. That kiss stayed on his mind during the entire flight to Florida and longer. He didn't know what to make of it and was afraid to ask her what it truly meant, for fear of finding out the truth. As the days went by, he had become too nervous to call her and decided to wait. Afraid that maybe he had misjudged the whole thing and was making it out to be more than what it was. So he tried to dismiss it altogether. Still, the constant thought of her kissing him with such intensity was wearing him down. He learned even before her that girls were too hard to figure out.

That night Sage thought about how much she missed Mark. He was a true and special friend, someone that she could trust and tell her inner most thoughts to and not be thought of as crazy or awful, especially how she felt about her mother. She had confessed to him how much she hated even being in the same room with her and could visualize strangling her. He would only laugh and at the same time, empathizing with her because he had almost come that close to strangling his own father to death. These feelings she could never discuss with anyone else, and even though she and Elesha had become very close friends, she could never explain to her or make her understand how she felt or what was driving her from within. She and Mark's circumstances were similar. They both had lived in abusive homes where feelings or the lack there of had cost them both lives devoid of the full benefit of what it was to love or be loved. She also thought about the kiss, which made her wonder if how she felt was more than just platonic. She even wondered herself and had no idea from where it had come from. In the weeks and months that she had been with him, there were never feelings of any desire to touch him with any kind of affection. They always hugged when they parted. Shaking hands she thought was a bit masculine and didn't think that it was an appropriate gesture for their friendship.

It was 11:00 and Casey had gone to bed and had already fallen asleep. Sage took her shower and got in bed as well. As expected, Ally came in with three of her regular drinking buddies. There was one unfamiliar guy that tagged along that had been at the bar most of the night and had been a really fun person that everybody at the bar seemed to like, so she invited him to come to her place to celebrate her birthday also. He had driven his own car so that he could leave whenever he wanted to, he explained, even though he was offered a ride and was promised a ride back to get his car. When they got inside, someone had playfully turned up the music.

"Shhhh," she slurred. "Hey, guys, keep it down if you want to keep this party going. The neighbors are going to call the cops."

"Shhhh," they all slurred in unison, spraying their index fingers with spattering saliva and laughing incessantly. The bottles and glasses clanked and were passed around the table for hours. Ally's boss had let her leave a little early to celebrate her birthday with a couple who had become regular patrons that she met early on when she was first hired and had befriended them.

Through all the drinking, laughing and giggling, the falling around on the sofa and chairs in the den, the kids did not seem to hear them. The four of them were drunk almost out of their minds. "Man, this is so much fun. I haven't had this many laughs in years," Ally said. They all laughed about that. Caught in the moment, she remembered something that she had kept stashed away for a long time. For what reason, she didn't even know, but now was the right time to get it, she thought. She wanted to impress her friends.

"Wait a minute. I have something that I know you guys might like." She got up and staggered to her bedroom. In an old pocketbook that she never used anymore stashed in a box way in the back on the top shelf of her closet, she got it and walked back out to her merrymaking friends. With the pocketbook hanging on her wrist, she strolled in front of them, trying to sway her hips from side to side pretending to be a model, but barely able to walk a straight line. They started laughing even harder.

"What's to like about that old pocketbook," her friend, Tina said.

"That's the ugliest thing I've ever seen."

"What are you talking about? This is a designer bag, I'll have you know," Ally said in defense.

"So what do us guys want with that? We're not women... unless that guy is one," Her old friend, Gary, said pointing to the new visitor. They laughed again. The new guy took the pocketbook and started strutting around holding it on his wrist, trying to walk like a girl. They all roared with laughter.

"Shhhh," Ally said. They all mocked her and snickered like little kids. Ally snatched the bag from him.

"Give me that back. She opened it and took out a little packet.

"Hey, what's that?" one of the guys asked.

"It's a little souvenir from my ex-husband."

The new guy asked, "Is that what I think it is?"

"Probably," she answered.

"Well, let's try it and see. You got a mirror?" he asked eagerly.

"Hey, you sound like a pro," Gary said.

"I've tried it before if it's the same thing I think it is. Get a spoon if you don't have any straws."

"Oh, you must know my ex. I caught him doing this on our living room coffee table," Ally said jokingly.

"Oh, give it to me if you don't want it," the stranger said.

"Hold on, I'll get a spoon." She staggered her way to the cabinet drawer then came back with a teaspoon.

"Give it to me and let me show you how." He tapped a little in the spoon and snorted it up his nose.

"Oh, yeah. That's it. Hey, your old man had taste."

"Let me try it," Tina said. She got the spoon and did the same. "Gad! Where am I? That's sweeter than wine,"

Gary grabbed the spoon from Tina. "My turn." He sniffed some of the white powder as well. "Mama Mia. That is nice. What is this stuff? I've never done this before."

"Well, Ally, it's your turn. Do you want to try it? Or maybe you and your old man did this together."

"Maybe not. Maybe that's why he's now my ex." They roared with laughter. "I don't even know what it is. I've never tried any drugs before in my life," she confessed. "That so? Well, you're drinking one." the newcomer said.

"This is alcohol, not drugs," she said adamantly.

"Same thing, honey. You're a drug addict."

"I am not," she emphatically responded. "I drink to have a little fun, and I'm celebrating my birthday, so let's enjoy. Okay, since I'm already a drug addict then let me try it." She sniffed some from the spoon. She was not ready for what was to come. The feeling went straight through her body. It was frightening to her. "Here, somebody take this stuff."

Gary and the new guy rallied for it until it was gone. The music seemed to have intensified even though no one had touched the volume. They started dancing around with each other, laughing and giggling until they were totally exhausted and totally wasted. Consequently, they each wound up stretched out on a chair or on the floor.

The bottles were empty. The bowl of chips had just a few crumbs left in it. Most of the chips were lying around the tray, rather than in it, and what was left of the dip was an empty bowl. Gary and Tina managed to get themselves together and got up off the sofa to make their way to the door. They didn't see Ally or the new guy, so they left with the music still playing and no one there to say goodbye. Barely making their way to the door, they closed it and left. Ally had somehow found her way to her bedroom sometime during the early morning hours. She was lying sprawled out on the bed, half-naked and asleep. Sage was in her room asleep next to Ally's bedroom, separated only by the bathroom that everyone shared. All of a sudden, she thought she heard a scream. It was muffled, but she thought she heard her daughter cry out to her, "Mom" as if struggling to say it. Then it was gone. She turned over thinking it was just a dream. Again, she heard it. It was clearer now. She jumped up and ran to Sage's room. There was the new guy lying on Sage, trying to hold her down. She ran over to him and pushed him off of her. There he was standing in the dimly lit room shocked and frightened with his zipper down, erect and exposed. Her underwear had been torn down, and her gown ripped, revealing her naked breast.

"What are you doing? Are you crazy? That's my daughter, you piece of scum! Get the hell out of my house!" Ally screamed. He pushed Ally against the wall, trying to make a clear getaway. Everything was happening so fast.

"Mom, call the police… please!" Sage yelled through her tears. She grabbed the sheet to cover herself. Sharon came bursting through the front door wearing a robe, as the guy almost knocked her down to get out. He started running for the stairs, barely holding his pants up with his naked buttocks showing as he grabbed the door handle with his coat tucked under his arm.

"Ally, what's going on in here?" she asked, looking terrified. "Ally, Sage, what happened? Casey came over banging on my door and calling for me to come over and fast. Who was that half-naked man who almost knocked me down running out of here holding up his pants?"

"He was a guy that was at my party. That's all."

"What do you mean, that's all? That man was in my room trying to rape me, Mother! He snatched off my underwear," Sage was sobbing.

Sharon told Casey to step out of the room for a minute and to close the door. "Tell me, Sage. What did he do to you?" Sharon asked as she sat next to Sage on the bed with her arms around her shoulder, holding her head to her chest trying to console her.

"That man came in my room. I was asleep and I felt his... his..." She burst out crying again.

"It's okay, sweetie."

"But Sharon, it was between my legs and he was holding my mouth. I tried to get him off, but he was too strong. I bit a part of his hand and when he moved it, I screamed." Ally walked away with tears streaming down her face. She stood facing the wall. She didn't want her daughter to see her. The person who had once again subjected her to yet more atrocity.

"Listen, Sage, did he rape you?" Sharon asked. She looked over at Ally's back and said, "You need to call the police, Ally. You know who this man is? He needs to be arrested for attempted rape of a minor," Sharon was angry. Ally turned around with her head down said with a soft voice, speaking through tears, she confessed,

"I don't know him."

"What? You mean you had somebody in your place that you didn't even know. ...at this hour."

"No... We... me and some friends met him at my job last night. He seemed like a nice guy."

"Really? How would you know?"

"What do you mean?"

"You know what I mean. Were you drinking?"

"It was my birthday and some friends and I were celebrating. There's nothing wrong with that... is there?"

"Look, Ally, we can talk later." Ally turned again. Looking back at Sage, Sharon said, "We need to deal with Sage right now. Sage can you identify him?"

"Not really. Only my nightlight was on. It was too dark." She was still upset, wiping away the tears. Sharon looked at Ally's back again.

"Ally, turn around." She looked old and haggard.

"Can you recognize him? You need to get the police involved. At least there was no penetration," Sage fell backwards on the bed, turned over and wept in her pillow at the thought of almost losing her virginity to a stranger. She didn't want anybody ever to know about this. This was one thing that she would never tell, not even Mark. "Sharon, can I speak to you in the kitchen?"

"Sage, are you okay?" Sharon asked.

Sage responded by nodding her head. Sharon got up and followed her. Facing each other Ally began to speak.

"Sharon, I am as upset as you, but I don't want to get the police involved."

"What are you talking about? There's a rapist running around free out there somewhere, free to rape someone else, even a child. He could even rape my daughter or somebody else's."

"I don't even know his name. I was pretty wasted. Look, Sharon, you know I'm one mistake away from losing everything."

"You could have fooled me," Sharon said, uncharacteristically sarcastic.

"If the police get involved, I could lose my son. Even though Sage is just about on her own, still, I could lose her, too."

"Truthfully, Ally, you already have."

"I don't want Sage to have to go through this either, Sharon. If this gets out, her father's family could find out. It would be an ugly scandal."

"Why don't you think of these things before you act, Ally?"

"You know what, Sharon? I think I need some help."

Sharon only walked away from her, back to Sage's bedroom. She had talked to Ally many times about her needing help, only to be met with denial and self-defense. On her way back to the bedroom, she could hear the shower water running. Sage had gone to take a shower. She felt so violated and filthy. She had the hot water on as hot as she could tolerate it. She wanted to cleanse the feel of those filthy hands and his smelly body off of her. Sharon went back to her apartment after she checked on Casey who had gone to his room. She convinced him that Sage would be fine and he was satisfied. She offered to let him stay at her place if he wanted to, but he assured her that he would be fine.

An hour later, Sage came out of her room with a suitcase. "Where are you going, Sage? You shouldn't go out now and where would you go this time of morning?" She didn't answer. "Sage? ... let's talk."

"We don't have anything to talk about. I'll be going away to college soon, and I will never come back here to live with you again."

"Sage…" she called as she was getting ready to walk out the door.

"I'm going to be staying with Sharon until it's time for me to go to Glasslane. She already told me that I could. I'll get the rest of my things as I pack up to leave for school at the end of summer."

"Sage… honey, I am so sorry."

"No, Mom. You're not sorry because your feelings are all for yourself. You have always only been sorry for yourself." She opened the door and walked across the hall. Sharon was waiting inside to let her in.

Chapter 26

Sharon and Ally's relationship had become more strained over the attempted rape incident. Sage continued working until she went off to college. Sharon continued to try to help the family as much as she could in spite of the sour atmosphere between them. Ally's behavior had not improved, even after that revolting incident. It was very disappointing to watch her continue to come home almost every day from work intoxicated, and nothing could deter her from her destructive behavior, not even a horrible criminal act such as what her own child had gone through. Even so, Sharon reached out to Ally and always invited her to come to church with her or go to counseling to try to get her life together. Ally never called the police to report the incident, and the culprit was never seen again. She even asked her friends who had been there that night if they had seen him again, but never revealed to them or anyone else what he had done after they left. Neither one of them had ever seen him before, or ever again, since that horrendous night, and admitted that they probably would not have been able to recognize him even if they had.

It was the same awful night after all the excitement had calmed down, that she realized there was some stickiness between her legs and on her bed saw a spot under the disheveled sheets. It was also wet and sticky to the touch. She then realized that he had taken full advantage of her in her extreme drunkenness. He raped her, and it terrified her. She had been too out of it to feel him penetrate her and carry on with his sexual criminal act. As she played back the events of that night, she remembered how she had to straighten out her own clothing when she rushed into Sage's room. It never occurred to her then what had transpired, but after finding out what he had attempted to do to her daughter and had succeeded with her, was when she later realized that she was not wearing any panties at all. This made her feel ashamed and disgustingly depraved. She thought that she was worse than a prostitute. At least they got paid. All she was left with was emptiness and grief. Thoughts of hopelessness, helplessness, and uselessness crowded her mind whenever she was sober. All that she could do was cry, constantly wondering what had she done to deserve the horrible things that had happened to her in her God-forsaken life. Suicide seemed to be the only solution to her irreparable existence. She had lost everything, including her children. Casey was there, but he had stopped talking to her as much as he had in the past. She knew that he had also been affected by what had happened to his sister, although he never mentioned a word to her about it. The only thing that stopped her was the disgrace and degradation she would leave for her family to have to endure. She never told anyone that the unknown man had raped her the same night. Especially, after she found out that she was pregnant.

A full month had gone by, and she had not had her period according to her timing. Sage had already left to start college. She, Casey, and Sharon's family took the train to Pennsylvania to see Sage off on her first day as a college student at Glasslane University. It was a happy day for everyone. Sage was happiest of all. They had lunch together and took the train that evening back to New Jersey. Ally had almost managed to forget about what had happened to her, until then. She checked the calendar again more carefully. This was something that she did not have to deal with anymore because she had not been sexually active since she and Colin had divorced. Ally was nearly forty-one and there was no way that she could get pregnant, or so she thought. When entering into the second month without a period, she decided to have a pregnancy test done at the clinic. The result was confirmed to be positive. She was devastated. She was carrying the child of a stranger who had raped her. Thinking of how this happened repulsed her to the point of nausea and her body filled with rage. Her mind scrambled with conflicting thoughts about what she should do. How could she face anyone? She didn't want to think about the embarrassment and shame to her family, friends, or the community. She imagined herself with a protruding stomach for nine months and everyone's curiosity about who the father might be. How could she explain this awful situation to anyone? Who would understand enough to accept her irresponsible predicament? She couldn't, so how could she expect anyone else to? The Tyler family's reputation would be smeared, tarnished and ruined in elite society, even though she had been divorced for years. She could not imagine how Sage would feel or what she would say or think if she carried out this unwanted pregnancy, although Casey may have been more sympathetic. The neighbors already looked down at her as an unfit and despicable parent, ready to report her to the authorities, as it was. In her imagination, she could see herself ripping this entity from her womb barehanded. She hated it already. Looking at it would be as strange as its father and she could not imagine herself cradling this thing or nurturing it in any way. The thought of adoption came to mind. There were many couples desiring to have a child, but she could not fathom carrying this thing for nine months. So why was she left in this calamity? Was there anything worse that could happen to her? She didn't want this creature growing inside of her and tried to get the thought out of her head that it was even there. Tormented by what was the right or the wrong thing to do, she decided that having an abortion was the only solution. It may not have been the moral thing to do, but there was no other way otherwise because the aftermath would be devastating for everyone. There were other matters of far greater significance in her life to consider. No one would ever know about it, but her and only she would have to live with her decision.

A few weeks later after the abortion, she and some friends had gone out to celebrate on her day off. Of course, they had no idea what the occasion was for. She told them that she was celebrating her children's scholastic achievements. One had already begun her freshman year at college on a full scholarship, and her youngest was taking all honors classes this year. Deep in her heart, she was relieved that she was rid of the "Thing" as she thought of it and it was finally out of her body. But in the back of her mind, deep in her subconscious mind, was the reality that a living being had been destroyed by her. The whole fake celebration was to help to obliterate the thought.
Walking to the subway, she thought she heard someone walking close behind. Ally and her friends were having so much fun that they managed to stay long enough to close the bar, so by this time it was early morning when they left. Wanting to take her time getting home to try to sober up a little by the time she got there, she declined a ride home and took the subway. Walking along, she saw shadows coming up from behind almost hovering over her, but when she turned slightly around, there was nothing. Her ability to walk fast was

hindered by her inebriant condition. As usual, she had had too much to drink. Clutching to her shoulder bag, she headed to her usual subway stop. Just as she was getting ready to walk down the steps, she was almost face to face with a tall, slender, bearded man. Having a heavy foreign accent, he apologized and kept walking. She turned around as quick as she could without stumbling and saw the back of a man wearing a military jacket, but had not seen his face. In her foggy memory, she thought of the man in her dream and on the street that day on her way to the bank while riding the bus. "Was that the man?" she thought. Obviously, he didn't recognize her. Dismissing the thought, she kept walking. "He could be anybody. There are more people other than that guy who wore military jackets," she thought. If he is really the man in her dream, what did it mean? Using her monthly pass, she went through the gate and waited. There were couples so into one another that they hadn't noticed her when she brushed against them as she staggered by. A burly old hunchback man stood waiting, holding a cane. She wondered what he was doing out so early in the morning. His hat was pulled so far down on his head it covered his ears and his jacket looked old and worn. He never looked anywhere except straight ahead, although there was nothing there except a brick wall. The train finally came, and the few passengers that were waiting got on. Her ride was not long, but she dozed off and missed her stop. "I can't believe this," she said out loud. The driver, who was scanning the cars, woke her and told her that she had to get off the train. He explained that she had to go to the other side if she wanted to get back to her stop. It was the end of the line and this train would not be turning around. She was not the only person there. Seeing the old man also waiting to go back, she thought was a strange coincidence. Now feeling somewhat uneasy and not that loaded, realized not taking that offer for a ride home was obviously a stupid decision and now she regretted it.

This time they were above ground, the old man only stared across again towards the reverse track. It was strange that she never saw the man walking; he was just always there, standing and waiting. She was afraid to say anything to him, so she kept her distance and continued waiting. Just as the train got there, he was now just there, right next to her. She never even saw how he managed to move. Making sure that he got on ahead of her and sat down, she could sit far away to watch him. But this man was old. What could he do to her? His back was hunched, apparently from age and she noticed how his cane shook as they waited for the train to come. So, why was she so afraid? When she got off at her stop, so did he. They even caught the same bus. This was becoming more and more bizarre. When she got off the bus, the old man got off too. She could now hear his cane hit the pavement as he walked not too far behind her. As she got closer to her neighborhood she saw Mr. Melmann's store and Nate's place, but they were both closed. The taps were getting closer and faster as she walked faster. After all this time, she had become more sober because of the frightening pursuit that was happening. By the time she got to the glass doors of the building and hopped inside, she could see him walk by. He looked in, but strangely, she could not see his face. She was so frightened that she was trembling. She nervously put her key in and opened the door. All that she could do was think about that frightening incident that had just happened. Why was he following her? She couldn't call the police because there was no crime. Again, there was no one who she could talk to. She would be blamed for being out alone in the first place. It always seemed that every terrible thing that had ever happened to her was her fault. What had she done? Was she being punished by God? If so, then which one,…which god? Not wanting to think about anything else, she got her glass from her drawer and her stash from the closet after taking a shower and poured herself a drink. Though her hand was a bit shaky, she managed to pour without spilling a drop.

At work a couple of nights later, her friends stopped by for Happy Hour. "How'd you do? You're here so I guess you got in okay." Gary asked.
"What are you talking about?"
"We sat in the car waiting for you to find your key."
"Yeah, you were taking so long, we almost left you standing there, but I persuaded Gary to wait a little longer," Tina added.
"What are you talking about? I got the subway."
"Tell me you're joking. Either we were dreaming, or you were dreaming. Me and Tina couldn't have had the same dream, so I guess it was your dream."
"I guess I was dreaming then."
"By the way, how was the ride?" Gary asked, joking around. They all started laughing, including Ally, but inside, she was scared. She couldn't believe that she dreamed the whole incident. Gary was at the bar jokingly telling everybody about Ally's dream. Fortunately, he didn't know any of the terrifying details.
"Do I drive so fast it feels like you're riding on the subway?" Everybody laughed, even Ally, but she didn't think it was a laughing matter. She continued to be bothered by her 'dream'. Were there other dreams that she thought were real or real events that were only dreams? She noticed again the slight tremor of

her hands.

"It has to be my nerves. Maybe I should see a doctor," she thought. At the end of the shift, her coworker offered her a ride home. She readily, and thankfully, accepted.

Chapter 27

Now in her junior year at the college, Sage had made many friends, but only a few had become close. For the most part, she had forgotten about the dreadful life that she had left behind, except for the short visits to see her brother. Mark stayed in touch as promised and had even, flown up to visit her a couple of times during the first two years of college, but the distance between their schools and obligations in other endeavors for both of them brought distance in their relationship. However, they still managed to stay in contact with each other by text or phone. She wrote Mr. Melmann brief letters when there was time and would send a card on special occasions. Even during the summer, Sage didn't come home. She found a job through the school that was related to her major of which there was also the potential of staying on after graduation. One of the faculty members had notified her of the opportunity and encouraged her to apply. Casey continued to do well in school despite his mother's relentless drinking and obnoxious behavior. He spent more time at Sharon's apartment rather than his own when he was not working at the store. When they were both at home, he buried himself in his studies, watched television or read. There was no real family-like relationship with his mother now, as she was working, or hanging out with her friends, or recovering from the usual hangover. There were days that she would try to spend time with her son, but during those times, she was too intoxicated to even have a sensible conversation with him. He never got the game system that she promised, nor did he expect to get one. Working at the store and not wanting to cause her any feelings of guilt or financial burden, he was able to save his own money and buy his own game system. Regardless of her actions, he loved his mother dearly and worried about her health. His Uncle Jack had tried to get involved in his life, but he was not receptive. Not that he didn't love his uncle, but being five years younger than his sister and just a little boy when his parents were divorced, he never got the chance to know any of the family as well as Sage had, except for his dad.

The dreams continued. The shaking and the numbness had come back. Finally, Ally contacted the clinic to try to see a doctor about her health issues. She was able to get an appointment with one of the doctors, who after her examination recommended that she see a neurologist. Through the examination, he could tell that she had a problem with alcohol. The neurologist, Dr. Hiemer, warned her of the consequences of continued and excessive drinking, which Ally denied as being excessive, but rather described it as having an occasional cocktail. But for as long as she had been drinking alcohol, her liver was not as damaged as he had first suspected after viewing her scans and receiving the results of her blood tests. On her return visit, the doctor spoke with her about her results, concluding with a caution to cut back on her 'cocktails.' Her interpretation of his analysis in her mind was a cause for celebration. The doctor had given her a warning, but the test showed differently than she had perceived to be his diagnosis.

That night at work was busy, but she was more lively and funnier than ever. Her boss commended her with a bottle of vodka to take home. Unfortunately, there was no one there who was able to give her a ride, so she had to resort to the subway to get home. The night had been busy and tiresome, so as she headed up that long haul going her same old route, thought about that old jalopy of hers that hardly ran and needed so much work done that she could not have afforded to keep going. With the money that Jack had given her, she would have had enough to get it fixed, but even so, it would have been a struggle to keep up with the insurance costs. So, one day a year before, she decided to put a "For Sale" sign on it and got an offer the same day. She got more than what she had expected even though it was not even running at that time, but still she never tried to buy another one. Subsequently, she wished at times such as these that she had had her own transportation.

That night as she continued her trek home, there were a few pedestrians walking along as usual. The stores had been closed hours ago. The streets were practically clear of traffic. This was a weekday, so there was not much going on downtown. Still a little tipsy from all the treats that night, wanted to get home. Having walked a ways up the street, from behind she felt someone coming up close to her. She could see their shadow overshadowing her own. "Oh, no," she thought panicking. "I can't be dreaming again. I know I'm not dreaming." Then a woman, her hands in her pockets hastily walked around her rushing up the street. The shadow was gone. Clutching tightly onto the bottle of vodka that was in her shoulder bag, she vigilantly continued up the slightly inclined street towards the subway looking out for any other shadows that might be coming up from behind.

The weather was rather chilly that early fall morning and the streets were quiet until out of nowhere a snarling black wolf-like dog appeared directly in front of her. She stopped dead in her tracks looking around for its owner to beckon it to come back. Its yellowing teeth were pointed and looked razor sharp protruded out of shiny black gums. The eyes looked angry and piercing. She looked around again to see if someone was coming to rescue her from this possible attack. No one was coming to the scene, and no one ever came. She was petrified. Its slender, muscular body began moving in slow mechanical cadence towards her, the black coat so shiny it looked hairless. An identical dog came out of this same abyss and joined in on the other side of her as both started growling and closing in towards her rapaciously snapping and gnarling as their narrow pointed tails whipped in unison seemingly in slow motion. Seeing that she had no other recourse, she whirled around and started running as fast as she could. No one tried to help. She started screaming for help and no one came to her rescue. They only scurried out of her way in fear. The dogs ran closely behind her, barking as she ran. She was running and screaming. There was no place to go for shelter. The stores were all closed; there was nowhere to go. With their strong-looking jaws and sharp teeth just feet away, she turned the corner, practically out of breath. Just then, a man with a huge dog was walking towards her, as she ran by him with a piercing cry for help, the dogs chasing close behind. As she ran, she heard him give out a command to his dog in a foreign language that she could not recognize. It went chasing behind them barking and growling charging after the two unrestrained menacing carnivores. His dog was huge, yet fast. She could hear the screeches from the other dogs in the distance as he apparently had attacked them. She stopped and turned around and watched the man as he gave out another command in the same tongue. Apparently, he called his name to return, because it came back immediately and sat at his side.

"Did someone put those dogs on you?" he asked. The accent, she thought, could be Middle Eastern. "Did you see anyone?" he continued to question her. She tried to explain to him how the chase started, how those taunting dogs confronted her.

"No, I was just walking to the subway. They came out of nowhere growling and barking at me for no reason."

"Well, I don't think they will come back. Go home and be careful Miss." She expressed how thankful and grateful she was to him and for his dog to stop to help her. Before they left, she told him that she liked his dog's name and asked him the meaning.

"His name means, Guardian." Afterwards, he said something to the dog, patted him on the head and walked across the street, the dog walking close to his side. When she got on the subway train, she suddenly remembered something. In all the excitement, she had not realized how familiar he looked. He looked just like the man in her dream with the big dog. It was him because this man was wearing a military jacket. Evidently, he lived in the area, otherwise, how else could she have recognized him after seeing him in a dream before she even met him? That was the only explanation. What was happening to her? Or could she have special powers? She could not understand any of it. If she told anyone, they would think she was crazy or say that it was from her drinking. She had to figure this out alone.

Chapter 28

Ally's financial woes had not changed. She still could not afford to leave her supplementary housing or could not even save one dime. This reality always took her back to her regrettable and prideful decision during her divorce so many years ago. It was the year of Sage's graduation. She wanted to be able to give her a very special gift. Something that money could not buy… the gift of sobriety. It was already February, and she had already been working painstakingly hard to lay off the alcohol for a couple of weeks now. Since her last ordeal, she finally realized that there needed to be serious changes made in her life. But one night out of nowhere the numbness in her hands showed up while she was at work, which resulted in a few glasses falling to the floor and breaking, causing a bit of a commotion. The shaking came right behind, almost causing her to lose her job on the spot due to a couple of embarrassing spills and the resulting customer's laundry expense. Had it not been for the kind patrons who she had known well, she would have. The manager sent her home early that night; however, with a threat to get herself together. This was the first time her boss had ever spoken to her with anything less than praise for her hard work and friendliness to the customers that he often commended her for.

It had been a long and arduous week of keeping herself devoid of any drink. In fact, it was about the third week without even a glass of wine. It was hard to keep a smile and be the fun person that her regulars had known her to be. The drinks that they offered, she either kindly refused or accepted them only to pour them in the sink behind the bar.

"You guys are too kind."

"Thanks, but no thanks."

"Not tonight. I don't have a ride home, but I'll take a rain check." Those were some of the excuses she used to decline their generosity politely and inoffensively. Now that was the first and second week, but by the third week, the shaking and numbness had started again. Even though she dutifully followed the instructions, that her doctors suggested, and had taken her meds as directed, it had all come back. She thought that by listening to them, she had almost lost her job. In truth, she could hardly tolerate the reality of it all while sober. All the way to the beginning, the constant tormenting remembrances of her haunting past and the menacing awareness of her thoughtless decisions came back reminding her of how their spiraling life began its perpetual doom and gloom. These always managed to creep into a sober mind.

Her early dismissal only made her angry, and her heart was defiant. Concluding that even when she tried to change to do what was right, it was all for nothing… it was fruitless and really didn't matter, so she was going to do it her own way. She decided she was not going home… anyway, not just yet. The night was young, so she decided to go to Manhattan to have some real fun. Casey was okay, he was following his usual routine when she had to work and then there was always Sharon. He practically never talked to her anymore anyway, so she was going to enjoy the night. She was going to deal with her issues her own way. "I'm not afraid. Whatever is happening to me, real or unreal, I'm going to do it my own way." she said softly, but emphatically, full of hatred and resentment. Maybe she was being taunted by demons, she sometimes thought, remembering from past church sermons growing up and learning that demons were real. But then again remembered that the Bible also taught that with prayer and petitioning to God that whatever you asked for any desire of your heart, He would give it to you. All you had to do was ask. She was sure that anything counted. "But, a lot of good that did," she thought, remembering those prayers she prayed for God to save her marriage. Even so, she was so disgusted and enraged about everything that she didn't care anymore about anything. If there was ever a demon in her life, it had to be Greg. Ever since Greg had come into her life, she had had nothing but hopelessness through no fault of her own. It turned out that meeting him at Huntington Beach that day was the worst thing that had ever happened to her in her entire life and marrying him brought every egregious moment after that, and she hated him for it.

While riding the subway to Manhattan, she randomly picked the Fifty-ninth Street stop to get off. So, this was Manhattan. Everyone seemed to be in such a hurry. On both sides of the street, there were numerous selections of delis, bakery shops, and restaurants of any choice of palate. Department stores and street vendors displayed their wares. Some were closing down because it was getting dark and the night's wind had picked up quite a bit, nearly blowing their goods right off the stands. About a half block in, a gust of wind practically pushed her into the foyer of a little juke joint where the music was blaring inside when she opened the door. It was small and very crowded. She looked around for a table or a booth and saw none vacant. Then, a couple suddenly had just gotten up when she glanced and saw them standing. Immediately, she dashed straight there. Just making it, she sat down. "Sorry," she said to the woman who obviously had also noticed the departing couple. Never saying a word, the woman looked down at her, rolled her eyes, and then walked away into the vast crowd. Almost as soon as she sat down, the waitress walked over to get her order. She had very dark, almost black lipstick with streaks of green and purple throughout her bleached blond, almost platinum hair. Her eye makeup sparkled and matched her style of dress. The colors matched the streaks in her hair. She handed her the food and drink menus, and asked, "Can I start you off with something to drink, maybe?" she said in a heavy, probably Brooklyn accent.

"That's okay, I don't need this," handing her back the list of alcoholic beverages. "I'll just have a gin and tonic with a slice of lime, please?"

Holding a pen with her laced gloved hand, she wrote. "Sure, I can get that for you. Did you want to order something to eat?"

"What, no freebees? I thought this was Happy Hour?"

"Are you joking? That went out in the nineties," Ally was only kidding.

"Okay, I'll look at the menu,"

"I'll be right back with your drink."

"Thanks," she saw her give the bar tender her order. Looking over the menu, she decided to have a cheeseburger with fries. It wasn't cheap, she thought looking at the other selections. She had to remind herself where she was. This part of New York was where the "haves" usually hang out. The waitress brought back her drink and took the order for her meal. The music was rocking, and the people were indulging themselves in food and conversation. Picking up her sandwich, about to take a bite, she heard someone trying to get her attention. There was a man, standing right next to her, asking if he could sit at her table. He was holding a drink in one hand with his overcoat hanging over the other arm and holding a briefcase. "There are no more seats and if you don't mind, I just want to sit have my drink and leave. Even the seats at the bar are all taken," he added to support his case. He was well dressed, wearing a dark colored suit. In the dim lighting she noticed the tie. Looking to be in his late thirties in age, he had evidently just stopped in for a drink after work. There was no way she could refuse, especially since her table held seating for at least four. Refusing, she would have appeared to be selfish, plus he looked harmless. "Sure. Have a seat," she said.

"Are you sure you don't mind?" At this point, she wanted to tell him that if she had wanted to say "no" she would have. But she remained polite and assured him that it was okay. "Thank you. I thought I'd stop in here before I go home."

"Yeah, same here." He started with small talk.

"Do you come here much?" Between bites, she tried to respond.

"Actually, no. This is my first time here." Again, she took another bite and began to chew.

"Are you just getting off from work too?" She held up her finger as a gesture to wait.

"Oh, I'm sorry. I'm disturbing you again." When she finished chewing and swallowed her bite, she said,

"No, my mouth was full at the time. I couldn't answer just then, sorry."

"No, I'm sorry. It's bad enough that I've imposed on your space."

"No, no. It's not an imposition. It's only me sitting here. I've taken up a table for four when it's only me…"

"That's okay," He interjected. "You obviously got here first."

"I did. In fact, I beat out some other woman who wasn't too happy about it. It was like musical chairs and the music was still playing." She burst out laughing. The man began to laugh too. The other patrons were looking to see what was so funny but turned back to their own affairs.

"That was funny after I thought about it." She got the attention of the waitress who quickly came over.

"Could you bring me another gin and tonic, please? Oh, and don't forget the lime, please."

The man also asked for another drink. "Oh… uh… do you mind if I sit for another drink?"

"Nooo. I told you this isn't my table. Have as many as you want. Would you like some fries? There's no way that I can eat all of them."

"No, thank you."

"Here, go ahead. I haven't even touched them yet." She slid the plate of fries over to him.

"Okay, I'll just have a few."

"Go on. Have them all. I can't even finish this burger."

"Okay, if you insist. And thank you. By the way, what's your name?"

"Ally, what's yours?"

"My name is Richard, but everybody calls me Rich."

"Oh, how fitting." She started laughing again, thinking that he looked as he if had some well-paying job. He laughed while wondering what was funny.

"Awww, I was only joking." The waitress brought their drinks and Ally had drunk half of hers already. She finally began to have a real conversation with the man. He wound up offering and paying for her entire order and then some.

"Ally, have you ever taken a ride…a carriage ride through Central Park?"

"No, but I've always wanted to." She had drunk quite a few drinks by this point and easily swayed.

"Okay. Do you want to go?"

"Go where?"

"On a carriage ride. Come on, let's go."

"Wait a minute. I don't even know you," she slurred.

"Yes, you do. We've been sitting here talking most of the night and about everything. I even know your family. I know your name, you have kids, and you know mine, so how about it? It's not even a block away. I'm not going to hurt you. Do I look like someone that could hurt anyone?"

"Well, no. You are wearing a suit and tie," she said with some doubt. He only laughed.

"Okay, but after that, just let me off at my subway stop to catch my train home."

"Sure. Okay then, let's go. I'm sure you're going to love this." He helped her to put on her coat and then grabbed his from the empty chair beside him. She picked up her glass and drank the last few drops. Then, they walked to the door.

"Wait right here. I'll be right back."

She saw him walk over to the bar and say something to the bartender. The bartender pointed to a direction adjacent to the bar and Rich went that way.

"Maybe he has to use the men's room," she thought. Standing and waiting thinking about how pleasurable her night had turned out, she thought of how Rich's inadvertent company had helped her to accomplish just that. Watching him emerge from the crowd walking towards her and smiling she thought, "He seems like a nice enough guy, so why not go along with him to Central Park."

There were quite a few carriages waiting when they got there. It was a weekday and cold, so business was slow. He let her choose the one that she wanted. It was already about midnight and well past the time that she wanted to be out, although if she had been working she would have been cleaning up and getting ready to leave for home after a couple more hours of work. "Hey, you didn't tell me about the smell." "Sorry, it won't be for long."
"You know it's really cold out here."
"Yeah, it is pretty cold. We'll just take a short ride, okay?"
"It's okay with me."
Out of her pockets, she pulled out a knit hat, some gloves, and put them on. She had forgotten all about them until she felt the cold wind blowing against her face and through her hair. The carriage took off with a slight jerk as they both went backwards against the seats. They laughed like little kids. Riding into the park quite a ways away, she noticed, "You know… this park is really beautiful. As long as I've lived in this area, I've never come to Central Park."
"Really? It's a great place to walk through just to admire its beauty, especially in the spring and summer months. A lot of people like to jog through."
"I can see why. It's even beautiful at night. I can imagine what it's like during the day."
"Did you know that there are paths through here that can lead you right to the New York Public Library on the other side? It's a beautiful building."
"No, I didn't."
"You know that library is almost the largest in the United States. You'll have to go sometimes."
"I will. Maybe I'll get my son to go with me. He'd probably like that."
"He is a teenager, you told me, right? A teenager who wants to go to the library…now that's different."
"Yeah, he likes history and things like that. He likes to read."
"Well, that's great. The world would be a better place with more kids like him." The carriage turned along as the path turned. "Oh, I almost forgot." He pulled out a bottle of brandy from his briefcase with two plastic cups. "Have some. This will warm you up." "Yeah, I can use something right now to make

me warm."

He handed her about a half cup. She drank it with a sigh of satisfaction.

"Don't worry, there's more if you like."

"That's great because I'm still a bit chilly." He knew that she was being facetious and they both looked at each other and burst out laughing. She did take him up on having another cup, though and another until she was practically drunk. They wound up at the statue of Alice in Wonderland. "Wow, look at that. It's huge," she said excitedly. "Hey look! There's the rabbit and the Mad Hatter!" she said with slurred speech. She chimed into the song from the Walt Disney movie that was sung by the white rabbit. "Yeah, I am late. I need to get back." Her words slow to come.

"Awww... we just got started.

"No, Rich, I need to get back."

"Oh, okay. But let's walk over and sit on the mushroom before we turn back."

"Okay, but I really need to get back to catch my train home."

They both got out of the carriage. He went to say something to the driver. They walked over to the statue and left the carriage on the other side of the road. She could barely jump. "That's okay. I'll just stand here and look at it. She started running her fingers over the large images and making faces at them. Rich laughed at how silly she was acting. He jumped off and started walking around the statue to the other side. She was trying to follow him fumbling and stumbling behind, but when she got to the other side, Rich was not there. She called out for him. "Rich…Rich where are you?" She started calling his name melodiously. "Ri-ich…come out now. This isn't fuun-ny." There was no answer. The driver of the carriage, who was on the other side of the road said, "Miss, I can't stay. I have to get back. I'm on a schedule and you didn't pay for a full park ride." He yelled from way across the road. He started turning the carriage around.

"No wait!" she shouted as the driver started heading back. She looked back around and called out again.

"Rich," she said sternly, but still intoxicated. "Rich, the driver is leaving. Get me out of here. I don't know my way around in here." She spoke softly and started walking away, looking for signs for directions. At one point when she looked back, she thought she saw the head of Alice turn a little in her direction. She knew that it had to be her imagination. Walking farther away when she turned to look back, hoping to see Rich, all of the characters were standing and facing in her direction. They all moved slowly in unison as if getting ready to run. She panicked and in disbelief, started to run. Not knowing where she was headed she continued to run. She kept running for seeming at least a mile stumbling and tripping almost falling with no sign of Rich. She didn't know what to do or think. Then she came to a statue of a dog that looked like a Husky. As she walked past it, she stared at it to make sure it didn't move. What was happening? It surely was not a dream. It had to be something demonic, something satanic. As she walked by the statue of the dog, it growled. She heard it clearly. Almost out of her mind in fear, again she began racing through the park as fast as she could to get away. She was running for so long and far that it seemed, and she hoped, that she was near the end where there would hopefully be people around. Where were those joggers and walkers that he talked about? Did they only come out during the day? Where were the police or somebody patrolling the park for security? She needed help. Was the alcohol causing her to see these strange phenomena? If Rich was a hallucination, then, how did she get here? She was confused, perplexed, and scared. But Rich was real. All of it had been real since the beginning. Not hearing anything from behind for a while, she desperately needed to take a chance and stop to catch her breath. Taking that chance, when she saw a bench she plopped down looking around in every direction. She was still holding on to the plastic cup that Rich had poured her drink into and could smell the brandy. "See…" the smell of the alcohol convinced her that whatever was happening to her had to be real. She didn't have any issues with alcohol and surely couldn't be hallucinating. The doctor never warned her or even mentioned anything about delirium tremens when she was being examined. But while waiting in his office, she read a pamphlet that explained that hallucinations could occur in alcoholism. This was surely not her issue, she thought. Still determined to envelop herself in denial and self-deceit she deliberately had not mentioned the dreams or the man in the military jacket to the doctor. Also, she didn't honestly answer the question "How often do you drink alcohol?" one of the questions on the medical history form. Why was she even thinking about delirium tremens or DTs? she asked herself. Could all of this have been a hallucination? Surely, that could not be her problem. Her problems were stress related.

"Need a refill?" She practically leaped off the bench, feeling as though she was nearly having a heart attack when she heard a voice coming from the bushes behind her. "Rich, is that you?" It was Rich stepping out from behind the bushes and laughing. "Rich that was not funny. You really startled me. In fact, this whole thing has been scary. I was so scared, I started imagining those statues had come to life and were chasing me."

"Alive? …statues coming to life? You mean you thought that statues could come alive. …and chasing you?" he started laughing harder.

"Yeah, I guess I was just so scared that my imagination just got away with me." He started laughing again. She stared at him laughing at her and was becoming quite annoyed at his finding her fear to be so amusing.

He stopped laughing and looked at her with now a more serious look. "Ally, maybe it wasn't your imagination."

"What do you mean?" she asked, now feeling extremely alarmed. He started to laugh again. His voice sounded strange. "Stop it, Rich. You running off and leaving me alone out here was not such a funny prank either." He kept laughing. "You're scaring me. Stop it…stop laughing and take me back. I need to go home." He continued to laugh. As his laughter became louder; he went back into the bushes. "Rich, come back. Take me out of here. This isn't funny." She followed his laughter into the bushes but didn't see him. Going deeper into the bushes, someone suddenly grabbed her arm. It was Rich. He gripped her so tightly that she could feel his fingernails through her coat. He slung her down to the ground and started trying to pull down her pants. "Rich, what are you doing? Let me go. Get off of me. What was going on?" she thought as she attempted to scream but couldn't because he held his hand over her mouth. He threatened and dared her not to scream when he removed his hand. His piercing gray eyes stared down at her and he started to grin showing his teeth. He tried to kiss her as she tossed her head from side to side. She felt as though she was going to throw up. She could not believe what was happening to her. He was going to rape her. She could feel his hand between her legs. She attempted to scream and again he covered her mouth again. He started to smile and laugh. She could not believe the sound. It was now not a humorous type of laughter, but sounded haunting. "You know you want me," he said, looking down at her. She looked in his eyes. They looked evil. What was happening to him? As she stared at his face, something was changing…his face, his mouth, and his hair dropping to the ground and on her. The man in the dream…it was him. Horrified at what she was witnessing, she somehow kicked him in the groin. Moaning in pain, he fell backwards onto the ground.

Quickly grabbing her purse which had been next to her, she took flight heading for some semblance of civilization… a building, a house, a car, someone…anyone. She could hear the frightening taunts from behind her telling her to stop and come with him. "Ally, my way is the way," he said. "Come to me. Only I can help you." Out of nowhere, she heard the barking and snarling of vicious dogs. The growling sounded angry. She heard the thing command them in his hair-raising voice, "Stop her." She somehow outran them and got to the end of the park. The New York Public Library was right across the street. She could see the statues of the two lions. The building was closed, but she thought that maybe someone would see her running and stop to help. She raced across the wide street and arduously tried to climb the high incline of steps. She had almost gotten to the top when one of the dogs caught up and snagged her on the shoulder from behind. She was horrified when she felt it touch her and began to tilt backwards. Down the steps she fell, hitting her shoulders and her head as she continued to slide downwards on her back. She could still hear the dogs' threatening and taunting growls coming towards her again. Overwhelmed with fear she desperately pleaded and cried out, "Dear God in Heaven, please help me." She had reached the bottom and still lying on her back on the steps. Her mind fuzzy from alcohol and the fall, her vision blurred when she heard a familiar voice. It was the same voice of the man in the military jacket speaking in his native tongue. She couldn't see him, but she heard him clearly. He commanded his dog the same way that he had done before when he helped her. She remembered the name. Then she saw the statues of the lions come alive. Her vision was still blurred, but she could see the outline of their huge shape clearly. One had stood up on its hind legs and leaped up over her, then the other one followed as they met in mid air with the dogs. The lions and the hellish looking dogs that were chasing her, clashed right over her in mid air. The lions' mouths were wide open as their paws leaped out towards the dogs whose forelegs were extended in the air for the counter attack. High above her, she saw the eight gigantic paws collide. There was a loud noise and a brilliant light that blinded her as she passed out.

Chapter 29

Ally had never reached home that morning. When she realized where she was, she had come to lying in bed at a nearby hospital. The police had gotten involved because a passerby found her sprawled out on her back on the library steps unconscious and called 911. One of the detectives found out the phone number and address of Sharon from the information on Ally's I.D. card and notified her that she was in the hospital. Casey was highly upset when he found out. This was the first time that something this terrifying had ever happened to his mother. Sharon contacted Sage. She told Sharon that she was unable to come. In truth, Sage did not want to come. She figured that her mother had made her own problems in her life and she shouldn't drag other people into them. She was tired of having to suffer for her mother's irresponsibility. She had her own life to live and didn't want to nor should she have to deal with her mother's blunders anymore. And it wasn't fair for anyone to expect her to.

"But Sage, she's still your mother. You have to care. I know you and Casey have been through a lot, but you should at least try to call her."

Diverting the subject she said, "Sharon, I don't want my grandmother to worry, so could you please not let anybody else know about my mother yet. Casey told me that she'd be leaving the hospital in a couple of days anyway, so it looks like she'll be okay. Listen, Sharon, I can't just up and leave school. This is my senior year, and I need to be focused. I have exams coming up, so I need to study."

"I know you do, but your mother needs you, too."

"You know, Sharon, I don't think she does. She never has in the past. Thanks for the call. Bye now."

Sharon took Casey to the hospital later that morning to visit his mother. While she was in the hospital, she asked Sharon if she could call her manager at work to let him know where she was so that she hopefully would not lose her job. At that time, Sharon had not known the full details of what had happened. The police only told her where she had been found and the hospital where they had been taken her. She wondered how in the world she could have even been in that part of the city if she had been working. But if what she was told was true, she knew that her drinking had everything to do with whatever had happened. In actuality, Sharon could understand Sage's insensitivity towards her mother's current dilemma, but was hoping that under these circumstances, she would have been more compassionate since the same thing had nearly happened to her.

From the examination at the hospital it was determined that there had been an attempted rape. She told the police the whole story of how she had met Rich and where the crime had occurred. Someone had seen a man running from the area of the scene and into the park around the time the incident allegedly took place but was too far away to see what he looked like. The witness had been the same person who found Ally lying unconscious on the steps of the library. During their search, the police found a briefcase in the bushes in the park with an empty bottle of brandy inside which were going to be examined in the crime lab for fingerprints. At the hospital, the detective tried to get a description of the man and asked her to come to the station when she was released from the hospital to look at pictures of known rapists to help find the person who tried to commit this heinous crime.

When Casey woke up that morning and didn't see any sign that his mother had been home, he became alarmed. Not knowing where she was, he didn't want to go to school until he knew her whereabouts. No matter how drunk she was she always came home at night. He called Mr. Melmann to tell him that he wouldn't be able to come to work. He didn't expound on the reason, only telling him that it was a family matter. Immediately, he went over to Sharon's house to tell her that his mother had not come home from work. Seeing how upset he was, she told him that he didn't have to go to school and was going to find out where she may have gone. She tried to assure him with explanations that would quell his anxiety and then persuaded him to stay at her place and have breakfast with the children. Her children went on to school, but Casey stayed behind. It was late that morning when Sharon had gotten a call from the police letting her know that Ally was in the hospital, but didn't discuss what had occurred. She called the hospital immediately to speak to someone to find out how she was if she could have visitors. Her nurse had been trying to find her next of kin. In her brief conversation with the nurse, Sharon informed her that Ally's daughter was away at school, but her son was with her and wanted to see his mother.

Sharon gave Casey the phone. "Hello?" he said nervously.

"Hi, my name is Judy, the nurse who's taking care of your mom."

"Is my mom all right?"

"Yes, she is fine. Don't worry. I'm taking good care of her. If you want, you can come to see her anytime you want. Now, may I speak to Sharon again, please?"

He handed Sharon back the phone.

"Hello, this is Sharon."

"Hi, Sharon, I was just telling Ally's son that he can come anytime to visit his mom, but he's under age for this unit and has to be accompanied by an adult."

"Oh, that's fine. I'm going to bring him when I come. And thank you so much."

"Oh, you're welcome. Now, you said that she has a daughter, also?"

"Yes, she does, but she's away at college right now in Pennsylvania. I'll get in touch with her."

"You know, Ally's isn't giving a whole lot of information about her next of kin."

"Don't worry. I'll take care of that."

When Ally was finally released from the hospital that Saturday, Casey was extremely happy to see his mother. He raced to the door as soon as he heard her come in. Hugging her tightly, he said, "Hey, Mom. How are you?"

"I'm okay. But, how are you?"

"I'm great now that you're home."

"Awww… Casey. That's so nice of you to say." She kissed him on the forehead. Now, she had to reach up to him as he leaned down to her. Casey was a tall teenager, almost sixteen now, but she still saw him as her little baby. "Have you talked to Sage?" reluctantly, he answered. "Yeah, I told her that you were in the hospital. …and that you were okay and would be coming home soon and not to worry." He knew that he had exaggerated about his conversation with Sage, because he knew that she was not at all interested in what had happened to their mother. Sage, not wanting to upset Casey by acting totally apathetic told him not to worry because she has always bounced back and would be just fine. He was grateful for what she told him but knew her true feelings.

During her three-day stay in the hospital, Ally had had the proverbial epiphany. How frightful when she realized that she had been in a possible life or death situation and had no one else to call except God. Relatively unscathed except for scrapes and bruises He answered her prayer. Even the attempted rape was foiled. She never believed that she would ever utter His name again. In that hospital bed, she saw her whole life laid out before her. Everything that she had ever done and all that had ever happened to her she could see, but now in a different light. She began to recognize that she was the reason for all of her difficulties, the transgressions she thought were against her, the mistreatment by those that she loved and thought loved her...all that had ever happened to her was of her own doing. She was not going to blame anybody for her mistakes and bad choices anymore. She realized that she was never forced into anything that she had ever done, not even her marriages. With opened eyes now and acceptance of her own wrongdoing, she admitted that she chose not to listen to good advice which deep within, knew was the right advice to begin with. Her decision to 'do it her way' was of her own volition. The intention was to prove to everyone that they had been wrong. She was going to show them how little she needed them, asking for nothing from no one, including their advice. Now she realized what a fool she had been. Her foolishness had caused her to hurt a lot of people, including herself, but worst of all her children. In her hospital bed, she cried and cried thinking about how horrible a mother she had been to them for so many years. No way could she fault Sage for not wanting to ever see her or have anything to do with her. She wanted to beg them both for their forgiveness and try to make things right if they would only trust her again.

After gathering enough nerve, she finally went to the police station to look at photos. Truthfully, she was not sure if she clearly could remember Rich's face without a doubt. Not wanting them to think she was a crazy drunk, she never mentioned to the police anything about the horrendous monster that she saw him become. But who could she tell? No one would ever believe her. Could she really be losing her mind? Now even she was not sure that what she saw was real. As she sat at the table with the detective who was handling her case looking through the book of photos, she tried to recall that night. Thumbing through, she remembered. "…but, what about the man in the military jacket?" She looked up and blurted out all of a sudden. Her out-of-the blue comment startled and confused him.

"He was there," she blurted out excitedly.

"Who?", he asked. It all came to her. She remembered that he was there that night with his dog and had rescued her again. So she began telling the detective about the mysterious man.

"He was there. Maybe this witness saw the man who helped me and could possibly identify Rich." Ironically, he was there…again, she thought. She decided that she had to tell the detective about him anyway, even though she had only heard him before she passed out. So she continued to describe what she had only heard.

"You know officer, I heard a man's voice just before I passed out. He had some sort of foreign accent. I didn't see him, but I knew his voice. Most of the time he has a dog with him and wears a military jacket…at least every time that I've seen him he's wearing it. I've seen him around before. In fact, he helped me out another time when I was being chased by dogs one other night on my way to the subway. Those wild dogs came out of nowhere barking and growling at me for no reason. Well, his dog went right after them; they ran like crazy."

"What? Do you work in a meat market or something… that dogs are always chasing you?" he said jokingly.

"No, but something is going on."

"So… what about this guy?"

"Well, evidently he lives in the city. Like I said, I've seen him around before. He would probably be able to identify the guy, Rich, who attacked me."

The policeman got up. He went over to a file cabinet and came back with a folder. When he sat down, he opened the folder and pulled out a photo. Placing it on the table in front of her, her eyes bulged with excitement. Seeing the expression on her face, he asked, "Is this the man in the military jacket that you saw or heard?"

"Yes, that's him!" she said, almost losing her composure. "That's the man!" Her fervor abruptly waned. "Wait a minute. Don't tell me that this man is a criminal. That man came to my rescue twice."

"No, he's not a criminal." Her emotions started to build up again. "Well, find him. Maybe he can describe the man who attacked me. He was there that night. I heard his voice. He sent his dog again to help me and…"

"Ma'am…ma'am, calm down," he told her, holding his hands up to wait for him to speak.

"I can't get him."

"Well, why not? He could be a witness."

"Ma'am… because this man is dead."

"What?" she said in disbelief. "That can't be. I spoke to this man." She couldn't believe what he had just told her.

"I'm sorry, ma'am, but it's true. He was the victim of a hate crime about four years ago." "That's impossible. I saw him with my own eyes, and he has a big dog. He even told me his dog's name when I asked him." She was blown away by this unbelievable revelation. She just stared into space completely astounded, repeating softly, "It can't be. It can't be true."

"You're not the only person who has reported to have seen him."

"I can't believe it. So how do you explain this then?"

"I can't. Nobody can," he answered with a surrendering intonation. "We just keep his picture for when we get a description of him."

"I have to admit, it is strange."

"Was he a soldier?"

"No, actually his older brother was a Marine interpreter in Baghdad who had gotten killed there days before he was to be discharged. Witnesses said that he was very close to his brother."

"Why was it a hate crime? What happened?"

"Evidently, the shooter didn't like seeing a Muslim in an American soldier's jacket. Anyway, that's what he said when he was arrested. Ironically, though they both were Christian. He came to this country because of religious persecution and death threats in his country. The other irony is that he came here to escape death, and it was here where he was killed."

"That's a horrible twist of fate," she sadly responded. "So what about the dog?" she asked, trying to make sense of what she was being told. "The older brother owned the dog and left him for his brother to care for when he had to go on the mission. They both had the same address, so apparently they lived together. After he was killed, several people tried to take him as a pet, but he would always run away. Because there were no other family members here in this country, animal control tried to catch him but gave up because he always found some way to escape. He's been seen many times roaming around the area where they used to live." She wouldn't dare tell him about seeing the lion statues come alive. "Ma'am, you said that you passed out when you heard dogs growling and barking."

"Yes. Anyway, that was the last thing I remember."

"Well, did you see anyone near the lions? We have photos that were taken by the crime team at the scene of the lions showing damage to their claws and ears, but the security cameras don't show any person or persons near the lions. Did you hear any noise or see anyone near the statues? Security at the library attests that there was no damage prior to this incident. No one can figure out according to your story, how this could have happened."

"No, I never reached the statues. I was pulled backwards by one of those dogs before I even got that far. That's how I fell backwards."

"Did this man…your attacker, have any dogs with him?"

"Not when I was with him."

The news about the man in the military jacket added to the puzzle. The mysterious events that were going on in her life were just that… mysterious. She wondered what it all meant. And what could be next?

Chapter 30

In her heart, she could feel that something had changed in her life. Since her encounter in the park, it seemed that her desire for alcohol was no longer there. Whenever she thought about her circumstances and her past, instead of feelings of self-pity and failure, she now had a renewed strength, a revitalization to overcome what had once been able to defeat her in the past. She wanted to regain what had been lost. Since she could now face her faults, she was going to live a better life that was now in store for them. Her real dilemma was her current job. How could she ever work there again? Serving alcohol only made her an accomplice to ruining someone else's life. She could no longer help them go down that road of self-destruction that she, herself had been on for years. But she needed a job. She also knew that she would lose a lot of her friends that she had met while working there. Thinking about those people, other than drinking together, truthfully they had nothing in common. They were kind people and generous to her when she needed a favor. A few had been her friends. It was not her intention to turn her back on them, condemn, or judge them as if she was any better than them, but they had to accept her new and different way of life. Moving back to California to live with her mother was an option that she seriously considered. Her mother would certainly be delighted if she did. But Sage would be graduating soon and from what Sharon told her would probably be staying in Pennsylvania with the company that she has worked for since college. Living that far away from her daughter was not something that she could feel comfortable with in spite of Sage's declaration of excluding her from her life. She had always loved her children even in her deplorable and disgraceful manner of life that she forced them into and had only caused them to feel abandoned and tossed aside like worthless baggage, for that she was liable and deeply distressed. So much valuable time had been forever lost. After the demise of her two marriages, she no longer tried to make any time to include them in her life. She resorted to submitting to alcohol because she found its effects had opened up a different world where she could live blamelessly. Usually, she was too intoxicated to even have a decent conversation or passed out. The other times she was at work and they were asleep. In her search for happiness and love, her foolish pride, adamant self-will, and then her over indulgence in alcohol had alleviated her pain enough to dismiss the ugliness in their lives and from this chosen path had totally devastated them all.

Ally and Sharon's relationship had become closer after her attack in the park. They began to communicate more and with honesty. Anyway, she had to because Sharon had always had high principles. Her invitations to come over for a meal or to come over if just to sit around and talk were now accepted. Multiple times, she apologized for her shameful and deplorable behavior in the past years that they had been neighbors and was also grateful for warding off the other tenants when they threatened to report her to the authorities, which probably prevented her from being evicted. Sharon even helped her to land a job at the nursing home where she was working. Soon enrolling in college, she began taking courses through a government education program that was offered through the same housing program.

Seeing the extraordinary change in Ally, Sharon again tried to persuade her to come with her to church. They had just been sitting around one evening reclining on the sofa after dinner talking about their school progress and their jobs when Sharon thought she would invite her again to come to her church the following Sunday. She promised that it would help her on her road to recovery and might even help to mend her relationship with her children, especially with Sage. But it was the shame that held her back. The thought of walking into a church made her have more guilt and feelings of unworthiness. She had turned her back, denied His very existence, and had even cursed God when she thought that her life was not going where she wanted it to go. How could a person like her have the audacity to step over the threshold of such a sacred place?

"Sharon you know what kind of person I've been. I was despicable. I can't go in there with those people. Truthfully, I don't even see how you would want someone like me as a friend."

"Look at me, Ally." She shyly looked at Sharon. "What are you talking about? Churches are full of nothing but sinners. So, I'm sure you will feel right at home with the rest of us. And when I met you, I didn't know what caused you such hurt, but I knew that you needed help...you needed a friend."

"Thank you, Sharon. Okay, I'll come." They hugged each other and leaned back again on the sofa then started talking about how good the chocolate cake was that they had just finished eating.

"Not to brag but, I think this was my best one yet."

"It is really good, but then all your food always tastes good."

"Go ahead...you're embarrassing me." Sharon responded, bashfully fanning her away. "No...really."

"No really." They said ping-ponging back and forth, about Sharon's good cooking as they chuckled about their childish playfulness.

Casey was utterly thrilled about his mother's amazing and wonderful metamorphic change in behavior. He noticed the changes daily after she returned home from the hospital. When he found out that his mother was in the hospital, he felt so alone and insecure. Seeing how she has changed now, he had to call Sage to tell her about their mother's miraculous transformation into a new person. Detailing the changes, he professed that she had not had anything to drink since coming home from the hospital. To appease him she tried not to sound doubtful or distrusting and went along with his enthusiasm. However, he did confess that he was being cautious about getting his hopes up too high, but he was still hopeful more now in their life than at any other time.

Through all those years of boozing, partying late nights, and not getting the proper rest and nutrition, Ally's body had taken its toll. Her face especially showed most of the damage of what her abusive behavior had done. Even her voice was coarse and sounded rough. But the mirror was her enemy. She hated having to look even to comb her hair. Her style of dress had also changed again. Now that she decided to go to church, she didn't have anything appropriate to wear. But this particular Sunday she felt compelled to go, so she thought about the outfit that she had worn to her father's funeral. It was for the summer, but she could wear a sweater and of course, she would have on a coat. The thought of her father suddenly tore open the wound in her heart and brought tears to her eyes as she quickly wiped them away with the back of her hand. Diverting from the past, she started thinking about the dress again and said to herself, "It's either now, never, or wait until I buy something more decent to wear." "But the church should accept you as you are with open arms." she continued in thought to affirm her argument. Having sold many of her dresses and shoes when she became low on cash, her choice of wardrobe was very slim to none as far as dressiness goes. Casey was thrilled when she told him that she would be going to church with them. He had continued through the years of going with Sharon and her family most Sundays. Sage had gone several times when she was in high school, but not as often as Casey. She had fallen into a state of its insignificance in her life. Like her mother, she found that going had been useless. Unlike her, Casey continued to go carrying the burden of both of them on his young shoulders. He and Dave had become very close friends and would always hang out together with the other kids their age. Because he stayed in their apartment more than his own, he had become very much attached to their family and Sharon always welcomed all of them at any time.

Sharon was elated and full of joy to see Ally with Casey that Sunday morning standing outside her apartment door. She had been a little doubtful that Ally would keep her word and felt bad that she had not trusted her until she saw her there through the peephole. But Ally's newness had been quite sudden and unusual to everybody who knew her. It was truly very difficult to adjust to her new life which kept them on edge with the possibility of reverting to her old ways. The parking lot was full to capacity.
"Is it always this crowded?" Ally asked, seeing how full the parking lot was.
"Every Sunday that I'm here it is."
Sharon gave her an encouraging hug and with one arm around her shoulders, they walked into the sanctuary.

The sanctuary was as crowded as the parking lot. It was almost standing room only as the minister began to preach. To Ally, it seemed as though he was speaking directly to her. He spoke about the world and its evil ways and how Christians are being pursued by real demonic forces. He continued his sermon in loud inflections. As she listened, she thought about her recent experiences of the seemingly supernatural occurrences that she had seen when she so desperately called out to God for help after being attacked and chased through the park. At the end of the service, the minister offered a Believer's Baptism for those who wanted to change their lives. Casey and Sharon were surprised when Ally made her way to the front of the church. She had been baptized years ago as a young child, but due to the life she had chosen, she felt filthy and unclean and wanted to have her old sinful life washed away. The congregation applauded and yelled praises as the converts walked down the aisle and prepared for Baptism. The pastor stepped in first then one after the other they stepped in having first confessed their faith, the minister submerged them while the congregation affirmed with shouts of amen, clapping, and humming intermittently, singing the old Christian song, "Take Me to the Water."

At the end of the service, so many members came over and hugged Ally, and launched her back into the world with reassuring confidence of words of inspiration. Casey called Sage to tell her the news about what had happened. She told him that she was glad for her, but didn't tell him that she still didn't trust her. She knew how sneaky and deceitful she had been in the past during all those years with her drinking in her bedroom before she went to bed, hiding bottles of alcohol all around her room. She had done that for years and she was not going to be fooled by her fabricated confessions of repentance and phony good behavior. She was not going to be tricked into opening her heart to her just to be disappointed again even though this change was what she had so many times secretly wished and even prayed for. Her hopes would be crushed every time she smelled her reeking of alcohol. Her hopes eventually had become hate.

Ally continued to go to church, but not every Sunday. After she was baptized, she sometimes felt a little weak and thought that maybe she had caught a cold. She also noticed that she had to wipe her eyes almost continuously. They would water a few times all during the day. If not both eyes, it was at least one. It became quite bothersome, especially while she was studying. One day while chatting with Sharon, she asked her if she knew if there were any chemicals in the baptismal pool water, because ever since the Sunday that she was baptized, her eyes would water. "I don't think it's any different than the water that's in any swimming pool, but I'll check it out." "Okay, thanks."
Sharon watched her as she was dabbing away a tear. "Ally, maybe you should have your eyes checked, especially if your vision is affected. You are getting to the age of needing to wear reading glasses."
"No, my vision seems to be fine except when I dry them I sometimes see a

glare." "Then you definitely should have that checked out. You shouldn't see any glare. Where do you see it?"

"It's usually at the periphery of my eyes."

"Is it always there?"

"No, but most of the time it'll go away after I blink a couple of times."

"Yeah, I think that's something that you should have checked out."

"I think you're right. I haven't had an eye exam in years."

"What about the kids? Have they had their eyes examined?"

"No, I don't think so. Not in a while. I have taken them to the dentist, though."

"Well, don't put it off. You should get your eyes examined as soon as possible."

"You're right. I will." After folding and packing their laundry up, they headed on their way back home continuing their conversation.

"Well, that's good and make an appointment for Casey, too. I'll ask Sage when I talk to her. That's another thing, Ally. You and Sage have got to fix your relationship. You have to reach out to her. I don't like being the go-between for the two of you. It's very uncomfortable for me, and it's been for too long."

"I know. I don't like it either. And I've tried to reach out to her, but she won't even talk to me not even on the phone. I want my daughter back, but she doesn't want me. I've hurt both of them deeply. I can understand why she feels this way."

"Well, we'll have to pray about this."

"Yes, we will. And thank you, Sharon, for everything. You have been such a good friend." They hugged and each went home to their own apartment.

Chapter 31

A few more weeks had passed by, and Ally continued to have to daily wipe away the tear droplets from her eyes. The glare was only in her peripheral view, obstructing a part of her vision, but still, it had not gone away. One morning while making the bed, from the corner of her eye, something appeared. She had been daydreaming and could see in her mind how happy Casey was when he saw her making pancakes for yesterday's breakfast. Wondering how she was going to top this morning's meal, her thoughts were interrupted by the shadow that had suddenly appeared on the side of her. "Casey, I didn't hear you come in." Turning her head towards the image as she continued talking,

"I was just think…" But when she looked, no one was there. There were other times that she thought and even felt, someone actually standing next to her. She thought for sure that what she saw was an image of a person, and since it was only she and Casey in the apartment, she knew that it could only have been him. She looked out into the kitchen and there he was sitting at the table with a book. "Were you just in my room?"

"No," he said, looking puzzled by her question. "Why?"

"Never mind."

"Are you going to fix waffles again?" he said, with a grin.

"Sure I am. It's your favorite, isn't it?"

"Yeah, thanks, Mom. One of these days I'm going to make breakfast for you."

"Awww Casey. That's so sweet." She was smiling, but inside she was bothered about the formed glare that she had just seen in her peripheral vision. Again, she began to try to rationalize what was happening to her eyes. Something had to have been in that water. She had never had vision or eye problems before until then.

Ally called around to find an ophthalmologist that could see her immediately even though the glare was usually very brief. This time she was no longer going to procrastinate, because recently whenever the shadowy glare appeared, it seemed to have a form, some image, or shape. It had been several months since she had been baptized, so her eyes should have cleared up by now. She had no idea what was causing this to happen. Sharon's report was that the water that was used was safer than pool water. A water sanitation company took samples to run in their laboratory on a regularly scheduled program and professionally maintained it. After that news, she had become a little frightened that she might be losing her vision or that it could be some kind of eye disease or worse, a tumor since nothing had improved.

The doctor that she found agreed to take her the following day, especially after describing the nature of the issue.
"You called yesterday describing a problem that could be quite serious which is why I decided to get you in right away. But the good news is it's treatable if it's what I suspect." She was speechless. He looked at her worried face."
"Don't worry. I haven't even done anything yet, and nothing has been confirmed. So just try to relax." After completing the exam, which took about forty-five minutes, he wrote a prescription for glasses.
"From what I see now, everything looks good… your measurements are normal. Right now, I can't find anything pathological. Except that, you may need reading glasses, but they aren't necessary right now. Other than that, everything else is okay. But there is a test called a Visual Field test that I'd like to do which measures your peripheral vision since that was your major concern, but you'll have to come back for that." "Stop at the desk to make your appointment for the Visual Field test. I won't be doing that test. A technician performs it; he will give me the results, so you'll have to come back to the office to discuss your results if anything abnormal shows up. You'll get a call to set up an appointment for the MRI based on the results, or if you are still having problems."
"Okay. Thank you, doctor."

Chapter 32

After her initial eye appointment, there had not been any more episodes of the glare for weeks. For that, Ally was cheerfully relieved. Added to her joy was that the visual field test was normal. Because her results were normal, her doctor told her that there was no reason for an MRI. Maybe later, but for now, all was well.

It was only weeks now before Sage's college graduation. The invitations had been sent, but not even an announcement had been sent to her. Sharon had come over all excited to make sure they both would be able to go together. That's when Ally found out about the date of the graduation.

"But Ally, you have to come. It's your daughter. She's graduating from college!"

"Sharon, I don't think she wants me there. I haven't spoken a word to her since she went away to college. Do you realize how long ago that's been? She won't even speak to me on the phone."

"I don't care. You are going anyway. What about Casey? You know he has to go…and what about your friend Toni? Have you spoken to her?"

"She mentioned that she wasn't sure just yet if she'll be able to make it. She would have to take a flight and plane tickets aren't cheap.

"Yeah, I can understand that."

"Anyway, Casey may have to go with you, Sharon."

"Look, I'm going to talk to Sage myself and find out just what happened that you didn't get your announcement and invitation."

"Sharon, please don't. I don't want to make matters worse."
"Don't you worry," Sharon assured her.

"You mean you're not going to invite your own mother to the graduation? Sage, that's not right. You're her first child to graduate from college."
Her friend said as they talked during a lunch break between classes. "Look, Grace, you don't know what I've been through with her."
"Yeah, but didn't you say that your brother told you that she's changed."
"Yeah, that's what he said, but he's always been defensive of her. And how many times have I heard that she's changed, even from her? I just don't trust her. Like I said, you don't know what my life was like as a child."
"You said your mother drank all the time, well, so did mine. Maybe not as much as you say your mom did, but just the same, they drank every day. Both of my parents drank and still do. … well, let's say they've cut back. At least your mother stopped."
"Anyway, I don't want to talk about it right now."
"All right, it's your decision. Remember you can't go back in time to make changes."
Sage had spoken to Toni on the phone many times during her stay at college. Even she mentioned how wonderful it was that her mother had changed her life and was doing so well. But Sage never mentioned to her that she had no intention of asking her to come to her graduation. Toni wanted to fly over to attend, but she was not sure if she would be able to for financial reasons, as she had told Ally. She also had a kid in college. Sage understood and assured Toni that she wouldn't be disappointed if she wasn't able to come.

It had been so deeply depressing for Ally to have to hear from others of how and what her own daughter was doing while being so far away from home. She tried to busy herself by studying for school whether it was doing extra papers or other projects for extra credit. Getting more involved more in church activities, and doing volunteer work with a woman's shelter also helped to keep her mind occupied and from going back to thinking and blaming herself, for the dreadful years of her self-inflicted deplorable living all resulting in years of living in some of the worst, disgustingly, and sometimes fearful, living conditions. What she had put her children through she was now reaping the consequences. But the years were gone, never to be recaptured to start over to rectify the damage. Still, no feelings of regret could steal away the joy she felt about her first-born about to graduate from college. Her heart was bursting with pride, especially when she found out that she would be graduating with honor. They were all so happy for her. But the thought of going in spite of knowing how Sage felt haunted her, and continually crossed her mind as graduation day came closer. She had had inclinations of going even before Sharon mentioned it, but knowing Sage's most likely negative response, caused her to rescind the thought. There was no way she would be able to bear the castigation from Sage if she showed up uninvited since she made it undoubtedly known and crystal clear to her that she never wanted to see her again. What could she do to convince her to trust her again? How could she prove to her that she was no longer the person that she was before? The closer it came to that day, the more nervous she became.

Sage found herself at her desk staring at the list. Her mind had momentarily strayed, reminiscing when she saw Mark's name and the talks they used to have. Getting back on track, she came across her uncle's name. He had reached out to her and stayed in contact with her all these years. There was no way that she was not going to invite him. All these years she never had his home address. As soon as she asked, he eagerly gave it, and let her know that he would be there.

Jack had long since broken away from the family's business to start his own. Breaking away had also freed him from having to live under any threat of disinheritance, which had come mainly from his mother. He was doing well on his own and did not need their help financially. In turn, Jack called Greg when he received the announcement to make sure that he knew about it and would not be able to use ignorance as an excuse not to show up. But as usual, he was full of excuses and cowardly feared rejection, not only from his mother but this time mainly from Sage. Sage had never expected her father to come anyway nor did the thought ever occur to her. Jack, however, never mentioned to her that he had asked his brother about attending, and was surely not going to tell her his answer. But secretly, she did want her mother to attend. She wanted so badly to trust her, so she did not send her an announcement, but left it up to her to make that decision. It didn't seem fair, but she, too, could not bear the disappointment if her mother was a no-show, even if it was what she expected. "If she really wants to come, she will," she thought. This was the safe way to protect her from any more feelings of rejection. This way if she did not show up, it would be just like old times.

A week before the graduation, Ally told Sharon that she had decided that she would go with them anyway. They got together at Sharon's apartment one evening and made their plans. After the graduation, it was decided that they would all go out and have dinner at a swanky restaurant to celebrate. When Sharon told Sage about restaurant plans, she asked her to pick the restaurant since she was more familiar with the area.

Staying in touch with his niece throughout the years and all through college, a closeness developed between them, so when she was told about their after graduation get-together dinner, she immediately told her uncle. He was so gracious and honored to have been invited but ashamed that her father, his brother would not be there to share in the moment of pride. When she was told that her mother would be coming and even to her graduation, she was not very convinced. Her response, when told, was, "We'll see."

Sharon and Ally had gone out one Saturday to buy special outfits for this most anticipated affair. The night before, Ally could hardly sleep. Not only had she not talked to her daughter in four years, she had not even seen her except for the pictures that Casey had shown her. That morning she was extremely nervous. She had become so stressed that her hands had begun to shake. When she looked in that all-revealing mirror, as always, she did not like what she saw and could think of nothing to do to make herself look any better, not even makeup. The damage was done, the years were gone, and she could think of nothing that she could do to appear more pleasing. She truly wanted to look her best. The bus would be leaving at 11:30 that morning, and it was already eight o'clock.

An hour had already passed when she peeked out of her bedroom and saw Casey. He appeared much taller in his black slacks and tweed sports jacket and looked extraordinarily handsome in his dress shirt and colorful tie. Almost seventeen now, she had not realized how much her son had grown up, and she praised him on his appearance when she walked out wearing just her robe. She had seen him looking around in the kitchen for something to eat for breakfast.
"My, how handsome you look."
"Oh, thanks, Mom. Hey, when are you going to get dressed?"
"I'm trying to, but honestly I don't know if I should even go." He stopped abruptly from pouring the milk on his cereal bowl.
"What? What do you mean? You have to go."

"Casey, you know your sister doesn't want me there."

"No, that's not true. She does want you there."

"Did she tell you that?"

"Well, no... not in those words. But I told her that you were coming and she didn't say anything."

"You see, she really doesn't." she contested.

"Mom, just go and get dressed, will you? I'm going over to Sharon's."

"What for? ...and what about your cereal?" she asked, as he was walking out of the door. Casey had gotten upset at the possibility that his mother might try to back out of going that he just jumped up and left. When Ally went back in the bedroom to finish getting dressed, the glare had appeared. She went to the bathroom and looked in the mirror, this time there seemed to be a shadow over her face. The mirror looked as if it was tinted. Looking up at the light fixtures, she thought that maybe a bulb had blown out. But they were all lit. "What's happening now?" she thought, with feelings of frustration and fear. She blinked her eyes in hopes it would clear, but it was still there. Her hands shook more as she tried to put on her makeup. Suddenly, she felt the right side of her face squeezing tightly. One side of her face felt as though it was paralyzed. She thought that she might be having a stroke, but when she looked in the mirror at her face, there was nothing wrong. It felt tight, but it looked normal. As she continued to peer in the mirror, her face began to feel normal again, but her hands were still shaking. She had not had the shaking hands in years. She attributed it all to the apprehension and anxiety she had about seeing Sage for the first time in four years and the most likely response of rejection which was more foreboding. She could not handle that. She had to leave. Hurriedly, she got dressed did her best with the makeup and quietly closed the door behind her. She went down the stairs so as not to be seen and left the building. Maybe if she could just get out, walk around for a while, and get some air, everything would go away. But as she walked, the shadow had only moved back in the corner of her eye and her hands shook so much that she had to hold them together, one holding the other. Tears began running down her face. She knew that Sharon and Casey would be upset if she didn't go, but she did not want Sage to see her like this. If she indeed decided not to go, she did not want them to try to persuade her and drag her there just to be humiliated and insulted in front of everyone. Walking up the street thinking about all of the tests, examinations, and medication that she had been through and taken, nothing had changed. She felt it was all for nothing. It seemed as though she was only getting worse. Her bouts of continuous fatigue and weight loss had up until now seemed to have replaced the shaking hands of which, she never bothered to mention to her doctors. He would only attribute her fatigue to working too much, going to school, and not getting enough rest to justify these new manifestations. Her spiritual strength was waning. How could Sage believe that she had changed? Certainly not by her appearance, no one would be able to tell that her life had changed with that face and scrawny body. She could not believe the torment that was beginning to fill her mind, nor could she stop it. She had not had any desire or even thoughts of alcohol in almost a year, but found herself thinking about the relief it had given her in the past. Filled with self-doubt, she began convincing herself that if she could just have a small glass of wine, it would help calm her nerves, and it could at least alleviate the shaking. Then she would be ready to go with them. Of course, it would be strictly medicinal, like taking a pill. "This would not be the same as before," she argued with herself. She would have just enough to get rid of the shaky hands and nervous feelings, and then head back in time to go to the graduation, and on Monday, she would make an appointment with her doctor to find out why her condition had returned. "Maybe it will get rid of this glare too," she thought.

In her anxiety, feelings of helplessness began to cause her to begin losing the newfound joy that she had gained by getting back in church after that horrible incident in the park. She began to doubt herself and her faith. Was it fear, that had changed her life, or was it faith? She tried to pray, but her mind was being barraged by other thoughts of regret and self-pity. As she walked past Mr. Melmann's store, she saw the "Closed" sign hanging inside of the door. The store had been closed because he too, was going to the graduation. "Even Mr. Melmann had been invited," she thought sadly, as she hastily passed by. When she looked over across the street at Nate's Tavern, she thought about going there, but was too embarrassed to go in after professing to have made such a change in her life. No one would believe that all she wanted to do was just get something to stop her hands from shaking. She needed to go somewhere where no one knew her. There was enough time, for now, so she thought, as she hurried by. If she had to, she would just go directly to the bus station and meet them there. Fortunately, she was already dressed. A bus was coming, stopping at her stop; she got on, having no idea where she would get off. . There were two empty seats where she sat by the window hoping that she could sit alone. She sat down and stared out the window contemplating her next move where she would get off. When the bus stopped, a man got on.

She was relieved to see that he looked totally unfamiliar. It was Saturday. She hoped that she wouldn't run into anyone that she knew. Again, staring out the window wanted to avoid looking at anyone who might recognize her as the bus proceeded on its route. From the corner of her eye, she saw that someone had sat down next to her. Just what she had hoped would not happen. They were so close that she could feel the person. Continuing to stare out the window to give an impression of nonchalance, she tried to ignore him until she felt that it had touched her on her leg, but when she looked next to her, no one was there. She looked around, and everyone was seated, waiting for his or her stop. She looked at her thigh and rubbed her leg where she could still feel the place where she felt had been touched.

Just when she glanced out the window again, there she saw a bar. The place was small, situated just between a deli advertising breakfast and a pizza carryout on the other side, which was closed. Quickly, she got up, pulled the string and made her way to the door just in time before the driver pulled off. Looking around and to see if anyone was watching, she went in after the bus drove away. There were only a couple of people in there. After getting the glass of wine that she quickly ordered, she went to a secluded corner to drink it. Having no intention of being there long, she tried to drink it fast, but not to look as though it was out of desperation. Checking the time, she was feeling pressed to hurry and get to the bus station in time to meet Casey, Sharon and the kids there. Just about finished now with her glass, she became utterly overwhelmed with guilt. Thinking of all the progress that she had made had been wasted and gone right down her throat in one glass of wine. Sitting there moping, she felt that she had betrayed and deceived every person that she had ever known. Toni, her long time and caring friend, was so proud of her when she told her about the great changes she had made in her life. Toni expressed how much she had prayed for this time to come in her life. Poor Casey, if he knew where she was, he would be devastated. He had been exhilarated ever since he saw how his mother had once again become the mother that he had missed for so many years. Sharon would also be disappointed. She had never seen Ally in any way other than what she was the day she first laid eyes on her. She knew that she needed to change to save her family and herself. So, when she recognized how Ally had transformed into a more selfless, loving and caring person, she was elated. Sharon had also seen how Casey had changed. In fact, he had stopped coming over as often as he had, although his part time job also took up much of his time as well as his schoolwork, but there was clearly a positive change in him as well. But Sage… she had only despised her even more. It seemed she would never be able to gain her trust and love, no matter what she did. Her thoughts of guilt became a mental soliloquy of justification. What had she done? Why was it that God didn't stop her? Was her faith true or were her actions motivated by fear? Whatever the reason, she felt like a fraud. She was worthless and unfit for anyone to love. At this time, she began to cry. She laid her face down into her arms on the table and continued to cry. She was crying so hard that her shoulders shook between sobs. "Ma'am, are you okay?"

With her head still down, she responded. "Yes, I'm fine."

"Are you crying? Can I get you anything?" the strange, yet kind voice asked again.

"Do you have a napkin?" she asked, still with her head down. She was too embarrassed to even look up at this kind gentleman who was talking to her. She heard him walk away and return to place a tissue in her hand. "Thank you." Covering her face with the tissue, she raised her head. "I'm sorry," she said talking through the napkin. "I didn't think anyone noticed me. This is so embarrassing."

"What, that you're drinking again?"

Did this person know her? The voice did not sound familiar. She was too frightened to look, but could not continue to keep her face covered. When she wiped her eyes and face, she could see the stranger. She could not believe her eyes. She was petrified. It was the monstrous creature. "Get away from me," she screamed. Immediately, she jumped up and ran for the door. A hand reached and tried to grab her. "Leave me alone." She thought she felt him try to grab her.

"Hey, lady, get back here," the bartender, yelled. "You didn't pay for those drinks. Stop, or I'm callin' the cops!" There was no way that she was going to turn around. What was wrong with these people, she thought. What was wrong that they didn't see that horrendous creature chasing behind her? Finally, she got out into the street. She ran and ran until she was practically out of breath, but she could hear the creature calling her by name. People were watching her as she ran almost breathless, never bothering to help. She watched how they all just looked at her, bewildered.

"Help me!" she cried, as she ran down the street.

"What's wrong with her?" she heard someone say.

"Who's she running from?"

She clearly heard the haunting voice behind her. Couldn't they see this grotesque man chasing her? She saw a church. It was a Catholic church. She heard the loud, frightening voice urging her not to go in. Running up the steps, she was so weak and scared that she was unable to open the door. Banging continually on the door and in tears, out of nowhere she heard a child's voice and a tug at her dress. She looked down and saw a naked, bloody child looking up at her with large sad eyes which seemed to be about four years old, holding its umbilical cord. "Mommy, don't leave me again," it said. The door opened just as she fainted and collapsed right into the arms of the priest.

Sharon and Casey had gone over to the apartment and found that Ally was not there. They waited around for as long as they could for a call or preferably for her to return. They both knew how nervous and worried Ally had become and dreaded the worst. Casey had become anxious and angry because he was counting on his mother going and feared now that all hope may be gone. Sharon could see how his mood had changed and tried to encourage him. "Casey, we have to go now to get to the college on time. You know how afraid and nervous your mom was about going."
"I know, but Sage would have been so happy to see that she, at least, came to her graduation."
"I know she would have been, Casey, but your mom didn't believe that. She was terrified of how Sage would react to seeing her there. You know, it may not have looked like your mom was sorry about your situation, but have you ever thought that maybe what she did was the only way she believed she would be able to cope with her life?"

At the graduation, seated now were all the prominent alumni and prestigious guests. Elegant classical music played as the enchanting school choir harmoniously sung. All of this was followed by the announcements of accolades, commentaries from some of the special guest speakers, and finally, the speech from the eminent guest speaker, rendering eloquent words of wisdom for their uncharted, but much anticipated, future. The applauses were constant throughout the entire ceremony. When the speeches were over, the graduates waited patiently, but anxiously, for their name to be called, which was the proclamation of their successful accomplishment, which brought them to the apex for final jubilation… the tossing of the caps.

It was not until Sharon, Casey, and the kids had gotten back home that they found that Ally had again been taken to the hospital.

Chapter 33

Finding out that her mother had been hospitalized the day of her graduation did nothing to soften Sage's heart towards her. She felt that her mother had never intended to come to her graduation in the first place. It was only more of her lies and deceptive excuses. How could she have been so cruel to deceive everyone? What had she proved? Only that she was still a lying, hopeless drunk. She knew her mother's choices in her life were the cause of her having so many health issues, and consequentially hospitalized. Thinking back on all those years of her alcohol abuse, she knew that someday it would catch up with her. She begged Casey to come live with her and finish high school in Pennsylvania, but he declined her offer. He could not abandon his mother, especially since she once again had to be hospitalized. He felt that she needed him more now than ever.

While Ally lay in bed of her most recent hospital stay, she was eating her heart out for missing Sage's graduation. It was her sincerest intention to be there. Now, there was no way that Sage would ever accept her into her life or would even give her a chance to explain why she was not there. Then again, what would she say? Lying there tormented by the frightening images that she saw that day. How could she explain to her or to anyone else those strange things that had happened, and had been happening to her? Who would believe her? But, these things were real; there was physical evidence to prove that something was happening. She never told anyone about the things she had seen. Why did she not tell anyone? Was it that she was trying to deceive herself because of the fear of facing the truth, that her drinking had affected her mind and body? Were these things only imagined? Maybe that was why those bystanders never came to her rescue when she cried out for help. And the only person who had ever tried to help her was a dead man. The horrid sight of that bloody child still made her body quiver with fear. Could all of this be the personification of guilt? Her conscience was reeling with remorse and guilt. With all of these thoughts going around in her mind, she became even more confounded and depressed. Truly, she needed help.

As soon as Sharon got home, she sent the kids in to change their clothes. She had not noticed the phone blinking with a message on her answering machine until she went to her bedroom. It was a message from the police department, stating that Ally was in the hospital. Right away, she grabbed the phone, took the message and called the hospital. After getting all of the information, she and Casey caught a cab right away and went straight there. Their ride was silent. Casey walked alongside Sharon looking down with his hands in his pockets. Approaching the room, they looked in to see her sitting in a chair looking down, with her sad face leaning onto one hand. Looking up and seeing her son's saddened face, Ally was disheartened and embarrassed. He went straight over to her. With outstretched arms, she reached out to him and hugged him long and affectionately, then immediately apologized for not showing up for the graduation. When he was satisfied that she would be all right, Sharon asked if she and Ally could be alone to talk.

"Casey, here, take this money and go down to the gift shop if you want." Sharon had taken money from her purse. "Or if you want, you can wait in the waiting room down the hallway."

"No, thanks. I'll just go to the waiting room." She waited until he was out of the room. "Ally, what happened to you? We waited for as long as we could."

"Sharon, I am so sorry. I know you think, that I backed out, but believe me I truly wanted to come."

"So what happened?"

"It's a long story, and I know I should have told you a long time long ago, but I didn't know myself what was going on, and I still don't." Sharon sat on the bed beside Ally, who was still sitting in the chair. "For some time now, I started getting tremors in my hands. At first, it seemed that if I had a little something to drink, it would go away. I almost lost my job at the restaurant one night because of the shaking."

"You know, I noticed your hands were shaking a little one day, but I didn't say anything," Sharon interjected.

"Well anyway, everything had been okay for a while. I started seeing a doctor and taking medication for it, but the morning of the graduation it started again."

"I'll bet it was because you were so nervous about going to see Sage," Sharon again interjected.

"That's exactly what I thought."

"Well, did you take your medicine?"

"No."

"Why not?"

"I don't know why, but I convinced myself that the medicine wasn't helping because it had started up again even taking the medicine. So I thought if I could just get a small glass of wine, it would stop. My hands were really shaking badly, plus, the glare had come back."

"I thought you went to see about that."

"I did, and it had gone away too, until that morning. Sharon, I couldn't go up there and let Sage see me that way. She would never have believed I had stopped drinking."

"What… Do you think she'll believe you now? Why didn't you just come over to my place?"

"I didn't even want you to see me shaking like that. I'd been able to hide it for years."

"Oh, Ally, how could you when you were doing so well?"

"I don't know. I was just going to get the one glass of wine, and then meet you at the bus terminal. I was already dressed and everything. I wasn't trying to get drunk. I was only trying to stop the shaking." She started crying to the point that her words were incomprehensible.

"Ally, don't try to talk now. Just get yourself together. I don't want Casey to see you upset. We can talk later when you get home and get yourself settled."

Before she was discharged, the doctor mentioned to her that he noticed her blood alcohol levels were very high. He was also referring to results from a previous report. Embarrassed about his comment, she tried to explain to him the reason why she had drunk the alcohol. She mentioned that the medicine her doctor had prescribed had stopped working which was why she had had only one glass of wine the day that she was admitted. He only smiled but cautioned her to tell her doctor so that he could prescribe a different medication and for her not use alcohol as a replacement for her medical treatment for any illness. Still, she told him about her incident, but never mentioned her pursuer's physical appearance, not even to the police when they asked for a description of the perpetrator. She was surprised when told that the bar owner said that he started running after her because she jumped up and ran out without paying, and was trying to stop her. He gave up his pursuit when she got out of the door and later even declined to press any charges.

A week later Ally and Sharon got a chance to talk again. She had made an appointment with the doctor that was recommended by the hospital physician and felt more hopeful that she would be able to get the help she needed. The coworkers at the nursing home welcomed her back, and the church members promised to keep her in their prayers. At Sharon's, she began to reveal the nightmarish events that had been plaguing her. "…so when I went to this place…a bar, a man approached me when I was crying. I was so upset with myself, for going back to this kind of thing, that I started crying. I had my head down crying when a man handed me a napkin. When I looked up, he looked like the horrendous beast that I first saw in a nightmare that I had had many times before. I jumped up and started running out of there and up the street. He was chasing me as he has always done…grabbing at me and calling my name. I ran directly to a church that I saw in front of me while running, and then I wound up in the hospital. After that, I don't remember anything about how I got there. Sharon, I have been seeing some horrible and strange things."

She continued telling Sharon about all the unusual and bizarre things that she had seen and the things that had happened, everything except the child that she was still dealing with. Since then, she had not been able to get a full night's sleep. After describing all of those eerie images to Sharon, she became quite frightened. She wondered if her friend had gone crazy. Or were these the final effects of what so many years of alcohol abuse had done to her brain? The only irony to Sharon was that she herself had seen what appeared to be scratches from animal claws and the bruises. She had actually seen the marks on her arms from the vicious grip that someone had had on her from the park incident that she had told her about, only she never described her assailant until now. Was she imagining these faces that looked like monsters because she didn't want to face her own reality?

"Ally, you really need to see a doctor. One that can help you figure out what's really going on with you." Ally's past behavior had been so careless, that she could have indeed easily subjected herself to such situations of vulnerability with men, but the scenes of wild dogs, a monstrous rapist with cat eyes were a bit too much for Sharon to grasp.

"I already have an appointment."

"Thank God!" Sharon said under her breath with relief.

After Ally's confession of her hellish nightmares and cryptic encounters, Sharon thought she should let Sage know what was going on with her mother. Ally did not want Casey to worry, although he was seventeen, she still thought it was best not to tell him the details of what she had been through. Sage was hardhearted. After hearing about everything that her mother had been going through with the physical condition and her possible mental condition, she was still not interested and thought that her mother had brought it all on herself by her actions. Sage had gotten away from her mother physically, but she still could not get away from her permanently. Why couldn't she be left alone? Why did she have to be dragged back into her mother's wretched life?

"Sage your mother needs help."

"Maybe she has DTs or something. I can't help her."

"Yes, you can. She really needs you. She doesn't drink anymore."

"Oh, really? So then, why did she wind up in the hospital again after running out of …a bar?"

"Who told you that?"

"Never mind who told me. I know that's why she didn't come to my graduation. She was too drunk. And yeah, I wanted her to come, but deep down I knew she wouldn't be there. Don't you think that I have feelings too, Sharon? I've had feelings for a long time and I'm tired of them getting hurt. So, please don't call me again if it's anything else to do with my mother."

"That's right Sage, she is your mother," Sharon uttered softly as they both hung up the phone.

Chapter 34

Another year had passed. Casey and Ally were still at the apartment. He had already begun his first year at Georgetown University, compliments of his Uncle Jack. Finally, through Sage, he and Casey had begun to have a closer relationship. Jack never had any children of his own, and they were his only niece and nephew. They met for meals, attended school basketball games together, and visited the gym to see the pictures of his uncle in his college years there as one of the star players on the team, and even got to meet his old college basketball coach who was still there. Sports had never been of much interest to Casey, although he played them on the video games. He was proud of his uncle's popularity as one of the school's top players. They got along very well, were even buddies. Sometimes they would get together and ride to Pennsylvania to visit Sage, of course, with his mother's permission. Ally and Sharon had both graduated from the community college and Sharon was in the process of searching for an opening at a nursing school. Becoming a registered nurse was now her new goal.

Trying to get her life jump-started again for a new beginning, Ally had begun seeing a psychiatrist, along with her other doctors. After many sessions with her, discussing her past even from a child, he concluded that her problems had probably stemmed from years of alcohol abuse and guilt, problems both physical and mental. This she had already known for years, but in her self-deception, she refused to accept responsibility for what her actions had caused.

As for the strange people that had assaulted her, he tried to convince her that what she had seen had been real, but to escape the reality, her mind would give her attackers images that were so inhuman that they would appear to be unrealistic so that she would not have to cope with being actual people and be able to escape what was truly happening to her. In order for her to go on with her life, she would have to acknowledge that her beginnings with alcohol were to cover and hide from the hurt she felt after being rejected by her first husband Greg. This was something she had never verbally admitted. After her sessions with the psychiatrist, at home in idleness, she would often replay in her mind how that out of love she had poured her whole life into her marriage to Greg, only to be cast aside as if she had meant nothing to him and then thoughtlessly, out of arrogance and pride, had married a drug abuser who managed to bring her to utter financial ruin. This only encouraged her continued and chosen companionship with the bottle, and its tasty yet harmful contents, whose only contents were destined to destroy.

In her subconscious mind, she knew that the continuance of her abusive drinking was because she could not face the social stigma and embarrassment felt by her and having to live an impoverished life that she had been left to live with her fatherless children. This same irresponsible thinking and behavior was what had placed her into such dangerous situations to be taken advantage of by malevolent predators out seeking such victims of vulnerability. But even so, after all the many times of consultation, it was still difficult for her to believe and accept that it was due to her choices and behavior which had caused all the grief and physical consequences in her life. But was she solely to be blamed for everything that had happened to her? Did Greg and Colin play any role in her downturn? Although, after weeks of counseling she agreed that all she had gone through had probably caused her mind to create those ghastly figures. Those horrible forms conjured up or not, even now, could not be forgotten. The fact that real people had committed those evil crimes continued to be difficult to comprehend. Why her? Why was she constantly being sought after? What about those other supernatural appearances and occurrences? Were they all imagined? How could they be explained? Could all of this have been in her mind… a dream? They had all been so real, even with physical evidence. She was so confused about everything. She did not know what to believe, what was real or imagined. Now every time she would see a dog, she became petrified. Rich was surely a real person and from that encounter, she was now leery of even a friendly greeting from a kind stranger. Then there was the man in the army jacket… what was the reasoning for him? He didn't even exist according to that detective at the police station. And the irony was that he had been the only one who had ever helped her, made things even more bizarre. Added to her fears now was the sound of that child's voice. She would cringe now at the sound of the remembrance of the baby that she had aborted years ago, which would have been about the age of that terrifying little image that she had seen on the church steps. Still holding onto that secret, she was now more riddled with guilt and shame.

One late evening after work, she got off the subway and while walking to her bus stop, heard someone with a cane whose tapping was coming from behind. It stopped very close to where she had stopped to wait for the bus. She was afraid to turn around to see who was standing so close to her. When the bus came, it wasn't crowded. Quickly, she got on looking around for someone to sit next to. The man with the cane walked slowly by with his face covered by the brim of his hat and hoodie. Just as she thought, he looked very similar to the same man who she thought had followed her before. It was the same black wide brimmed hat and hoodie, which concealed his face, the hunched shoulders, and that haunting tapping of his cane. She reluctantly thought back to that terrifying night when she was so drunk that she fell asleep and missed her stop on the subway, then rode to the end of the line with the hooded stranger. The next evening at work, she was told that it was a dream. Even so, dream or not, that night, she thought he was following her and apparently he was. She was horrified then, as she was this night. She had forgotten all about that scary episode until now. She hoped that there would be someone, at least one person, who would be getting off at her stop. As luck would have it, she was alone. When the bus stopped, she saw the large hat at the back exit looking down while she was at the front exit. Quickly stepping off, she began a fast pace down the street. The tapping cane sounding behind her was just as fast. As she passed Mr. Melmann's store, suddenly the glare appeared in her left eye. She couldn't tell at that time where the man was except for his clacking cane or if it was that man. Mel's Tavern was open, she heard the noise as the door opened and closed and thought about running in. She did not want to yell for help. Suppose it was someone else behind her. Suppose this person was not pursuing her. But then she saw a shadow that seemed to be growing into some unnatural form. Then out of nowhere, a huge dog came running from across the street. She froze in place. It came barking and growling across the street towards her. It was déjà vu. Thinking that she was going to be attacked, she was about to give out a loud scream, but then she recognized the dog. He was the same one that had belonged to the man in the military jacket. It wasn't running towards her, but raced quickly behind her, evidently to chase after whatever had been coming up behind her. She could not believe it and looked around for the man, but saw no one, nor did she hear anyone. The dog came back and walked by her side all the way home. She called his name.

"Hey, what are you doing around here? I don't know where you came from, but I'm sure glad that you were here. Thank you." She didn't reach out to try to touch him, but only spoke gently and praised him for helping her. He made her feel protected as they continued to walk. That was when she noticed that the glare was gone. As soon as she got to the double doors, she rushed in and looked back outside. No one walked by, not like what had happened before and she was relieved. The great canine had already turned around to leave as soon as she went inside. She listened as the automatic latch locked. This was no dream, she thought. She could not call the police, because again, there was no crime. Having told Sharon about all the other strange events that had happened to her and by the look on her face could see that even she was frightened, decided not to tell her about this latest incident. She just thankfully prayed for protection.

This was not the last of the strange and unusual occurrences that were going on in Ally's life. They were not often, but continued, and there was always the glare. She had been through many tests and all showed no reason or evidence for such a phenomenon in either eye. Brain scans were done which all had shown to be normal. These sightings were intangible and seemingly supernatural in nature. She thought that she was being taunted by demons, but no matter how much she prayed, they continued to torment her, but this time, she never resorted to, nor even thought to go back to her old means of dealing with the upsetting and distressful complexities in her life, even though she was deathly afraid when they happened. No one believed her before. Even she wasn't sure if what was happening was imagined, dreamed, or otherwise. The doctors attributed everything to some psychological reason for the "hallucinations" as they called them, and only prescribed medication and dismissed any reality of these occurrences.

Closing her eyes in prayer and then opening them, the crazy images would be gone. There were also faces in the mirror as if looking back at her even with accusing taunts to lure her back to her old life. Most of the time she would awaken and find that it had only been a dream that she thought was true, only to see the glare in one eye or the other. She was always terrified by these sightings. Even walking along on the street, some people at a glance appeared to her to have demonic faces and eyes that were staring directly at her. She also saw Guardian, the dog, who seemed as though he was protecting her when she saw those things. She thought that maybe he could see things that she no longer could see. No longer did she try to run. The sightings were usually brief, usually in the blink of an eye. She sometimes thought that she was truly losing her mind. After speaking to her doctor about all the strange and weird things that she continued seeing, he determined that the medication might have been the cause. Hallucinations had been one of the many side effects of some of the medications for that problem. So why would he prescribe something that could possibly augment her problems? Now as a pharmacy technician, she should have read for herself and questioned his treatment.

Once she stopped taking the medication, she had been given a reprieve. The strange sightings abruptly stopped, except for the annoying glare, which began soon after she was baptized. It still, remained in her mind that maybe there was something in that water. Except for that, for the first time in a long time she was able to live somewhat of a normal life. Now coping with her past and looking more towards the future, she was able to feel hope and happiness for a change. Ally began calling her mother more often, which made her mother happy to hear her daughter's voice every time she called her. Toni was just as excited. She could tell that there had been a drastic change and was blissful about her friend's comeback. They even talked about her going soon to California to visit her mom who was getting too old now to travel.

It had been Ally's intention to move out of those apartments some day and into a better part of town once Casey graduated from college. She was extremely grateful for what Jack had done for her son, but she was still unable to fully trust that his generosity would continue even though he had proved himself many times over to be a most trusting, generous man who was worthy of her confidence. Even so, for financial purposes, she thought it safe to remain at the apartment in case of any unexpected financial circumstances that could occur. Over the years, he and Casey had built a bond between them. He had invited her several times to accompany them as a gesture of his sincerity to mend their familial relationship, which had been severed so many years ago. Only once she accepted his invitation and that time was only because of Casey's insistence.

Sage had since moved back to New Jersey in a community of small townhomes, a forty-minute drive from their old neighborhood. With her outstanding resume and high recommendations, finding a job had been easy. Casey was glad that she had moved back. He thought that with this arrangement there would be a better chance for her and Ally to reconcile their relationship. Casey was still hopeful, but also displeased with Sage's refusal to try to make amends and he let her know it under no uncertain terms. Ally had sought help and was gaining progress on her road to repairing what once had been broken in their lives; he could not see why Sage was so determined to allow the past to control her future. She would not listen regardless of who spoke to her about the matter; she vehemently refused to relent.

Chapter 35

The people at the company where Sage had worked for the past two years were truly sad to see her leave but understood her family situation. They sent her off with an amazing farewell party and excellent references and recommendations for her new pursuit of employment. Of course, to add authenticity to her reason for leaving, she told them about her mother's delicate health. Sage knew she was being deceitful for using her mother as an excuse because her feelings for her were emphatically empty. She felt like a hypocrite but eased her conscience, since there was some truth to her story. Her mother was a bit crazy, she thought to herself. At her farewell party, she gave a heartfelt speech thanking everyone for hiring her from the time she began in college through and after graduation. To her college counselor and now friend, who guided her along while she was a college student, she gave a special thank you. Then she vowed to stay in touch with them as she had done with her college buddies. Before leaving Pennsylvania, she had already received a great offer from a prominent company in New Jersey and accepted it immediately. Having been able to save during those years, she was able to buy one of the newly built two bedroom townhomes just outside of New York.

Mark was well on his way as a professional basketball player, still single, but greatly pursued. He kept Sage updated on what was going on in his life as they had always done throughout their friendship. He had even gone to Pennsylvania to visit her occasionally, especially when he was there for a game. She and Casey had been to some of those games courtesy of his affiliation with the team and he was always in awe of the privilege they had of being so up-close and personal with the team. She admitted to herself long ago that she still had a special place for him in her heart, but was not sure how to deal with what or how she truly felt towards him. Sometimes he wondered if his reluctance and avoidance to get involved in any serious relationship was because maybe he was waiting for her. He truly believed that he loved Sage, but never told her for fear of getting hurt if her feelings toward him were not the same. Somehow, in all the time that they had known each other, she never showed any real affection towards him, but for that last day years ago when she kissed him in the taxi. Sometimes during dinner while visiting, Mark thought that maybe he had seen a glimpse of some special feelings for him, especially when he mentioned how much he had to ward off his female fans. In all truth, Sage truly enjoyed being with Mark, but had not felt the spark that she felt the night he was leaving for college during that airport taxi kiss. Neither one had forgotten about it, and neither one had ever spoken of it.

A few years later one evening after a game, Mark had stopped by to pay Sage a visit before leaving for the airport. They hugged and were happy that they had gotten another chance to see each other once again. During their short conversation, he mentioned that he had heard how well her mother was doing. Some time ago, he had found out that Sage wouldn't visit her mother and had not even spoken to her. He had no knowledge that this nonsensical behavior, as he saw it, was still going on. Knowing she was still harboring raw feelings toward her mother, he also as everyone else would try to persuade her to take some time to go and visit her, maybe surprise her. That being a touchy subject, he would look for a chance to sneak in the suggestion during some of their other talks while catching up on each other's lives. This particular day, he had sat down briefly for a bottle of water and a slice of chocolate cake that she so wanted him to try, having to confess that it was Sharon's recipe.

"Umm... this is good, even if you did bake it yourself," he said in between bites.

"...so, Sage you mean you haven't spoken to your mother since you left for college? You never told me that in all this time. I thought we never kept any secrets from each other."

"That wasn't something you'd call a secret. What was I going to say? I'm still not talking to my mother. How could the subject ever have come up anyway?"

"What do you mean? I asked you about her every time we've talked."

"Yeah, and I told you that she was okay," she answered, as she forcefully put the cake back into the refrigerator.

"All right, Sage, I'm not going to argue."

Turning back around and looking into his eyes, she retorted, "I'm not arguing. But don't you remember how upset I was that day and told you that she couldn't stay sober long enough to even come to my college graduation?"

"Yes, and didn't you also tell me that she had gone to the hospital that same day? Sage, how could she get to the graduation if she was in the hospital?"

Putting his dish in the sink, she answered,

"That was her fault." She turned around again this time looking up because he had stood up. "Look, the reason why she wasn't there was … because she was too drunk to get there," she said angrily.

Holding her by her shoulders, he tried to convince her.

"It doesn't matter. She was in the hospital. Look at how long ago that was, Sage."

Though she walked away out of his grip, he continued,

"Well, evidently she realized that she needed help which is why she's a much better person today and deserves another chance if just for trying. I'm sure she's still heartbroken about what she'd done in both your lives. …and you won't even talk to her?" He pleaded with her, trying to make her understand how futile her grudge was. At this point, she left him in the kitchen and had gone into the living room.

When he walked in, she was sitting on the sofa deep in thought. "If he only knew," she thought, recalling that horrible night years ago. She wanted so badly to tell him about that night in her bedroom when she had almost been raped because of her mother's self-indulgence and drunkenness, but never wanted to remember nor utter the words to describe that terrifying scene of what she had been through and felt. She didn't want to, but she could remember and visualize in utter disgust the darkened room where that filthy intruder had attacked her. His smelly body was pressing against hers and with his knee trying to pry her legs apart. That stranger's hardness pressing against her body was forcefully pushing, prodding, trying to aim his way in to penetrate and steal away her innocence. The alcoholic smell on his breath and the rancid stench of his body was something that she could not forget. Then to protect herself, her cowardly mother refused to call the police. Never did she want to ever tell anyone about that deplorable ordeal. The thought of it had rekindled the anger and disgust, which culminated in her decision to move out in the first place.

"Mark, I've been through more than you will ever know or imagine and then having to hear again how broken she is just makes me want to..." He cut her off.

"Look, don't bother explaining. That's your mother and that's between you and her. But don't do something that you may someday regret. Remember, she's not getting any younger and truthfully, Sage, neither are you." That last comment was hopefully for her to ponder. He was also hinting about their many years of not making a commitment to have a closer and more serious relationship. Sage did not respond which was always her way to end the direction of where a conversation was going.

After that last visit and conversation, they never called each other again. What he had witnessed was that she was relentlessly unforgiving, unmerciful, and malevolent. From conversations throughout the years, she never had one kind thing to say about her remorseful mother. If she could not be forgiving and kind to her own mother, then what chance would he have in an eventual disagreement if they were ever a couple? As he had known for years, her mother had stopped using alcohol. He would stop by himself for a short time every now and then when visiting the old neighborhood and they would have the most pleasant talks about all that was going on. She told him how she had even graduated from the community college and had become a pharmacy technician and that she had been working for a while in one of the local pharmacies in the city. When she told him that she was also an active member at a church, he was nearly blown away even though others who knew her had told him, but this was straight from the horse's mouth. What more evidence did Sage need to prove her mother's good intentions? But her miserable past still festered within her, leaving her hard-hearted, devoid of any ability to forgive or maybe even to fall in love. What he could see was only resentment and hatred. Finally able to see past his own feelings, he thought it was best that they only remain friends and for him to go on with his life. What more evidence did he need of Sage's true character, especially when he found out that she had moved back to New Jersey and had never bothered to tell him?

Chapter 36

Even before Casey graduated, it seemed that Ally's health had begun to decline even more. She continued with the medication as prescribed, but she was beginning to feel weaker and more tired by the end of the workday. The shaking had long stopped, but the glare had been back ever since the day of Sage's graduation and had never stopped showing up with its unpredictable occurrences. She thought it was happening now even more frequently. Several different specialists who she had been referred to examined her, but they too could find nothing.

Stopping by Sharon's one day after work, she just needed someone to talk to. Sitting in their usual places during their chats on the sofa, Ally began. "Sharon, I am getting so tired of seeing this glare in the corner of my eyes. It's like I can almost feel it as well as I see it."
"Did you tell the doctor about this?"
"Yes, but I didn't mention that I felt a presence. I did tell them that the shape of it had changed. They don't even believe that anything is there, so why would they believe that now it looks different?"
"Maybe you should get another brain scan or something...and Ally, you have to pray for healing. Doctors have their limits."
"I do pray, but it seems the more I pray, the more I see it."
"Well, try not to dwell on it so much. Maybe there's a small spot in there somewhere on your eyes that those machines just aren't able to pick up right

now."

"That could be, but it's still scary. I hope it's not a tumor or anything growing in my eye or on my brain," she said sadly.

"Oh, Ally, don't say that. You don't even have those kinds of symptoms for something like that."

"Yes, but I also know that I don't have the energy that I used to have either. How does that fit in?"

Sharon got up. "Let's have some tea. Do you want a cup of tea?"

Ally only sat there. "Sure, I'll take a cup."

"Are you hungry? I know you haven't had anything to eat yet."

"No, I'm not hungry right now. I'll fix something later."

"You know, Ally… I think you're just depressed about Casey not living at home anymore."

"I guess I could be. I do miss him. I miss him a lot, but he wanted to live on his own. He is a grown man now."

By this time, she had gotten up and sat at the table while Sharon finished pouring the hot water in their cups.

"Hard to believe, though. I miss Sage, too. I pray that someday she will find it in her heart to forgive me."

"She will. Just keep praying," She patted Ally's hand as they kept drinking their tea.

Even though, Sharon never told Sage how egregious she thought her behavior was toward her mother. Nor did she tell her how terribly awful she was to continue to shut her out of her life, especially now that she was not doing well. Whether Sage wanted to hear it or not, Sharon kept her updated on her mother's life, as did Casey.

For Casey, finding a job wasn't difficult, just as it had not been hard for Sage. He decided to major in computer programming which was the type of business his uncle's company was involved in. Jack had offered him a job with his firm, though he was grateful for the offer, he wanted to spread his wings and find his own way. With his first paycheck, he wanted to treat everyone to dinner. Everyone was there, except Sage, although she had been invited. Even Sharon and children were there. They were grown up now. Elesha was there with her brothers to celebrate Casey's graduation from college and now to celebrate getting his first paycheck. They both had completed college, so the only one left at home with Sharon was little Ben who was no longer little. He was a teenager now, taller, and anxious to get into college with everyone else.

Sage knew that everyone would be there, but just could not bring herself to be in the same room with her mother, so she made up an excuse, but everyone knew. This time, Sharon did not even try to persuade her.

The night of Casey's dinner celebration, Sage was disgusted with herself over her rebellious behavior of not attending, even though, she sincerely wanted to be there for her brother, as she had always been all his life. She had been a surrogate mother to him while their mother was living her own wasteful and reprobate life, seemingly with no consideration for them at all and for all those years. She may have changed, but so what? She couldn't give in to her now that she has gotten older and has run her body down to the point of ill health and her mind to almost insanity. By giving in, she felt defeated; her mother would be the true winner. She didn't want to lose to a loser, not even for Casey. She had debated with herself that whole evening. "What kind of thinking was this?" she asked herself. This was not a game. But she had been so deeply hurt and ashamed for so many years of heartache and feelings of abandonment, so what should anyone expect? A mother who showed no concern whatsoever for her children who had to contend with this wretched impoverished lifestyle throughout their childhood in their school years, by their peers, the teachers, their neighbors, and even some other family members was unforgivable. Because of her past, she had developed into this hardnosed, insensitive, and apathetic individual. Her toughness had been her shield and weapon to guard her heart against any insults or slander before it even started, or shut it down if it had. As she matured, she could prevent herself from having a broken heart ever again. Now, after having wasted their young lives and squandering away their childhood, she now thinks that everything should just disappear or be erased as if nothing had ever happened. Well, something had happened, and she could not ever forget it.

That night after Casey got home to his apartment, he called Sage. He spoke to her before about leaving the past behind, so he never chided her or tried to make her feel guilty, but only told her how everyone had missed not being able to see her, especially Elesha and David, now living out of state. Everyone had been affected by Sage's absence. They could all see how Ally's facial expression had changed when she found out that Sage would not be coming. She thought for sure, for this occasion, Sage would surely come. She knew how much it meant to her brother and how proud he was to be able to pay for it all. Even her Uncle Jack had been there, who seemed to be at all of their gatherings now. Ally was happy and yet also sad that Greg had never been to anything that involved his own children. She was not proud about anything that happened after their marriage failed, nor did she hold anything against him anymore because of its demise. But her heart ached for her daughter. She loved her so much and prayed for the opportunity to tell her so and beg for her forgiveness for all that she had done. Even Elesha and David spoke with their mother about Sage's unwillingness to forgive her mother. Sharon wanted in the worse way to reprimand her herself for her reprehensible behavior towards her mother, but she was a grown woman and had to live with her own decisions. Not only had she hurt her mother, but also her actions were a letdown to her brother and almost put a gloomy cast over the whole affair. She wanted to, but none of her talks mattered anymore anyway. Sharon would always reflect back and could see the image that had been forever embedded in her memory of the angry looking teenager's face the day they first moved in. The only time that she had ever seen her happy in her mother's presence was the evening of her prom. She was so grateful to have captured that shot with her camera of that night of Ally pinning the bouquet on her daughter's gown. Sage had mellowed to such obvious tranquility, as her mother was almost breath to breath with her while she stood still and close with tenderness as her hands slightly touched her daughter's shoulder. Sharon didn't know, but that was the first time in years that Sage had allowed her mother to get that close to her, and that closeness never happened again.

Even Jack was greatly disappointed about Sage not attending. But there was no way that he could ever mention anything to her about her behavior or her treatment of her mother. His brother had no badge of honor as a father. He had abandoned them completely almost as soon as their divorce was final. He didn't want to do or say anything that could jeopardize his relationship with them. Already he was grateful that they both had accepted him into their lives. As usual, whenever he had seen his niece and nephew, he would blast Greg about his abominable behavior as their father, only to hear the usual excuses and apologies. That night after the dinner, when she got home, Ally wrote Sage a letter.

A few weeks had passed since Casey's dinner, and it seemed as though everything was back on track. That next day, Sage had gotten a chance to speak to Elesha and David while they were still at their mother's apartment but was just about ready to leave. Again, she apologized for not being there and wished them well and a safe trip back home. "Tell your mom I said hello." Too embarrassed to face Sharon, she decided to call to avoid seeing the disappointed look on her face.

She loved being at work. There she could escape into a world where there were no family members, no friends, and no neighbors. There were no intimate issues or interactions. Sage had made a great impression at work with her innovative ideas. Her status of employment had opened many opportunities to meet many available and successful men in the business world. Some who were quite handsome and eager to settle down in a more stable relationship, as even some die-hard bachelors had divulged to her over dinner or while meeting for lunch that she most times had struggled over to agree to go. Some of those available callers, whose titles were commensurate with their salary, were genuinely sincere admirers. But money and status were not what she wanted nor needed, especially from the efforts and accomplishments of someone else as her mother had done. Never able to shut out the memories of her once affluent life to the abject poverty and the deprivation of anything decent, the meagerness in how they had to live because her mother chose to marry into richness knowing that she had nothing to equal to or ever contribute to. The life of that wealthy, gutless wonder, who having no courage to stand up for what was right as a husband and father, just stood by and did nothing as their lives went into shambles. All her mother had to give to him was her love, her heart, and life only to be tossed away like an old rag and in her selfish pride was blinded of common sense. She was never going to let herself fall into the clutches of anyone whose empty promises of 'being together always' and 'only death could separate promise'. A change of heart and those promises could be broken. After so many years still deeply marred by her father's abandonment and his family's refusal to recognize his children as their own, Sage had never felt affection for anyone. When her father left them never bothering to contact them with a call, a birthday card, or a Christmas gift, he took away her trust and the ability to love.

Chapter 37

Ally wanted so much to drive again, but every time she took the driving test, she failed the vision portion. Not knowing when the glare would appear, she thought maybe it was not a good idea to even try to drive anymore. She wanted so badly not to have to rely on public transportation anymore, but now when the glare would appear she was almost blinded by it …at least in one eye. It would not be safe for anybody on the road for her to be at the wheel. As long as she was able to get to work, there was always the bus, the subway, or both. It had not been often that she would see the great dog anymore, but from time to time there he was, walking or running by somewhere in the city, nor had she seen the hooded stranger. Occasionally, she would notice Guardian walking right next to her, which may have been why she had not seen the stranger. She swore that he could see things that she could not. Probably things that she had once seen before…things that maybe she was now not aware of anymore, but as usual the glare would appear in an instant and gone the next. Very rarely did it block her vision for any length of time. She could not remember when, but the watery eyes eventually stopped, seemingly replaced by the glare.

At the drug store, the volume of work and customers had begun to pick up. Because of this, the manager hired a new pharmacist to try to keep their customers satisfied by minimizing their wait time. This particular gentleman was a middle-aged man who had been a pharmacist about thirty years. Kurt was a handsome man with a charming and pleasant personality. He was single, but not necessarily looking for a relationship, he told Ally this during one of their conversations while having lunch. His wife had passed away a few years ago, after twenty-seven years of marriage, due to an extended illness. Ally thought that he was a nice person, but a bit too talkative for a man. When the pharmacy department would close for one hour for lunch, he would sometimes ask her if she would join him, or go out to a nearby restaurant for lunch. Sometimes she would go, but had gotten so used to eating alone and would mostly use this time to catch up on her reading. At times, he would even give her a ride home for which she was most grateful. Whenever she thought the conversation was getting too personal, she would try to avoid him by declining lunch or even his offer of a ride home to get a little space between them. In no way did she want him to start asking personal questions that ultimately would lead to her past. But he seemed to be a truly nice person and she enjoyed talking to him.

After a few months of getting to know each other and many times being asked, she agreed to go out to dinner with him, but let him know that she, just like him, was in no way looking for anything other than just being friends. He was in complete accordance because he wasn't looking for another wife, as he reiterated, but only a friend who he could talk to and go out with sometimes. The conversation continued as he drove her home after dinner. He had only moved into the area in acceptance of the job that he had seen advertised in a medical magazine as he had begun to explain over dinner that evening. "After my wife passed away, I wanted to move because the house was too big just for me. My son lives so far away, it wouldn't matter whether I moved or not."
"Oh, you have children?"
"Just one son…after him, nothing else happened. How about you? Do you have any children?"
This is what she was afraid of…the personal questions. "Yes, I have a son and a daughter."
"Really? Do they live with you or nearby?" The conversation was becoming one-sided, and she was going to divert the direction.
"No. They both have graduated from college and are on their own, and both are doing well. So, how did you wind up here, so far from where you're from?"
"Well, like I said before, I subscribe to a medical magazine and saw this ad in the job section. I've always read them to see what is available. Since I wanted to move, it didn't matter where I went. So, I wound up here. It's nice where I

live now and just enough room for me and a couple of guests."

"Yes, that part of the city is a nice place to live."

"So, then why do you live here in this community where you are? I'm sure you can afford something better than this."

"You know Kurt since you asked I'm going to tell you. No, at one time I couldn't afford anymore than this. And at one time, I had more than I would have ever have needed or wanted, but things changed for the worst after my divorce and even went into a worse downward spiral after the second one. And you know whose fault it was? It was mine. My pride took me down to squalor. I went from almost a palace to living place to place in dumps worse than these, and the worst thing is that I dragged my poor kids with me. I was a horrible excuse for a provider and a more dreadful example of motherhood. I was so into my own hurt and heartache, trying to put the blame on everyone else except myself and I started drinking to ignore my life…to abandon my life and not have to feel the pain. The only way that I was able to cope was to blot it all out, going on drinking binges and hanging out with people who were just as perverse as I was… living my kind of pleasure seeking, self-absorbed, corrupted life. Forgetting my sorrows in feeble drunkenness, I left my children alone while I basked myself in what had brought me merely temporary bliss, day in and day out, but this was only the covering of my perpetual gloom and emptiness inside."

"Wait, Ally…You don't have to tell me…"

"No, I need to tell you this because sometimes people are so busy holding their noses up that they can't see all the progress that's going on down below them. But you know what… those people in that community took care of my children and me when I wouldn't and couldn't take care of them or myself. They fed us and looked out for us when I was too out my drunken mind to do it myself. They watched out for them with their schoolwork, made sure that they were safe, going to and from school. And when I finally managed to keep a job…probably because I was a barmaid, who at that time was where I wanted to be; they continued to help because I was never there when my kids were home. But there I was in my haven, and I loved it. Yes, I loved it, but only while I was in it. Being there helped me to think that I was happy. I didn't want to come out of it for fear of seeing the truth… the truth about myself and what I had done to my family. So, please don't say anything about those people or that community. They were by my side all the way. Watching out and trying to talk some sense into me to help me to save myself and keep my children. I had been so close to losing them because of my alcoholism. Yes, I had become an alcoholic. I lost the love of my daughter, who hasn't spoken to me in years. And that's what it took. It took years for me get my act together, but maybe a little too late to get back her trust and love."

"Ally, I'm so sorry if I've offended you. Please accept my apology."

"It's okay. You know this is the first time that I ever confessed to anybody, the events about my personal life in that way. Not even to my doctors. Usually, they were telling me how I felt."

"Probably, you needed to get it off your chest."

"Maybe." They had finished their conversation while sitting outside of her apartment building. "You know, I feel good and energetic. Thanks for dinner."

"You're welcome. Have a nice evening." Slowly he drove away after waiting to see that she had gotten inside safely. She waved goodbye while standing inside the glass doors.

Chapter 38

The phone kept ringing over at Ally's apartment. It was already 11:00 in the morning. Sharon had gotten a call from Casey, asking her if she had seen his mother. Having not seen her, he asked if she could go over and check on her. Her supervisor called him because they had been trying to call her at home to see if she was coming to work. She had never called in nor was ever late, so they became worried and called him, since he was listed as an emergency contact. Sharon immediately went over and knocked on the door. Usually, she could hear her leaving for work in the morning but recalled this morning that she had not heard a sound, but had paid no attention and went on with her morning routine. Now she was alarmed. Ally had been saying how tired she felt of late, but both of them had blown it off as probably depression from living alone since Casey had gone to live in his own apartment. After knocking several times with no answer, she called the office manager explaining the emergency and to have someone come to open her apartment to see if she was there. "Please hurry. Something could be wrong," she cried. "She may need a doctor or something. Please, please hurry," Sharon pleaded.

"Ma'am, someone is on the way right now," the office manager assured her.

When the maintenance attendant opened the door, Sharon burst in, heading straight for the bedroom, calling out her name. When she saw her lying on the bed, she rushed over to her calling and gently shaking her. "Ally, Ally are you okay? Wake up!"

She moaned and was barely audible, "Sharon." Ally lay almost still on the bed, barely breathing. She put her ear to her chest and listened for a heartbeat. She heard the gentle and irregular beats.

"Call an ambulance! Hurry up, please!" With haste, Sharon called the ambulance as well. She was so upset that she was not able to do any more for her friend. She had no equipment necessary to make her own assessment. Not being a nurse yet, she didn't have the knowledge to perform anymore than CPR. Having no other alternative without the proper direction, equipment or medication, she continued until the ambulance came. Neighbors had begun to gather in and around the door of the apartment. After calling for an ambulance, she called Casey back.

"Casey, your mom will be going to the hospital. She was still in bed, but she seems weak. The ambulance is on the way."

"Why? What's wrong with her?"

"I don't know. Her breathing is light, but I think she saw me. She said my name, so she's not unconscious or anything."

"Where are they taking her? Do you know?" Casey asked, his voice trembling in fear. "I'm sure to the hospital, closest to us.

"I'm coming right now."

"No, don't bother coming here. By the time you get here, she'll probably be at the hospital. Wait a minute Casey they're here. Let me call you back."

"No, I want to hold on."

"Okay." She really didn't want him to hear all that might have to go on, but she held onto the phone anyway. They both heard and she saw policemen ordering onlookers to move aside and out of the apartment.

"Casey, I don't think you should hang on to the phone. She's going to be all right." Sharon said to quell his already heightened emotional state and encouraged him to go to the hospital as soon as the paramedics tell her which one they would be taking his mother to. She heard them outside the apartment, bustling their way through the hallway. They rushed in and began their quick assessment and emergency treatment. "Which hospital are you taking her to?" she quickly asked, letting them know that her son was on the phone, waiting to find out. One of them blurted out the name of the hospital.

"Casey..." Before she could say any more, he told her that he heard the paramedic and hung up the phone. After first giving a shot of medication in her arm and carefully placing an oxygen mask securely over her nose and mouth, she was hoisted onto a stretcher and hurriedly taken to the waiting ambulance outside of the apartment building. By this time, more policemen, spectators, and neighbors had gathered and were waiting to see who would be lying on the stretcher as they were being pushed back to make room for the out coming rolling stretcher. With red lights flashing, they took Ally to the hospital with Sharon right by her side. As she looked at Ally, whose weak looking eyes were opened now, her tiny thin figure lay there strapped to the stretcher, she thought about Sage, but didn't want to hear her unemotional, indifferent, and crass comments. She had heard them before time and time again whenever Ally had wound up in the hospital, mostly due to her own careless and reckless behavior, but still, she was her mother, in spite of her thoughtless actions. Sharon was afraid of what she would say to Sage. She had had enough and had grown impatient and unsympathetic to Sage's unyielding determination to hold on to the hate and bad memories of her past. Ally looked so fragile and pale lying there. What could have happened so quickly to bring her to this state? Other than the weakness and occasional sight of that glare that she so often complained about, she seemed to be doing well. She was thinner, but then again she was always petite. She smiled at Sharon and closed her eyes out of complete exhaustion.

The call had already been made to the hospital, so they were prepared to treat her according to the report of her condition from the paramedics. Politely, but hurriedly, shoving Sharon aside, someone whisked her quickly into the waiting area while the emergency team took Ally to the back for treatment. There were only a few people in the huge waiting room. Casey who was already there saw her and went over to find out what had happened along with his Uncle Jack, who had come as soon as Casey called and told him what had happened. They both greeted her. "Hi, Sharon."

"Hi, Casey…Jack," she replied and hugged them both.

"Sharon, what's wrong with my mother?"

"I'm sorry Casey, but I really don't know. I rode with her in the ambulance. When we got here, they told me to wait in the waiting area. They're not going to talk to me anyway, since I'm not a family member. But try to stay calm. Have you called Sage yet?"

"I tried, but I'm only getting a recording."

"Is she at work today?"

"I guess, but she could be anywhere. She's out of the office most of the time at conferences or meetings. I left a message with her secretary for her to call me as soon as possible."

"That's good. I guess all we can do now is wait to hear from the doctors,"

Sharon said sadly.

Sage had not known about this meeting until a last minute call at her home the night before. Arriving early that morning at the office to pick up what was needed for the meeting, she dreaded the hour-long drive that she would have to travel to get there. As she was packing papers, she thought about Grace her good friend from college. Since she lived and worked in the area, she thought that maybe they could meet for lunch. On the way, she called. Grace was surprised and gleefully anticipated their lunch date.

Turning off her phone, so there would be no interruptions during the meeting, decided to leave it off while having lunch with Grace. They could better enjoy their time together not having any phone interruptions during the little time they had to catch up on all the happenings that had gone on in their busy lives since the few calls after graduation. Grace hardly had a chance to wait when Sage walked through the glass doors of the restaurant. The hostess watched amusingly as they hugged and giggled rocking from side to side. As soon as they were seated, the waiter came with the menus. The minute he turned to walk away with the drink orders, they simultaneously began talking and laughed about the silly incident.
"You go first." Sage urged.
"Sage, I can't believe it's been this long."
"I can't believe it either. You look so...so glamorous." Grace said.
"Well, now that I get a paycheck, I can afford to buy a little glamour," they both laughed. "So, Sage what's new with you. I thought for sure that you would have called me by now about a wedding."
"Wedding? ...to who?"
"Oh come on... to that tall, handsome basketball player in Florida, that's who. I heard he's a professional player now."
"Yeah, he was drafted right after graduation. Listen, Mark is a nice guy. But he's only just a really good friend, nothing more than that. I don't have time to get involved in romantic relationships. I'm too busy."
"You mean you're too busy to take a little time out for yourself to share with a friend?"
"No really, I'm hardly at home. I travel a lot. I go to work early, and I get home late. With deadlines to meet... who has time?"
"Well, you're not getting any younger. Your biological clock is ticking away, you know." Grace said jokingly but serious.

"Excuse me, ladies, here are your drinks. Would you be you ready to order yet?"

"Can you please give us a little more time?" Sage asked.

"Sure, I can come back." Picking up where they left off Sage responded,

"Well, so is yours. Are you romantically involved with anyone?"

"Funny you should ask." Grace said with a big grin and practically throwing her left hand right into Sage's eyes. Sage was amazed to see such a gorgeous and large diamond ring. Grace was not a pretty girl, not very sociable, but smart, and had a very charming personality. And her new look… she had to admit, she was quite attractive. Thinking back when they were in college, she had never even seen her with a guy before that she could recall.

"Wow! It's beautiful. Grace, this is awesome. When were you going to tell me? And when did this happen? Do I know him? Did he go to school with us?"

"Slow down. It's only been two weeks that he proposed."

"What's his name? Do I know him?"

"No, his name is Drew… Drew Stewart. He didn't go to college with us. In fact, he's a few years older. He moved here from upstate New York a few years ago after accepting a job down here. That's where he went to college."

"So how did you two meet?"

"Through my sister Fran. They work at the same company where he's an engineer."

"Oh really." Sage said with surprise. "Yeah, when he first started working there, she saw that he was always eating alone and one day she just plopped down with him and they had lunch together and a great conversation. You know how outgoing she is. Well, he told her everything about himself …that he was single and had no friends down here, only a few where he's from, and not even a girlfriend. Actually, his family is in California. So she invited him out with some of her friends and practically begged me to come along to meet him. So, we all met at a club for happy hour. Can you believe we met on a blind date? I really didn't even want to go. Right away, we seemed to hit it off. Can you believe it? We dated for about two years and the rest is his-story…as they say." They both laughed.

"Oh wow, Grace. That is fantastic. Congratulations. So, when's the big day?"

"We're looking at fall of next year. I was going to call you because I want you to be one of my bridesmaids."

"Oh sure. I would love to be." Sage didn't know if she was happy for her friend or a little jealous. She thought about Mark, and how she knew that he wanted to be more than just friends and that she was the person blocking the growth of their friendship. She honestly couldn't understand herself why she continued to let the past make her always avoid getting romantically involved with men. She allowed her hurtful past to prevent her from allowing herself to trust anyone with her feelings. She had no ability to forgive or forget. Or maybe it was fear. People controlled their own behavior and actions, and they knew the consequences that might result from them. She didn't want to be involved in the yo-yo, seesaw modes of a romantic relationship. That was her sentiment. Her thoughts would always revert from romance to her mother's behavior. There was no way that she was going to wind up like her. Why should she have to give in to someone else's selfish behavior and easily let them off the hook after ruining the lives of others? These thoughts had been relegated from how her mother's past choices which seemed deplete of the loving care and affection that a mother would have for her children that had so egregiously affected their lives, especially hers. These thoughts always held her back from any true desire for romance in her life. Snapping out of her deflected thoughts, she said. Realizing this, she wondered if she'd missed any of what Grace was saying.

"Time is really flying. I guess we'd better order."

"Yes, you're right." Looking at the menu quickly, by the time the waiter reappeared they were ready to order. They chatted throughout the meal barely eating while asking about their other friends and family members.

"So, how's your mother, Sage?" Grace finally asked. "You mentioned everyone except her."

Sage stopped abruptly from lifting her fork. Immediately she became annoyed even a bit irritated. "I'm sure she's fine."

"What do you mean? You sound as if you're not sure." '

"Well, no news is good news. Anyway, my brother and a family friend from the old neighborhood keep me informed and up to date."

"Sage, don't tell me that you're still angry with your mother."

"No, I'm not angry with her. I just don't talk to her. I don't have anything to say to her."

"Doesn't she ever try to call you?"

"No, but she did mail me a letter a couple of weeks ago. I guess since we don't see each other which is probably why she sent it."

"Are you kidding me? You mean you're still feeling this way after all these years. Is she still drinking or something? I know mine is…not as much. Not like before."

"No… from what I've been told she stopped years ago after her physical and mental health began to fail."

"Sage, you're going to let your past rob you of any happiness in your life."

"I'm happy." She said in a stoic manner. "Look, Grace, I told you before that she practically ruined our lives."

"I can't see where your life has been ruined. You got a free college education, two great jobs. You didn't even have to take any handouts from your rich uncle." Grace said sarcastically. "And you could be married to a professional basketball player if you wanted to. What more could you ask for? You know Sage, you were very young and totally oblivious to the realities of life during that time when you were a kid. Ignorant of what adults have to go through just being adults, especially in marriage. You saw everything through the eyes of a child. You never understood the emotional roller coaster and sometimes traumatic heartbreak in relationships, especially in committed ones like marriage. Most people want to love and be loved. But finding that perfect partner to share your life together with is almost impossible to do. It's a gamble. You try while dating to learn who your partner really is, which is what dating is all about. In different situations, good or bad notice how things are handled. And when outside influences work their way into your lives only working together can save a relationship, and that's in any type of relationship." That brought back memories of her grandmother, her father's mother. She could tell as a child that she never wanted them in her life. With her obvious display of indifference whenever they went for a visit she could now imagine the hurt her mother must have felt having to get along with a person like that. Grace went on talking trying to help Sage see her life from a different perspective.

"The uncertainties and unpredictable circumstances in our lives can destroy what may have at one time seemed to have been the perfect union. Some people can handle riding the proverbial 'emotional roller coaster' and others are devastated. My mother was one of them.

"How do you know so much about relationships, Grace? You're no older than I am. You sound as if you've had experience?"

"I learned from my mother when she had had a few too many drinks after a huge argument with my dad. When he walked out, she'd come moaning to my sister and I. We were young and probably shouldn't have been told about such grownup things, but I got to understand that my mother had feelings and that they both loved us. My parents certainly weren't perfect. No parents are. And every family is dysfunctional. Divorce was always in the air in our house, but they somehow managed to work things out. You know Sage, it's time that you sit down with your mother now that you are an adult and find out just what really drove her in the direction that she took and I'm sure you'll find just how sorry she still is for any hurt and regret the horrible circumstances that she put you guys through. Your mother loves you very much. Give her a chance to tell you." Sage was practically in tears. For the first time she could remember, she felt empathy for her mother.

Still holding onto the unopened letter that her mother sent her, Sage now felt childish and shameful for refusing to read it. Several times, she attempted to throw it away but decided she should at least read it one day before throwing it.

"What did your mom write in her letter if it's not too personal?"

"I haven't read it yet."

"Sage, are you kidding me? Please read the letter. It can be a start towards a real conversation with your mom. You have to forgive her and go on with your life before you miss out on your own true happiness and a future." By the end of their conversation, Sage decided that she was going to visit her mother. She promised Grace that she would. Noticing the time, they realized that they both had overstayed their time. They hugged and promised to stay better in touch. Sage promised to be available for any help needed for the wedding plans.

"I'll call you," Sage promised as she got into her car. She turned on her phone in case there were any messages that she may have missed from the job. There were several calls from Casey.

Seeing so many calls back to back, she called him right away, thinking that maybe something was wrong.

"Hello Casey, what's going on? I've had my phone turned off ever since early this morning."

"It's Mom. She was rushed to the hospital this morning." She was shocked and in fear when she heard the news. A great sadness came over her as she thought of her past reactions whenever she had gotten this type call. Now she felt deeply ashamed.

"What's wrong? Is she okay?"

"I'm not sure. No one has come out to tell us anything yet. I'm at the hospital now."

"Oh, God," she thought with regret.

"They're still running tests."

"What hospital is she in? I had to go to a meeting early this morning at one of the other branch offices, which was about an hour away. Casey, I'm so sorry that I'm not there with you."

"Well, Sharon and Uncle Jack are here, so we'll see you when you get here. Are you coming?" he asked cautiously.

"Yes, I'll be there."

"I'm sure she'll be admitted, but right now we're still in the ER waiting room."

"Okay, I'll call my manager and let them know where I'm going. I'll see you soon." "Okay... oh...and Sage...thanks." He hung up. She knew why he thanked her. Before, her response would have been annoyance and indifference. She shuddered to think of how she must have appeared to them back then and tried to blot out those thoughts from her mind. As she drove, she thought of the letter.

Chapter 39

By the time Sage reached the hospital, Ally had been admitted to the intensive care unit. She was on a respirator with IVs and monitors seemingly all over her body. Ally was in a semi-comatose state that was drug induced to calm her body and brain activity because she had had a seizure in the ER. Seeing his mother lying there on the hospital bed with monitors beeping and neon graphs moving, waving up and down measuring her vitals, Casey was deeply distressed and feelings of guilt began to overcome him for having left her to live by herself alone in that apartment. But Casey always looked out for his mom. Sharon was still across the hall.

While he was standing at the side of the bed, a nurse came in to check her IV bag. "Looks like this one's just about empty," she said rhetorically. "Hi, my name is Cheryl. I'll be taking care of Mrs. Jacobs for now. Are you her son?"
"Yes." He saw her name on her nametag. "How is she doing?" he asked as he backed away from the bed.
"As well as can be expected for now, her tiny body has been through a lot. For right now, she's stable, but we have great doctors here who are treating her."
He hadn't gotten a chance to speak to the doctor in the ER and inquired about speaking to the doctor on the floor.
"Well how can I get in touch with the doctor while she's here on this floor?" he reiterated. Finishing the adjustment on the IV, she wrote down the name and number.

"Usually, the doctors come around later in the evening, especially when it's a new admission. But a team of doctors always comes in the morning around seven o'clock which is part of their normal rounds schedule." Before sitting, he looked at her again and shook his head in sorrow. Taking a seat in the chair beside the bed he checked his watch to judge about the time Sage would probably be arriving. Before speaking to a doctor, he wanted to wait until she was there. Sharon and Jack had been allowed to come in; however, very briefly and only two visitors were permitted at a time. Sharon left in tears, but became elated when he told her that Sage was on her way to the hospital. She even shouted "Hallelujah" as soon as she heard the words.

"Casey, please keep me posted." It had given her so much joy and relief to know that Sage had finally come to her senses. She wasn't sure about her attitude, but was happy that at least she was coming this time. Casey would be there to keep her in line and that gave her some assurance.

When Sage got to the intensive care at her mother's room, she immediately stopped at the door. She could not move seeing all the tubing and cords coming from everywhere on her mother's body, leading to beeping monitors with their neon green screens of graphs in motion with corresponding flashing numbers changing from electrical pulses coming from the patches stuck on her body. It was a frightening sight. She was shocked with the reality that this was her mother who was the person lying there. She had never been admitted for more than two days at the most, but this time she dreaded that this case would be different and more serious.

Then she looked over at Casey, elbows on his legs, his face down covered by his two hands.

"Casey," she said softly. He practically leaped off the chair when he heard her voice and went right over and hugged his sister. Holding her, he felt a sense of comfort and relief.

"Oh Casey, I'm so sorry. If I hadn't turned my phone off, I would have gotten here sooner."

"It's okay. Nobody knew that this was going to happen." Holding each other's hands, they walked over and stood by the side of the bed. Sage was devastated to see her mother lying still with the tubing from the respirator taped to her mouth. Her eyes were closed, but she could see that they were moving as if she could be looking for something or maybe someone. She wondered if she was conscious enough to know that she was there. That is what she hoped for. She hoped that her mother would realize that she had finally come to her, although regretful that she had to be in an intensive care unit before she would come. This very thought she expressed to Casey.

"Sage, please don't do this to yourself. Mom always understood why you never came to see her. She never held anything against you. She just wanted so much to tell you this as she told me so many times. You know, she really had hoped that she would get a chance to see you at my dinner…"

"Oh, God if I could bring that day back," she interjected. "You don't know how many times I wondered over and over whether I should go or not, never thinking that not going was a bad decision. In fact, I thought I was well within my right not to go. You know… that's probably why she sent me that letter."

"Mom sent you a letter?"

"Yes, it was not long after your dinner… maybe a week or so after, I got it in the mail."

"Well, what did it say?"

"Casey, I'm so ashamed."

"Ashamed… ashamed of what?"

"I never even opened it," she confessed.

"Why Sage? Why wouldn't you open it?"

"I don't know. I guess I stupidly wanted to hold on to my bitterness, which was so childish. My whole life I've been behaving like a child. I didn't want to forgive her. I guess I wanted her to suffer the way that I had suffered."

"Well, you're here. Even though you didn't read it, you're here. That means that you forgave her before she even got a chance to ask you to. Don't you see?"

"Yes, but look how sick she is. This is why I'm here."

"No, it's not. You didn't know how sick she was when I called you, but you came anyway."

Tears rolled down her face. She wanted so badly to hug her mother… to now ask her for forgiveness. Trying not to focus on her own feelings, she asked,

"Casey, have you eaten anything today. It really doesn't sound as if you have. So, you've been here since this morning?"

"No, actually it was around twelve when I got here."

"Why don't you go to the cafeteria to get something to eat? I'll stay here with Mom. I'll read the letter while you're gone."

"You have it with you?"

"Yeah, it's so strange that ever since I got it, I've kept it with me." She didn't want to confess that she sometimes thought about ripping it up and throwing it in the trash.

"Then, that's a great idea." He rubbed his mother's leg gingerly as he walked out. She then sat in the one chair that was next to the bed. Looking over at her mother, she took the letter from her purse and looked at the handwriting. It was a little different from what it had been years ago. Her mind drifted back to when she was in their gorgeous home, sitting together at the table practicing her handwriting while her mom cooked the evening meal in between helping her. It was strange thinking about that house. She had not thought about it in years. Opening the envelope, she took out the letter and started unfolding the lined papers and began to read with feelings of anxiety of what she was about to find out.

My Dear Sage,

I am so sorry that I have taken so long to tell you that I love you and how much I have missed you. I can't blame you for hating me and not ever wanting to see or talk to me. For many years, I had thought only of myself, even though I loved you and Casey more than you can imagine. I know it sounds crazy and I didn't show it, but I did, and I still do. When your dad and I divorced, even before then when I saw our marriage crumbling, I was devastated and felt as though my life was ending. In truth, I wanted it to end. I loved him more than life itself and couldn't face what was ahead without him, but I would have been the worst kind of person to leave my children behind. I'm not trying to make excuses for myself to make you feel sorry for me or try to get you to talk to me again or even care about me again, but in all honesty, I wanted to quit. But I was the grownup, and I should have been strong, able to do whatever I needed to do to be the best parent that I could and make your lives better, even if it had to be without a father, but I failed. I failed you both in the worst way. You and Casey had nothing to do with any of the horrible things that happened in our lives. You were the innocent victims and aftermath of the mess that selfish and thoughtless grownups create.

I let my pride get in the way of common sense. Your father gave up his responsibilities as a father, but when I had the chance to make sure he upheld his parental responsibilities, in my resentment, anger, and pride, I decided that I didn't want anything from him. I didn't want his family to think that I married him for their money and to prove it, I didn't. I didn't want or need their money. But I shouldn't have cared about what they thought of me or try to prove anything to them, because as a parent, he should have owned up to his responsibilities, which are you and Casey. I made a stupid, selfish, and prideful decision not to take a cent from him, which would have helped us continue to live the life you were used to. We could have had a decent life. Even your grandfather offered to pay for you and Casey to stay in private school; I wanted nothing and refused his offer. I went to public schools, and if they were good enough for me, I thought they were good enough for my children. But, schooling was not the real issue. The real issue was that my one and truthfully my only love no longer loved or wanted me, and sadly, neither his children. So, to cope with my feelings of broken heartedness, abandonment, and loneliness, I started drinking. I couldn't sleep those nights when your father didn't come home until late so a glass of wine calmed my nerves, and I was able to sleep. I didn't want to face the unbelievable reality that was happening to me, so alcohol helped to get rid of the truth. After the divorce, I tried to escape by not being in my real senses and having to see the consequences of my pride. It helped in the beginning, but if I had had a backbone, I would have faced my life and not try to hide behind a bottle. We could have made a life for ourselves, probably not at the level that you were used to, but we would have made it because we had each other. But again, I let pride deceive my sense of what was right and indulged myself in alcohol and reckless living with total disregard for how you and Casey felt. All of this only made your lives more of a shambles because of my bad decision-making.

Then I married Colin. I was revengefully trying to show your dad that I wasn't defeated. I could live without him. I refused to listen to anyone when they tried to discourage me from getting married too soon. They warned me that I hadn't known him long enough to take such a serious step. Again, my pride got in the way. Even you tried to tell me. I should have listened to you. Even as a child, you had more adult sense than I did and I, without reason distrusted you and believed him when my jewelry was missing. For that, I am also truly sorry. He squandered most of our money, leaving us with little to live on at the level we had readjusted to. I don't have to tell you where that took us. I never had any real work skills. When I met your father, I was barely out of high school and about to start college that fall, so when he asked me to marry him, there was no reason to pursue my plans.

The terrible thing about all this was that I dragged my children down with me in the most dreadful way of living. I didn't think of how embarrassed and ashamed you two must have been to have a mother seen staggering home night after night from drinking too much. But it was the alcohol that I needed. It had allowed me not to think about, or face, what my foolish actions were doing to our family, which was why I didn't try to stop. As long as I was drunk out of my mind, I wasn't able to think about the horrible life that I made for my children. It became a much needed companion, which probably caused me to create in my own mind those imagined companions, good and bad. Anyway, this was how my doctors explained them to me. They finally diagnosed it as delirium tremens, which is also called DTs, although it seems I can still feel where some of those apparitions touched me. What a life for a once upon a time church girl to have succumbed to. That was so embarrassing and is the reason why it was so difficult to face my parents. I never wanted them to see what I had done with all that they had taught me and now living almost in squalor because of my alcoholism and other physical ailments that came along because of it. I never wanted them to visit to see where we lived, and how we were living. Toni either. I was pathetic.

Sage, I understand why after the night of my birthday, the most terrifying thing in your life and mine to happen, why you would never want to see or talk to me again. Believe it or not, out of all the bad decisions that I made, that was the worst. I caused that to happen to you. I don't blame you for hating me. I hated myself. And again, it was my fault. If I could give my life to erase that awful night and memory out of your mind, I would. I know you wanted me to call the police, but if they had come and seen the state that I was in, I would have possibly lost you and Casey, the apartment, probably everything, which wasn't much because we really didn't have very much. You were my children and you were everything to me. I wasn't the most ideal example to have for a good neighbor in our building. Some of them had already threatened to report me, so I was already in trouble. Thanks to Sharon, they didn't. Sharon has been such a true friend, just like Toni. And for this dreadful experience, I beg you to forgive me. I had no idea that anything like that would ever happen. It's still so very hard for me to deal with what could have happened to you and I was the person solely responsible for such a thing. That night I wanted to be the one to hold you and comfort you, but I knew that you would never allow me to get anywhere near you, especially since that whole disgusting incident was my entire fault.

The day that you graduated from college, I wanted so badly to be there. I was so very proud of you. You had worked so hard for that day as you had done in high school. For weeks I had stopped drinking. Also I was seeing a doctor to help me stay on my road to sobriety. I finally made up my mind seeing all the devastation that alcohol had caused in our lives, so I made up my mind to stop drinking. I wanted to surprise you even though I knew that you didn't want me to come. Sharon and Casey also encouraged me to come anyway. For your graduation gift, I wanted to give you the gift of sobriety. Sharon and I had even gone out to buy special outfits to wear. I was reluctant. It was hard not knowing what you would say if you saw me there, especially because I knew that you didn't want to see me. I guess that's why I became so nervous. My hand-shaking problem started that morning and even after taking my medicine, it only got worse. So, it came to mind, stupid as it was, to have a little sip of wine, which always seemed to help in the past, and I would be okay. I had gotten rid of all alcoholic beverages from the apartment, so I went out in search for just a small glass of wine. Again, that was the dumbest thing that a recovering alcoholic could think of to resolve a problem, but I did. I found a bar and then afterwards felt so embarrassed and guilty that I couldn't go to your graduation, not like that. Then my mental state had gone so twisted that I thought I was being taunted and chased by demons, but it was the owner, yelling for me to pay for my drink. Anyway, that's what I was told later in the hospital, but it still seems real in my memory. Alcohol is a horrible and sometimes hallucinogenic drug. That incident is what caused me to wind up in the hospital that day and caused me to miss your graduation. Again, I'm not trying to make excuses, but I am asking for your forgiveness. I had been trying to make up for every awful thing that I had ever caused in your lives after I accepted and faced myself for what I really had been. I had never seen myself as an alcoholic. Now I'm proud that I haven't had a drink in years. I have a good job, and I have been saving to move into a more decent part of town, although I have met a lot of good people and found good friends here at our complex.

I know at Casey's dinner, it wouldn't have been the place to ask you to forgive me, but I still hoped that you would have been there. I thought we would have at least had a chance to talk and I could invite you out for lunch or dinner someday, so that we could have a mother/daughter talk that I missed so much, just you and me. So, I hope that after reading this letter, you would consider having a meal with me sometimes. If not, I hope that you can find it in your heart to forgive me for all the wrongs that I have done that caused all the heartache and misery that you and Casey had to go through in your young lives.

You know Sage, I also had grown to hate. My feelings of deep love for your father had become feelings of disgust and hatred. I blamed him for the downward turn that our lives had taken after he left, no longer wanting me as his wife and then to give up his role as your father made me despise him even more. I hated him for being such a coward and too weak to stand up against his controlling mother, who had somehow managed to convince him that I wasn't good enough or the right person for him to be married to. But it wasn't his fault. I forgave him many years ago for his actions. He was who he was and I took him for better or for worse as the marriage vows say. I couldn't change him. He was my choice. I had convinced myself that he would be different once we were married. In the beginning, I thought that he had changed, but as things turned out, he hadn't. The problem was that he had no faith and nowhere to go in time of need, except to his mother. My problem was that I knew where to go, but instead, I blamed God and turned my back on Him when He didn't answer my prayer to save my marriage. My faith was in man to provide my needs, but money and material things will never be enough to sustain a marriage. Your grandparents tried to warn me, but again, I didn't listen.

415

Sage, please try to find it in your heart to forgive him as well. Hopefully, one day he will come to you and Casey himself and ask you himself. But don't wait, you go to him. I'm sure he probably fears that he would be rejected for abandoning you and is remorseful and ashamed just as I am. I know that I'm asking a lot. Your father and I have been two fools who are, beyond a doubt, unworthy and deserve nothing, let alone forgiveness. But from the bottom of my heart, I'm begging you to someday find it in your heart to forgive me for all the wrong that I've done and for the horrible mother that I've been. God knows I would give my life if I thought I could change a second of the heartache and suffering that I have caused you and Casey. You certainly didn't deserve any of it. I'm sure by forgiving me, you will find that a weight will be lifted and you will have an enjoyable and more fulfilling life. You will be able to replace all the hatred and animosity with love. Love, that maybe someday you will be able to share with someone else. I love you and Casey very much more than you could ever imagine and always have.

I know this letter seems more like a story, but these words are years of conversations that we were never able to have to let you know that I never intended to hurt you, but love you.

With Love,
Mom

Sage kept wiping away the tears as she read the pages. Sorrow and pity came over her as she looked in her mind's eye and remembered those horrible days. She felt empathy thinking about that young woman being swept off her feet by a tall, handsome, rich bachelor, so full of promises and then marrying him only to have to contend with years of rejection by her controlling and uppity mother-in-law, who saw her as unsuitable for her undeserving son. As she thought about her mother, she could envision her living at her own parent's home as she remembered from their visits. She imagined her mother living there as a child and then growing up into a beautiful young woman still in the comfort and safety in that same home with her parents right up until the day she got married. This had to have been a frighteningly huge change from her meager means to step right into an entirely different way of life of wealth and sophistication. She was sure that it also had to have been a difficult decision to have to make of leaving behind her parents, who were on the opposite side of the country, where the fastest and closest connection to them was only by phone. Coming back to the circumstances at hand, she thought about her poor grandmother, who was now too old to travel and now alone.

How could she ever be told that her only child is lying here in an intensive care unit in a hospital? God forbid if she didn't pull through. That probability brought abject fear to the realization of that possibility. Even before reading the letter, after talking to her friend Grace, she thought about going to see her mom, or at least calling her. Feeling vilely low about the manner in which she had treated her throughout the years, Sage now desperately wanted to have the chance to ask her for forgiveness for her stubborn, and unrelenting, refusal to even speak to her. Knowing there was a possibility that she might not have the chance filled her with immense sadness and fear. After putting the letter into the envelope and back into her purse, she stood up and looked down at her mother, her eyeballs still moving under the lids, as if she was trying to look around or that she was aware. Sage leaned over and said, "Mom, can you hear me? It's me, Sage. I'm here, Mom," she said, as she took her mother's hand kissed it and held it gently. "Mom, I'm so sorry for being so selfish and childish." Her head and shoulder seemed to twitch, but barely. Sage thought she felt a slight clinch from her mother's hand, and her eyes continued to move around as if she was trying to open them. With her other hand, she tenderly stroked her hair back on the top of her head, seeing strands of gray mixed into her light brown hair that she did not know she had. They made her realize that her mother had grown older, although she was only in her late forties. Her hair was soft to her touch. She was crushed into utter ignominy, realizing that she had not touched her mother in years. She looked away up at the ceiling, wiping away the tears, then bowing her head as she prayed silently for her recovery.

Casey was now standing at the opened glass door of his mother's room. An hour had passed since he had gone and come back. He saw Sage leaning over near her head. He was moved seeing his sister treating their mother so affectionately. A vision that he had so many times in his life prayed for.
"Sage, I'm back," he said softly, trying not to startle her. She raised her head and quickly stood up suddenly hearing his voice.
"How's she doing? …any change?"
"Not really. I guess we really won't see much until they bring her out of the induced coma that she's in."
"So… did you get a chance to read the letter?" he asked.
"Yes, I did." The tone of her voice had changed to solemnity. "It was so sad. There were quite a few pages." She began to walk slowly away from the bed and towards him with her head down.

417

"You know, it was like a confession. It broke my heart. Casey, I've been such a jerk all these years." Casey was surprised, yet happy to hear her say those words, but he made no comment. She kept asking me to forgive her over and over again. She even mentioned that we should reach out to Dad. Her words were like the mother that we had years ago. You can read it if you like."

"I feel so badly about the way I treated Mom through the years. I have to ask her to forgive me. I need to ask her," looking straight into her brother's eyes, "Casey, she's got to get through this."

Hugging his sister as she cried on his shoulder, he tried to console her.

"She will. We just have to keep praying. Go on, sit down."

Sitting on the chair now as she dried her eyes, she asked,

"Have you talked to Uncle Jack since he left the hospital? I think he should let Dad know what's going on."

"Actually, he told me earlier in the ER that he was going to do just that. He said he'd call as soon as he left."

"What about Grandma? What do you think? Do you think we should tell her?" she asked.

"I don't know. I've been thinking about that same thing myself."

"I haven't even called Toni yet," she added. "We have to at least let her know what's going on."

"Yes, maybe Toni could help us to decide about whether to tell Grandma or not. Toni has been such a wonderful friend to Mom…taking care of Grandma like she has." "She's been a friend to all of us. Who else would do what she's been doing for Grandma all these years?" Casey added.

"Yes, we're going to have to get there more often to visit our grandmother and give Toni a break."

"You're right, that's something we have to do."

"I think before I call her, we should speak to the doctor to find out more about Mom's condition, that way we could tell her exactly what's going on. Have you tried to call the doctor?"

"No, but I have the number right here."

Another hour had passed, and it was now after six. They talked about what could have possibly led to their mother's seeming sudden and critical episode. They wondered who had seen or spoken to her last before this happened… whether there were any signs that anything was wrong, and if so, what were they? Casey recalled that she had been so happy about how well her life was going now and how really proud she was about her job at the pharmacy. Sage was embarrassed and ashamed that she had nothing to contribute. She had not spoken to or seen her mother in years. Remembering again, her past behavior was crushing. Because she gave herself the capacity to harbor that much anger and hatred in her heart for so long, made her feel despicable. The disgustingly, unimaginable evil thoughts that had come into her mind were now hard to believe that she could not see the wretchedness that was within. How could she have justified such actions and thinking? She needed to release the anguish that was building up seeing her mother lying there, possibly dying and acknowledging now that her past terrible treatment to her mother made her realize it was all unwarranted and downright mean. Feeling desolate and crushed with guilt, she could hardly hold back the tears. If she hadn't been waiting to see the doctors; she would have left in shame.

Two men walked into the room wearing white jackets, one holding a metal clipboard under his arm. Both Sage and Casey stood up and walked towards them. The men reached out and shook their hands. "Hello, my name is Dr. Sullivan, the head of cardiology, and this is our chief neurologist, Dr. Anston. After introducing himself and his colleague, with a friendly smile, he proceeded with the discussion. "Is this your mother?" the taller and apparently older man asked.

"Yes." They replied in unison. "I'm Casey, and this is my sister Sage."

Dr. Anston appeared to be most knowledgeable with his graying temples, clean-shaven face, and a stoic persona that made him stand out as one with experience.

"Doctor, what's going on with our mother? What happened to her?" asked Sage. She stared directly into the young doctor's face, waiting for a response.

"She was fine… now all of a sudden she's in the intensive care unit," Casey, in a somber voice, chimed in. The doctor glanced at the small frame lying still under the sheets, connected to a plethora of wires and tubing attached to bags of fluid and flashing monitors. Through the years, he knew that this sight brought a lot of skepticism and concern to see a loved one in this condition. Seeing their look of fear and concern, he wanted to give an answer that would not give them unrealistically high expectations, but then, not leave them hopeless with no chance of a recovery.

"Well, right now your mother is still in stable condition. As you know, she had a seizure in the E.R; we had to give her medication to prevent any more episodes for now, or at least until we get the tests back that would show that her responses are back to normal, such as normal breathing pattern, heart rate, brain activity…things like that. Her heart rate was very weak when she was admitted. We are still running tests for that. For now, there is nothing that we found or that we have done, which indicates to us, what is causing your mother's body to malfunction the way that it has. Her history shows that she has been here before as a patient a few times in the past, but all of her blood work is normal, so there is nothing in her history that could relate to what is causing the symptoms now. To tell you the truth, right now, we really don't know what's wrong with your mother. And, at this time, we are just treating the symptoms and keeping her comfortable. She'll probably be out of it for the next twenty-four to forty-eight hours, and then we'll try to wean her off the seizure medication and maybe the oxygen later on to see how she does on her own. Hopefully, we'll be able to know something more when we run more tests after she's awake." The other doctor spoke.

"I'm sorry that we don't have anything more definitive, but so far she's responding well to what we've done so far, as my colleague, Dr. Sullivan has said. We should be back in the morning to check on her. Please feel free to call us if you have any other questions or concerns." They both walked over to Ally and glanced over all of her connections and bottles, and momentarily stared at the monitors. They spoke inaudibly to each other, and then both walked past Sage and Casey into the nurses' station. After another short conversation with each other, one of the doctors left the unit. Doctor Sullivan sat down in front of a computer screen looking and tapping on the keyboard.

Sage and Casey went to their mother one on each side. Rubbing her hair back, Sage bent down and kissed her forehead.

"Mom, I'll be back to see you tomorrow," she said softly. Casey took her hand and kissed it, and then he too kissed her forehead.

Both silently walked out together past the bustling nurses' station. The scene was a cluster of people standing, walking, or rolling around on office chairs, moving about inside the huge cubicle of counter tops filled with piles of papers, scribbled-on notepads, sticky notes hanging about, computer screens filled with data, beeping monitors, and telephones ringing non-stop.

Chapter 40

When Toni got the call from Sage, she became very distraught. Her words and her voice were filled with tears. She could not believe what she had just heard.

"How can this be? What happened? Oh my God. I don't know what to do…? What about your grandmother? Ohhh… poor Mrs. Morris…oh, God," she cried.

"Toni…Toni, please calm down." Sage pleaded through Toni's sobs.

"Right now she's stable." Sage could hear her fighting back the tears, crying softly, sniffling as she tried to listen.

"The doctor said that she's responding well to how they're treating her so far, so don't get yourself upset. We just wanted to let you know that Mom was in the hospital and what was going on with her. Right now, we don't know for how long she'll be here."

"Well, from what you've told me, it doesn't look like she'll be leaving any time soon."

"No, she won't be, but she's going to get better. I know she will," Sage said, holding back her own tears, thinking about how desperately she needed to ask for her mother's forgiveness for the horrible way that she had treated her for so long. Toni knew about their strained relationship and had only tried to persuade Sage to forgive.

"How's Grandma doing? Casey and I were just talking about coming to see her and helping out with her more. Toni, you have been such a true friend to my mom... really to all of us. You've treated Grandma as if she was your own mother. We all love you and appreciate everything that you've done for her. Thank you Toni for everything."

"Listen, your grandmother has treated me like a daughter and has never been a problem for me at all. All of us have enjoyed her company when she comes over. The neighbors have also pitched in and have looked out for her as well. They do a lot while I'm at work. So, she's doing okay. I just don't know if she should be told about Ally yet." "Truthfully, Casey and I were hoping that you would be able to help us with that. Probably not just yet...huh?"

"No, I think we should wait until they know a little more about her progress first before we say anything."

"Yes, I agree."

"Listen, don't you hesitate to call me. Keep me posted on everything that's going on. Gosh, I should be there," she solemnly added.

"Toni, there's no need in you coming all the way here. There's nothing that you can do for her right now. Truthfully, there's nothing that any of us can do right now, except pray."

"Amen," said Toni. "That's about all we can do."

"You take care, Toni. I'll be talking to you soon."

After talking to Toni, Sage felt exhausted. Anticipating her reaction, she knew that it would be better to wait until she had gotten home before calling her. She sounded calm, but on the inside, she was a wreck. She had not even spoken to Sharon but wanted to let her know that she had gone to see her mother, if only to let her know that she was no longer the angry person that she once was.

Chapter 41

Casey and Sage continued their daily visits to the intensive care unit. It had now been two and a half weeks since Ally was first admitted to the hospital. She was off the seizure medication, but was still on oxygen and still out of it. Her eyes would open sometimes, and she could move her head, but didn't seem to be focusing on anything. The doctors had no definite prognosis still. They believed that there might have been brain damage due to lack of oxygen, because of the low heart rate that she had when the paramedics arrived on the scene. No one knew exactly for how long she had been in that condition. Since she showed no signs of progression and remained in stable condition, they discussed discharging her from the intensive care unit to an upgraded recovery unit the following week, but continue monitoring her to see if she would show any signs of improvement while still there. Regretfully, they admitted that nothing more could be done for her in the intensive care unit. Even though the move was an upgrade, that news was not what anyone wanted to hear.

Everyone was still in a state of shock. They could not believe that this was happening. One day after their hospital visit, they all sat around at Sharon's, talking about what had transpired the weeks prior to the seizure. It occurred to Sage how eerie it seemed that everyone was there except her mother. This made her think of the worst thing that could happen. That dreadful reality she tried her best to subdue, but still crept into her mind. She wiped the tear before anyone would notice. Tuning back to the conversation, she heard Sharon talking as she recalled the last conversation she had had with Ally the night before the morning she found her almost unconscious. She had told her about a new employee Kurt that had been asking her out almost from the time he started working there. She had had lunch with him off and on, but he kept hounding her to go out for dinner one evening. They listened intensely as she spoke. "Finally, she gave in and decided to go out with him that particular night." The only thing, as she remembered while talking very slowly, appearing as if she was looking at the scene as she recalled it, was that she never heard a sound in the hallway that whole evening. Usually, she could hear the door when it closed. She had heard it for years, she teased. But to her recollection, had not heard a sound and wondered if maybe she had called off the date since she was so reluctant to go in the first place. After a while, she got busy and thought no more about it.

"Well, did she tell you anything about Kurt? Maybe we should call her job talk to him about what may have happened to Mom," Sage said to Sharon. Under the circumstances, Sharon was deeply depressed, but yet so full of joy that Sage had finally let go of her resentfulness towards her mother. In similar times, she had held on to her impervious attitude. She could see love and tenderness as she spoke about her now, something that she had never seen before. From the time, she first met them years ago; Sage was a very angry teenager and had only shown animosity towards her mother. She thought that after going to college, her attitude would have changed. Sharon understood well why Sage felt so angry, especially after nearly being raped; forgiveness was not in her heart. But after so many years of separation, she thought that she might pardon her mother since her life had changed so drastically for the better. With Ally's condition seemingly not improving, she could also see the guilt and remorse that she was now feeling and was worried about how she would cope with a possible dire outcome.

"I think that's a good idea. Maybe that guy Kurt might know something," Sharon finally responded.

Later, Sage and Casey continued to discuss over the phone what Sharon had told them about their mother's co-worker and decided to go together to speak to him personally. Calling first, they got permission from the manager to come, but did not divulge what the meeting was about or who they wanted to speak to. When they arrived, a young man, who was refilling shelves of candy, led them to the pharmacy area. After introducing themselves, as did everyone else, they were swarmed with well wishes, words of hope, and promises of continued prayers.

"Come into my office. Did your mother leave anything here that you came to pickup?" she said as she led them to her office for privacy. "Her paycheck is direct deposit if you didn't know," the manager, Mrs. Edwards said.

"Oh, no, we didn't come to pick up anything. We came to speak to one of your employees."

"Oh, really?" With a look of puzzlement, she said, as she pointed to the chairs in front of her desk for them to sit down "Here, both of you have a seat. Now, what is the employee's name that you wish to speak to and what is this all about?"

"His name was Kurt, and we were told that he went out with my mother the very night before she went to the hospital," said Casey.

"Is that so?" she asked, her brow wrinkled by confusion.

"Is he here today? We just thought that maybe he could tell us something that could help us figure out what may have happened to her."

"Yes, maybe she wasn't feeling well, or maybe it was something that she may have eaten…since they had gone out to dinner that night," Sage added.

The manager listened, but looked at them very strangely, then spoke. "Did you say the name was Kurt?" she asked looking confused.

"Yes, Kurt. I don't know the last name, but how many Kurt's could be in one place at the same time?" Casey added with a little chuckle.

"Well, I'm sorry, but no one by that name works here," she answered.

"Are you sure? Mom told her neighbor, a good friend, all about him. He's a new employee that she had eaten lunch with a few times and he had begged her to go out to dinner with him. When she finally agreed to go out to dinner with him was the night before she got sick."

"Well, I'm sorry, but the only Kurt that has ever come here was an applicant that I called in for an interview about a month ago… Kurt Randolph, but he was never hired. I decided after the interview that I'd rather have someone who was more experienced.

This person was young… right out of pharmacy school."

"My God…" Sage said under her breath, as she and Casey looked at each other in complete bewilderment. Embarrassed, they both apologized for the mistake and imposition on her time and then quickly left.

"Casey, what's going on? We need to talk to Sharon again. Maybe we missed something or probably she could think of something else that she may have left out." "Yes, I'll give her a call a little later. I need to go home and think about this."

"Are you going to the hospital today?" Casey asked.

"Yes, I'd planned to go later this evening. I'll call you from there."

As they walked to their cars, they continued talking about this developing mystery. They both knew about their mother's past with strange experiences that she told to explain her unacceptable behavior …encounters with strange people, even animals that seemed to be too extraordinary to exist, and insisted that those events had truly happened. But for years after her recovery from alcoholism, she had not spoken of anything like this. Her life had changed dramatically. Even though Sage had not spoken to her mother, Casey and Sharon managed to keep her informed even through her resistance to know. He was still living at home well after her last recovery had begun and had not seen any signs or anything indicative that she had reverted to her old ways.

Having changed her mind about waiting until later, she called Sharon as soon as she got in the door. She retold the whole unbelievable conversation that they had had with Ally's manager that there was no Kurt at her job. Sharon was shocked and dumbfounded.

"Wait a minute. What do you mean he doesn't work there? Ally told me that he was a new hire who was from out of state and had been there for about a month. I know I'm not crazy. I didn't dream this whole thing up."

"Well, according to her manager, Kurt was a younger man who was never even hired. He had only come in one day for an interview about a month ago."

"Now that is strange," Sharon responded. "…real strange."

Sage then asked Sharon more questions about Kurt, her mother's complaints, or if she noticed anything that would lead her to end up in the hospital.

"Sage, I didn't notice anything wrong. With both of us working, we didn't see each other as much or even got a chance to visit as much like we used to do. But she did tell me that she had met a man at work who was about her age who kept pestering her to go out to dinner with him and that his name was Kurt. I didn't ask what his last name was. I didn't even think about it. She even said that she had eaten lunch with him a few times, but most times tried to avoid him. I can't believe this."

"We couldn't believe it either. So, what do you think?"

"At this point, I don't know what to think." She was as perplexed about the report as they were.

"Well, the only person that knows what really happened that night is Ally"

Sharon answered. "Have you talked to your mom's friend Toni? Maybe she talked to her about Kurt… or told her how she has been feeling."

"You know, I hadn't even thought about asking Toni. I'm going to call her right after I hang up with you."

"Yeah. Go ahead and call her because I don't know anything more than what I've already told you. I don't know what to think now."

"All right, I'll let you know what she says."

Checking the time zone, she figured that Toni had not gotten home from work yet.

She had taken the day off from work not knowing what to expect had they been able to speak to Kurt. Every time she thought of her mother lying unconscious in that hospital bed swept her into such guilt. In her mind, she tossed around theories of what could've gotten her into this state. With no improvement in her condition, she still wouldn't allow the worst-case scenario to enter her thoughts, even though, in her subconscious, she knew that was a possible outcome. She prayed continually. Every time the horrible reality entered her thoughts, she prayed for the chance to be able to ask for her forgiveness. At this point, she did not know what to do or even think. Standing at the kitchen sink, washing her dish along with the many from the previous days' meals, she thought probably if she knew the name of the restaurant they may have gone to, she could find out for sure if this date had even occurred, or if Kurt was actually a real person. This whole development of events was mysterious and even bizarre. She was beginning to wonder if maybe there could have been foul play, or have even been self-inflicted since her mother's episode was so sudden and unexpected. According to Casey, she was still required to take medication because of the years of alcohol abuse that had taken such a toll on her small, fragile body, oddly on everything except her liver, but she never showed any signs of depression. Thinking about the latter, the letter that she had written came to mind. Was it a suicidal last words confession? Could her long alienation from her mother have caused her to want to kill herself? She was dreadfully afraid to know the truth if that were so. How could she live with herself if she was the cause of her mother committing suicide? She refused to let her mind believe that possibility. Her imagination was beginning to get out of control, with so many thoughts and explanations of what could have happened that night. She desperately needed her mother to wake up, so that she could tell her how much she loved and needed her. She had always loved her, but her hatred of her actions helped to shield her from the hurt she felt during those years of feeling neglected, mistreated, and unloved.

Chapter 42

Later that evening, Sage went to the hospital. She found out that her mother had been upgraded to a floor with lesser care. Since her condition had not changed, she did not know if the move was good or bad. She was still unable to eat or drink, being nourished only from the hanging bottles and bags connected to her body. Still in a semi-comatose state, her doctors' diagnosis hadn't changed. They were still vague. It was becoming frustrating trying to keep up with them to find out exactly what the prognosis was, or what was really going on. There seemed to have been a different team every time they came to visit her.

Now as always, sitting in the chair beside the bed, she would gently stroke her mother's hand and speak to her in a soft tone about her many friends who were praying and hoping for her speedy recovery. As she named some of her closest friends, she looked to see if maybe there would be a sign of consciousness. Maybe a flinch or a twitch... some movement, which would indicate that she, was aware to show some hint of brain activity. Seeing nothing, she walked over and began looking on the board at the many cards reading the names to see who had sent them. The flowers on the windowsill had begun to cover the view. Taking down a few cards, she began to read them and tell her the names of the people who had sent them. What do you think?" she asked, as if to get an answer. Again, looking over at the small frame under the sheet, she saw no movement. She sighed and walked back to the bedside. Leaning over, she kissed her forehead and stroked her hair. "Mom, please forgive me," she said softly as a tear fell onto her mother's cheek. When she attempted to wipe it, Ally's face twitched as if she felt something. Her shoulders moved and her eyes were moving under the lids. "Mom," Sage said in a louder tone. "Mom, can you hear me? It's Sage." She tapped her hand and wiped her cheek hoping to see the movement again. But the movement had stopped and she lay there still as before. Sage sat down and cried. The days that followed were the same although the doctors had already taken her off the medicine that had kept her in a semi-coma; even so, she remained unconscious. They assured Sage that there was brain activity, but were not sure how functional she would be even if she did regain consciousness. The following week they spoke to her and Casey about placing her in a nursing home or hospice. This was surely not the news that anyone wanted to hear. Sage was devastated. Her hopes of being able to speak to her mother were vanishing quickly, being replaced with gloom and pessimism. Sharon was sadly reminded of her husband's ordeal, and Toni was out of her wits with this update of somber news.

Casey and Sage talked about the possibility of taking her with them and caring for her themselves, but they knew that her care far exceeded their ability to accomplish such necessary attention. It was more feasible to place her in the best facility there was for her needs. Sage became more distraught over what had transpired over the weeks and months since the event. Through this whole horrific ordeal, she never could fathom that this would be the final outcome. Her only comfort was that at least she was still alive. By the end of the week, Ally had been moved to one of the best healthcare facilities in the state, which had been recommended by her doctors. If there was any opportunity for a recovery, it was there, the doctors told them. They wanted a place where she would be kept comfortable, a pleasant atmosphere with outstanding professionals, up to date medical technology, and location as close to them as possible. Approaching the magnificent structures was intimidating as they stood together, the tallest in the middle. This particular healthcare facility specialized in similar cases such as hers and had had very successful statistics considering their patient clientele.

At this medical center, all visitors were welcome, unless otherwise stated by the family to which Casey and Sage had no objection. Her visitors had become sparse because of the distance, but the cards and flowers continued to flow in. Sage and Casey's visits were not as often as before but remained frequent. They agreed to alternate their visits. Both had missed many days from work initially, since the onset of Ally's grievous illness and needed to catch up with the backlog. Whenever Sage went to the facility, she would sometimes ask at the desk if she could check the log to see who had come to visit. Jack had been many times. Ever since Ally was first admitted, he never stopped going to the hospital to see her. She was especially surprised to see that her father's name was even there… a few times, in fact. The nurses were always ready to give her an update of the report and found that her mother had begun to move her arms such as bending the elbow and had some movement in the shoulders, but nothing significant. They thought that the movements were only reflexes, nothing intentional, as one of the doctors had described it. She was now breathing on her own, a crucial step and very encouraging in her progression. It had been the second week of testing her independent breathing and found that the oxygen mask could be removed. This improvement allowed her to be more able and free to move. It was also reported that she had opened her eyes briefly, not focusing on anything, yet to Sage, these were all signs of hope, which gave her encouragement. The doctors also boosted their spirits when he told them that there were more tests to be performed to find out what might be the cause of her unconscious state. Every day she earnestly prayed that God would allow her to hear her mother's voice. She had begun to have nightmares and would wake up in tears because she would wake up not having the chance to speak to her.

Several months had passed that Ally had been transferred to the Neurological Medical and Research Center. Always met with pleasant greetings, Sage and Casey had become very familiar with Ally's Nurse Team. Devoted to the family's concerns, they dutifully kept them abreast of her progress. The reports were sometimes encouraging, but most times remained the same. They continued to visit alternating the days to relieve each other.

As the days went by Sage had gone deep into a state of hopelessness, riddled with guilt and draped in loneliness. When at home, she tried listening to music as a distraction or watching a movie or some ridiculous talk show that she thought anyone with a brain would not even bother to allow on their television. Over the years, Sage's hatefulness had caused her to emotionally detach herself from any pursuers, so as not to lead them to the slightest notion that there was any minute possibility of becoming her significant other. In her life, there was no desire to share her life. That type of relationship required trust and trusting anyone with her emotions was not something she felt was worth the gamble. She had seen and inadvertently experienced the destructive capabilities of what falling in love could do in some poor gullible romantic's life. Consequently, she was left alone with only memories and regrets. If only there was someone who could have mentored her during those turbulent and grievous times. Her mother was that victim. How could she have told her anything? Trying to justify her behavior, she thought to herself, that there was no adult around to help quell her anger, none of which she would listen to anyway. All she could do now was to admit her guilt and pray that her mother would come out of her coma. Bored with the television, most times she would go to bed early and empty hearted. Lying in bed, not able to sleep she would imagine how her mother must have felt when her dad left. Now she was depressed and alone. There was no one to hold her hand, no one whose arms she could sink into who could reassure her and give her the support and encouragement with love and compassion, which now she so desperately longed for. Many times she thought about Mark, how such a wonderful and loyal friend he had been throughout the years. Now he was married and with children. That could have been her. She could have been his wife. Knowing how he felt about her, but refused to reciprocate and allow herself to love him back or anyone else for that matter. Remembering herself as she had been back then, so full of rancor, bull-headed, and stubborn, did not even want to imagine how difficult it must have been for those around her. She could remember all of their warnings and pleadings to find forgiveness, but chose to blot out their voices and only fester on her anger. Her satisfaction was watching her mother suffer for all the years of misery that she felt her mother had so selfishly put her through and finally was getting that wish to watch her suffer, only to realize that now she was even more miserable than she had ever been in her whole life. At the end of it all, when reality set in, she had let hatred snatch away years that could have been spent trying to help her mother, rather than punish her. She had deprived herself of having a mother. One that she knows now would have loved her in whatever state of mind she may have been. Knowing this now, she curled up in her bed and prayed silently, "God please if only she could just hear me. I just want to ask her to forgive me for shutting her out of my life. If only I can hear her voice."

Nothing had changed for Ally. Everyone had hoped that there would be some sign of progress by now. Sage and Casey had to continue their visits for fear if not, could possibly miss any sign of her awareness, especially Sage.

She continued with her own personal treatment by combing and caressing her mother's hair and polishing her fingernails. By giving her updates on the weekly neighborhood gossip that she would get from Sharon, she hoped that maybe by hearing a familiar name, it might spark some neuron in her brain that would wake her. She read the cards from well-wishers and told her who had sent flowers, putting them in front of her as if she could see them. Sage had named every person that she thought her mother was familiar with, even names from the past, all to no avail. Nothing even caused a flinch. Every visit she would perform the same routine hoping for even a murmur of consciousness.

Casey had spent his time, and now it was Sage's turn to visit again. For some reason, this day she had been very apprehensive about going. As went the routine after arriving from work and stopping by the nurses' station, she proceeded down the hallway after seeing a report of having seen the usual, 'no sign and nothing significantly different' in the progress report. This had been going on for months now and had thrown her into a deep state of solemnity. Sleep for her was almost nonexistent, no restful sleep anyway. Even her coworkers had picked up on her listless mood and tried to get her out of her slump with a funny story or some corny joke. Some even offered their time if she needed someone to talk to or just a listening ear. She had become somewhat reticent during company conferences, barely attuned to the discussions at hand. They had even seen her wiping away tears as she sat staring at the computer at her desk, aloof from her surroundings. Her secretary had of late, had to walk into her office rather than buzz the intercom to inform her of incoming calls. Because of this, her manager called her into his office to speak to her about these reports. Knowing the family issues and the gravity of them with compassion and sympathy, he encouraged her to take a leave of absence. He knew that her actions or inaction was clearly not characteristic of her. As she had always had a tenacious drive, always eager and ready to answer questions, offering new ideas to resolve old issues, pertinent suggestions, and always having a new vision for the advancement of the company. With some hesitation, but with his persuasion, she agreed. Because of her dedication, she was reluctant, but found this to be an opportunity for her to spend more time at the medical center and could also relieve Casey on some days, although he wanted to continue to come, maybe not as often as he had. He knew his sister's grief and was suffering in their mother's silence. This time was most needed to spend with her mother, if only to recapture what should have been, which was her being at her mother's side in her troubled life. She had confessed to Casey how much she regretted the opportunities that she had thrown away to reignite their relationship that had been lost because of her childish behavior and vengeful attitude. Feeling her pain, there was nothing he could say that could console her.

Before her leave of absence began, she had not been able to spend a full day there since the first day of admission. It had been a week since her leave that she had begun that long and lonely drive on the highway to the medical center. As always, she filled the car with upbeat music to help keep her mind occupied and her spirits high. Even in these lowly circumstances, she still looked forward to spending her time with her mother. It had been days since the new treatment had started. She and Casey had been informed by the doctors that they wanted to try a different treatment, which was an injection that had been used on some patients whose conditions were quite similar to their mother's and had shown much success. It had brought them out of their comatose state, even after months of being non-responsive with other treatments. With forewarning that this was a dangerous step forward, the doctors still thought it necessary as another alternative because there had been no change for months in her condition with the current direction of treatment. They both had to attend the consultation, because necessary consent papers had to be signed to go forward with the treatment.

Drearily walking around the room, there seemed to have always been a new flower or plant delivered every day, and Sage happily told her incognizant mother. She continued with her one-way conversation with her about the many people who loved her and were continually praying daily for her recovery. Rattling on and on about mounting the flowers and cards filling the room, consequently had to be given away. Every day someone would be leaving with plants to take home. Many were given to other patients and some even sent to nursing homes. Now able to be there all day, she could now see the intricate care that was necessary to sustain her mother in her fragile condition. Although off the ventilator, she was by no means out of the woods as the doctors had told them. Her breathing and heart rate had to be carefully monitored before going forward with any other type of testing or medication and because all had gone well, the new regimen had begun. Still in a semi-comatose state, nourishment was continually done through a feeding tube during which times Sage would leave the room because witnessing such a procedure was gut-wrenching to watch. It only increased her guilt.

Days after the new treatment, she would stare at her mother looking and staring, expecting for something to happen. She so anticipated that at any moment she would see some hint of arousal, that when nothing happened she would go home even more dejected. At home, every time the phone would ring, her stomach would sink thinking and hoping that it was a call that her mother was awake. The anxiety was becoming almost unbearable, in so, she had to find a way to cope. If she was not there when it happened, there was no way to witness it. After the treatment, she was certain that any day now her mother would be sitting up in her bed wide-awake and talking. But the days continued as usual, empty with no real change except more eye movement. On this particular day, she felt strangely saddened even more than at any other time. Sitting next to her mother, forcing herself to be upbeat tried to continue with her usual conversation about the flowers, family, and friends, she became so incredibly overwhelmed with painful regret that she stopped talking and her head fell over gently on her mother's chest. She began to cry softly, pleading for her to wake up, imploring tearfully for forgiveness. Then out of nowhere, she felt a hand patting her gently on the head and heard her name softly called in a raspy voice. She was almost afraid to move, but carefully moved her head from under this hand and rose up locking the sidebar in place. Looking at her mother, she was shocked. Her eyes were open, but only staring at her. Her hand was still where she had put it. Sage stood up and looked right in her mother's face, waving her hand in front of her eyes. "Mom, Mom, it's Sage. Can you hear me? Can you see me?" There was no response. Her mind was racing with thoughts of what was happening and what to do.
"She touched me. I know she called my name," she whispered to herself. "I need to get the nurse. I need to call Casey." Turning towards the door, she heard again,
"Sage? Sage, is that you?" She was blown away to hear her mother talking. Turning around, seeing her sitting up in the bed was even more astonishing. "Mom," she cried out with excitement, going back to her side. "Mom, wait. I need to call for the nurse."
"Who is that with you?" she asked. Sage looking side to side then behind saw no one.
"Nobody, Mom. It's only me."
"No, somebody is there with you. I can see him." Her voice sounded frightened.
Awakening out her deep sleep, Ally could see that form again, but now she saw

it standing next to Sage, and it was more than just a form.

"Oh, no, it came back. It's the glare! Who are you?" Ally looked terrified, as she kept rattling on about seeing a glare. Sage tried to calm her as she began to move around in the bed as if something was getting closer to her. The sidebars were locked as she began pressing against them, moving away from the form. "No, Mom... please... Nobody is here. It's only me."

"Make it go away. You have been following me for years. What do you want?" she asked.

"Mom, who are you talking to? I'm going to get the nurse."

"Sage, don't you see it?" Sage finally pressed the nurse alert button and ran out up the hallway towards the nurses' station. She could not wait until they came. Her mother was getting more excited and more frightened.

"Couldn't they hear her alarms going off?" Sage said, as she was running up the hallway. But as she was rushing towards the nurses, they were rushing towards her with the Code Blue team. In all the excitement of Ally awakening, she couldn't hear the code blue that had been called out over the intercom. When she caught up with them, the door was closed as they were performing CPR. She had apparently gone into cardiac arrest. She called Casey to let him know what was going on.

"Casey, Mom woke up, but now the Code Blue team is in the room."

"What?" he said. His whole body reacted to her words sending signals of panic to his nervous system in nanoseconds, forming sweat droplets from every pore on his body.

"She started carrying on about seeing a glare and she was getting scared and…" Quickly regaining his own composure, he tried to calm her.

"Wait, Sage…slow down. Now what happened?"

"I put my head on Mom's stomach, and she put her hand on me and…and…" Nattering on without taking a breath, Casey interjected.

"Wait, Sage, I'm coming there right now."

"Okay, and hurry. Please hurry," she exclaimed.

Chapter 43

The funeral was beautifully done, but very somber. The obituary was tastefully written. Flowers filled the front of the church on both sides of the shiny wooden coffin. There were so many viewers during the wake that there was a delay in starting the funeral. There were so many different faces known and unknown. Bemoaning her grief and overcome by guilt, seeing her paternal grandparents walking around the casket had no effect on her. There were no more feelings left to feel. Many of their coworkers and friends were there, of which was most gracious of them to do, to make such a sacrifice. Some had traveled long distances, just to give their last respects. Having this knowledge brought tremendous joy to both Casey's and Sage's hearts even for such a sorrowful occasion. Their attendance showed how much their mother meant to so many people. As was stated in the obituary, she had reached out to many as a volunteer in many public programs and at church. Many had come to share their wonderful remembrances about Ally and did so during that part of the service. The choir loft was almost full as well as the church. There seemed not to have been a dry eye in the sanctuary as the minister gave the eulogy. Sage too, could barely stop her tears as she and Casey sat side by side. Toni still had not come to grips with her friend's death and sat close in her husband's arms, as he tried to console her. Sharon and her children were all there. Their friendship was also credited in the obituary of those left behind. Almost throughout the entire service, there were pockets of mourners' audible crying, but from somewhere, within the congregation, there was intermittently from the same person loud, mournful whaling of grief. Sage could not imagine who it could have been. Looking back at the procession of cars that was following behind them on the way to the cemetery, Sage and Casey were truly amazed at the number.

Many had volunteered to help and participate in the program that it had become heartbreaking to have to make a choice, once Sage and Casey had begun to prepare the church program for the funeral proceedings. Because of the limited time for the funeral in order to keep the scheduled time at the cemetery, there had to be a limited number of participants in the funeral proceedings. It had been a very difficult task, emotionally and physically, to even get started having to make the initial calls to tell family and friends of their mother's passing and then calling again with the final arrangements. Sage was still distraught, not having the chance to ask her mother for forgiveness. She had gotten so close to the opportunity to make amends, but that chance was gone in minutes. The pain of missing that chance was beyond belief. The pain of guilt was almost constant and was causing her to suddenly burst out crying. Sharon tried to be with her as much as possible while at the apartment and was most helpful by informing the church, classmates, and former coworkers of Ally's untimely death. Because most of her mother's business and personal papers were at the apartment, they tried working from there, but it had become unbearable for Sage. Being there, looking around where she had once lived with her mother, only reminded her of the hatred she once harbored, and the years that she had been away after vowing never to go back there again. Sharon understood her plight, encouraging her not to come back to her mother's apartment until she was ready.

Jack, who had called as soon as he heard, was willing to do whatever was necessary to help. For Toni, the impact was so shocking when she heard the upsetting news she fainted right on the spot. Sage could hear the noise of clambering and then screaming that was going on in the background and did not want to hang up until she found out if Toni was all right. Finally, someone picked up the phone. It was a male's voice. Toni's husband had picked the phone up from the floor when she fell and assured them that she would be okay. Sage apologized for upsetting her and explained to him the dreadful news.

"Don't worry. She'll be okay. It was just such a shock to her. I'm sure she wasn't ready for anything like that."

"I'm sure, and again, I'm sorry. I'll wait until she calls me."

When Sage had to repeat those words, it made her recall how devastated she had been when told that her mother did not make it. In her mind's eye, she could see the Code Blue team running past her in the hallway. Someone had stood in front of the window of the door to block her from seeing what was going on inside the room. She eventually walked away in anguish and waited for Casey to arrive. They had been in the room for at least a half hour or more trying to revive her. By the time Casey had gotten there, their mother was gone. It took days for her to get to a place where she could even start thinking about making funeral arrangements.

News traveled fast. She and Casey were both receiving calls of condolence and sympathy from people, who neither of them had even thought of, Mark being one of them. He, like everyone else, was in utter disbelief when hearing the sorrowful news and also offered to help them in any way needed. Sage was truly happy to hear from him. Hearing his voice had briefly brought her out of her sadness. She had not heard from him in years. In fact, she was still living in the apartment in Pennsylvania on his last visit. He remembered that last visit and their conversation but never said a word about it. He could hear in her voice how grieved she was and knew that part of her grief was due to guilt and remorse. He had never forgotten about Sage. They had been friends for so long and knew each other's deepest secrets. She had been the first girl that he had truly fallen in love with. After their last conversation though, he felt that he needed to move on with his life and accepted that his life was going to be without her. He felt that he had already waited long enough, and when he heard nothing else from her after that he knew.

The gravesite ceremony had been the worst for Sage. The very thought that her lifeless mother was in that box was devastating. Even then still could not believe that she was gone. So grief-stricken, her mind was not there. She had not heard anything that had been said. "How could this be?" she thought. She was still young and they had been given such hope. At the church, seeing her lying there so beautiful in her pale yellow dress, holding a small bouquet of flowers, her painted fingernails, and hair revealing the few gray strands that she had seen that she had so gingerly stroked. How peaceful she looked, as though she was only asleep. The whole eventful episode was surreal, from the first ambulance call to the apartment, to the Code Blue call at the medical center. Holding the half-used box of tissues, the tears continuously streamed down her face. Why was she even here? She thought if she had only been more kind and understanding, maybe her mother would still be alive. She knew that some people remembered how she felt about her mother, especially the neighbors. Embarrassed now, about how wrongful she had treated her, hung her head down low and wept. It was all her fault, and now she was paying in sorrow for every mean and nasty word that she had ever said and every evil look that she had ever given her. At one time, she had even longed for a time like this. She wanted her mother to die and felt that she deserved it and thought these things without an inkling of guilt. So now sitting there, recalling her past behavior became appalling to her, to the point of nausea. She could not believe that she could have ever felt that way in her heart. If only she had not been so filled with wrath and revenge, she would have read the letter and talked to her mother. The letter…the last conversation her mother ever had with her.

At the repast, Sage was able to personally thank those friends and family members who had come from near and far to pay their respects. Looking at all the food that had been brought and sent to the house brought back memories of her grandfather's funeral. She thought of her poor grandmother left behind in California. They had decided that it was best not to tell her. It would probably destroy her to know that her only child had died. The neighbors were looking out for her while Toni was away. She and Casey had gotten many calls, cards, and even some telegrams as well. When Toni was finally able to cope with the news, she asked them never to even mention Ally's name to her. They understood and vowed to comply with the family's request. Heartbroken about his grandmother, Casey reminded Sage that they would have to take a more active part in taking care of her.

As more familiar faces came to the house for the repast, Toni and Sage had gotten much better emotionally, but Sage continued to wipe her tearing eyes. Toni was able to introduce her and Casey to the few people who had come from California. They were thankful that they would come so far for their mother. Some family members and many friends Sage had introduced to Toni, as her mother's best friend for many years. "She was like a sister to my mom and is an aunt to me." Finally, Sage got a chance to ask Toni about those wailing cries at the church. "Did you know who that might have been?"
"I was told that it was an acquaintance of your mother's. A former coworker named Jessica."

"She must've really liked my mom."

"I think all that crying were cries of guilt," Toni responded but did not elaborate and Sage wouldn't dare ask why. She had no room to be critical of anyone. She had cries of guilt of her own and worse, being Ally's daughter. Jessica had only been a coworker. But Toni knew all about the incident at Jessica's. Ally had told her all about it. Ally's two closest friends Sharon and Toni finally got to meet one another, both regretting the circumstances. She had seen both Nate the bar owner and Doris the barmaid, but not at the house. They both knew how she felt about her mother's drinking, especially because she had spent much of her time and money at his bar. But she couldn't hold anything against them. They had nothing to do with what went on in their lives and she would have welcomed them both. Now that she had come to her own sense of accountability, she was beginning to look at life from a different perspective. Even so, she still could not shake the guilt she felt not having had a chance to tell her mother how sorry she was. Sorry about missing them after the service, she was surely going to send them a Thank You card, she thought. Many from the old neighborhood came as well as did their coworkers, some college classmate, family and so many friends. She wanted to personally thank them all for their presence and support. Casey pitched in with his words of gratitude.

While still standing with Mr. Melmann and Mrs. McFarland, Casey joined them. He thanked him for coming, and for letting him work at the store during his high school years.

"It sure helped me out. Keep up the good work and nice seeing you, sir."

"Sage, have you seen Dad and Uncle Jack?"

"Not lately and then only long enough to ask Liz's name and if she's single," she said looking at Mrs. McFarland with a smile. You remember Mrs. McFarland, don't you?" "Yes, how are you?" he shook her hand as well. "Thanks for coming," he added and left the group.

"…my Uncle Jack. Don't mind him. He's still single and apparently so is my dad." Mrs. McFarland smiled uncomfortably. "You know, Sage, I'm going to leave soon. It's still pouring out there and I have so far to drive."

"Okay, thanks for coming, Liz."

"Sure. I'm around if you need me. …and don't bother, I can get my coat." After they hugged she rushed away towards the closet. Soon after, she left. Jack caught Sage by the table still filled with an array of comestibles. Just as she was about to bite into a deviled egg, Jack stopped her to ask where her counselor friend had disappeared to, declaring that he somehow remembers her from years ago and asked for her phone number.

"I can't do that… not unless she gives me permission."

"Okay, that's fair," he said and walked away.

Driving away, Liz McFarland hoped that Jack and Greg hadn't recognized her. Thinking back to when her family worked summers at the club, she never thought that they would ever recognize her in a million years, especially Jack. She never thought he had even looked at her long enough to see anything other than a frump to make fun of. What could he possibly see now? And his brother, he left his wife just like he had left her…empty and alone. Being on the scholarship committee at Glasslane, she was in a position to reach out to help Sage get the full scholarship that was for low-income families since she had no other offers. She never wanted any of them to find out how she got it. Working there would have been the only way that she would ever set foot on that campus again, after what had happened there. Through the years, she had followed the Tyler family in Forbes and the celebrity magazines and knew about Greg's divorce with all his gallivanting afterwards, and then Jack's breakaway from the family business. Poor Ally, now she will never find out that she was one of those unknown uninvited guests that were sitting at a table at the wedding reception of her second marriage. She wanted to remain Sage's friend, but from now on had to be careful when accepting any future invitations.

The crowd had dwindled. It was still raining. Sage pleaded with everybody to take at least a plate of food with them. By the time Toni and her husband left, she was again beginning to feel the grief, still unable to believe that she would no longer hear her closest friend Ally's voice ever again. Sage also urged Casey to leave as well. Sharon and her family had left a while ago. As everyone was leaving, the gloom of the day began to fill the house again. Wiping the one continuously tearing eye again, she relived everything from beginning to end to find some way to go on, to find some relief from her guilt. How did her mother become that sick just overnight? Her mind flashed back to the ride from the cemetery. Even in the rain, she could clearly see the pharmaceutical emblem and name on that tombstone, Kurt Randolph, born 1960. Casey caught the epitaph, that read, "Whatever the sore, he had the cure." She remembered the eerie feeling she got. They only looked at each other. And that huge dog, she thought. She had never seen a dog running around in a cemetery before.

BJ Watson

www.ingramcontent.com/pod-product-compliance
Lightning Source LLC
Chambersburg PA
CBHW070735120726
47910CB00001B/103